"Page-turning, breathtaking reading... Once I started reading this tale of redemption I didn't want to put it down... Grace Burrowes enchants."

—*Long and Short Reviews*

Pierpont opened his eyes, Sebastian gazed into loathing so intense as to confirm his lordship would rather be dead than suffer any more of Sebastian's clemency or sermonizing.

Sebastian walked up to him and spoke quietly enough that the seconds could not hear.

"You gave away nothing. What little scraps you threw me had long since reached the ears of French intelligence. Go home, kiss your wife, and give her more babies, but leave me and mine in peace. Next time, I will not delope, *mon ami*."

He slapped Pierpont lightly on the cheek, a small, friendly reminder of other blows, and walked away.

"You are not fit to breathe the air of England, St. Clair."

This merited a dismissive parting wave of Sebastian's hand. Curses were mere bagatelles to a man who'd dealt in screams and nightmares for years. "*Au revoir*, Pierpont. My regards to your wife and daughters."

The former captain and his missus were up to two. Charming little demoiselles with Pierpont's dark eyes. Perhaps from their mother they might inherit some common sense and humor.

"Cold bastard."

That, from Captain Anderson, one of Pierpont's seconds. Anderson was a twitchy, well-fed blond fellow with a luxurious mustache. Threaten the mustache, and Monsieur Bold Condescension would chirp out the location of his mother's valuables like a nightingale in spring.

Michael Brodie snatched the pistol from Sebastian's grasp, took Sebastian by the arm, and led him toward

One

THE BULLET WHISTLED PAST SEBASTIAN'S EAR, COMING within an inch of solving all of his problems, and half an inch of making a significant mess instead.

"Die, goddamn you!" Lieutenant Lord Hector Pierpont fired his second shot, but rage apparently made the man careless. A venerable oak lost a few bare twigs to the field of honor.

"I shall die, *bien sûr*," Sebastian said, a prayer as much as a promise. "But not today."

He took aim on Pierpont's lapel. An English officer to his very bones, Pierpont stood still, eyes closed, waiting for death to claim him. In the frosty air, his breath clouded before him in the same shallow pants that might have characterized postcoital exertion.

Such drama. Sebastian cocked his elbow and dealt another wound to the innocent oak branches. "And neither shall you die today. It was war, Pierpont. For the sake of your womenfolk, let it be over."

Sebastian fired the second bullet overhead to punctuate that sentiment, also to ensure no loaded weapons remained within Pierpont's ambit. When

This book is dedicated to those teachers and students for whom the traditional classroom has been a battlefield.

their horses. "You've had your fun, now come along like a good baron."

"Insubordinate, you are. I thought the English were bad, but you Irish give the term realms of meaning Dr. Johnson never dreamed."

"You are *English*, lest we forget the reason yon righteous arse wants to perforate your heart at thirty paces. Get on the horse, Baron, and I'm only half-Irish."

A fact dear *Michel* had kept quiet until recently.

Sebastian pretended to test the tightness of Fable's girth, but used the moment to study Pierpont, who was in conversation with his seconds. Pierpont was in good enough weight, and he was angry—furious—but not insane with it. Nothing about his complexion or his eyes suggested habitual drunkenness, and he had two small, adorable daughters who needed their papa's love and adoration.

Maybe today's little exchange would allow them to have it.

"You fret, *Michel*, and one wants to strike you for it. The English are violent with their servants, *non*? Perhaps today I will be English after all."

"The French were violent with the entire Continent, best as I recall, and bits of Africa and the high seas into the bargain. You ought not to begrudge the English some violence with their help from time to time. Keeps us on our toes."

Michael climbed aboard his bay, and Sebastian swung up on Fable.

Burnished red eyebrows lowered into a predictable scowl. "You would have to ride a white horse," Michael groused. "Might as well paint a target on your back and send a boy ahead to warn all and sundry the Traitor Baron approaches."

Sebastian nudged his horse forward.

"Fable was black as the infernal pit when he was born. I cannot help what my horse decides to do with his hair. That is between him and his God. Stop looking over your shoulder, *Michel*. Pierpont was an officer. He will not shoot me in the back, and he will not blame you for sparing all others the burden of seconding me."

Michael took one more look over his shoulder— both the Irish half of him and the Scottish half were well endowed with contrariness.

"How many duels does that make, your lordship? Four? Five? One of these honorable former officers will put paid to your existence, and where will Lady Freddy be, then? Think on that the next time you're costing me and Fable our beauty sleep."

He took out a flask and imbibed a hefty swallow, suggesting his nerves were truly in bad repair.

"I am sorry." Such flaccid words Sebastian offered, but sincere. "You should not worry about my early outings. These men do not want to kill me any more than I wanted to kill them."

Michael knew better than to offer his flask. "You didn't kill them, that's the problem. What you did was worse, and even if they don't want to kill you—which questionable conclusion we can attribute to your woefully generous complement of Gallic arrogance—the rest of England, along with a few loyal Scots, some bored Welshmen, and six days a week, an occasional sober Irishman, would rather you died. I'm in the employ of a dead man."

"Melodrama does not become you." Sebastian cued Fable into a canter, lest Michael point out that melodrama, becoming or not, had long enjoyed respect as a socially acceptable means of exposing painful and inconvenient truths.

⤳

In Millicent Danforth's experience, the elderly, like most stripes of human being, came in two varieties: fearful and brave. Her grandmother had been fearful, asking incessantly for tisanes or tea, for cosseting and humoring. Like a small child, Grandmother had wanted distracting from the inevitability of her own demise.

By contrast, Lady Frederica, Baroness St. Clair, viewed her eventual death as a diversion. She would threaten the help with it, lament it gently with her many friends, and use it as an excuse for very blunt speech indeed.

"You are to be a companion, not a nursemaid. You will not vex me with your presence when I attend my correspondence after breakfast. You will appear at my side when I take the landau out for a turn in the park. Shall you write this down?"

Milly returned her prospective employer's beady-eyed glower calmly.

"I will not bother you after breakfast unless you ask it of me. I will join you when you take the air in the park. I believe I can recall that much, my lady. What will my other duties involve?"

She asked because Mr. Loomis at the agency had been spotty on the details, except for the need to show up at an unseemly early hour for this interview.

"A companion—you keep Lady St. Clair company!" he'd barked. "Step, fetch, soothe, entertain. Now, be off with you!"

The way he'd smoothed his wisp of suspiciously dark hair over his pate suggested more would be involved, a great deal more. Perhaps her ladyship tippled, gambled, or neglected to pay the trades—all to be managed by a companion whom the baroness might also forget to regularly compensate.

"You will dine with me in the evening and assist me to endure the company of my rascal of a nephew if he deigns to join us. What, I ask you, is so enticing about a rare beefsteak and an undercooked potato with a side of gossip? I can provide that here, as well as a superior cellar, but no, the boy must away to his flower-lovers' club. Never mind, though. He's well-mannered enough that he won't terrorize you—or no more than I will. Are you sure you don't need to write any of this down?"

Yes, Milly was quite sure. "I gather you are a list maker, my lady?"

Blue eyes lit up as her ladyship reached for the teapot.

"Yes! I am never so happy as when I'm organizing. I should have been a general, the late baron used to say. Do you enjoy the opera? One hopes you do, because nothing is more unendurable than the opera if one hasn't a taste for it."

Her ladyship chattered on about London openings she'd attended, who had conducted them, and what she had thought of the score, the sets, the crowd in attendance, and the various solos, duets, and ensemble numbers. Her diatribe was like a conversational stiff wind, banging the windows open all at once, setting curtains flapping, papers flying, and lapdogs barking.

"You're not drinking your tea, Miss Danforth."

"I am attending your ladyship's recitation of my duties."

The baroness clinked her teacup down on its saucer. "You were estimating the value of this tea service. Jasperware is more practical, but it's so heavy. I prefer the Sèvres, and Sebastian likes it too."

Sebastian might well be a follower. Milly had stolen a moment while waiting for this audience to glance over the cards sitting in a crystal bowl on the sideboard in the front hall. Her ladyship's social life was quite lively, and by no means were her callers all female.

"The service is pretty," Milly observed, though it was more than pretty, and perfectly suited to the pastel and sunshine of her ladyship's breakfast parlor. They were using the older style of Sèvres, more easily broken, but also impressively hued. Her ladyship's service boasted brilliant pink roses, soft green foliage, and gold trim over a white glaze. "Meissen or Dresden aren't as decorative, though they are sturdier."

The baroness used silver tongs to put a flaky golden croissant on a plate. "So you are a lady fallen on hard times?"

She was a lady who'd blundered. Paid companions did not need to know that fifteen years ago, Sèvres was made without kaolin, fired at a lower temperature, and capable of taking a wider and more bold palette of hues as a result.

"My mother was a lady fallen on hard times. I am

a poor relation who would make her own way rather than burden my cousins any further."

"Kicked you out, did they?" Her ladyship's tone suggested she did not approve of such cousins. "Or perhaps they realized that underneath all that red hair, you're quite pretty, though brown eyes are not quite the rage. One hopes you aren't delicate?"

She passed Milly the pastry and shifted the butter a few inches closer to Milly's side of the table.

"I enjoy excellent health, thank you, your ladyship." Excellent physical health, anyway. "And I prefer to call my hair auburn."

The baroness snorted at that gambit, then poured herself more tea. "Will these cousins come around to plague you?"

They would have to bother to find her first. "I doubt it."

"You wouldn't be married to one of them, would you?"

Milly nearly choked on soft, buttery pastry. "I am not married." For which she might someday be grateful.

"Then I will regularly scandalize your innocent ears and enjoy doing it. Eat up. When Sebastian gets back from his morning ride, he'll go through that sideboard like a plague of locusts. If you prefer coffee, you'd best get your servings before he comes down in the morning. The man cannot abide tea in any form."

"The plague of locusts has arrived."

Milly's head snapped around at the mocking baritone. She beheld...her opposite. Whereas she was female, short—*petite*, when the occasion was polite—red-haired, and brown-eyed, the plague before her was male, tall, green-eyed, and sable-haired. The divergence didn't stop there.

This fellow sauntered into the parlor, displaying a casual elegance about his riding attire that suggested time on the Continent. His tailoring was exquisite, but his movement was also so relaxed as to approach languid. The lace at his throat came within a whisker of being excessive, and the emerald winking from its snowy depths stayed barely on the acceptable side of ostentatious, for men seldom wore jewels during daylight hours, and certainly not for so mundane an undertaking as a hack in the park.

This biblical plague had…sartorial éclat.

Again, the opposite of Milly, who generally bustled through life, wore the plainest gowns she could get away with, and had never set foot outside London and the Home Counties.

"Aunt, you will observe the courtesies, please?"

This was the rascal of a nephew then, though as Milly endured his scrutiny, the term *rascal* struck her as incongruously affectionate for the specimen before her.

"Miss Millicent Danforth, may I make known to you my scamp of a nephew, Sebastian, Baron St. Clair. St. Clair, Miss Danforth—my new companion. You are not to terrorize her before she and I have negotiated terms."

"Of course not. I terrorize your staff only *after* you've obligated them to a contract."

If this was teasing, Milly did not regard it as humorous. Her ladyship, however, graced her nephew with a smile.

"Rotten boy. You may take your plate to the library and read your newspapers in peace."

His lordship, who was not a boy in any sense, bowed to Milly with a Continental flourish, bowed again over Lady St. Clair's hand, tucked some newspapers under his arm, and strolled from the room.

"He's been dueling again." The baroness might have reported that her nephew had been dicing in the mews, her tone truculent rather than aghast. "They leave the poor boy no peace, those gallant buffoons old Arthur is so proud of."

For all his smoothness, something about St. Clair had not sat exactly plumb, but then, what did it say about a man if he could face death at sunrise and appear completely unaffected by the time he downed his morning coffee?

"How can you tell he was dueling?" For ladies weren't supposed to know of such things, much less small elderly ladies who lived for their correspondence and tattle.

"He's sad. Dueling always makes him sad. Just when I think he's making some progress, another one of these imbeciles finds a bit of courage, and off to some sheep meadow they go. I swear, if women ruled the world, it would be a damned sight better place. Have I shocked you?"

"Several times, my lady."

"Excellent. Have another pastry."

Milly munched away on a confection filled with chocolate crème—one could learn to appreciate such fare all too easily—while Lady St. Clair waxed enthusiastic about the affairs of Wellington—for who else could "old Arthur" be?—and his officers.

And still, something about the Baron St. Clair lodged in Milly's awareness like a smudge on her spectacles. He was quite handsome—an embarrassment of handsomeness was his to command—but cold. His smile reached his eyes only when he beheld his elderly aunt.

Perhaps dueling had taxed his store of charm.

"…and the ladies *très jolie*, you know?" Lady St. Clair was saying. "Half the fellows in government claimed they needed to go to Paris to make peace, but the soiled doves of London went into a decline until the negotiations were complete. Making peace is lusty work, methinks."

"I'm shocked yet again, my lady." Though not by the baroness's bawdy talk.

St. Clair—a baron and peer of the English realm—had spoken with a slight aristocratic *French* accent.

"Excellent. We shall get on famously, Miss Danforth, provided you aren't one to quibble about terms."

"I have not the luxury of quibbling, my lady."

The baroness peered at her over a pretty teacup. "Truly odious cousins?"

"Very. And parsimonious in the extreme."

"My condolences. Have another pastry."

⤜∘⤏

A properly commanded garrison relied on a variety of types of soldiers. In Sebastian's experience, the ideal fortress housed mostly men of a common stripe, neither too good nor too evil, willing to take reasonable orders, and possessed of enough courage to endure the occasional battle.

They were the set pieces, announcing to all and

sundry that a war was being prosecuted, and they deserved as decent conditions as their commander could arrange for them. The decent conditions minimized the chances of rebellion or petty sabotage, and maximized the possibility of loyalty and bravery.

Equally necessary to the proper functioning of any human dwelling place were the women. They were the more interesting of the foot soldiers, usually good for morale, diversion, clean laundry, cooking, and—in a manner that comforted in the midst of war—of maintaining the peace. To Sebastian's way of thinking, they were also the intelligence officers most likely to pass along information that would allow him to sort out bad apples from good, and sheep from goats.

Though a few bad apples were utterly necessary. A few who enjoyed inflicting pain, a few who could be counted on to serve Mammon rather than France. The first group—the brutes—were useful for enforcing discipline and *more* useful as an example when they themselves had become undisciplined, which they invariably did.

The second small group—the born traitors—were invaluable for their ability to disseminate false information to the enemy, to start rumors among the troops, or to undermine the stability of the local populace. When Sebastian had come across such a one, he'd cultivated that resource carefully.

And now it was time to determine what manner of soldier Miss Danforth would be.

He found her not in the library, which had been the preferred haunt of *Tante*'s previous companions, but in the music room, arranging roses.

"Good morning, my lord."

Four words, but they told him much. Her greeting was accompanied with a slight smile, not quite perfunctory, not quite warm; her tone had been halfway between dismissive and respectful.

She was accustomed to dealing with her social superiors and to dealing with men.

"Good morning, Miss Danforth. May I join you for a moment?" Because a proper interrogation was conducted with proper respect for the person questioned.

She glanced at the open door so smoothly it did not interrupt her attention to the roses. "Of course."

And then she did not chatter, which was interesting. He was permitted to join her only because the proprieties were in place, and that told him worlds. "Those roses are quite pretty, if one enjoys the color red."

Not by a frown or a pause did she show a reaction. She tucked a sprig of lavender between green foliage and surveyed the effect.

"I've never understood the allure of the rose," she said. "They are pretty, as flowers go, but most have little scent, they make a mess all too soon, they have thorns, and people are always reading arcane significance into them. May I have those shears?"

He passed her the shears and took a seat on the piano bench a few feet away. He did this because an English baron would not likely ask a companion for permission to sit, but also because something about her recitation, the frankness and intelligence of it, appealed.

"The lavender is an unusual touch."

Miss Danforth wrinkled her nose. She had classic bone structure about the brows, cheeks, and chin, the sort of looks that suggested outcrosses in her lineage. Scandinavian, Celtic, or Teutonic, based on her hair. The nose itself hinted of ancient Rome, though her coloring was too fair for that.

"The lavender isn't working," she pronounced, scrutinizing her bouquet. "Somebody left it as waste in the conservatory, though, and that is an abomination I cannot abide."

He opened the lid of the piano and considered. Something innocuous and sweet. Music by which to lay bare a soul—her soul, for he hadn't one to his name. "You cannot abide waste?"

"Not the waste of such a useful plant. The very scent of it quiets the mind. Lavender can soothe a wound, liven up a bland pudding, brighten a garden."

She had good taste in flowers. Many knaves and whores did, as did some traitors. "Do you mind if I play?"

"Of course not, my lord."

A slight misstep on his part. If he didn't ask permission to sit, he probably ought not to ask permission to use his own piano. He started off with a few scales, mostly to draw his not entirely quiet mind from the scent of lavender and the sight of graceful female hands toying with flowers and greenery.

"Might I inquire as to your last position, Miss Danforth?"

She clipped off a few inches of a thorny rose stem. "I was companion to a pair of my aunts, my lord."

Again she did not chatter. She was a woman who understood the proper tempo of an interrogation. Sebastian started up the keyboard again, this time in parallel sixths in the key of F major, the scale made a bit tricky by the nonsymmetric placement of the B flat.

"And what were your aunts' names?"

"Millicent and Hyacinth Hathaway, my lord."

"They dwelled here in London?" He kept to the small-talk tone that a wise prisoner knew signaled relentless patience rather than civility.

"Chelsea. The air is better."

A single volunteered detail, which was a significant step. She was acknowledging that he was in pursuit of her truths. He abandoned the happy key of F major—Herr Beethoven called it the pastoral key—and switched to his personal favorite, A-flat minor. Because of the intermingling of black and white keys, this key required a deeper penetration of the hand into the keyboard, and more dexterity. He particularly preferred it after sunset.

"Why did you accept a position with my aunt, Miss Danforth? She is noted to be difficult under the best circumstances, even eccentric, according to the intolerant majority. Your days here will be trying, and your evenings no less so."

Miss Danforth took a step away from her flowers. "The container is wrong."

He brought the scale to a smooth conclusion, and though he knew it would not serve his investigation into her character, flicked a glance toward her bouquet. "I beg your pardon?"

"That..." She waved a small hand toward the vase, which was a cheerful, pastel urn sort of thing from *Tante*'s collection of Sèvres. The scene depicted was some gallant fellow bowing over a simpering damsel's hand. Courtly grace surrounded by gold trim and fleurs-de-lis.

"It's pretty enough."

Sebastian was treated to the sort of look women bestowed on men too thick to see the obvious. This look was the same across every nationality he'd encountered, and every level of society, though it hadn't been aimed at him by any save his aunt in years.

"What has pretty to do with anything?" Miss Danforth asked. "It's a vase, of course it's pretty. Also too tall, too busy, too elegant, too impressed with itself. If you would fetch me that jar?"

Some long-dormant gentlemanly habit had him rising—she was that good at balancing polite request with implied command—and crossing the room to reach above her head and fetch down a simple bisque container.

As if he were any footman, she did not move from his path, but busied herself with removing the flowers from the offending—and quite valuable—vase. When he presented her the jar, she smiled.

Too tall, too busy, too elegant, too impressed with itself.

Oh, she was quite good.

"My thanks, sir. This plain vessel will serve the flowers to much better advantage." She hefted a substantial pitcher and filled the plain vessel with water.

His estimation of her rose yet more—and this was not a good thing—because of that smile. The smile was a *coup de grâce*, full of benevolence, understanding, and even *sympathy* for a titled lord who'd done a mere companion's bidding without hesitation. His intent had been to dissect her like an orchid on the examining table.

Time to be about it. "You have not answered my

question, Miss Danforth. Why choose a position with my aunt? The air in London is inferior, after all."

Her shrug was as eloquent as any Gaul's. "The wages are better in London, and your aunt is not confined to a sickroom. Her company will be lively, and her terms generous."

That those terms *could* be generous was no small relief. "It wants organization—your bouquet."

Why couldn't she see this? He removed all the greenery and stems she'd tucked willy-nilly into the vase and started over. Greenery mostly, a few sprigs of lavender next.

"It *wants* to be pretty," she countered. "It wants to have a pleasant scent."

"Balance and proportion are pretty, grace and harmony of the colors are very pretty."

He added roses next, here, here, and there. She was right about the scent, though—the lavender dominated, mixing with the scent of greenery. The roses were invisible to the nose.

He paused, the last rose in his hand. "You're wearing lavender, Miss Danforth."

"And you are making an English bouquet, all tidy and symmetric. I would expect…"

How lovely, to see her stumble over her words, to see her gaze shift to the single rose in his hand. "*You* would expect?"

"A more Continental approach, more free and loose, a bit off balance but more interesting for it."

He could go on the offensive now, but he didn't. "I am in an English household, and I am an English baron. I will have an English bouquet for my pleasure."

She took the rose from him and considered *his* bouquet. "Here, I think."

He'd reserved the longest stem for last, and she'd used it as the centerpiece of the arrangement, English-fashion.

"Very nice, Miss Danforth. Now where will you put it?"

Her scent was very nice too, mostly sweet lavender, reminding him all too powerfully of summers in Provence. An English baron in his English household ought not to be homesick for old monasteries and French sunshine. He leaned in and sniffed the delicate purple flowers anyway, right there in front of her.

"Your aunt wanted an arrangement for your piano. She said you play a great deal, and she wanted them where you could see them. Does that suit?"

"No, it does not." The last thing he wanted was a reminder of his past when he came to the piano for solitude and solace. "Water and musical instruments are not a prudent combination."

"Then you decide, my lord." She passed him the vase, roses, lavender, and all, and began tidying up the detritus of his design.

He set the bouquet aside and took a step closer, an impulse intended to intimidate a small, plain woman who did not understand with whom she tangled. He considered how best to acquaint her with her multiple errors in judgment.

"Blast!" She did not apologize for her oath, but brought the fourth finger of her left hand to her mouth.

"A thorn?"

She nodded and drew her damp finger from her

mouth, frowning at it. "Roses are overrated, I tell you. No wonder we equate them with true love."

Her comment, the scathing tone in which she'd delivered it, told him much. He wrapped his handkerchief around her finger, and thus had a means of ensuring she didn't flounce off before he'd achieved his objective.

"The bleeding will stop momentarily, Miss Danforth."

"I know that."

Her composure was jeopardized by their proximity, which should have pleased Sebastian. The simplest form of intimidation was physical, though to use his sheer size and masculinity against her was unappealing.

Unsporting, to use the English term.

And yet, he did not step back or turn loose of her hand. "Who was he?"

She glowered at their joined hands, her loathing not quite hiding the hurt in her eyes.

"My cousin's choice, one I'm far better off without." Hurt was there in her words too.

"I will tell my aunt that should any gentlemen followers come calling on you, she is not to leave you alone with them, no matter what flattery or tricks they attempt, or how strongly she is tempted to matchmake, for matchmaking is one of her besetting sins."

If Sebastian had been asked, he would have said the emotion in Miss Danforth's brown eyes most closely resembled sorrow. "Thank you."

The flattery and tricks that had gone before had been bad, then. Bad enough that she'd given up much in the way of a genteel lady's comforts to find refuge in service. Englishmen were a disgraceful lot when their base urges beset them, which was to say, most of the time.

He unwrapped his handkerchief and inspected her hand. "You will live, I think. Keep the handkerchief. It is silk and has my initials on it. When your cousins come to call, you shall wave it around under their noses, and not too subtly, yes?"

Every person in a garrison, every mongrel dog and mouser in the stables, was the responsibility of the commanding officer. Sebastian had still not ascertained quite enough to let this soldier get back to her appointed duties.

"I will flourish it about indiscriminately, my lord. My thanks."

He did not step back, but continued to study her. Her eyes were really quite pretty. "And if these cousins realize the mistake they've made? If this sorry choice of theirs comes to his senses and tries to woo you into his arms again?"

She did not step back either, and sorrow turned to dignified, ladylike rage—a fascinating transformation.

"That will not happen, my lord. In any case, I would not go. My fian—*he* made it plain that my shortcomings will not be overcome to his satisfaction, whereas your aunt offers me a decent wage and comfortable surrounds in exchange for my simple presence. For all her friends and callers, my lord, I think Lady St. Clair is lonely. One does not turn one's back on a woman who can, however indirectly, admit she's lonely."

Quite the speech. Quite the speech from a woman who knew what it was to be abandoned by those who'd given her promises of constancy. He spent a moment pretending to examine the bouquet while he analyzed her words.

"Then you expect to be in *Tante*'s employ for some time?"

"She offered me employment when I badly need it, my lord, and has done so on little evidence other than my characters. I am in her debt. To toss aside her faith in me would be ungrateful, also foolish."

She marched across to the piano, closing the cover over the keys and relieving Sebastian of her lavender scent.

"One admires your pragmatism, Miss Danforth. Perhaps the flowers should be set in the window. They will appreciate the light, and passersby can appreciate your bouquet."

She liked that idea, or she liked any excuse to keep moving away from him. The sorry choice of a former fiancé sank further in Sebastian's estimation. Englishmen knew nothing of how to appreciate women. Not one thing. Most Frenchmen knew all too much about the same topic, though.

Miss Danforth nudged the flowers to the center of a windowsill behind the piano. "Will that do?"

"Lovely. And send a footman to clean this up. I cannot be responsible for further injury to my aunt's newest companion." Though he'd injure her without hesitation if his judgment of her proved overly optimistic. "I will take my leave of you, Miss Danforth."

He bowed, she curtsied, and as he left the room, she was tidying up the mess they'd created, despite his orders to the contrary.

No matter. He'd ascertained what manner of

addition his aunt had brought into their household. Miss Danforth was the kind of soldier whose loyalty was earned, and once given, was not rescinded except for excellent cause. Had she been an English officer, she would have given her life to keep her troops safe.

Sebastian decided that for now, Miss Danforth would do. His next task was to head to the conservatory to see what fool had put lavender clippings in the trash.

Two

HENRI ANDUVOIR DISLIKED ENGLISH TAVERNS, AMONG many other aspects of "perfidious Albion." He disliked the scent of raw fish, and England had so much coastline, the entire sorry country stank of fish, or manure, or some diabolical, dank, rotting combination of the two.

He disliked the growing bald patch at the top of his head, to the point that the last time a woman had remarked upon it, he'd slapped her into silence.

A small lapse of control, though the encounter had turned out pleasurably enough for them both.

He disliked the ubiquitous dish of the English common man, which paired an overcooked, dead fish of indistinguishable species and ample bones with an equally overcooked heap of dead potato. Not a sauce, not a spice to be found anywhere in the vicinity, unless excessive salt merited consideration.

Though decent ale was at least at hand to wash it down, which was fortunate, because no wine should be expected to bear such an insult.

When former Captain Lord Prentice Anderson came

through the door, Henri had one more thing to dislike—the expression on *mon capitaine*'s face.

Anderson had been pressed into service for two reasons. First, while held at the Château, he'd never laid eyes on Henri Anduvoir, and thus could make no inconvenient connections. Second, Anderson was not burdened with excesses of intellect, but could be counted on, like the loyal soldier he was, to follow orders.

Anderson had been cavalry, which meant he could also be counted on to move about and conduct himself with the subtlety of a horse. He stopped immediately inside the door, thereby announcing to all and sundry that a fellow had arrived who was not a regular patron. He glanced left; he glanced right. Nervously.

And then—may the merciful God have pity— Anderson put his hand up to his face and brushed his fingers over an overly groomed mustache, as if to say, "and don't forget this aspect of the tall, blond, expensively dressed, gentleman stranger's appearance, should any passing constable need a description."

Amateurs were a trial beyond endurance. Henri took a hearty swallow of his ale—Englishmen did not sip ale—and, as intended, the movement drew Anderson's attention.

The captain did not go to the bar—of course, he did not—but rather, clomped straight over to Henri's table, hung his hat and cape on the nearest hook— lest his exquisitely tailored riding ensemble also go unremarked—and scraped back a chair.

"I do not have good news."

Henri offered the man a blazing, toothy smile.

"Perhaps your not-good news can wait until the tavern wench has come trotting by?"

Another twitch of the glorious manly mustache, also a nod.

"The ale is surprisingly good," Henri said as he caught the serving maid's eye, lifted his tankard an inch, and jerked his chin toward Anderson. She moved off toward the bar, and Henri realized he'd erred. An Englishman would have bellowed, but then an Englishman would have sounded like an Englishman.

Anderson's jaw firmed. "English ale is the best in the world."

So subtle, this glossy English gelding. "*Bien sûr*, else I would not have come this distance to enjoy it."

Anderson's drink was put before him, and he spared the maid neither an appreciative look nor a thank you, lest he be mistaken for a relaxed swell— that was the English word—enjoying a casual tankard with an acquaintance.

"Pierpont missed. St. Clair deloped. Again."

Bad news, indeed.

"Drink your ale, *mon ami*." Because Pierpont *had* missed and because Anderson's usefulness was not yet at an end, Henri made his tone consoling. "One did not expect success on the first or second attempt. Our governments are prepared to be patient."

Anderson eyed his drink, which sported a head of foam only gradually receding from the rim.

"Then you need to find somebody else to assist you. The word in the clubs is that St. Clair has deloped three times, and outright refused to fight when the Duke of Mercia challenged him. He tells them all to go home to their womenfolk, and that the war is over."

A conscience was a great complication in a subordinate, but then, Anderson in no way saw himself as Henri's subordinate.

"You found it difficult, to see a man fire into the air when his life had been threatened, even when threatened by one who had a right to take that life. This does you credit, Captain. Nobody disputes that St. Clair has courage."

The baron had rather too much courage, in fact, which Henri might have regretted, had he been interested in retrieving his conscience from the dusty confessionals of his long-distant boyhood.

Anderson relaxed fractionally and reached for his ale, then set it down untasted.

"It *was* difficult—bloody damned difficult, and St. Clair is right. The war is over, so you'd best find somebody other than me to aid you. I've agitated twice now for St. Clair's victims to challenge him. If I second at another duel, my involvement will be too conspicuous."

This flare of scruples was tedious, like a mistress who pretends she must be wooed and aroused as well as paid. Henri manufactured what he called his French Philosopher look. Soulful, understanding, wise, and sincere—it required tired brown eyes and a thin nose to be carried off properly. A graying beard would have been nice, but that had been sacrificed in the interests of anonymity.

"Your government selected you to work with me in this venture, Captain. My government chose me to see it through." He considered a biblical allusion

to removing this cup from his lips and rejected it—
his objective was murder, not martyrdom. "We are
patriots, we have that in common, and both England
and France want to be rid of the embarrassment that is
Monsieur le Baron St. Clair."

Anderson scrubbed a hand over his face, tweaked
the mustache, and peered at his drink.

"One more. I'll see if I can talk one more former
prisoner into calling him out, and I'll find others
to serve as seconds, but then, that's it. To hell with
England and France. If God wants St. Clair to survive
five challenges and four duels, then who am I to question the verdict of the Almighty?"

A comfort, to know that at least the hand of God
provoked an Englishman to humility.

"Then we will choose our next champion carefully," Henri said. "There are eight candidates that we
know of. Eight more officers who suffered abominably
at St. Clair's hands, eight men who will never sleep
as well, or feel safe even in their lovers' arms. Who
among them do you think has the best aim, the steadi-
est nerves, and the greatest chance of ridding the world
of the blight of St. Clair's existence?"

Anderson took a prissy sip of his ale, but hadn't
waited quite long enough, because his mustache now
sported evidence of his libation. "Dirks or the other
Scotsman, MacHugh."

The Scots were bloodthirsty. Despite their propensity for drinking whiskey, this was something Henri
admired about them. He attributed a pugnacious
nature and tolerance for strong drink to having to
share an island with the English.

He passed Anderson a plain linen handkerchief and tapped a finger above his own lips. As Anderson daintily blotted ale from his mustache, Henri sorted through options.

"Approach both Dirks and MacHugh and assess their receptivity. We can afford to be patient and careful, but not too patient."

Henri tossed a few coins on the table, including a bit extra for the wench, and rose. He did not settle his greatcoat around his shoulders with a subtle flourish—that would be French of him—but rather, put his arms into the sleeves and left the coat hanging open, English fashion.

When he'd also tugged on his gloves, he clapped Anderson on the shoulder in a hearty parting gesture. Because remaining unnoticed in a foreign country started with walking in exact imitation of the locals, Henri strode out the door like he'd just spent time with a pretty, conscientious whore.

Which, in effect, he had.

⁓

"No matter how many times you glance at that door, I will catch you at it every time, and *Tante* will not join us."

St. Clair's voice was not exactly accusing. Milly regarded her breakfast companion over a plate of sinful lemon pastry and saw something in his eyes though. Humor? *A challenge?*

She lifted the pot—more old-fashioned Sèvres. "Tea, my lord?"

"If you please."

He had a way with silence, just as Aunt Mil had had. Milly poured but did not ask him how he preferred his tea. She set the pot down, went back to savoring her lemon tart, and did *not* glance at the door.

The lemon pastry was lovely—flaky crust cooked to an even, golden brown, the sweet, rich filling still warm. The very scent of it proclaimed wealth and ease; the taste of it comforted in ways the jingling of coins never could.

"What will you do with your morning, Miss Danforth? It appears we're in for that most rare of English treats, the sunny day—or a sunny morning, at least. One doesn't want to tempt the gods of English weather."

He picked up a slice of bacon and tore off a bite with his teeth, appearing both savage and elegant even in so mundane an activity.

"If your lordship is going out, I thought I'd spend some time with the piano. Lady St. Clair said I might use the music room when she has no duties for me."

The bacon was dispatched in about three bites. He paused with a forkful of eggs halfway to his mouth.

"She will not have use for you this morning. She is resting, and also plotting. Tonight is that bacchanal known as Lady Arbuthnot's card party. Like witches, the coven gathers on the Tuesday nearest each full moon. They tell everybody they're playing whist, but in truth they're casting spells on fashionable bachelors for all their nieces and granddaughters."

He was…teasing. Like any other nephew might tease about an elderly aunt upon whom he dotes.

"And has Lady St. Clair spared you from her

magic, my lord? You would seem to qualify as a fashionable bachelor."

The baron also qualified as titled, wealthy, handsome, and at a marriageable age without an heir to his name, which constituted a puzzle.

He held up another crispy, aromatic strip of bacon as if regarding a bottle of wine or a fine miniature.

"This is curious, now that you mention it. Aunt has powerful magic—she claims Gypsy blood on her dam side—and yet I sit before you unscathed by holy matrimony." He bit off an inch of bacon and crunched it to oblivion. "Much like yourself."

Milly took refuge in her pastry, because just possibly, that was a rebuke.

Very likely that was a rebuke.

He waved his fork with an elegant gesture of the wrist. "Who is your favorite composer?"

"Herr Beethoven."

"You prefer a German over your native talent?"

Not "our" native talent. Perhaps that was why he was unmarried. He did not favor English beauties, and they did not favor him. He was large, dark, and French, after all.

Milly considered her lemon pastry. "Herr Beethoven's music balances abundant technical talent with abundant passion. He's not afraid to rage or laugh or grieve in his music, though one is told the man is stone deaf."

She braced herself for another tease/rebuke/challenge, but St. Clair only twirled his teacup a quarter turn by its tiny handle.

"Well put. Would you like a few pages of the paper, Miss Danforth? The society pages, perhaps?"

He was neither teasing nor rebuking nor challenging, and yet his polite question was worse than if it had been all three.

"No, thank you, my lord. Would you pass the jam pot, please?"

The question came out too brightly, and Milly endured a baronial perusal before he moved the raspberry jam closer to her plate. Raspberry symbolized remorse, and it was her favorite flavor of jam.

"I enjoy Beethoven as well," St. Clair said, getting back to his eggs. "Though Clementi is a pleasure for the hands, and Mozart can be a wonderful confection for the ear. More tea, Miss Danforth?"

"Please."

She wasn't used to him, was the trouble. He seldom came down for breakfast and had accompanied his aunt on an evening outing only once in the two weeks since Milly had accepted this post. He'd joined them in the coach as far as Haymarket, seen them deposited at the theater, then gone off on some gentlemanly errand and sent the coach back for them.

Which meant he'd walked home alone through the streets of London in the dead of night—or spent the night with his mistress.

He poured for her, set the teapot down, and added cream and sugar to her cup. "What else will you do with your liberty, Miss Danforth? One can play Beethoven for hours, of course, but a day is also livened by variety."

Milly appreciated that making small talk with the paid companion was gallantry of a high order for a baron at his breakfast, so she mustered a response rather than commit the public eccentricity of applying raspberry jam to her lemon tart.

"If the day holds fair, I'll likely walk in the park."

"Take a footman, at least. Take Giles, in fact. He enjoys the park and is sent stepping and fetching all over Town the livelong day because he's such a brute."

Giles was a genial giant, and his company would be pleasant, but the idea that Milly merited such an escort was absurd.

Also...flattering. "Yes, my lord."

He stirred her tea and set the spoon on the saucer, another nicety, done with both elegance and a casual ease.

"And if it rains, Miss Danforth? Will you let the footmen make you a blazing fire in the library, order a pot of chocolate, and curl up with one of Mrs. Radcliffe's novels?"

His tone invited a confidence, and his green eyes were so grave as to invite all manner of nonsense. He was being French, for all he'd served her tea like an Englishman.

The image his words evoked, an image of an afternoon spent in a world of fictional adventure and happy endings, was painful nonetheless.

"I might sketch, my lord. I also enjoy paper cutting, embroidery, and knitting."

He downed his tea in one gulp, then shuddered. "Knitting. You are a paragon of domestic virtue, Miss Danforth, and as such, I pronounce you entitled to apply that jam to your tart. You've been staring at it with shameless longing, you know."

No, she had not. She'd been thinking of an

afternoon in the library with shameless longing. "Yes, my lord."

Her response was the most innocuous ever manufactured on a pretty English morning, and yet, St. Clair narrowed his eyes at her.

"You have been good for *Tante*. She's laughed more in the past fortnight than in the previous season. She flirts with the help, and she dwells less on me and my endless shortcomings, matrimonial or otherwise." He came to an internal conclusion. "She *worries* less. I am in your debt, Miss Danforth."

He was not an easy man to spend time with, but he knew how to give a sincere compliment. The occasion was so rare for Milly, a blush rose up, along with a pleasant warmth in her middle.

"Thank you, my lord. One wants to be useful in this life." One also wanted a decent place to sleep and some food, too, and the St. Clair household provided that in generous abundance, along with a tidy bit of coin.

Aunt Hyacinth had been right. A good position could be far better than the crusts and criticism handed out among one's own family.

"One does want to be useful." He slid the jam pot closer to her plate and rose. "If you will excuse me, madam. Like my aunt, I have correspondence that demands my attention, though your company has been a delight."

He might have bowed to her, but Milly was staring at the jam, trying to ignore his meaningless flattery. She heard him move off toward the door, and reached for the preserves.

"Miss Danforth?"

He'd stopped by the door, a big, elegant man who could carry off lace at his throat and wrists even in riding attire.

"Sir?"

"You must not begrudge yourself that rainy day in the library. Nobody can be a paragon all the time."

And then he strode off, while Milly dipped her knife into the jam, and wished—and wished and wished and wished—she might someday have that afternoon with Mrs. Radcliffe.

❧

Though Sebastian wished it were not so, another infernal duel was brewing. He could feel it, could sense it in the way the members of his club barely met his eye when he nodded to them across the reading room.

They would not speak to him if they could avoid it. That he even had membership was only because the Benevolent Society for the Furtherance of Agrarian Science had been too unsophisticated to realize that Sebastian St. Clair was the Traitor Baron himself. By the time they'd become aware of their blunder, Sebastian had made a contribution of unignorable proportions to their experimental farm out in Chelsea.

He'd spent those precious funds because a man needed the company of his fellows, even if it was silent, nervous company lured close with coin, and tacit acceptance of the fact that he was merely tolerated in their midst.

"Ah, there you are!" *Tante* came fluttering into his

study without knocking, a gleam in her eyes Sebastian had learned to respect. "You look quite intellectual, St. Clair. Those spectacles are deceiving."

"The spectacles are necessary if I'm to make sense of your figures, madam." Years of figures that she'd kept meticulously in the absence of husband, son, nephew, or grandson.

She settled into a chair opposite his desk, a sparrow coming to light. "I wear them too, when I'm at my correspondence, but spectacles become no one. Will you accompany Miss Danforth and me to the Levien musicale?"

No, he would not. "When is it?"

"Next Tuesday. Tuesday evenings are when all the best events take place. I'm having some new gowns made up for Milly, and the woman adores music. There's a pianist on offer, a single gentleman who's the son of a duke. I think he might do for your cousin Fern, or perhaps Ivy, though not Iris. The girl can't carry a tune, tipsy or sober."

God help the pianist. *Tante* would set loose an entire flower bed of eligible young ladies on him before his recital was complete.

"I'm afraid I must attend a meeting at the club Tuesday evening. I'm trying to convince the members that peaches are worth investing in."

They were not, particularly. Peaches liked a sheltered location, a good lot of sunshine, and a mild but discernible winter—exactly what half the valleys in Provence offered, but not quite the English climate.

"Peaches." Aunt rose, a wealth of scorn in one word. "You would rather take up breeding peaches than pursue your own succession. The war is over, Sebastian. You've been pardoned for your errors, and life moves on. You were just a boy when the Corsican resumed his nonsense, and you can't be held responsible for your family making an unfortunately timed visit to relatives in France."

How did one breed a peach? Sebastian set that conundrum aside and prepared to deal with being The Despair of the House of St. Clair, as his aunt would no doubt term it in the next five minutes. *Tante* did not lack for accuracy in her scolds.

"I beg your pardon."

The paid companion stood at the door, which would normally have been a pleasant sight. She diverted *Tante* from pestering Sebastian for the most part, and she was a pretty little thing in a not-very-English way.

"Miss Danforth, you must join us. *Tante* is preparing to deliver one of her more rousing sermons, and such eloquence deserves an audience." Though Freddy would pull in her horns about the succession if a damsel were present—Sebastian hoped.

The young lady remained in the doorway, her hand on the jamb as if for support—which put Sebastian's instincts on alert. Her mouth, a full, often-smiling mouth, was grim at the corners, and her eyes...

"Come, sit, Miss Danforth. You are upset." Sebastian had no intention of being in the vicinity when her upset got the better of her. She would not appreciate him witnessing any loss of composure, and he would not like her for subjecting him to such a display. "I'll find a footman to bring the teapot. I'm sure whatever troubles you, *Tante* will want to know of it."

He escaped with all dispatch and closed the door behind him, sending the tweenie trotting down the steps for the ubiquitous pot of tea. Rather than a scepter and orb, King George ought to rule the empire with a teapot and sugar tongs.

Sebastian was about to call for his horse—the morning was pretty enough to inspire riding out both before and after breakfast—when Freddy emerged from the study.

"There you are. Summon the phaeton, Sebastian, and prepare to drive Miss Danforth to Chelsea."

This was an order. Freddy enjoyed giving orders, but Sebastian could not oblige her.

"I'll have the coach brought around instead, the weather being unpredictable. The press of business is such that—"

Tante advanced on him, hands on her hips. A line of Shakespeare flitted through his head, about the lady being small but fierce.

"She has lost her only friend, Sebastian. Miss Danforth's aunt, her only supporter in this world, has gone to her reward, and the girl buried her other aunt only three months past. She is *alone*, but for what kindness we can show her."

An aunt. *Merde.* It would be an aunt. "John Coachman knows the roads—"

She jabbed him in the sternum with a bony, surprisingly painful finger. "*You* are competent to get the girl to Chelsea. John Coachman's gout is acting up, and the undercoachman takes a half day today, along with the footmen. Call. For. Your. Phaeton."

Four more jabs right to the sternum. Sebastian had

never had any call to jab a man in the breastbone before, but if he were still in the interrogation business, he would have added it to his repertoire of torments.

"Perhaps she should wait a day, *Tante*. Her composure will benefit from waiting a day." And the under-coachman would be back from swilling his wages or spending them on a pretty little tart.

She smoothed a hand down the lace of his jabot. "Coward."

Ruthless besom.

"Such an endearment will surely addle my wits." Though her epithet was not strictly fair, unless she referred to his unwillingness to take his own life.

"Please, Sebastian? She says if she doesn't retrieve a few mementos from her aunt's cottage, her cousins will sell them all, and there's some elderly fellow who was sweet on the aunt. Milly is desperate to look in on him."

Milly. He'd forgotten that was her name—put it from his mind the way he could put entire years of his life from his mind—and he was *not* a coward.

He was a dutiful nephew and a gentleman. In this case, it mattered not whether he was a French gentleman or an English gentleman. Either doomed him to surrender.

"Have a hamper packed for the bereaved old fellow—a bottle of spirits to ease his loss, a decent blanket against the winter cold, comestibles, sweets, that sort of thing—and tell Miss Danforth to be ready in half an hour."

In half an hour, he hoped the English weather might oblige him for once and produce a steady downpour.

Alas, that hope, like most of Sebastian's hopes to date, was not to be realized.

❧

Milly did not want to tool out to Chelsea in the baron's smart phaeton. She did not want to sit beside him in all his understated elegance, while she presented as the dowdy poor relation she was, an insult to the glorious, sunny day in her drab brown. Most of all, she did not want to risk her cousins catching sight of her.

The neighbors had not sent word of Aunt Hyacinth's death until Milly had no chance of attending the services or the wake, which was likely a mercy, but one Milly bitterly resented.

"Do you have need of my handkerchief, Miss Danforth?"

The baron posed his softly accented question as he clucked the horses into a relaxed trot. His manner suggested that a few blocks past Grosvenor Square, they might turn into the park, their outing no more than a lark.

"I have my own, thank you." Her reply was ungracious, but that too—like every one of her disgruntlements—was a symptom of the anger that so poorly disguised grief.

They trotted along in silence, until his lordship turned the vehicle south on Park Lane.

"I would be lost if Freddy were to abandon me for the celestial realm." His tone was contemplative, as if he were only now acknowledging the truth he'd admitted. "I would have nobody to scold me, nobody to hold me accountable for my numerous small lapses, nobody to look upon me as if I were a particularly exquisite arrangement of roses, when I am nothing but a man who scratches and swears and wears his muddy boots into the parlor on occasion."

For the baron, this was a speech, and also a bit of a eulogy for a woman not yet dead.

"She is formidable, your aunt. My aunt was too, but in a much quieter way."

They both had been, Hyacinth and Millicent. They'd protected Milly as long as they could, and made the world think Milly was the one looking after them.

"When Aunt Millicent died, Aunt Hyacinth began planning my escape into service. I would have been prey for my cousins without Aunt chiding and encouraging and plotting."

Mostly chiding.

"You were named for your aunt?"

She was pleased he would remind her of this. "Yes. I have her red hair."

"Auburn. I am certain your hair is auburn, in proper light. Tell me about your Aunt Hyacinth." He was being kind, and the magnitude of Milly's loss was such that all she could do was appreciate his compassion.

"I call her—I *called* her—Aunt Hy. Everybody did, and that was a shame. Hyacinth is a lovely name."

Traffic was moving along, like it would not at the fashionable hour. The spring breeze brought the pungent scent of Tattersall's. Life, as both aunts had said often, goes on.

"You do not want to talk about your loved one,"

the baron said. "As if that somehow makes them more deceased. Soldiers do not reminisce about fallen comrades easily at first."

She'd forgotten he'd served. Forgotten he would know a great deal about loss and about life going on.

"Aunt Mil loved laughter, Aunt Hy loved beauty. Ours was a happy household. Aunt Hy could hardly see toward the end—I felt like a traitor for leaving her—but she said she could still feel the beauty with her hands, still smell it with her nose, still taste it in a perfect cup of tea."

"You did not feel like a traitor for leaving," the baron said, slowing the team to let an enormous traveling coach lumber past. "You felt like an orphan, an angry orphan with no good choices and nobody whose guidance you could trust, because nobody had trod the path you faced. Your aunts had not been in service; they had not been married. They could suggest, but they could not *know*."

As the phaeton rolled along the park's pretty green perimeter, the most fashionable addresses in the world on their left, Milly realized the baron was speaking from experience.

She would rather talk of his experiences than her loss—much rather. "You felt that way. You're English, and you ended up in the French army. You had to have felt that way."

He wrinkled his grand nose, the gesture Gallic, and Milly's observation clearly unwelcome. She expected he'd absorb himself in managing his horses, though he drove with the instinctive ease of a born whip.

"I was a boy when the Peace of Amiens came

about, and my mother was desperate to visit her relations in France. I spent the summer in Provence, at my
grandparents' château, and I had no concept that the
Corsican and old George both were merely regroup-
ing for another decade of war. When the truce ended,
my father, of course, had to leave or face internment.
Getting him out of the country was a difficult proposition. My mother would not leave me behind, but
we could not safely travel with Papa. Very soon, we
could not safely travel at all. Mother died that winter,
without ever seeing her husband again. She was my
first experience with the casualties of war, for I believe
she died of a broken heart, not a simple ague."

So he'd gone from being an English schoolboy,
albeit a wellborn schoolboy, to a Frenchman's grandson with inconvenient paternal antecedents, all in the
course of a few bewildering months.

He steered the phaeton past Apsley House, that
imposing edifice inhabited by no less personage than
the Duke of Wellington.

"Tell me more about these aunts," St. Clair said.
He did not so much as glance at the duke's handsome residence. "Did they tipple? Did they flirt with
the curate? The baroness would lose all heart had she
no flirts."

What to say? That Milly did indeed feel like an
orphan—more of an orphan than ever? That she was
frightened to be so alone, more frightened than she'd
been since her own parents died? He'd listen to those
sentiments, and he would not judge her for them.

St. Clair viewed the world with a surprising sense of
compassion, and yet, despite her own need for silence,

despite the lump in her throat, Milly launched into a spate of chattering about Aunt Hy's flowers and Aunt Mil's shortbread.

To spare St. Clair from his own thoughts of an orphaned, angry, bewildered past, she talked.

Three

As Sebastian listened to Miss Danforth prattle on about quilting parties and old women who held "knitting meets" with their familiars, he wondered if Wellington himself might not be behind the recent series of duels.

Sebastian's first year of repatriation had been calm enough. The worst he'd suffered had been scornful looks, the cut direct here and there, a smattering of snide asides—the very same fare served him during his initial months with the French Army. A few months ago, the tenor of the abuse had become more lethal, as if somebody important had gone down a list of post-war grudges and come to Sebastian's name.

"I have not seen you knitting, Miss Danforth, for all that you claim to have won these knitting races." Inane talk, this, but she was trying not to cry, and Sebastian would aid her as best he could.

"I knit at night now, when I can't sleep. I do the piecework during the day, when the light is better."

"I have seen the old sailors, sitting with their tankards, knitting away as if their hands belonged to somebody else. I have seen the old women, too, knitting while cannonballs flew over their heads. Knitting must be powerful medicine for the mind."

"Why on earth would old women be knitting in the midst of cannon fire? Why would old women even be within hearing of cannon fire?"

Her indignation was a tonic. Every soul on earth ought to regard the combination of old women and cannon fire with outrage. The human race should go to bed each night praying to *le bon Dieu* such a tragedy never befell any of their members again.

Though it would, human nature being incorrigibly foolish.

"I commanded a small garrison in the mountains of southwestern France. For much of the war, we had little to do but serve as a place for troops going into Spain to eat and rest." He told this lie smoothly, because he'd rehearsed it often in his mind, which made it no less mendacious. "Some officers brought their wives to the post, and we had our share of laundresses and cooks, the same as any army."

Whores, most of them, and God bless them for it.

"I cannot fathom women in the midst of warfare."

Miss Danforth looked less grim and peaked to contemplate this topic than to contemplate the loss of her aunts. Sebastian brought the phaeton to a halt in deference to a donkey disinclined to proceed into an intersection. The ragman at the beast's head was cursing fluently, but in such a thick Cockney accent, Sebastian doubted Miss Danforth could comprehend it.

"Look around you, Miss Danforth. You see the

strolling gentlemen, the shop boys, the tigers and grooms, the fellows milling about outside that tavern? Pretend they're all gone—not a fellow left in sight. Now pretend your job is to kill the enemy, or be killed by her, day in and day out. How long do you think it would take for that combination, of warfare all around and not a single member of the opposite sex among you, to become untenable?"

The ragman lifted a whip from the cart's seat and came around to brandish it at the donkey.

"War is untenable," she said. "I cannot see how anybody stands to raise a weapon at somebody who has done them no wrong, much less pull the trigger."

The whip came down on the beast's shoulder, viciously hard, and Miss Danforth turned her head away. Had she not been beside him, Sebastian would have already been out of his vehicle. He passed her the reins, leaped down, and approached the donkey. The beast was tiny, its hide scarred and its tail matted with burrs. Outside the tavern on the corner—the Wild Hare—bets were being placed, probably over how many lashes it would take to get the animal moving or kill it.

The whip came up again.

"How much?"

At Sebastian's question, the ragman lowered the whip and turned a puzzled frown over his shoulder. "Beg pardon, guv. I'll have the beast moving directly, see if I don't."

He raised the whip again, but Sebastian forestalled the next blow by the simple expedient of snatching the whip from the man's hand. "How much for the beast?"

Simon gestured for his tiger, and the boy came to

heel quickly, no stranger to these encounters. Simon passed the lad the whip, because sometimes a man needed two fists on short notice.

"Yer want t'buy 'er?"

"*How much?*"

The ragman dressed to advertise his trade in an assemblage of fabrics that, had they been clean, would have been colorful enough for any tinker. Rheumy blue eyes turned crafty. "I've met your kind. You like to beat 'em, like to beat the wenches too."

The donkey stood quietly, head hanging, while the gallery at the pub had gone silent.

"I do appreciate the necessity for the occasional display of violence," Sebastian said, stroking a hand over the animal's shaggy gray fur. "But I like my opponent to be able to fight back, not trussed up in harness, a bit in her mouth, and a whip in my hand."

On the seat of the phaeton, Miss Danforth was perfectly composed. The team stood placidly in the traces, suggesting not even her hands conveyed nervousness.

"Two quid."

Exorbitant for a beast broken in spirit, foundered, and underfed. Sebastian flicked a glance at the tiger, who produced the requisite funds. "You have two minutes to unhitch your cart."

He climbed back into the phaeton, and before he could retrieve the reins, Miss Danforth signaled the team to walk on. His geldings—a young pair given to occasional fits and starts—moved off smoothly.

"You were discussing your aunts, Miss Danforth." He came off sounding like a headmaster trying to restore decorum to a classroom overtaken by chaos.

"*We* were discussing the civilizing influence of women on men compelled to make war. If I hadn't been here, you would have trounced that fellow, wouldn't you? I would have liked to have seen that."

He liked the sight of her, her posture the perfect, relaxed, graceful pose of a lady comfortable with the reins. Had her knitting aunts taught her how to drive? "You like seeing men behave like animals?"

"Of course not. I like seeing justice done. I like that very much. The donkey was afraid of the dogs hanging about the tavern."

He thought of her cousins, who hadn't had the decency to notify her of her aunt's death. Oppressed and bloodthirsty were not the same thing. "Justice is a fine objective, bloody knuckles are not. Will you give me back the reins?"

She looked down at her hands in surprise, then over at him. "Must I?"

The smile she turned on him was complicated. Winsome, chagrined, a bit sad, and entirely feminine. Were she French, she'd learn to use that smile, because it made her not beautiful—her coloring was too vivid to be beautiful—but alluring.

"No, you need not. My horses have decided they like you. This is a great compliment."

He liked her. He liked that she hadn't turned up sniffy because he'd threatened a ragman, discussed money in the street, and taken up for a homely jenny who was—to all appearances—merely exhausted and in want of courage.

Sebastian propped his foot on the fender and decided to make a clean breast of matters. "It is a failing of mine to interest myself in the fate of fractious animals. I will find the little beast work at the Chelsea farm if she can be made sound in body and spirit."

Miss Danforth cooed to the horses, and they lifted to a spanking trot. "You get it from your aunt, then. I'm a fractious animal, and she's found work for me."

"You are not wearing driving gloves." Miss Danforth was poor enough not to have a good second pair, and yet, Sebastian didn't take the reins from her.

"Your geldings have velvet mouths. I was dreading this trip, but I'm enjoying it now. Aunt Hy would like that."

Her smile was muted, but because he'd achieved a distraction from the near occasion of tears, Sebastian let her keep the reins and remained silent until they'd reached their objective less than an hour later.

Chelsea was little more than a village enjoying a spate of growth owing to its proximity to London, and yet, it was still a pretty village. Miss Danforth drove them down one of the quieter streets, to a tidy Tudor house set amid a riot of daffodils.

Sebastian saw many an Englishman's dream in the snug, tidy cottage—many an Englishwoman's too. "I am not cheered to think you left this for the stink and pretense of Mayfair."

She gave him a look, suggesting his observation was unexpected. "I am not cheered to think of you watching over old women while cannonballs whizzed overhead. The key is around back."

The cottage was more substantial that it appeared from the lane. Miss Danforth maneuvered the phaeton around back, where orderly gardens backed up to pastureland. When he'd set her down and tied up the geldings, she extracted a key from between two loose bricks and opened a back door.

She gestured him inside, which was a surprise. A man and an unmarried woman ought not to be in an empty house together, not according to the strangling list of proprieties adhered to by Polite Society.

"I am worried about Peter," she said, taking off her bonnet and gloves. "The house might already have been let, and the next tenants are not likely to look kindly on him."

A soldier learned to appreciate simple things— quiet, order, solitude, and cleanliness. The house offered these gifts in abundance. The kitchen was spotless and full of light from back windows overlooking the gardens. The copper-bottomed pots gleamed, the andirons were freshly blacked, the mullioned windows sparkled.

The curtains sported embroidered borders of pansies and morning glories, jewel-tone colors in riotous patterns. As Sebastian moved with Miss Danforth upward through the house, the same peaceful, pretty aesthetic prevailed.

"This is a happy house." He could feel it, just as he'd felt the misery, pain, and despair in the cold stone walls of the Château.

"My cousins could not understand how we could be happy here, three spinster ladies with only modest means. My aunt's bequest is in here."

He followed her into a bedroom, and knew immediately this was where Miss Danforth had slept.

Except in this house, she'd been Milly. She'd been

loved, and confident of that love. Her ease showed in the way she moved through the rooms, sure of her destination and her place. She knelt before a bed covered by an elaborately embroidered counterpane, peacocks and doves, beauty and peace in a pattern of green, blue, white, and gold.

"This was to be my trousseau," she said, dragging a trunk from under the bed. The bed was raised; nobody would have thought to consider the underspace as storage, and the trunk was not small.

She'd flaunted propriety in the interests of availing herself of Sebastian's muscle—practical of her. "Is there more you would retrieve before we depart, Miss Danforth?"

"A few small things."

"Then I will leave you to make your farewells." He hefted the trunk to his shoulder, happy to depart before grieving sentiments could overtake pragmatism. The trunk smelled slightly of cedar and camphor, and was surprisingly light, suggesting her trousseau did not include much silver.

"I'll be along soon, my lord."

He left her sitting on the bed, alone in a pretty house that by rights should have come to her. This thought bothered him, because he was glad her cousins had cheated her out of her inheritance, for it meant his aunt had a cheerful, practical companion who was easy to look upon and competent with the reins.

❦

The baron had hefted the trunk holding her trousseau as if it had been no more weighty than a wicker basket full of clean sheets. In his absence, Milly sat on the bed where she'd slept most every night of her adult life until recently, and inventoried her emotions.

The very exercise the baron had no doubt given her solitude to undertake.

She was in the grip of a sense of loss, but the loss had started two years ago when Aunt Mil had begun to fade. The aunts had known they were leaving Milly, and had done what they could to safeguard her future.

The house was just a house, as Aunt Hy had said. When the baron had escorted Milly up from the kitchen, the house had felt small and empty.

In addition to the feeling of loss was a sense of satisfaction, because the aunts' plan was successfully implemented. Milly was safely ensconced in the employ of a Mayfair baroness, one who understood about dreadful cousins.

And Milly was relieved too, because even if those dreadful cousins should surprise her on the premises, his lordship would deal with them, as Lady St. Clair had no doubt intended.

St. Clair would not come back inside to retrieve her, either. His ease with difficult emotions meant Milly would not have to rush her farewells.

Though neither would she prolong them, because the final emotion Milly could not ignore was loneliness. She had been happy with the aunts, and she had been lonely.

She was lonely still.

"You can come out now."

Nothing, not even a rustle. Perhaps Peter was downstairs, hiding from Alcorn and Frieda, who'd probably inspected the house before Hyacinth had been measured for her shroud.

Peter did not lack for the self-preservation instinct. "Peter Francis Danforth!"

Still nothing. Milly turned her steps down the hallway, to Hyacinth's sitting room, and there she found her quarry in his customary spot in the window, as if waiting for the next quilting party when all and sundry would make their obeisance to him before the workbaskets were opened.

"There you are."

He glowered up at her in feline indignation, flicking his great black tail as if to ask, "Where on earth have you been?"

"I came as soon as I could, and while I appreciate that you've maintained the order of the household, it's time to go now. Aunt Hy wanted you to come with me. It's the only thing she asked of me."

Milly spoke not for the cat's benefit, but for her own. She picked him up, surprised as always at his sheer weight. A cat so fluffy ought not to weigh so much. Predictably, he began a rumbling purr.

"You are a fraud, Peter Francis. You glower at the world, switching your tail and promising doom to all who cross you, and then you start that purr..."

Aunt Hy had claimed the purr helped her rheumatism. She'd sat with the cat in her lap, stroking his soft, dark fur for hours while Aunt Mil had read and Milly had done piecework.

"The baroness will love you," Milly said around the lump in her throat. "But you're mine now. And I'm yours. You may love her ladyship, too, but you'll always be mine."

She tucked the cat against her and walked through the house, looking neither left nor right. She'd slipped a bottle of Aunt Hy's perfume in her skirt pocket, but left everything else as she'd found it, knowing Alcorn and Frieda would note anything substantially out of place.

When she passed through the back door, she set Peter down for a moment while she worked the key. On impulse, she slipped the key in her pocket too, then picked up the cat.

The baron had secured her trunk to the back of the phaeton and was lounging by his vehicle, the picture of a handsome man enjoying a pretty day in the country. He pushed away from the phaeton at the sight of Milly.

"That is a cat." His tone was a combination of consternation and banked hostility.

"This is Peter. Peter Francis Danforth. He was Aunt Hy's dearest friend, and if I don't collect him, my cousins will banish him to the stables or worse."

"I drove the length of the city to retrieve a cat. A black cat."

"He is black." Wonderfully, unrelievedly, marvelously black with piercing green eyes and plush, long fur. "He's very friendly."

That a cat was friendly was no particular recommendation. Milly should have said Peter caught a prodigious number of mice, except he'd never caught a mouse in his pampered life. As predators went, Peter was an utter failure.

The baron's expression did not soften, and now—now when she could not reach a handkerchief because of the burden she held—Milly's tears welled.

"I can find a home for him, if you insist, but the baroness assured me…" She could *not* find a home for this cat. He was lazy and friendly, two mortal sins for an animal who ought to survive by hunting. He was convinced dogs were his intended companions, after old women, children, and Mr. Hamilton down at the Boar's Tail.

Milly brushed her cheek over Peter's head. "I thought that's why we brought the wicker hamper."

Her voice had wobbled. She buried her nose in Peter's rumbling warmth and wondered if the baron were susceptible to begging, because Milly could not lose this cat. She would sell her trousseau, face her cousins, pawn the little bottle of scent, give up her last links with the aunts—

A hand landed on her shoulder. "The error was mine. Of course your friend cannot be left alone in his grief. I take it he is old?"

St. Clair's voice was gruff, and yet his hand on Milly's shoulder was gentle. She ran her nose over Peter's neck. "Five."

"In his prime, then. He will make a lovely addition to Aunt's sitting room, and soon have all her confidences."

The baron moved off, taking the warmth of his hand with him. Milly watched while he removed a peculiar assortment of items from the wicker hamper: A thick wool blanket, a bottle of wine or spirits. A wrapped loaf of bread, a small wheel of cheese, a jar of preserves, a quarter ham in cloth.

He piled these offerings on the seat, and Milly realized the morning had passed. "Were we to picnic, then?"

Dark brows rose over unreadable green eyes. For a moment, the most distinct sound was Peter's purring.

"Would you *like* to picnic, mademoiselle?"

❦

Somebody sought in a methodical, determined manner to kill Sebastian, and yet, he had offered to picnic with a sad young lady on a gorgeous spring day. Because surviving the tender mercies of the French Army had absorbed his most callow years, he'd never made such an offer before.

Was one picnic in the English countryside too much to ask of an adulthood otherwise devoted to war and its aftermath?

"I would like a picnic," Miss Danforth said. "Peter would like that as well."

"Then the vote is unanimous. Have you a location in mind?"

Of course, she did. She had Sebastian turn the horses out in an overgrown paddock across the alley from the house. While the cat followed Miss Danforth around the yard, she picked a bouquet of daffodils and disappeared for a time up the lane. When she returned, she no longer carried the flowers.

Sebastian had spread their blanket in the spot she'd designated in the shade of the back gardens, a place not visible from the alley or the home of the one neighbor the property boasted.

"I would have gone with you, you know," he informed his companion as she lowered herself to the blanket.

"With me?"

"You went to the churchyard, to pay your last respects. One wants to do this alone, and yet one should not have to."

One, one, one. He was leaning toward his English side today, which was odd, because all of his funerals, including the many he'd presided over as any commanding officer might, had been in French.

Miss Danforth opened the hamper, which Sebastian had repacked as best he could.

"Aunt told me I was not to wallow in my grief. She was quite stern about that. I was to find a good position and make the most of it. We have no utensils."

Sebastian withdrew his everyday knife from his left boot and presented the handle to her. Based on Miss Danforth's expression, this was not *comme il faut* at a picnic.

A cessation of hostilities left a soldier hopelessly behindhand, though it had been some time since Sebastian had felt so very out of step with his surroundings. "Shall we retrieve napkins, forks, and such from the house?"

She examined his knife, a serviceable, bone-handled blade whose twin reposed against the small of Sebastian's back. He kept his smallest throwing dagger in his right boot, that being the handiest location for quick retrieval.

"I'd rather not go back into the house, thank you." She took the knife from his palm without touching his bare skin. "A knife is all we really need."

"A knife is often sufficient for the moment." Also silent, reusable, and capable of being hurled at one's enemies as they retreated, with more accuracy than most small pistols afforded. "If you'll pass me the bread?"

They managed sandwiches, and then came to another awkward moment over the Madeira.

"You must not go thirsty on my account, Miss Danforth. Drink from the bottle, and I will manage." Though his morning coffee was but a memory, and the ride back would be dusty.

He'd been thirstier. He'd once gone nearly three days without much water, and the results had produced all manner of useful insights for a man whose business had been prying the truth from unlikely sources.

Miss Danforth considered the bottle, then her companion. One or the other must have found favor. "We'll share."

She tipped the bottle up and took a swallow of wine fortified with brandy. Even genteel elderly ladies might have such a drink on hand for chilly evenings and special occasions. Miss Danforth was not shy about enjoying her libation, her throat working as she took another swallow, then another.

Was she trying to drown her grief?

She wiped the lip of the bottle on her handkerchief before passing the drink to him. "It's quite good. Very restorative."

Abruptly, the moment shifted, at least for Sebastian. Miss Danforth's tidy bun had slipped on their journey. A dusting of dark cat hair graced her otherwise spotless bodice, and she wore no gloves. Her lips were damp from the wine, and perhaps because she'd been crying earlier, her brown eyes were…luminous.

Sebastian took the bottle, wondering if there were *ever* a convenient time to be ambushed by lust. He drank deeply and passed the bottle back. "The cork is around here somewhere." He'd seen the cat batting it about, in fact.

She produced the cork, jammed it in the bottle, and then sank back, bracing her weight on her hands, turning her face up to the sun. "You are being very kind, my lord. I appreciate it."

Sebastian did not want her gratitude. Of all the inexplicable, inconvenient impulses, he wanted his bare hands on her naked and possibly freckled breasts, alas for him. Such were the burdens of being half-French that the freckles had something to do with his unruly impulse.

"Do you think it's such a trial for me, Miss Danforth, to enjoy the company of a pretty lady on a lovely day? Do you think bread, cheese, wine, and some viands cannot satisfy my appetite because some ancestor of mine survived a foolhardy charge into the enemy lines for his king centuries ago?"

Any subordinate under his command, any prisoner in his keeping would have known that soft tone presaged temper or worse.

Miss Danforth closed her eyes, making her complexion an offering to the sun. "You sound very English when you're in a pet. Your consonants when you conversed with that ragman could have cleaved gems, and I know good and well I am not pretty."

No, she was worse than pretty, as Sebastian had had occasion to conclude earlier; she was *alluring*. Her attractiveness came from slightly disheveled red hair—not auburn, not titian—eyes that slanted a bit, a complexion that bore a hint of porcelain roses, and a mouth...

Sebastian looked away. A commanding officer became very skilled at looking away. After a few years, it was nearly a reflex.

"A woman need not be blond and blue-eyed to appeal to a man's aesthetic sensibilities. More wine?" Much less appeal to his ill-timed and completely illogical lust. The French side of him was overcome with hilarity at the expense of his dignity, while the English side tried to think of Aunt's collection of Sèvres bud vases.

"No, thank you. No more wine for me. Who was the last person you lost, my lord?"

Maybe she was unused to any spirits at all, or maybe she was trying to distract herself from her grief. Two feet beyond the blanket, the black cat stretched itself out to an enormous length, then curled up and commenced vibrating.

"Who was the last man you kissed, Miss Danforth?"

As an interrogator, he knew the value of a sneak attack, knew the value of a question lobbed at a flagging mind from an undefended angle. His inquiry, however, had emerged without any warning *to him*.

Her lips quirked; she did not open her eyes. "I kissed Peter. That is not an appropriate question, my lord."

He shifted on the blanket, so he could undertake his folly properly. When he slid a hand into Miss Danforth's hair, she opened her eyes, and up close, Sebastian could see flecks of gold in her irises.

"I cannot bear to talk of death, Miss Danforth. Not now."

She regarded him, her expression putting him in

mind of the cat. Unreadable, unafraid, unblinking. Something in her vibrated too, with intelligence, warmth, and feminine awareness.

He would never again picnic on a lovely day with a pretty girl, not because his death warrant had already been signed, but because the occasion provoked him to odd behaviors.

Sebastian leaned forward another inch. "No more talk of dying and grieving, no more tears and suffering. I cannot bear it. Do you hear me?"

Though when a grieving woman could not cry, she was a much more worrisome creature.

He kissed her, perhaps because he hadn't cried since his mother's funeral, but more likely because the unreadable depths of Miss Danforth's chocolate-brown eyes shifted and became, if not warm, then at least curious.

For a kiss that bore more than a little anger on Sebastian's part, the touch of Miss Danforth's lips on his was sunlight-soft. She scooted closer, one of her hands wrapping around the back of his head, the other cradling his cheek.

She tasted of the wine, of sweetness, and a little of grief. He kissed the grief then nudged it aside by stroking his fingers over her cheek, her throat, her temple. Though she was a redhead, her hair was silky soft, and her skin…

No human female ought to have skin like that, warm and smooth, and a sheer pleasure for a man to drag his fingertips over. He wanted to taste her everywhere, and that he'd never have the chance was the only thing that made him ease out of the kiss.

"You are alive," he growled. "Be grateful for that. Don't tempt fate by questioning your good fortune, because one day it will be you who lies in some churchyard."

Or on a muddy battlefield buzzing with flies, or at the bottom of some ravine in the freezing Pyrenees, or blown to bits when a cannonball hit the powder magazine by merest lucky—tragic, horrible, unendurable—chance.

"You are alive, too." Miss Danforth was much better at scolding with a kiss than Sebastian would ever be. She pressed her mouth to his, all business, though her hand on his jaw was gentle.

Before he marshaled his wits to react, she took her mouth away and patted his cheek, putting him in mind of his recent meeting with young Pierpont.

"Have some more wine," she said, and Sebastian did not argue. When he'd finished, he passed the bottle to her without wiping the lip, and she too indulged in a healthy tot.

He was supposed to apologize for kissing her; he was sure of it in both the English and the French parts of his mind. He might as well apologize for the beautiful weather, for her aunt dying, for being a man, for Miss Danforth's own glorious red hair. The kiss had been relatively chaste, at least compared with his thoughts.

The Frenchman in him decided he would not apologize for it.

Sebastian tossed the cat a few bits of ham, then wrapped the uneaten food in its cloths and stowed it behind the seat of the carriage. The blanket went into the hamper followed by the cat, and in short order, the team was headed back to Town at a spanking trot.

And now—of course—the sky was sporting the sort of low, sulking clouds that would only gather more and more closely, until rain was inevitable.

"We'll beat the weather," Miss Danforth said as they reached Earl's Court. "When a storm threatens, it clears the traffic, so you can make excellent time. Thank you for taking me, your lordship."

He hadn't *taken* her, though had they kissed much longer, he would have wanted to. That kiss hadn't been entirely meant as a scold or a lecture. He was too out of practice with lust to know where desire ended and anger began.

Anger or loneliness. He barely knew the woman, which seemed to be the primary prerequisite for an erotic encounter in his life.

"You will not rail at me for taking liberties, Miss Danforth? I might have made the same point without molesting your person."

In the basket, the enormous cat shifted, making the wicker creak. The damned beast probably understood every word of English spoken in its presence.

"I do not consider myself molested, my lord."

How he hated the my-lording, and how he approved of her answer. In the distance, off to the south, thunder rumbled. He could not tell her that he was lonely, though the notion had strutted into his thoughts with the unapologetic confidence of a personal truth.

Not a very useful concept, loneliness.

"You never did answer my question, Miss Danforth."

She smoothed her gloved hand over her skirts, a hand that Sebastian now knew bore freckles across the back. The gesture told him she recalled exactly which question he alluded to: Who was the last man she'd kissed?

"I hadn't any answer. You were my first."

Another rumble of thunder, though thunder on the right was supposed to bring good luck.

"*I* gave you your first kiss?" The notion pleased him inordinately, and confirmed his sense that the men of England were a troop of witless apes. No wonder their womenfolk were such a twitchy, high-strung lot. "How did I do?"

She smiled a patient, female smile. "You were awful."

Ah, but that smile told a different story. "Perhaps in the future, you will provide me an opportunity to improve on my performance."

He winked at her, to show he was teasing and could be trusted, utterly, and because the day had abruptly become much less about death, scoldings, and shoving aside bad memories.

She did not wink back, but neither did her smile fade entirely from her eyes until they reached home.

Four

MILLY WAS ACQUAINTED WITH ONE VALET, HER COUSIN Alcorn's servant, Winslow. She knew not whether Winslow was a first name or a patronymic, and had never heard the fellow say more than, "salt, please," or "good day, mum."

Michael Brodie would make at least two of Winslow and was likely half his age, but those weren't the only reasons Mr. Brodie made Milly uneasy.

"Good day to you, Miss Danforth. I understand condolences are in order."

He stood in the doorway, unsmiling, her trunk in his hands, the only sound the rain pelting the window of the little sitting room outside Milly's bedroom.

"Thank you, Mr. Brodie. If you would please put my trunk there by the wall?"

Not in her bedroom. Not even in broad daylight with the door ajar and the rest of the household likely to stroll by did she want to open her bedroom door to this blond, green-eyed Irishman.

As he walked past her, Milly caught the distinctive scent of vetiver. Valets were not to bear such a fragrance, nor were they to hoist trunks about like second footmen or porters.

"It's a pretty trunk," he remarked, setting it down and dusting his hands. Michael Brodie had big hands, and they were callused. Milly was certain Winslow's hands were not callused.

Though the baron's were.

"The baroness reports that you've lost the last of your family," Mr. Brodie said, taking out a handkerchief and wiping off the lid of the trunk.

Peter chose that moment to appear from under the brocade skirt of the small table in the corner.

"Not the last of my family. I have a married cousin, and he has been blessed with three children." And she had Peter.

"Who's this fine lad?"

She wanted Mr. Brodie out of her sitting room, wanted back the last of the solitude guaranteed her by the baroness's nap.

A brogue or a burr had whispered through Brodie's question. *An' who's this foin lad?*

Mr. Brodie was trying to be friendly, and despite the chill in his green eyes, Milly felt compelled to acknowledge the overture. "Peter is a bequest from my aunt."

He picked up the cat, and a predictable rumble underscored the rain against the windows. "A friendly fellow."

"My aunts treasured that about him, as do I."

Mr. Brodie glanced out the window, to the damp gardens beneath. The spring flowers were ebbing, and the summer blooms not in evidence, and yet Milly found the scene soothing.

"I am friendly too, Miss Danforth. Now, don't be pokering up like that. All I mean to say is that if you've need of a ride out to Chelsea, next time you might ask me. His lordship would have spared me for such a task were I not from home."

She wanted to snatch her traitorous cat out of his arms, but Peter was shamelessly snuggling against a broad male chest. "Thank you, Mr. Brodie. I took my request to her ladyship, and she assigned my driver. I trust his lordship was not too discommoded."

"His lordship would ride to hell on a lame horse for his auntie, but you have to know…"

He paused and scratched Peter under his hairy chin, rendering the feline nigh cataleptic with bliss.

"What do I have to know, Mr. Brodie?"

He turned and sat on her trunk, cuddling the cat like a baby. The sight should have been charming. Milly instead found it presumptuous that Mr. Brodie would make himself so comfortable in her sitting room.

Mr. Brodie cuddled the cat more closely. "His lordship served in the French Army."

"I know that. He was abandoned by his family after the Peace of Amiens—his English family—and had no real choice."

Brodie stopped scratching the cat. "Abandoned? He told you that?"

"He offered it, I did not ask. A person's past is their own business." Every person's, including Mr. Brodie's—and Milly's.

"Aye, 'tis, but many don't see it that way. There are those who'd hold a boy's tragedy against the man he became."

Abruptly, Milly felt the need to sit as well. Mr. Brodie was trying to warn her of something, something uncomfortable.

"I know about the duels, Mr. Brodie. Her ladyship knows of them too, somehow."

He muttered something in...Gaelic? "Her ladyship probably knows what flavor of jam Wellington had on his toast this morning, but she cannot stop the fools who challenge a man, though all he wants is to tend his acres in peace."

Was that all St. Clair wanted? Milly thought of him looming over the ragman, thought of his kiss, and hoped Mr. Brodie was wrong.

"What are you trying to tell me, Mr. Brodie?"

He rose and passed her the cat, but continued to stroke its cheek with two fingers. "I'm trying to tell you that it isn't safe for anybody to be too close to St. Clair. He has enemies, and they would destroy anyone and anything near him to end his life or simply to torment him. For some, the war will never be over."

"Are you threatening me?"

He dropped his hand. "No, lass. I'm warning you. You've noticed St. Clair doesn't escort his auntie if he can help it, noticed he never takes a groom when he rides out. You will notice that his aunt doesn't press him to socialize beyond the perfunctory meddling of an elderly relation."

Peter leaped from Milly's arms without warning, his powerful back legs imprinting an ache on her chest.

"That is no way to live. His lordship cannot help that he served for his adopted country. He's not the only person for whom the Corsican's bloodlust resulted in impossible choices."

Mr. Brodie studied her for a moment. He was not only big, blond, green-eyed, and muscular, he was also handsome, particularly with that sad light in his eyes.

"Your principles do you credit, Miss. See that they don't get you or the baron killed."

He bowed and left her alone, with more to think about than ever. She closed the door behind him and poked up the fire, wanting instead to beat something or somebody with the poker.

"Is St. Clair to live the rest of his life like a leper?" she asked the room in general.

Peter sprang to the windowsill and commenced to bathe himself.

"Alcorn and Frieda have resented me my entire life simply for being born. Some people delight in carrying grudges, but I do not think my cousins would attempt to kill me."

In pursuit of his ablutions, Peter adopted an indelicate pose most humans would find impossible, if not uncomfortable.

"They would encourage me to find a husband, though, and then sabotage my chances in that regard." Humiliating her endlessly in the process.

Thoughts of marriage were enough to send Milly into her bedroom for her workbasket. She wanted to think not of marriage, but of the baron's kiss, of the mischief in his eyes when he winked at her, of the novelty of feeling feminine, desirable, and cherished, if only for a moment, if only by a near stranger.

A handsome near stranger who knew how to scold

and comfort both, in a single kiss, then how to tease so neither the scold nor the comfort ached much at all.

Milly drew her workbasket out from under the bed. Something made her pause as she straightened, a sensation like being watched. She turned slowly, trying to place the origin of that feeling. The room was small, furnished with comfortable, mismatched pieces that nonetheless felt cozy. But something…

Vetiver. The scent of it was concentrated here by the close air of a small upper room on a rainy afternoon.

Michael Brodie had already been in her bedroom, the same Michael Brodie who'd warned her the baron had unseen enemies.

❧

"Michael, I have been foolish." Sebastian had kept this announcement to himself for the entirety of three days, for the distance of several long walks in Hyde Park, for the duration of two morning hacks that had taken him, of all places, to the Agrarian Society's experimental farm outside Chelsea.

Michael spread his cards on the table. "You have been nothing but foolish, lately. I've a double-double run, and I shall beat you handily if you don't start minding the game."

Michael was ferocious about his cribbage, and about as subtle as a cavalry charge when provoked on certain topics.

"You are working up to a speech, my friend." Sebastian advanced his peg one point, because he'd pulled the jack of the same suit as the cut card. "Let me guess. I'm overdue for 'Why survive five years in the Pyrenees with Henri breathing down our necks, the English pounding at the gates, and rations bordering on poison, only to be killed by an excess of English vengeance now?'"

Michael turned over his crib, another hand of four cards. "Not a point to be had. There being no hope for you whatsoever, I was thinking more along the lines of, 'Are you trying to get your aunt's companion killed too?'"

Sebastian gathered up the deck and let the cards riffle through his hands. "She was safe enough."

From English vengeance.

Michael rose and went to the decanters across the library. "Miss Danforth is an innocent. Innocents have a way of getting caught by stray bullets." Michael had younger sisters, one of whom he'd never met, and all of whom had been born with red hair, much like Miss Danforth.

"We're in London, Michael. English officers do not fire upon innocents in broad daylight, and I tell you, they don't want to kill me. I'd be dead four times over if they did. If I'm killed, then some old English general will die in retaliation, and nobody wants to provoke such an embarrassing feud now that England and France are great good friends again."

Though Michael had a damnably valid point, and they both knew it.

Sebastian tried to tattle on himself again. "I was referring to foolishness of a different order."

Michael paused mid-sniff over a decanter. He preferred whiskey that didn't reek of peat smoke, and Sebastian made it a point to keep some on hand.

"Your aunt has been tippling my favorite whiskey," Michael said, bringing half a glass to the table. "That is foolishness. The woman is no bigger than a minute and ought not to be indulging so freely."

Aunt could probably drink Michael under the table. "She has her reasons. Soon she'll have another."

"Because she'll be measuring you for your shroud?" The question was cheerful, as only a peevish, tired Scot could be cheerful.

"Because she'll be in want of a companion."

The good cheer in Michael's eyes died, though he took a respectful moment to sample his whiskey before asking the inevitable. "How did Miss Danforth find out about you so soon? You didn't tell her yourself?"

"I told her I'd served in the French Army."

"Many did. The parole towns are full of Frenchmen still. That alone wouldn't drive Miss Danforth off. She needs the coin, her heart's aching for the loss of her aunties, and she has no family worth the name."

An accurate summation, one that inspired the guilt roiling in Sebastian's gut to burn up from his belly toward his throat. "All true. Shall we finish this game?"

"You shall finish unburdening yourself first. I believe the words, 'Bless me, Father, for I have sinned…' might get you started. Particularly if you told the girl about the nature of your duties on behalf of the *République*."

"Papist."

Michael winked and lifted his glass, though Sebastian knew the rosary worn under Michael's shirt was in memory of his middle sister, and not an indication of popish sentiments.

"I did not tell Miss Danforth what went on at the Château. What I did was worse than that, though I've come to think I did the woman a kindness."

Michael set his drink aside and shuffled the cards. The sound was familiar to any former soldier, and should have been a comfort. "I am not likely to be impressed with this great kindness of yours, am I? And she's a lady, not a woman."

"I kissed her, Michael."

This admission did not result in a deluge of guilt and remorse, as Sebastian had been half hoping it would.

"She's pretty, though she tries to hide it. Any sensible woman in service hides good looks," Michael said, his tone sympathetic. "As long as we're confessing our misdeeds, you need to know I searched her room."

Old habits died hard, particularly when a fellow enjoyed indulging them—old bad habits.

"On whose authority would you violate a young lady's privacy, Michael? I cannot recall giving any such order. Or do we make war on small, defenseless women now?"

When Michael should have bristled and returned fire regarding the weapons available to females of any nationality, he instead cut the deck then shuffled again.

If Sebastian's enemies had finally succeeded in compromising Michael's loyalty, then matters had come to a sad pass indeed, for Michael alone was privy to the battles Sebastian had fought, won, and lost in the bowels of the Château.

"If she's a spy, she's a damned good one," Michael said when the cards were neatly organized. "Six dresses, all turned at least once, each one plainer than the one before it. One pair of boots, two pairs of house slippers, not a new heel on any of them. Underlinen so thin I could practically see through it."

Michael's recitation was disinterested, but Sebastian disliked the idea that Michael—that *anybody*—had seen Miss Danforth's underlinen. "What else?"

"Lavender sachets, a few letters from some soldier boy, a lock of blond hair, bits of household lace, and the most unbelievable quilt you'd ever want to see."

What would Michael consider an unbelievable quilt? "Anything else?"

"Her workbasket is large and well organized. I couldn't get to her reticule because she was off seeing the sights in Chelsea with some fool who's trying to get himself killed. No lap desk, no jewel box, no dancing slippers." Michael set the cards aside and took another swig of his whiskey. "Why can't you find a mistress to dip your wick? Fine English gentlemen have mistresses."

"No mistress for me." Some English officer might bribe her to poison her protector. Sebastian had reason to know such tactics might be attempted—again.

"So you'll dally with the companion until she realizes what you are?"

Michael clearly did not like that option, but he wouldn't blame Sebastian for considering it. Michael was a tolerant soul, despite much posturing to the contrary.

"Dally is such a frivolous word." A frivolous, *wrong* word where Milly Danforth was concerned, though there were no right words.

"You'll ruin her? That's all right, then. The brave English officers won't get a chance at you because your own auntie will finish you off straightaway, assuming I let her have the first shot. You need practice at this confession business, St. Clair. One doesn't announce one's sins, one repents of them."

"I'll not ruin her." He might kiss her again. He might drive out with her again.

Michael finished his drink and slid the cards across the table. "I'm vastly relieved to hear of your virtuous intentions, but you're right: you've kissed her, and that's bad enough. When your reputation catches up with you, she'll give notice, and your aunt will be left with out a friend by her side, and it will be your fault. Again."

"You are such a cheering influence, Michael. Take yourself off to bed, there to dream of the end of the world or whatever gives a nice Catholic boy comfort on a long and cold night."

Michael snorted. "I'm as Catholic as Miss Danforth's cat. I'm also from the North, and I know damned good and well what comfort works best on a long and chilly night—as do you."

Sebastian let him go, relieved to have solitude. Given the chance, Michael would shadow him every-where, the man's loyalty in France a backhanded gift from a God not inclined to deal kindly with soldiers who outlived their wars.

Though now, Sebastian resigned himself to keeping a close eye on his former subordinate. Even an angel could fall prey to such envy as would see him cast from heaven. Michael was a good man, but by no means an angel.

As for the quick tumble Michael prescribed to deal

with virtually all of a man's ills...Sebastian didn't fancy it. Never had. He'd never known Michael to indulge in that sort of folly either, but then, Michael could be as discreet as death at three in the morning.

A sense of being watched plucked at Sebastian's nerves. He glanced around the room, gratified to find his instincts still functioned.

"What are you doing here?"

The cat needed no more invitation than that to hop down from the back of the sofa and spring up onto the card table.

"You have no manners, sir."

And no dignity, either, for the beast was purring as it stropped itself against Sebastian's chin. Sebastian collected the cat into his lap.

"Am I your next project, cat? The next harmless old dear you intend to cozen for your meals?"

To be an old dear was a humble ambition, one Sebastian could not allow himself to aspire to. "Miss Danforth no doubt misses you, beast. You should go to her."

Sebastian wanted to go to her and be calmed and comforted by her pretty, female scent—lavender and bergamot. He wanted to kiss her again, to touch her hand, to forget for a few minutes that he was a man with a price on his head. He wanted to watch her brown eyes light with humor and surprise as she told him his kisses were tedious and awful.

"She is lonely, too, cat. She and I would not speak of that. We would not have to." They'd kiss, though, and that was the same discussion in a more efficient language—a language even a spinster companion might understand if Sebastian were patient enough.

For her, Sebastian could find oceans of patience.

"Your lady has no lap desk, my friend. Did you know that?" Sebastian had made a point to learn this before the woman had been under his roof four hours. "Every lady has a lap desk, and she keeps her journal in it, and her billet-doux, but your lady has nobody left to write to."

Sebastian set the cat out in the chilly corridor, closed the library door, and returned to the table. He could tell Miss Danforth that she'd been kissed by the Traitor Baron, and tell her exactly what he'd done to earn that sobriquet.

In which case, she'd be gone by the week's end.

He picked up the deck of cards and dealt himself a hand of solitaire.

&

"I have neglected my duty to St. Clair," the baroness announced. "Milly, you must aid me in making reparation."

Milly considered the seam she was working on, a curving arc between two swatches of velvet, one purple, one black. "I am yours to command, my lady."

Across the music room, Professor Baumgartner cleared his throat but did not look up from his scribblings. The professor was a tall, dapper Prussian who said little, smiled occasionally, and generally trailed her ladyship about of a morning, though he did not live in.

Her ladyship shot a tolerant smile at her secretary. "Herr Doktor Professor is laughing at me. He can do it in at least seven languages."

He paused in his writing long enough to smile back

at her. "Nine, and a smattering of several others, if your ladyship will please recall."

Nine languages that he not only spoke, but read fluently—and her ladyship thought such a thing a teasing matter.

"St. Clair has neglected his duty to the succession," her ladyship went on, and from her tone, she was not teasing in the least. "We must guide him toward holy matrimony, Milly. It is our duty."

"Of course, your ladyship." Though Milly felt no such duty. St. Clair was as deserving of the blessings of marriage as the next wealthy, handsome, dashing baron, but guiding him anywhere was a doomed undertaking.

"He said he'd escort me to the Devonshire musicale, and His Grace tends to assemble a more forward-thinking lot. I'll get a peek at the guest list and—"

Milly knew it was futile, but she spoke up anyway on behalf of a man who protected frightened donkeys and flirted with grieving spinsters.

"That is not what he said, ma'am. His lordship *said* he would ask Mr. Brodie to consult the schedule and see if his lordship was available to join in your frivolous pursuits—though he referred to Mr. Brodie as 'the ever-competent Michael.'"

Her ladyship glared down her nose at Milly, and the effect was surprisingly daunting given how delicate that nose was.

"One wants support from one's subordinates, Milly, not lecturing. St. Clair cannot fill his nursery without first taking some sweet young thing to wife. She need not have the skills to run his household—I have that much well in hand—but she must be biddable and fertile, in other words, the typical result of English aristocratic inbreeding. We shall make a list."

And abruptly the morning became perilous, for her ladyship wanted a list.

A written list.

Milly bent her head over her piecework, the better to suggest her hands were too well occupied to deal with pen, ink, and paper. "Perhaps the professor could serve as our amanuensis?"

"Capital! Baum, *attendez-nous*."

He went on scribbling. "Always, my lady."

"Aggravating man. The fate of the house of St. Clair rests on this list, and you scoff."

"I scoff as well, and I bid the company good morning."

St. Clair himself stood in the doorway, attired in subtle elegance and the tolerance of a long-suffering bachelor nephew. "Rather than hunting a bride for me, Aunt, we must find a husband for you. You are becoming obstreperous."

The baron sauntered into the room, while the baroness came to her feet. "I had a husband, I'll thank you to recall. A dear man whose memory leaves no room for successors, and if anybody is becoming obstreperous, it is you."

His lordship kissed his aunt's cheek. "I know you mean well, and your devotion to my welfare is much appreciated, but there will be no lists, my dear."

Milly's piecework lay forgotten in her lap, because there was more to this little exchange than either party was acknowledging.

Lady St. Clair fluffed the folds of his lace cravat. "Sebastian, why must you be so stubborn? A French girl wouldn't offend anybody, except possibly the French, and they do not signify."

"A French girl would be torn to pieces, Aunt, and well you know it."

Torn to pieces by whom?

"She would not, not if you kept her at St. Clair for a few years first, and got some babies on her. Three or four babies don't take that long, and there's little enough effort for their papa involved in the business. You could fuss with your plants and canter about on that white beast of yours and nobody—"

His lordship kissed his aunt's other cheek and murmured something in her ear. It sounded French to Milly, and stern. Whatever it was, it sent her ladyship back to her chair by the fire.

"Play for us, then," she said, waving a hand toward the piano. "Something to soothe an old woman's tattered nerves and broken heart."

St. Clair's smile turned indulgent. "But of course. And something to cheer an underpaid companion at her needlework, and an overworked secretary at his letters."

He folded back the cover over the piano's keys and took the bench, the picture of an elegant gentleman at a drawing-room entertainment. Milly expected him to offer various pieces for the baroness's consideration, the better to placate the old dear with opportunities to carp, criticize, and refuse, but he placed his hands on the keyboard.

And Milly held her breath.

He began with a soft turning melody in a minor key, arpeggios rippling beneath. Milly clutched at the velvet in her hands, missed her aunt, and wanted to close her eyes and simply absorb the torment of such aural beauty.

"Milly, if I'm to be denied an opportunity to aid my nephew, then I will at least be entertained. Fetch me some Byron from the library please. For all his sins, *he* at least knew to take a wife."

How was one to find a single volume of poetry in a room full of books? "Wouldn't you rather listen to the music, your ladyship?"

"For goodness' sake, child, I can listen to poetry and music at the same time. Baum can no doubt listen to poetry in one language and a song in another while the conversation takes place in a third. Be off with you, and have the kitchen send up some tea."

"Of course, your ladyship." Milly took great pains to fold up her sewing. Perhaps if she could find the butler, or even Mr. Brodie…

No, not him. He was a sneak and not to be trusted.

"If you're looking for *Childe Harold's Pilgrimage*, it's on the third shelf above the atlases," the baron said from the keyboard. "A little volume bound in green, and much used, owing to my aunt's preference for racy verse. There's a volume of poetry bound in red which you open at your peril just beside it."

"Thank you, my lord." Milly rose and set aside her sewing. *Thank you, thank you, thank you.*

She retrieved the volume based on his lordship's exact directions, and based on the fact that her own middle name was Harriette, which sounded a bit like Harold at the front end, and—she hoped—looked a bit like Harold as well.

Milly was back in her seat, the professor scratching away, the baron playing his soft, mournful tune when she realized she ought to have lied and said the book was nowhere to be found, because now...

Her heart began to thump, began the slow dirge that presaged humiliation and the possible death of any independence from her cousins' schemes. Milly wanted to hurl the little green book into the fire.

The baron brought his piece to a die-away cadence and rose.

"Aunt, you cannot mean to make Miss Danforth read that tripe. She is gently bred, proper, and has done nothing to deserve such a punishment. You are upset with me, and I shall read your naughty poetry."

Her ladyship looked pleased. "Yes, you shall. *Milly* is working on her trousseau, while you are idling away your morning."

Milly passed over the book, but the baron hesitated for a moment before taking it from her hand. His eyes held humor and resignation.

"Miss Danforth, my thanks."

He took the seat directly to Milly's left, bringing with him his masculine fragrance and a reading voice as lovely as his music had been. When he recited Byron's sad, sly whimsy, he did not sound French, and yet, there was a lyricism to his words that transcended public-school English too.

Occasionally, as he'd turn a page or finish a stanza, his lordship would glance over at Milly, and invariably, he would find her neglecting her stitchery. When she jabbed herself in the finger for the third time, Milly gave up all hope of progress on her mending—not

her trousseau—and surrendered to the pleasure of the
baron's naughty verses.

Five

BEHIND BYRON'S WORLD-WEARY, DISSIPATED INNU-endo lay the heart of a man bewildered and exhausted by the world's disappointments. His poetic lordship had traveled the fringes of war and lived at the heart of the beau monde. He had seen what violent and greedy impulses run amok could do, and had probably reflected at too great a length on the same impulses manifest in himself.

All of which was to say, Sebastian did not enjoy Byron's poetry. He maundered on anyway, mostly from memory, not so much to placate his aunt, but rather to enjoy the sight of Milly Danforth plying her needle beside him.

If Sebastian narrowed his eyes, the colors of her fabrics blurred and blended, like the colors of a slow sunset—reds, oranges, and yellows shifted through green to blue, purple, and the next thing to black. Her hand had a rhythm to the way it formed stitches, like a violinist with her bow or a poet with a line of verse. Byron made sad jokes with his words; Milly Danforth made soft, unlikely beauty with her sewing.

"I beg your ladyship's pardon!"

That expostulation came from Helsom, the butler, who puffed indignantly near the door. A corpulent fellow in gentleman's attire stood at his side, a man losing the battle against brown hair gone thin and a middle gone thick.

"This person disregarded my insistence that the family is not receiving. Your ladyship, your lordship, I do apologize."

"I'm not calling upon the family."

Beside Sebastian, Miss Danforth's head bent closer to her piecework, though she'd ceased stitching.

Aunt remained enthroned by the fire, but Baumgartner had taken up a post behind her chair.

"Sir," her ladyship said, "I do not know you. I will thank you to leave a card and be on your way."

"The Honorable Alcorn Festus Upton, at your service."

Sebastian lifted a finger toward the door, and Helsom melted away.

"Were you honorable," Aunt replied, "you would observe the simplest civilities of Polite Society and take yourself off. I will have you removed forcibly should you fail to mend the error of your ways."

Upton took hold of the lapels of his own coat, like Mr. Garrick taking center stage. "I will remove myself happily, madam—happily!—provided my misguided and vulnerable cousin removes herself with me."

Well, of course. Unease dissipated as Sebastian set the poetry aside and resisted the urge to pat Miss Danforth's hand. This was not a French emissary bearing knives or poison; this was that most universal of nuisances: the Interfering Relative.

Sebastian rose and marshaled his best Etonian accents. "St. Clair, at your service. Perhaps, Upton, you expected to find Miss Danforth in the employ of a short, hunchbacked, squint-eyed little frog?"

Miss Danforth shrank further at his words, and that... it more than aggravated Sebastian, it enraged him.

"I did not address myself to the likes of you, sir," Upton sniffed. "Millicent, gather your things. You cannot realize the extent to which you've blundered this time, and I refuse to tarry here while I explain your missteps to you. Trust me, dearest, most misguided cousin, when I assure you those missteps are egregious."

Michael slipped into the room, Helsom beside him. A glance assured Sebastian that Baumgartner was also prepared to act.

Aunt took a considering sip of her tea. "Sebastian, you will recall there are ladies present, even if this cretin does not." No violence, then. No broken furniture, no spilling of English blood on Aunt's pretty carpets.

Ah, well. A man learned to live with his disappointments.

"Aunt, I will accede to your judgment. Miss Danforth, would you perhaps like to accompany her ladyship up to her sitting room?"

The little companion rose slowly, her piecework clutched in her fists. "Alcorn, explain yourself."

"And be quick about it," Sebastian suggested pleasantly, "because you inconvenience my aunt, and I suspect you embarrass your dearest cousin—to say nothing of aggravating me, Mr. Brodie, and Herr Baumgartner."

Upton lost his grasp of his lapels, apparently noticing for the first time that he faced not only one little old lady, a smallish cousin, and a disgraced Frenchman, but three stout fellows who all topped him by at least half a foot.

"Millicent, come with me," Upton snapped. "You really don't know what you've done by accepting this post. If you come quietly, we may be able to keep your little frolic in service from anybody's notice, though if Vincent gets wind of this, your chances will be permanently queered. Another opportunity is not likely to come along for one of your limitations. I beg of you, heed my direction this instant."

Sebastian had heard such self-assured *direction* before, usually from commanding officers about to send their men into needless danger.

"Alcorn, I am content here. Your concern is appreciated but unneeded. You should go."

"I cannot leave you in the hands of…of the *Traitor Baron*, Cousin. Not when I know you are of limited understanding and ability. I would be remiss—"

He fell silent as Miss Danforth swished up to him, her sewing trailing out behind her like a regimental flag.

"The Traitor *Baron*, Alcorn? What about the traitor *cousin*? You pledge my hand in marriage to a man three times my age without a word to me? You expect me to step and fetch for your wife and daughters without any remuneration, to be grateful for every crumb, when Uncle Stephen charged you personally to ensure my happiness? You destroy any chance I have of maintaining a good, decent post among people who at least show me civility, and you…you failed to inform me of Aunt Hy's passing?" Her voice rose on that last question, rose and broke.

"I didn't want to upset you, and Aunt's demise was a foregone conclusion, as anybody with any sense would have known."

Which disclosure meant Upton had known exactly where to find his cousin, and he'd chosen not to, until now. Sebastian silently implored the cupids cavorting in the molding to imbue him with restraint.

"Upton, you have exceeded my patience," Sebastian said. "If Miss Danforth chooses to remain in my household, then that is where she will remain." And because he was a bad man, as was known by all, Sebastian could not resist adding, "We're rather fond of her, truth be known. She is the very soul of patience and Christian charity."

Sebastian took the soul of patience by the elbow and guided her back two steps, out of range of her cousin's worst notions. She glowered up at him for this gallantry, but Sebastian didn't turn loose of her.

"Of course Milly is a good girl," Upton retorted. "My wife and I saw to her welfare and ensured no waywardness emerged, but Milly is not of sound faculties and must be sheltered from the demands of a cruel and intolerant world. I cannot answer for the sorry influence two elderly ladies had over her in recent years. Millicent, for the last time, come along."

Sebastian wanted to drape an arm around Millicent's shoulders. Her expression suggested she would have bitten him had he dared such overt protectiveness.

"Alcorn, please leave. I am content with my post, and her ladyship's employ is hardly cruel or intolerant. Just the opposite, in fact."

The ladies exchanged smiles, a compliment sincerely rendered and much appreciated.

"Then her ladyship does not know of your limitations, and we must add mendacity to your list of shortcomings, Cousin."

Sebastian did tuck an arm around Miss Danforth's waist. "So my aunt's companion cannot read. *What of it?* Many well-bred ladies don't trouble themselves with that effort, and my aunt employs a very competent secretary to deal with letters and the like. If you're done befouling our morning, Upton, I suggest you allow Brodie and Helsom to escort you from the house."

Beside Sebastian, Miss Danforth was gratifyingly quiet.

"It's worse than that," Upton sputtered. "Her faculties are comparable to that of a simpleton. She cannot read *at all*, can barely write her name, cannot read her Bible even, and that is despite every effort by competent governesses and tutors, and even my own lady wife."

Sebastian twirled a languid finger. "Out. Now."

Helsom and Brodie took a step closer to Miss Danforth's relation, and that fellow, likely because he was as endowed with a taste for self-preservation as the next bullying coward, jerked his coat down over his paunch and spun on his heel.

"Don't go after him," Sebastian muttered, keeping his arm around Miss Danforth. "Don't apologize, don't plead, don't mend fences. Don't."

"I want to plow my fist into his belly."

"Don't do that either. All that lard means he won't feel your blow. You're better off breaking his nose, which will hurt, and the blood will also scare him—messy business, breaking a nose, but he's the kind who'd be more alarmed with the blood than the pain."

She peered at Sebastian, and where he might have expected revulsion at his lapse into the thoughts and vocabulary of an interrogator, Miss Danforth instead looked intrigued.

"I would like to see him scared. I would like to see dear Alcorn terrified, and of something other than his wife."

For her fierceness and her understanding, Sebastian wished, in the corner of his soul that loved the scent of lavender and missed Provence in summer, that he could give her what she wanted. Anything that she wanted, he wished he was able to give it to her.

⌇

He knew. Somehow, St. Clair had divined Milly's worst secret, her greatest sorrow and most profound humiliation. He knew, and yet he stood there, all elegance and unconcern, his arm around her waist as if they were about to promenade the perimeter of some ballroom.

While Milly clutched her piecework and felt sick, Lady St. Clair bounced to her feet. "Professor, you will join me in my sitting room. I must send out inquiries regarding this Upton creature. Sebastian, a medicinal tot for the poor girl. That is a dreadful cousin if ever I beheld one."

She patted Milly's arm as she swept past, the professor at her side.

"Some brandy, Miss Danforth?"

The solicitude in St. Clair's voice nigh undid Milly. She must thank him, decline, and offer her resignation. Packing would not take long, but she'd have to send for her trunk later. "I want Peter."

St. Clair gently disengaged her sewing from her fingers and set it aside. "You want to learn to read."

The hurt went through Milly, old, brutal, and mean. "I am too stupid. I have this on repeated, emphatic, unassailable authority, though sometimes I manage fairly well with it."

He shifted so his arms rested around Milly's shoulders. On some other occasion, his presumption might have made her feel trapped.

On this occasion, she was tempted to rest her head on his shoulder and weep.

"They tried to beat your letters into you?"

How did he know these things, and why did it matter to him?

"Yes. I wore letters about my neck, as if one can learn to recognize letters upside down more easily than right side up. I stared at them repeatedly, endlessly, in chalk, pencil, and ink. I recited them, and that went swimmingly—I can spell many, many words out loud, like reciting so much poetry—but I cannot read or write nearly well enough, especially if I am tired."

His scent was a comfort, not as great a comfort as velvet fabric between her fingers, or Peter's purr against her chest, but a comfort. And when the baron held her like this, in a loose, undemanding embrace, Milly could hide her face against the lace of his cravat.

"If I teach you how to write your name, Miss Danforth, to write it beautifully, confidently, will you stay? Will you stay for at least another month, so I might find a successor to replace you in my aunt's affections?"

Milly stepped back to peer up at him, because his lordship wasn't making sense. "I don't want to leave. I told my cousin the truth—I am content in your employ, more than content."

He did not return Milly's regard, but instead appeared to study the bouquet in the window. The lavender was in good repair, but the roses were going quite to pot.

"I am the Traitor Baron, Miss Danforth. You heard your cousin plainly enough. I served the Corsican loyally for years and have made no apology for it. I held English officers captive from time to time, and this is not something easily forgotten. You ought to take your cousin's concerns seriously."

Milly stepped away and closed the cover over the piano keys. "Yes, I ought. Alcorn is not concerned for me and never has been. When my uncle grew ill, he specifically charged Alcorn and Marcus to look after me—uncle never read very well either—and Alcorn took that to mean I was his unpaid help, his cross to bear. I do not enjoy being anybody's cross, my lord."

She did not want to be Lady St. Clair's cross either, but was confident that good dame would never entertain such a notion.

"Marcus is another cousin?"

The roses were beyond help, so Milly took the bouquet off the windowsill, set it on the sideboard, and began removing them from the vase. Petals fell all about, but there was no help for that.

"Marcus was my cousin, Alcorn's younger brother. Marcus did not survive the Peninsular campaign."

His lordship went to the desk and rummaged in a drawer. "I might have held your cousin as a prisoner, Miss Danforth. Might have questioned him most rigorously. Are you still content to remain in my employ?"

The baron held a pair of shears, and despite his lace and grace, he looked—and sounded—very severe.

"Marcus was never taken prisoner. He fell off his horse and suffered a blow to the head. I ought to change this water. Roses always leave such a stench." And why did his lordship look so relieved at Milly's answer?

He passed the shears to her, which meant she could trim up the stems on the sprigs of lavender. "Peter is not your only ally, Miss Danforth."

Milly tossed the roses in a dustbin near the desk and swept dead petals into her palm. "You use a military word—ally. I hope I'm not engaged in battle with Alcorn."

St. Clair stalked closer, nothing comforting at all about his expression or his posture.

"Your dear cousin beat you, when he had to realize that beatings were unavailing toward the furtherance of your education. He denied you wages for your labor. He belittled you and suffered others to do likewise. He limited your access to your aunts until you were of age—or am I wrong?"

Milly sat abruptly on the piano bench, a bunch of dead rose petals in her hand, soft as velvet, but not the same thing at all as a plush fabric. "You make it sound as if I was a prisoner."

He sat beside her, causing the bench to creak. There was barely room for the two of them, because St. Clair was no delicate flower.

"You felt like a prisoner. Your imagination and determination were all that sustained you, and possibly, the occasional visit from your aunts. Will you stay with us, Milly Danforth?"

Allies were not friends, but they could be loyal and useful. If one had allies, did that imply one had enemies as well? "I should cut more roses."

He took her wrist and pried her fingers open, then turned her hand palm down, so the rose petals fell into his larger hand. Because Milly had been holding the petals in a warm grasp, their scent wafted to her nose.

"Aunt would be heartbroken to lose you, and nobody in this house cares one whit if you can read or write. Nobody."

"*I* care if I can read or write. I've tried to tell myself that it's like singing—some people have a natural talent for it, and others do not. I have no talent for letters and words."

He swore. Milly's ear for French was more than passable, because she'd always liked the sound of it—as if velvet had a sound—and his cursing was creative and vulgar.

"I can teach you to write your name, Millicent Danforth, but not if you let Alcorn win."

She had no intention of letting Alcorn remove her

from this household, but that wasn't what St. Clair had referred to. "How will you teach me, when governesses, tutors, Marcus, and my aunts were unable to?"

He stood peering down at the rose petals in his hand. "It's not complicated. You will learn your name by stitching it."

~~~~

"Confound it, Sebastian, you are uncanny. How could you know such a thing about my Milly?"

Aunt paced the elegant dimensions of her sitting room, Baumgartner looking on from the corner desk.

"I didn't know it, not until Upton started with his buffoonery." Aunt's sitting room was pretty, full of lemony light from the yellow silk on the walls, the mirrors, and the gilt, but the room held no flowers.

"Do sit down, Sebastian. Were you guessing?"

No, he'd not been guessing. He'd been relying on the same instinct that allowed him to reduce grown men—brave, determined grown men—to weeping, undignified children. Sebastian appropriated the rocking chair by the fire and tried to fashion an answer.

"English cavalrymen riding dispatch were forever getting caught with orders in their boots, their shirts, their hats, their sleeves. A few were clever enough to make hidden slits in the leather of their saddles, or false compartments in their saddlebags. A very few admirable patriots secreted orders in their underlinen."

Aunt liked that part about the underlinen. She lit on a cream-colored sofa and poured herself a cup of tea. "Do go on. Tea, Professor?"

"No thank you, my lady."

"Most of those riding dispatch had simply accepted sealed orders and gone galloping off with a tidy packet of intelligence just waiting to be captured and deciphered."

Aunt looked thoughtful while she stirred sugar and cream into her tea. "I gather you took a different approach?"

He'd taken many different approaches. "When I needed information sent to a higher command, or sent"—he shot his cuffs and did not look at Baumgartner—"*elsewhere*, I relied on the peasantry, the unlettered and the unremarkable, to relay my messages."

"And this worked?"

"Not always." No method, no procedure, no clever scheme had been without its failures, some of them spectacular. "I found, though, that those who could not write had prodigious memories. They had far more accurate recall of what they'd been told than those who'd merely shoved a packet of paper into their kit bag and ridden away."

"And Milly Danforth has such a memory." Aunt held out a plate of tea cakes to Sebastian, but not to Baumgartner, who would not bother with sweets when there was business to be transacted. "She can recite anything she's heard practically word for word, sometimes when I'd rather she didn't."

Sebastian had listened to Miss Danforth often enough over breakfast, but her ability to recall conversations hadn't registered, not until her cousin's visit.

"She has no lap desk," he said, "and she didn't send written word to her aunt when she arrived here that she'd found a decent post. She has no Bible, no Book of Common Prayer with her name inscribed in it. She neither sent nor received any written communications. The neighbors got word to her not by sending a note, but by word of mouth when somebody had an errand in Town and could stop by the kitchen door to pass along the news in person."

"To have no letters, none in any language, is a sad, sad poverty," Baumgartner observed.

"To have that Upton swine as your sole male relation is a worse poverty yet," Aunt snapped.

"To have the Traitor Baron as your nephew is the saddest poverty of all," Sebastian said. "And yet, Miss Danforth has agreed to remain in our household, despite that unhappy connection."

"Of course she did," Aunt said. "I pay well, and my company is agreeable."

Both men remained silent.

"I pay *very* well, and my company is *not* disagreeable," she amended. "And you two are no gentlemen. Sebastian, be off with you. The professor and I have letters to write."

He rose, exchanging a look of sympathy with Baumgartner. The German was in every sense in Aunt's confidence, not a particularly comfortable honor.

And Baumgartner's sympathy for Sebastian? To claim the Traitor Baron as one's only male relation was indeed a sad, sad poverty.

❧

Parisians were sensible people. They appreciated the great blessing of living in one of the most beautiful, vibrant cities on earth, and assembled at cafés and along the boulevards when social inclinations overtook them. An occasional stroll in the ordered and civilized surrounds of the Tuileries sufficed to assuage their bucolic impulses.

Parisians did not feel compelled to associate with cows, geese, rabbits, deer, and other beasts in their very parks, while the Londoners—yeomen all, at heart—did. Henri nonetheless chose a shaded bench in Hyde Park for his next assignation with Captain Lord Anderson, in hopes that his lordship might be less remarkable in such an environment.

Anderson did not disappoint. He came striding along in the uniform of the English gentleman—shiny boots, close-tailored doeskin breeches, blue waistcoat, brown topcoat, hat, and walking stick. His watch fob was a tasteful wink of gold, and his gloves were spotless, dyed or chosen to exactly match his breeches. He took a seat on the bench as if enjoying the pretty day, not an ounce of imagination or idiosyncrasy in evidence in his dress or his demeanor.

"Have some gingerbread, *mon ami*." Henri passed over a slice of sweet that would never compare with his own sainted grandmother's recipe, but did not offend when decently covered with butter. "It's still warm, and I bought more than I should have."

Anderson looked momentarily nonplussed, no doubt because one did not eat with gloves on, but the English schoolboy won out over the man of fashion. He took off his gloves and accepted Henri's offering.

"My thanks." Anderson popped a bite into his mouth, managing to get a crumb lodged in his moustache. "Quite good."

A bit heavy on the ginger, and a hint of cloves

would have smoothed out the aroma nicely. "English gingerbread, like English ale, has no equal," Henri said. "Have you anything to report?"

He wasn't about to compliment the English weather. Even Anderson would pick up on that tripe.

"Dirks told me to take myself the hell off. Those were his very words." His lordship stuffed the last of his gingerbread into his mouth, and damned if the man didn't even chew like an Englishman—all business, like a bullock with its cud, as if food were not akin to sex in the sensual pleasure it might afford.

"Dirks is Scottish, and you are English. Does he want you to beg, perhaps?"

"I *served* with him, Henri."

And such was the bond among Wellington's former subordinates that it even, apparently, transcended centuries of national animosity. Henri took another bite of warm gingerbread and decided not to chastise Anderson for using his name. Half the French nation was naming its babies Henri, and he hadn't given Anderson any other means of addressing him—nor would he.

"What about the other one, MacHugh?"

Anderson dusted his hands. "He was sitting right there when I spoke to Dirks and didn't say a word. Dirks isn't the man's name, you know."

No, Henri had not known. This Dirks fellow had enjoyed the hospitality of the Château for a mere fortnight, and at a time when Henri's attentions had been absorbed by happenings in Paris.

"Why is he called Dirks, then?"

"Because no matter how many knives you find on

him, he always has one more in some location you'd never think to look. I expect he's bloody competent with a sword too."

"Which means if St. Clair chose pistols, Monsieur Dirks might not prevail. Why not challenge St. Clair yourself?"

Henri put the matter as a tactical question, when what he wanted to do was goad Anderson into the sort of idiocy upon which brave English officers prided themselves.

The frustrations of fieldwork on English soil were without limit.

"I won't do it." Anderson spoke not with bravado, but with the sort of quiet that suggested the bedrock of his Saxon stubbornness supported his words.

"And why will you not rid two sovereign nations of the traitorous embarrassment that is Sebastian St. Clair?"

Anderson brushed the crumb from his moustache and pulled on his gloves. "He had me soundly beaten, more than once. That is not reason enough to take a man's life."

"You were bound hand and foot. You could not fight back. Your wounds were not tended, and your womenfolk were left to think you dead."

His lordship stood. "My wounds were tended more effectively than they would have been in any English field hospital. I know it was part of his strategy, to alternate care and abuse, but it was not part of his strategy to work out a ransom for me. He didn't have to do that."

This was...this was the confounded illogic of English honor, and yet Henri attempted to argue with it. He rose, lest Anderson try to stroll away from a discussion not yet concluded.

"St. Clair extracted from you every useful detail of intelligence he could, and then extracted coin from your family for the privilege of burying you on English soil, despite the fact that neither France nor England wanted any part of official prisoner exchanges. You were abused in more ways than you'll admit."

Though at the time, Henri had approved whole-heartedly of the ransom. Paris did not need to know everything that transpired hundreds of miles distant, after all, and the *République* had seen some share of the coin. Occasionally.

"I am alive, sir," Anderson said, tapping his hat more firmly on his head. "And while I will happily meet any man on the field of honor for just cause, my lady wife would rather I not keep fighting a war now concluded. If this makes me a traitor, then have an English officer of the Crown take me to task for it. I bid you good day, and my thanks for the gingerbread."

He sauntered on, swinging his walking stick, the picture of English manhood in full bloom. Henri fell in step beside him, sparing a moment's thought for the knife in his boot.

Buried between *mon capitaine*'s shoulder blades, it would make a lovely addition to his so-fine and boring wardrobe.

"You'll talk to this Dirks again?"

"I will talk to MacHugh, and then you can find another accomplice, monsieur. If England wants St. Clair dead that badly, then many should be willing to assist you."

"Good day, then, and my compliments to your lady, and to your small daughters."

Because he could not abide insubordination, Henri gave those last civilities just the slightest ironic emphasis. Let Anderson understand that his cooperation was not discretionary, but rather, as imperative as, and *nearly* identical with, his loyalty to the damned English Crown.

Six

"YOU WILL NEED YOUR CLOAK AND BONNET."

Milly admired the perfect seam stretched across her embroidery hoop, though St. Clair's tone suggested she was to pop to her feet, salute, and trot off for the front door at double time.

"Since when does one need outdoor apparel to learn to write one's name, my lord?"

He remained standing over her—a male tactic she'd long since lost patience with—until Milly realized he was not trying to intimidate with his size and muscle, he was studying her sewing.

"Your stitchery is very pretty, Miss Danforth."

Flattery was a male tactic with which she'd had little experience. "Thank you."

He drew his finger over the flowers she'd embroidered along one hem—purple irises, red tulips, an occasional spike of yellow gladiolus, and a froth of greenery. "You have sketched the pattern on the fabric, and this tells me you can copy what you see. Your colors are accurate for the subject, and I haven't seen you wearing spectacles."

He continued to stroke a single finger over the linen, and Milly realized that, all unaware, the baron was admiring her new summer nightgown.

Saints abide. She set the hoop back in her work-basket. "My vision is quite functional, though I will occasionally use spectacles when I'm fatigued, your lordship, and I am most eager to learn my signature."

He straightened, but not before Milly noticed that her froth of greenery was the exact same shade St. Clair's eyes had been when he'd dealt with Alcorn.

"Then prepare to walk with me. When one's decisions can result in men losing their lives, one learns to gather information before choosing a course. I would hear from you about your previous efforts in the schoolroom."

Escaping the house held vast appeal, even if it meant marching about with St. Clair. Milly was tying her bonnet ribbons when his lordship joined her in the foyer, his expression disapproving.

"English women do not see themselves," he said, brushing her fingers aside. "You look in the mirror, and you think, 'Ah, my hat is upon my head, exactly where it should be. The bow is secure, and I will not have to chase my bonnet in a sudden wind.' You should look at the picture you make with that hat, and adjust your appearance accordingly. If there's a sudden wind, the young English gentlemen should all be trying to peek at your ankles anyway."

Already he was lecturing her, so perhaps there was hope for the project they were to undertake. He set her bonnet back an inch farther on her head, and retied her ribbons so the bow was off not to the right, where Milly generally tied it, but to the left and more loosely, the ribbons curling down over her heart.

"That sudden wind might carry off my only every-day bonnet, your lordship." Though as Milly regarded herself in the mirror, she allowed that the results of St. Clair's fussing were somehow *fetching*—even on her.

"Then I shall look a proper smitten gentleman when I go tearing down the lane after it, will I not? Come along."

If Milly had been concerned for the propriety of walking out with her employer, her concerns were put to rest. Mr. Brodie fell in behind them, as did Giles the footman, and Rumsfeld, the senior upstairs maid.

"Are we all to learn our letters in the park, my lord?"

"We are all to enjoy a bit of fine weather while it holds," he replied. "Aunt runs Giles about merci-lessly, and the maid—Clothilde, Chloe, I forget her name—is enamored of him."

"Her name is Rumsfeld."

"Not to Giles it isn't." This observation was made with no humor whatsoever, merely another detail to be managed as St. Clair supervised the subordinates under his authority.

"What would you like to know about my attempts to read, my lord?"

"Everything."

Everything took them to the park, along the Serpentine, and past children playing with the loud good cheer engendered by a sunny spring day. Everything included a recitation of tutors, punish-ments, and more punishments, humiliations, and small glimmers of hope doused by buckets of despair.

"Shall we sit?" St. Clair asked, gesturing toward a bench in the shade.

Giles and Chloe—Chloe Rumsfeld—had taken a bench a few yards off, and Milly did not see Mr. Brodie anywhere about.

And still, the baron put more questions to her: Was a slate any more helpful than pencil and paper? Did memorizing a recited spelling inform her attempts to make the letters with her hand? Could she recognize words without being able to name the letters in them?

"This is not easy for me to discuss, your lordship."

"Do you suppose this recitation of beatings, beratings, and deprivations is easy for me to listen to?" he retorted. "If I lamented your miseries, waved my handkerchief at you, and allowed my distress to become obvious, would your story be less painful?"

He sounded testy. The way Milly's aunts had often sounded when their aches and pains were troubling them.

"I think you marched me away from the house, away from what's comfortable and comforting to me, to shake loose my confidence. I am much attached to what confidence I have, your lordship, and I can assure you, if teaching me to write my name involves surrendering my dignity into your hands, I'll keep my ignorance a while longer."

Milly's only sign that he'd heard her was a slow blink and a pursing of his lips, while across the path, Chloe laughed at something Giles said.

"I cannot like—" The baron paused and glanced around. "You should not have been beaten. A gratuitous beating will have the opposite of its intended effect; witness, the beating intended to humiliate you only made you more proud."

At the oddest moments, he turned up French—or something.

"I'm not arrogant."

"Proud, Miss Danforth, is no relation to arrogant. Come along, you have caught me at my game, and I have a sense of how to start on our objective." He assisted Milly to her feet and kept her hand wrapped around his arm.

"What have you learned that you didn't know when we left the house, my lord?"

Milly asked, because *she* had learned things. When he'd taken his hat off and set it beside them on the bench, she'd learned that the sun could find red highlights in his dark hair. Because that same sun caught the fatigue etched around his mouth and eyes, she'd learned that he was tired, even this early in the morning. She'd learned that his scent was a pleasure that eclipsed the rare day of fresh air in London's often odoriferous surrounds.

She'd learned that in the deceptive openness and pleasantry of a sunny morning, she would tell him things she hadn't shared with anybody else—about birchings, about days of bread and water, about having her knuckles smacked until they were red, swollen, and bleeding.

About typical schoolgirl tribulations that had felt like the torments of the damned.

"What I know now, Miss Danforth, is that you are resourceful, determined, and clever, though one certainly had suspicions in this regard previously. I *know* you will soon be writing your name."

His utter assurance—his arrogance—on this point was lovely.

"I want the whole thing, you know, complete with Harriette."

His forward progress never faltered. "I beg your pardon?"

"Millicent *Harriette* Danforth. I want all three names, not some little squiggle in the middle that stands for Harriette. *H*'s aren't that difficult. They look like divided doors when both halves are fastened, the kind you see in stables and dairies."

"So they do. What other letters have you noticed lurking in odd locations?"

Milly prosed on as they passed blooming lilac bushes, though she did not tell him that when a lady stood with her arms at her sides in an evening gown, her décolletage resembled the letter *M*, particularly if she were well endowed. How a poor relation spent her evenings among the wallflowers was not his concern.

"Miss Danforth, you will not take offense when that blond gentleman offers the cut direct."

The baron's voice had changed, gone smoother and harder, more English and more commanding officer both. A tall, trim fellow came striding toward them. Every aspect of his attire, every aspect of his bearing shouted that he was Quality, and likely titled Quality at that.

She saw the moment when the man recognized St. Clair, saw not a hesitation in his stride, but a slight angling forward, as if a chilly wind had arrived of a sudden. His gaze flicked over St. Clair then landed on

Milly, to whom he offered the slightest gesture in the direction of a finger to his hat brim.

"St. Clair."

"Mercia."

The encounter was over in an instant, and yet Milly suspected her escort was not merely surprised, he was astonished.

Milly used their linked arms to tow him onward. "Steady on, St. Clair. I expect he was but an earl or a viscount. They tend to frequent the park on pretty days, the same as the rest of us, and being a useless lot, they have all the time in the world to perfect their manners."

"That, my dear, was no less personage than His Grace, Christian, Duke of Mercia, a man whom I hold in the highest esteem."

"Not a bad-looking fellow," Milly said, and then she chattered on because she had the sense St. Clair was so rattled, he needed her words to focus on. "One sees the occasional duke, and it's often a disappointment. They go bald, get fat, have bad teeth and nervous laughs just like the butcher and the coachman. Duchesses are no better. They're supposed to be nigh to royalty, but the association doesn't seem to lend them any immunity from human foibles. One need only look to the Regent himself—I suppose I'm flirting with treason—but the man's stays are said to *creak*, and that can hardly—"

"Millicent, I've met dukes before."

Millicent. His pronunciation of the *i* suffered a bit crossing the Channel, but she liked it—Meelicent. Doubtless, St. Clair had met that very duke before, and not under ideal circumstances.

"His Grace was in want of charm," Milly said. "You and he have that in common."

They walked for a few more paces. At some point, Mr. Brodie had rejoined their little foot patrol, while the baron remained thoughtful at Milly's side.

His silence was convenient for Milly, because she had much to consider. The thoroughness of the baron's questioning, the care with which he'd staged his interrogation, and the ease with which he'd adopted the role of interrogator suggested familiarity with that terrain—and Milly had been questioned before.

"Why can't you learn, you *stupid* girl?"

"*When* will you apply yourself? Children half your age learn this easily!"

"Are you *trying* to earn a beating? *Another* beating?"

All in aid of imparting to Milly an ability to read her Bible. Such Christians, her cousins.

And yet, the question that lodged in her mind as she made her way home beside a silent St. Clair was different from the ones shouted at her in the schoolrooms of years past. What remained to plague her was St. Clair's question.

"Do you think this recitation of beatings, beratings, and deprivations is easy for me to listen to?"

She'd seen the care St. Clair took with his aunt, seen the way he inconvenienced himself for an intransigent donkey. Milly had even tasted the man's kiss, and yet, she had thought that very thing.

She had thought, and part of him had wanted her to think, that her suffering mattered to him not at all.

❧

"You thought to show Miss Danforth how Polite Society torments its outcasts," Michael said. He paused as if to admire the shine on the boot he was polishing. "She didn't even notice when Lady Hutchings snubbed you."

Michael was a caring soul, which would be his downfall one day, if it hadn't been already. He assiduously polished a tall boot that was not exactly dirty, so the dear fellow would not have to look at Sebastian at the mention of Lady Hutchings.

"Why do you not leave those for the boot boy? I pay the lad good coin, and he does a decent job."

Michael remained firmly planted on his humble bench in the saddle room. "When a fellow—a valet sort of fellow—has only one pair of good boots, he likes to care for them himself. Rather like when he has only one horse or one wife."

Sebastian took down a bridle that hadn't been tied up properly. "Have you a wife, Michael, secreted away somewhere? A fiancée perhaps?"

Michael set his boot down *carefully*, suggesting he'd perhaps wanted to hurl it at his employer—which was interesting.

"You had a fiancée, my lord, and she gave you the cut direct this morning before Miss Danforth and half of Polite Society."

"Not for the first time, and not quite. Dear Amelia will be trying to give me the cut direct when she's doddering about on her canes and I'm in my Bath chair—assuming I live that long, which I shall not. A true cut requires that one pass the glance over the object to be cut, a distracted, unseeing glance—as if a faint stench has been detected—and then one turns the eye on the middle distance. Amelia has some way to go before she perfects it—there's too much of the shop about her antecedents, I'm thinking."

Michael stuffed his hand into his boot, dipped a rag in boot black, and started at the toe of his footwear.

"She's damned pretty, your Amelia, but she would have been a chilly night's work in bed. The point is, Miss Danforth didn't notice. She didn't notice when the Pierpont whelp turned off the path rather than cross his steps with yours. She didn't notice when Lady Fleming and both of her escorts turned their backs on you."

Sebastian looped reins through bridle parts in an intricate arrangement, one that would keep the leather supple, ensure no parts were left trailing, and look pretty hanging on a shiny brass hook—rather like tying a woman's bonnet to show off her features to best advantage.

"Lady Fleming is some relation of Amelia's. You will polish a hole in the toe of that boot, *mon ami.*" Sebastian moved on to the next bridle, which happened to belong to Fable.

Michael dipped his rag again and held the boot up over his arm, the better to spread polish over the calf, heel, and vamp.

"Miss Danforth passed your test with flying colors. Nobody would cut her when she's out with Lady Freddy. You were examining her reaction to being out with *you*, and she earned top marks."

Fable, being a rambunctious fellow in his prime, generally sported about Town in a double bridle, one having both snaffle and curb bits. The bridle was heavy, handsome, and perfectly clean, but something was amiss with it.

"Miss Danforth flunked miserably, Michael. The outing was intended to show her why association with me is not a sound idea, to give her a distaste for my company, but she was too distracted by the brutalities in her past to notice. She accused the Duke of Mercia of wanting charm. Who maintains these bridles?"

"Your head lad would know, a Kerryman named Belton. Why?"

"Because somebody has filed the curb chain on Fable's bridle to a dangerous sharpness. The first time I brought my horse to an abrupt stop, the underside of his chin would be cut, and I would likely be sent sailing halfway back to France."

The boot Michael had held aloft slowly lowered. "You aren't even angry."

Had Mercia cut Milly Danforth, Sebastian would have been angry. For the first time in years, he would have been angry and had difficulty keeping that anger in check. Mercia would have been pleased to know this.

Sebastian detached the curb chain and dropped it into the pocket of his riding jacket.

"Nobody rides the horse but me, and this mischief is tiresomely predictable, though it underscores why Miss Danforth must keep her distance. Many a domestic takes her employer into dislike, and she ought to be able to manage it with a little encouragement."

The boot was subjected to some vigorous buffing.

"You could simply tell the woman it isn't safe to

be seen with you. She'll comprehend the whys easily enough. I've already hinted as much to her."

Sebastian moved down the line of bridles, finding the next one had been hung up without the bit being cleaned off.

"You likely lectured her cross-eyed. Send Belton to me when we're done here, please. It's time to install more locks." And put the fear of the brooding, violent, Frenchie Traitor Baron into his stable master, though Sebastian had long since found that charade tiresome.

"Mercia didn't cut you," Michael said. "His Grace tipped his hat to the lady and exchanged greetings with you."

Michael, Michael, Michael. He was a brave man and a friend, and Sebastian wished him back to the Highlands daily—if the Highlands were in fact still his home.

"Mercia *should* have cut me. He, of all Englishmen, should have put out my lights twenty times over." The leather on the next bridle was so stiff Sebastian had trouble getting his little arrangement to work with it. "His hand looks to have healed." Though when a fellow wore gloves, one couldn't tell if his fingers worked.

"His marriage is reported to be happy."

"God be thanked." And this was a heartfelt prayer, for if anybody deserved happiness and a long, sweet life, it was Mercia. "I owe him whatever remains of my life, Michael."

"When I kill you," Michael said, *very* pleasantly, "it will be because I am puking sick of your Gallic fatalism. You're in good health, the war is over, and

you've survived more challenges than any man ought
to suffer in a lifetime. Your auntie loves you, and
you've apparently enough manly humors left to take
notice of her companion."

Michael liked to be right, and an aggravating per-
centage of the time, he was.

"Of course I like Miss Danforth."

"So polite, Baron. You 'like' her—you like Cook,
you like the old fellows at your flower club, you like
your aunt's card-party coven. You *want* Milly Danforth,
want her naked and panting, spread beneath you while
you rut yourself into forgetting your sorry past. That's
what all this wandering around the park is about. You
don't need to protect her from Society, you need to
protect her from you and your mighty sword."

His *flower* club? And yet, Michael was not overstepping, he was *worrying*, and he was prodigiously good at it.

Sebastian began an inspection of stirrup leathers
next, saddle by saddle. "If Wellington's boys are tena-
cious about their vendetta, I won't live long enough
to take advantage of the girl's curious nature, Michael.
You censure me for fancies any man with blood in his
veins would entertain about the woman."

Too late, Sebastian realized what he'd admitted.
He *did* want Milly Danforth, badly. She was brave,
loyal, and possessed of a kissably stubborn mouth.
Worse yet, she bore the fragrance of Provence and
understood how shame could corrode a soul.

"So marry her, why don't you? You must have an
heir, or the St. Clair holdings revert to the Crown.
If Miss Danforth is so oblivious to gossip, then marry
her, get some babies on her, and set her up at the

family seat. Twenty years from now, your son should be able to barter his expectations for an heiress, new wars and new traitors will have arisen, and your infamy will be forgotten."

Rather than tell Michael he sounded much like a certain elderly aunt, Sebastian straightened a saddle blanket folded carelessly on a trunk. "I would be condemning Miss Danforth to widowhood."

"You weren't this gloomy when we survived on bad rations at that frozen rock pile of misery known as the Château. Do you even want to live?"

"Oh, I do want to live. Increasingly, I do." For months he hadn't, but Aunt Freddy had bullied, pouted, sulked, and cajoled him along, and eventually, Sebastian had accepted that he might not want to live, but neither did he crave death.

He did, however, want to swive Millicent Danforth. This would be an encouraging step away from those first bleak months back in England, except wanting any woman was inconvenient as hell.

Complicated as hell, given the price on his head.

"Do you ever consider going back to France?" Michael asked as he set the second boot beside the first. "You might be safer."

"France is a wasteland, Michael. What Napoleon's army didn't decimate, the invading forces did, and I do not trust the populace's newly resurrected affection for royalty. The people are starving, angry, betrayed by their republican leaders, and unhappy with the alternatives."

While much of the English populace was also starving, angry, betrayed by their royalist leaders, and unhappy with their alternatives, too.

Michael rose, his polished boots in hand. "More relevant than all that balderdash, you would miss your aunt and torment yourself for abandoning her. God knows, you missed England."

"True."

Michael started for the door, then hesitated. "Anderson is the bellwether, and MacHugh will likely come after you next, but Mercia could be the one agitating for all these duels. He might have shown you civility merely to throw you off the scent."

Interesting theory. Sebastian shook out and folded the next saddle blanket. "I know Mercia, Michael, even better than I know you. I know his mind, I know his heart. I know him in ways his own duchess never will, if God is merciful. His Grace would look me in the eye, as he did once before, slap his glove across my cheek—soundly, not viciously—and call me out. Subterfuge is beneath a man of his honor."

Michael snorted. "You hope. Considering the damage you did to him, the scars you left him with, I'd say relying on his honor is a risky bet. If you'd put me through what he suffered, I'd be mad for your blood any way I could spill it."

Such honesty required no reply. Sebastian let Michael go, finished tidying up the saddle blankets, then followed Michael out of the stables. As he crossed the alley to the back gardens, the curb chain jingled in his pocket like so much loose change.

❧

"Close your eyes."

Had St. Clair spoken in tones of command, Milly

would have defied him easily. Instead, he used tones of seduction.

"Why?"

"Because I do not want you to use your eyes to learn the shape of your name, Miss Danforth. I want you to learn it the way you learn a seam, the way you learn a pattern of notes, by feel. I want you to be able to make these patterns in the darkness, the way you could sew in the dark, or play a favorite serenade on an instrument you've loved for years."

Perhaps he was making some sophisticated innuendo, but it was more likely that Milly's naughty imagination found mischief where none had been intended. St. Clair's theory was worth exploring, in any case, though Milly had wanted to watch as his hand guided hers over the paper.

"I can make the *M* easily enough."

His fingers glided away from her knuckles as he held up a sheet of foolscap covered with her scrawling. "Most of the time, you can write the whole business legibly enough."

"Legibly, like a child toiling to make it just so. When I'm tired, it's nearly impossible. Spaces pop up in the middle of words, the ink blurs, sometimes the letters look like they're swirling down a drain. If I must attempt to read or write, I never attempt it in the evening."

He sat back, making the gilded chair creak. When the professor sat at this desk in that chair, he looked studious. St. Clair in the same pose looked elegant.

"Why would you deal with the reading or signing of documents when you were tired?"

"Because that's when my cousin would ambush me with them. I never did sign, though. My aunts rescued me."

He flicked the foolscap aside, rose, and crossed to a bouquet of red, white, and yellow tulips near the window.

"Explain."

"I came into a competence from my mother's settlements when I was eighteen. Alcorn sought to manage it for me, and there were documents involved. I never signed them. I could not satisfy myself as to what the documents said, not truly. The solicitors drew them up, and I'm sure everything was in order, but Marcus told me never to sign anything unless I was confident of its import. Because it was Marcus who told me that, Alcorn had to tolerate my delays."

St. Clair rearranged the tulips, so the several white tulips were more in evidence, then stuck his finger into the blue ceramic vase they stood in.

"Go on."

"A green vase would have gone better on that table, and with those colors."

He shook a drop of water from his finger. "So it would. What else did your dear cousin want you to sign?"

Milly picked up a pen, dipped it in ink, and tried for an *M*.

"Nothing of any significance. Just the occasional correspondence, that sort of thing." She brushed the feathery end of the quill over her nose, which had developed a slight itch, though the first *M* turned out passably well.

As far as she could tell.

"What of this competence, now, Miss Danforth?"

Another *M* went even better, so Milly became daring.

"The funds sit in the cent-percents, gathering interest. My aunts assured me the sum was tidy, and while I did not trust Alcorn, I did trust my aunts and their solicitor."

St. Clair used the pitcher on the sideboard to add water to the vase. "Who might that be?"

Vowels were difficult, because they all consisted of curves. Curves could go awry more easily than straight lines. "Mr. Dudley. He's in the City on Clockminster Court."

Which was none of the baron's business, but Milly had given up resisting his questioning, because she sensed his inquiries intended no harm to her.

"May I ask you a question, my lord?"

He'd wandered to the fire, which he was poking up, though the day was cool rather than cold. "You just did."

"When we passed your fiancée in the park yesterday, and she gave you the cut direct, did it hurt?" She hadn't been the only one, but Milly would have thought a man was owed some civility from a woman the newspapers claimed he'd been engaged to since childhood. The aunts had read the society pages out loud, and Milly was nothing if not an attentive listener. She was sure the papers had said not one word about the baron's military past, though.

St. Clair stood by the hearth, the poker in his hand. When Milly dared to peek up from several attempts on a lowercase *r* and that perennial rascal, the letter *g*, his expression was amused.

"Noticed that, did you? Or have the servants been gossiping?"

"When a titled lady jilts a fiancé of long-standing, the gossip goes beyond the servants' hall, my lord. She's very pretty." In a blond, blue-eyed, wealthy, titled sort of way—with a narrow nose.

He set the poker back on the hearth stand, then moved it to the other side of the ash broom.

"Would she and I have suited, Miss Danforth? She told me in no uncertain terms what she thinks of a man who would serve the Corsican. She and her family might well have dubbed me the Traitor Baron."

His tone was light, still amused, while Milly wanted to hurl the ink pot and overturn the flowers.

"She's an idiot. Had you been a French boy sent to England for an education, then drafted to serve under Wellington, I doubt the French would be so judgmental. I do hate the letter *e*."

"A woman of violent passions never fails to hold a man's attention. Why does the letter inspire your ill will?"

Something was provoking St. Clair to smile, and not a charming smile, but rather, a private, pleased smile.

"Don't make fun of me and my letters, sir. You waged war against England. I wage war against being unlettered, and hostilities are not yet concluded. When a letter consists only of a narrow little loop, one loses track of it. When I drop a stitch, I know it. When I drop a letter—"

Some helpful, overbearing soul invariably pointed it out to her.

"Come here, Milly Danforth." He held out a hand,

the way a gentleman might offer a lady assistance into or out of an elegant coach. Milly rose, because that was what one did when St. Clair issued his orders.

She took his hand, and he arranged her in waltz position. "Close your eyes."

Why not? She closed her eyes, the better to enjoy his fragrance, the better to enjoy the fiction that they might, even in this parlor, indulge in a few steps of the dance.

The door was open, in any case. Let the footmen think what they would.

"You will let me lead you in an exploration of the letter *e*." He gathered her closer and moved off with her, slowly but confidently. Three steps up, a little shift, and three steps back. Another shift, and the same pattern, again and again.

"You're making a chain stitch with me."

"You have maligned a perfectly agreeable letter, Miss Danforth. A simple loop exists not to confound you, but to pleasure your hand in its making."

Or her entire body. He danced wonderfully, and to be held like this—Milly's opinion of the letter *e* underwent a drastic revision.

"I think you have it, madam, but now we will venture on to the letter *l*."

She liked the letter *l* even better, because it was six steps up, and six steps back, a more ambitious under-taking in the small parlor.

"There are two *l*'s in Millicent," she said. And for no reason, no reason at all, this inspired her to lay her cheek against his chest. They *e*'d and *l*'d and *o*'d (as in Danforth) a while longer before St. Clair came to a gliding halt.

"Keep your eyes closed, my dear."

Milly could feel the breath of his words against her forehead. He grasped her by the wrist and led her a few steps closer to the window—the cooling temperature told her that much.

"Sit, if you please." He scooted her chair for her, and then a pen was placed in Milly's hands, her fingers arranged around it. "Now our hands will dance a bit."

His fingers closed over hers, and he waltzed the pen across a paper, one-two-three, one-two-three, first *e*'s, then *l*'s, then a few *o*'s. "Do you feel these letters, Miss Danforth? Could you play them like notes in the dark?"

Milly could tell he was standing bent over her, could sense the heat and size of him as he guided her hand across the page, but she shoved those distractions aside.

"I want to peek."

"Not yet. You must solo first." He took his hand away. "Dance me some pretty letters, Miss Danforth. One-two-three, one-two-three…"

He dropped into French dancing-master—"*un, deux, trois*"—to count off the waltz, and Milly struck off across the page.

"Stop."

Before Milly could open her eyes, he'd whisked the paper away from her and held it up above her line of sight. "We have a few more dances ahead of us, Miss Danforth."

She could tell nothing from his schoolteacher inflections, so she snatched the paper away from him and put it on the desk before her.

Only to see a perfect, curling chorus line of *e*'s, *o*'s, and *l*'s looping over the page.

"They're beautiful." She beamed up at her instructor, amazed, terrified, and thrilled at the results of his tutelage. "I made beautiful letters. We did. We danced the letters onto the page."

"Well done, Milly Danforth. Perhaps I shall call you Milly Danceforth?"

What a lovely nickname. Milly stared at the page, comparing her previous efforts with the ones St. Clair had inspired. Her *g*, *r*, *i*, *m*, *a*, and *e* were recognizable, but not flowing, not elegant.

Those letters did not dance.

St. Clair picked up the paper again as if to admire it, then turned and sat on the corner of the desk, an informal pose, and not quite friendly.

"This is odd. These letters you chose to work on while we were talking earlier, they are a peculiar collection of consonants and vowels."

The joy suffusing Milly evaporated in an instant. She could not rise, because St. Clair had effectively blocked her in. She took out another piece of paper and tried to recapture the feeling in her belly of the looping, pretty letters, but it was no use.

"It's just a collection of letters."

"The very collection of letters used to spell the word 'marriage,' my dear." He leaned closer, and this time, his elegant scent was not so comforting. "I think you had better tell me who Vincent is, hmm?"

Seven

A SKILLED INTERROGATOR COULD USE FEAR LIKE A powerful lantern aimed in the direction of truth, a far more accurate source of illumination than physical pain itself. Pain was a crude and inexact tool, though some—Henri Anduvoir, for one—had been all too eager to use it.

And for what? To reveal that a man's deepest truth was that he did not want to die? That he longed to see his mother? That he yearned to apologize to the vicar's daughter with whom he'd taken liberties before buying his colors?

Sebastian regarded Milly Danforth as she pretended to draw her letters—because she did draw them, they were art to her, not sounds—and accepted the fact of his own fear.

He did not want her to be engaged to this Vincent fellow. He was *afraid* she was spoken for, afraid she'd given her heart to some buffoon unworthy of her—not that she ought to consider Sebastian worthy.

"Vincent is a friend of Alcorn's and some distant relation of Frieda's."

"That is two strikes against him. Waltz those letters, Miss Danforth."

Another source of illumination was silence, though Sebastian doubted it would be effective with Milly Danforth. She'd been schooled at the knees of old women, and what they knew about silence could ambush entire armies—witness, Aunt Freddy.

"One cannot waltz the letters with a large, scowling fellow looming over one," Miss Danforth replied, considering her work. "One needs room to dance."

Strong spirits could loosen a reluctant tongue, as could hunger or thirst. With Major Pierpont, fatigue, fear, and a few well-placed blows had been enough to render him a babbling imbecile in less than three days.

Sebastian leaned closer.

"The English alphabet includes twenty-three more letters, my dear, and they each come in upper- and lowercase. You've told me *what* Vincent is, but not *who* he is to you."

She scooted out of her chair so quickly, the top of her head nearly whacked Sebastian's chin.

"Vincent Aloysius Fontaine. He holds the living at St. Andrew the Apostle in West Hamley, Surrey."

Any fellow who'd spent formative years in France would know Andrew the Apostle was the patron saint of unmarried girls and old maids.

"You're making that up." Lying, she was, while wandering off toward the tulips.

"He arrived to St. Andrews from a series of smaller congregations, and to hear him talk, Bishop of London will be the end point of his ecclesiastical itinerary."

Sebastian's nose twitched as Miss Danforth bent

to sniff at a tulip. Tulips had virtually no scent, once picked, which further convinced him she was prevaricating. "He wanted to marry you, wanted to get his hands on your competence."

In typical female fashion, she nudged a red tulip a bit this-a-way, lifted a yellow tulip from here and replaced it there, so the entire bouquet acquired a more symmetric appearance. She crossed her arms, when Sebastian knew she longed to put the flowers back the way they'd been.

"Vincent wanted to marry poor, slow, dim-witted, eager Milly."

The humor in her voice cut at him. "You are not dim-witted, Miss Danforth." She was clever in the extreme, but if he stated that obvious fact, she'd leave the room.

"I am dim-witted, at least when the test of my readiness for marriage consists of reading a passage of scripture verbatim. I faltered, and much worse than Vincent anticipated I would. I hadn't realized it was a test, you see."

Sebastian shifted from his perch on the corner of the escritoire, the better to keep the errant Miss Danforth under surveillance.

"So you were supposed to be sweet, slow, and hardworking, but not entirely unlettered." And doubtless she was also to have been abundantly curved, adequately dowered, and the complete dupe of her cousins.

She came to light on the piano bench, opened the cover, and ran a finger silently over the keys.

"I did not want to be a burden to anybody, and

marriage is how a lady generally resolves that dilemma. Vincent is comely, and…comely."

Saint Calculating-and-Comely had no true religious vocation was what Milly implied. He did, however, have excellent taste in women and had probably been smart enough to assure Milly his vicarage would be overflowing with the sound of small feet on the stairs and childish laughter in the garden. Sebastian moved off, away from the piano bench toward the hearth.

"You were in love with this scion of piety?"

"I was infatuated. At the time, I thought my only alternative to living with my aunts would be to return to Alcorn's household. Then too, Alcorn had been extolling my virtues to an older fellow, some gouty baronet without an heir to whom I was nearly engaged, and me all unaware."

She pressed a lone chord—A minor, in the tenor register—and abruptly, Sebastian wanted to play her something cheerful.

"Move over."

When he thought she'd scamper off, she shifted a few inches left. "Are you finished with your questioning, my lord?"

"I was born to question. My own grandmother assured me of this, as did my tutors. In the army, it was not an asset." At first, it hadn't been an asset. "The Fontaine buffoon, is he of a mind to pursue you?"

Sebastian launched into the slow movement from Beethoven's Concerto in E-flat major, which, while not ebullient, had a sanguine beauty that had become dear to him.

"Alcorn certainly hopes so. That is a lovely piece."

"I heard it while I was hiding in Vienna, then I found Kramer had published it here."

Sebastian hadn't meant to say that, but sitting next to Milly Danforth, a man became distracted by the warmth and fragrance of her, by her willingness to freely compliment him on what little he could give her, by her thigh casually pressed against his.

As Sebastian played on, one lyrical, sweet phrase after another, insight struck: one could also unearth truth with the tool Sebastian had forgotten, the tool he'd never quite managed, except in some peculiar manner with Mercia.

That tool would be trust. Trust could move mountains, topple edifices, and win wars.

"Milly Danforth, I want to keep you safe from this idiot who would use you in his race to acquire a miter and stole, and from your thickheaded cousin. You must tell me what I need to know so I might achieve my purpose."

She was quiet for so long he thought she wouldn't answer. He could feel her swaying slightly beside him, enraptured by the music.

"Why were you hiding in Vienna, my lord?"

The arrangement called for crossed hands, and this allowed Sebastian to lean into her, albeit fleetingly.

"Not truly hiding. Everybody knew where I was. I was dithering, putting off my return to England because I knew it would be complicated. France was not safe, and England had no appeal."

"You love England."

He stopped playing mid-phrase. "How can you say that?"

"I saw the way you looked at the countryside around Chelsea. I see how you work at your ledgers and reports. I hear the servants talking about what a decent master you are, despite your Frenchie ways. You are not a man embittered by your English fate."

Sebastian decided what he'd take from that observation was not the truth of it—if any truth there was— but rather, satisfaction that she'd made a study of him.

"I love my aunt, which is probably a Frenchie thing to put into words. I came back when Michael established it was reasonably safe for me to do so."

Sitting on that piano bench, however, was not safe. Not for Sebastian, and not for Miss Danforth. He played a four-octave arpeggio in the key of C major, and this too allowed him to lean into her.

"How did you meet Mr. Brod—Michael?"

And when had she become the interrogator?

"Michael deserted from the ranks of one of Wellington's underlings. He showed up at the Château and demanded to be taken prisoner or given a post. I still am not sure if he's more Irish or Scottish, but either would account for both his folly and his bravery."

Miss Danforth watched his hands, and Sebastian liked even that attention from her.

"Isn't a deserter worse than a traitor? You were at least consistent in your loyalties once you established them, and yet I don't see anybody meeting Mr. Brodie over pistols at dawn."

He faltered at the top of the arpeggio, completed it, and again stopped playing.

"You make an interesting point." Why hadn't Sebastian come across this question previously? Every other officer, save Mercia, had eventually found his way back to English forces, except Michael, who'd declared his loyalty to England defunct upon the death of a younger sister.

"Perhaps nobody troubles Michael because he is not of the same social station as the men who are so eager to disturb my mornings. One only calls out another of comparable rank, if the rules are strictly observed." He shifted to C minor and wished pianos had longer keyboards. "Michael is protective of me. An Irishman is like a dog with a bone once he's championed a cause. Nothing will sway him. The Scots are worse."

Miss Danforth tucked her hands between her thighs, a particularly submissive and demure pose for all its impropriety. "I vote Scotsman. He wears the occasional bit of plaid. You seek to protect me, my lord, but I would protect you as well."

She suspected Michael?

"I'd trust Brodie with my life." Though Sebastian did not trust Michael with all of his truths.

"Will you finish the piece, my lord?"

Miss Danforth was wise. She sought to put an end to the discussion, and before she'd yielded up any more substantial confidences.

Before Sebastian had too.

He closed the lid over the keys and rose, because he could be wise too. He could protect Miss Danforth from her scheming relations, and he could take her caution regarding Michael to heart.

As he stood, Miss Danforth's shoulders slumped, and not in relief. She was disappointed that he would not play for her, would not give her any more of

Herr Beethoven's musical consolation for a world run amok.

Sebastian lowered himself beside her, but this time he straddled the bench. Slowly, he settled his arms around her, and more slowly threaded his hand into the hair at her nape.

"You should flee, Milly Danforth, for I am about to kiss you." *Again*, and make a proper job of it, because he surely would not repeat this folly a third time.

She rested her head on his shoulder. "You should stop lecturing me, St. Clair, for I won't run off."

Stubborn, fierce woman. He settled his mouth over hers, like coming home from war, like all the beauty in all the slow movements to all the tender concerti in the world. Miss Danforth sighed into his mouth and snuggled closer.

Sebastian's last coherent thought was that he would die to protect this woman from her scheming relations, from any harm whatsoever, but he was helpless to protect her from himself.

&

A man who is born to ask questions is a man enthralled with life, just as Milly was enthralled with St. Clair's kisses. She wanted to understand them, wanted to take them apart sensation by sensation until she comprehended the beauty and danger of them.

St. Clair knew exactly how snugly to hold her, so she felt cherished rather than confined.

He knew what a comfort his hand in her hair could be, what a novel and dear intimacy.

He knew—he was likely born knowing, to borrow

his phrase—how to use his mouth, so his lips clung and melded with her own, so her entire body poured itself into kissing him back.

St. Clair's kisses were fierce and tender, and they made Milly *feel* fierce and tender. She sank her fingers into his hair, brushed her thumb over his ear, and squirmed as close to him as their position on the piano bench would allow.

"Open, *chère*. Let me taste you." He challenged rather than commanded, and followed up with a brush of his tongue—hot, wet, entreating—against her lips.

Open her mouth. The meaning sank in as Milly ran her free hand over his chest, over the lace of his jabot, over the soft wool of his paisley waistcoat, over the silk of his shirt. He was a slow movement of a man, monumental, beautiful, all lyrical lines, rich textures, and—

She tasted him back, traced the contour of his elegant mouth with the tip of her tongue, and the soft, pleased sound he made—a chuckle, a groan, a sigh—reverberated through her.

"Again, *petite tigresse*."

He thought her a tigress. Pleasure blossomed beyond the physical, giving Milly leave to consume the man she'd plastered herself against. He tasted of bergamot, which blended wonderfully with the sandalwood and spice scent of him, with the lace and silk of his attire.

Milly got an arm around his waist and cupped his cheek against her palm while St. Clair returned her explorations.

"You taste of lavender. Of course, you taste of lavender."

He lapsed into French, telling her he'd like to lay her down in lavender fields and make endless love to her. For eternal summer nights under a soft full moon he wanted to—

Milly's French was not quite up to the literal translation, not when St. Clair's hand had traced down from her throat to her décolletage. He ran a slow, knowing finger over the tops of her breasts, along her sternum, and back up to her collarbone. She arched into that touch, needing his French extravagances, needing that full moon and those endless summer nights with a mindless determination that some distant part of her reasoning mind regarded fearfully.

"St. Clair, *please.*"

"You beg. I would never have you beg, not ever."

His tone, the seriousness of it, the Englishness of it, penetrated the haze of wonder and lust clouding Milly's brain. She pulled back, her hand still on his morning-smooth cheek.

"For God's sake, Sebastian, stop mauling Miss Danforth this instant!"

Lady St. Clair's voice cracked like musket fire through the room, but Milly perceived the words only dimly. When St. Clair's arms loosened, she wanted to haul them back around her. Her hand did not want to leave his cheek, to the point that she traced a finger over his lower lip as she parted from the feel of him.

He's not mauling me.

St. Clair's back was to the door, so maybe Lady St. Clair didn't see the kiss he brushed to Milly's cheek when Milly's reply was muttered aloud and not merely stated in the privacy of her mind.

St. Clair pivoted, so his back was to Milly, shielding her, though he remained beside her on the cushion.

"Aunt, you will excuse me if I remain seated. Was there something you required of me?"

How cool he sounded, how amused, while Milly's mind was unable to form thoughts, and her body unable to comprehend that her interlude with St. Clair was over.

"I *require* you to keep your randy hands to yourself. Honestly, Sebastian, it's difficult enough for me to keep a companion about without you exerting your charms to scare them off. Milly, you must not allow Sebastian's untoward advances to overset you. He's half-French, and allowances must be made."

Milly's emotions resolved themselves into bewilderment.

"I am equally responsible for this…for this lapse, my lady. You should castigate me as well, and I do apologize."

She would have scrambled off the piano bench, except St. Clair was as immovable as the piano itself.

"I did not intend to offend the lady," St. Clair said—the lady being *Milly*, "nor will I allow her to take responsibility for my trespasses. You have my apologies, Aunt, as do you, Miss Danforth."

He sounded sincere—too sincere. Milly shoved at his back. "Excuse me, my lord. I'm sure your aunt has need of me."

Now he rose and extended a hand to her, as if she couldn't manage to get her backside off a piano bench unassisted. "You do accept my apology, Miss Danforth?"

Milly stood in the pretty little parlor, Lady St. Clair

looking on, and wanted to kiss his lordship again. Wanted to climb into his embrace and taste his passion, because in those moments—those few, fleeting moments—she'd been with the real man. This Gallic fellow who looked both grave and mocking, this English lord of the manor with precisely appropriate words, she did not know him, and wasn't sure she'd like him if she did.

"I accept your apology. I accept that, *too*."

His brows rose, and something came cool into his eyes. Admiration, perhaps, but not pleasure. He bowed and dropped her hand.

"Then I am content that no significant harm has been done. Ladies, you will excuse me."

He departed, a lingering whiff of sandalwood assuring Milly she hadn't dreamed his presence or his kisses—if the frown on Lady St. Clair's face weren't proof enough.

"I don't know whether to celebrate or mourn. You do not seem discommoded, Miss Danforth, but we ladies grow expert at masking our worst hurts. If Sebastian was doing more than stealing kisses, you must tell me, and I will deal with him severely."

If only it had felt like theft—on his part.

"Some would say I was overstepping, my lady. Trying to gain the notice of my betters."

Alcorn would certainly say that. Milly dropped back onto the piano bench and considered Alcorn might have been—as he often was—*somewhat* right.

Lady St. Clair crossed the room to open the drapes farther, so a shaft of sunlight fell across the tulips, making the choice of a blue vase more tolerable.

"I vow you did not leap upon St. Clair and render him helpless with the powers of your charms, Milly dear. He was a soldier, for God's sake, he knows how to fight back."

Fight back against what? Or whom?

"We made progress with my letters."

"I daresay you did." Lady St. Clair snapped open another set of drapes, the light falling this time on the piano. "Well, no matter, but you must not allow any more such nonsense. Sebastian is not as sturdy as he believes himself to be. I can't have you trifling with him."

Trifling with *him*? He thought himself either indestructible or expendable, and Milly was not sure which was worse. "Do you suppose he was trying to scare me into quitting my post?"

Lady St. Clair's gaze fell on the tulips. "Those flowers go so well in here. And no, Sebastian was not trying to scare you into quitting your post. Were he intent on that end, you'd be writing out your notice this instant. Sebastian will, however, believe I'd think him capable of such machinations. Come along, my dear. You must assist me to choose my jewelry for the Hendershots' musicale. Early evening wants tact, and tact has never been my strong suit."

She swept from the room, while Milly shot a longing glance at the escritoire. Her *e*'s, *l*'s, and *o*'s lay forgotten, no obliging shaft of sunshine to illuminate them where they looped and swooped across the page.

Thank God Milly had had the sense not to attempt any *v*'s.

❦

A duke generally ascended to his title knowing exactly how many princes, royal dukes, and other dukes stood between him and the British throne. In order of precedence, Christian, eighth Duke of Mercia, far outranked the first Duke of Wellington, and yet, when the summons came from Apsley House, Mercia did not tarry.

He kissed his duchess good-bye, kissed her good-bye some more (the roads being unpredictable between Surrey and London, and his duchess being the affectionate sort), and presented himself in Wellington's soaring foyer well before supper.

"Married life agrees with you," Wellington observed with the slightly puzzled, wistful air of a man whose own duchess was seldom on the premises.

"It emphatically does, Your Grace." *This time*, for Christian was a widower whose fortunes had improved with his second foray up the church aisle. "My duchess sends her regards, and charges me to invite you to Severn whenever you're inclined."

"Pretty little thing, your duchess."

Wellington was an observant man, and a favorite with the ladies. From Christian's perspective, His Grace was making the transition from general officer, to politician, and even statesman with enviable ease.

"More to the point, sir, my duchess puts up with me. I'd like to return to her side before nightfall, if possible."

His Grace led Christian up the ornate staircase to the floor above. "You young fellows, haring in all directions, galloping about under the full moon... How's the hand?"

Wellington was also a man who took the welfare

of his staff—his former staff—seriously, which was not always convenient.

"Well enough. I can write with it—I can write with either hand now, thanks to Girard—thanks to St. Clair's—guards and their penchant for violence."

Wellington ushered him into a high-ceiling parlor that sported walls full of portraiture and other art. "It's about St. Clair that I wanted to speak with you. Shall I ring for tea, or would you like something stronger?"

If they were to discuss St. Clair, then a tot of the damned poppy wouldn't go amiss.

"Something stronger. The roads were dusty." Not too dusty to dissuade a man from traveling home by moonlight when that man slept ever so much better beside his duchess.

Christian crossed to an open window, where the fragrance of stabled horses came wafting in from Tattersall's not far upwind.

"To your health," Wellington said, extending a small glass to him. "And to the Regent's damned health."

Christian took a sip of excellent Armagnac. "You're spending time at Carlton House these days?"

"Not if I can help it, but I have ascended to the status of universal expert, you see. If there's a bit of scandal brewing, then I must sit on the committee to investigate same. If a charitable commission is to be got up, then we must have old Wellington's imprimatur on the thing. One doesn't miss the battlefield, but one does sometimes appreciate what an honest, efficient place it was."

No, one did not. In the strong afternoon sunlight, Wellington's age was showing. He was a handsome man, his posture impeccable, and his nose, in particular, worthy of some of the nicknames given to him, but Wellington was also no longer young, and that… made Christian sip his drink.

"Excellent libation, Your Grace."

"Thank Lady St. Clair, of all people. She knows my weaknesses, and indulges them from time to time. Our paths crossed in India when she was married to a younger son who never expected to inherit the title."

Christian took a larger swallow and moved away from the window. "How does she deal with having St. Clair for a nephew?"

"Easily. He's the last of his line, she loves him and will hear no wrong spoken of him. Nobody would dare cross her in this publicly." Wellington's tone suggested *he* wasn't about to take on the elderly baroness either. Not directly.

And Christian hadn't recalled, hadn't wanted to acknowledge that St. Clair's title was teetering toward escheat.

Which St. Clair alone was in a position to rectify.

"I saw St. Clair in the park the other day. He was walking out with a woman." For her sake, Christian hoped the lady was some unassuming Continental, or even an American, a woman whom Society's scorn would leave largely untouched.

"She was not…her origins looked humble," he went on. "Humble but decent."

Also lamentably English, though Christian could not have said why he reached that conclusion.

"The ladies tend to be more practical than we gentlemen." Wellington fell silent as a footman arrived bearing a cold collation. A second footman brought along a tea tray, though Christian would have preferred more of Lady St. Clair's Armagnac.

"St. Clair's situation is not resolving itself." Wellington settled on a gilt love seat upholstered in rose velvet, a delicate piece for a man of his height and bearing.

"What has St. Clair to do with me? My dealings with the man are over, and I intend that they stay that way." Christian resisted the urge to rub the fingers of his left hand, also the urge to make a fist with it.

"Several others have challenged him since you slapped a glove across his face. They've all missed, and then St. Clair has deloped. My officers are excellent marksmen, but St. Clair's luck thus far exceeds their skill."

Christian returned to the window rather than remain where his host could see his expression.

"St. Clair is a perverted excuse for a human being, one who could inflict suffering on his captives and watch that suffering without so much as flinching. His immediate superior at least took obvious pleasure in our humiliation, and under the circumstances, that humanity—evil though it was—was far preferable to St. Clair's disinterest."

St. Clair *had* watched that suffering, day after day, and then ensured the most competent doctors and best available rations were reserved for the prisoners he'd abused.

"This is, of course, loathsome behavior," His Grace observed, arranging slices of cheese and ham on a plate. "Also the same treatment French officers captured out of uniform were shown by our own forces, minus the medical care and food."

Christian heard the philosophical thread in the duke's voice and recalled this was the same fellow who'd reportedly once been given a clear shot at Napoleon himself, and had declined to fire on the basis of battlefield protocol. *General officers do not fire upon one another.*

"I should tell you I hate St. Clair," Christian said, "and the truth would be that I do, but I also don't know what to make of him. As you point out, his treatment of me was loathsome, though consistent with the situation." Christian clenched and unclenched his left hand, grateful that he could. "St. Clair gave me my freedom when Toulouse fell, though he left it to his pet jailer to unlock my cell. I owe him my life, and that is…complicated."

Owed him his life many times over, and owed him every single damned nightmare he'd had in recent years as well.

"Complicated, yes," Wellington said between bites of cheese. "The French share your consternation. He's an embarrassment, a traitor to both of his heritages, and an intelligence nightmare from which two countries would like to waken. Have some food, Mercia. One must keep up one's strength."

One must keep up one's strength. The same admonition St. Clair had used to coax Christian into eating, when Christian had once again decided to die rather than endure more of St. Clair's abuse.

Christian took a chair at an angle to Wellington's pretty love seat. "Just some cheese, please, and a slice of buttered bread."

"You've become abstemious in your dotage,

Mercia. I'm sure your duchess would want you to eat more than a schoolboy's ration."

His duchess. Even the thought of that dear lady soothed something that discussion of St. Clair had set amiss. "A spot of tea to wash it down, too, then."

Wellington loaded up a plate with three kinds of cheese, a few slices of ham, and three slices of bread slathered with butter.

"We must do something about St. Clair. More duels are in the offing, and while his death under such circumstances wouldn't be remarked, there's the off chance he might injure an opponent, and then all hell will break loose." His Grace paused with the teapot poised above a jasperware cup. "Cream and sugar?"

"Neither, thank you. You're sure more duels are in the offing? There's little honor in challenging a man who has deloped on three previous occasions."

"Little honor perhaps," the duke said, passing Christian the steaming cup of tea, "but significant satisfaction. Eat your food, Mercia, and pay attention. You are not yet acquainted with all of the salient aspects of St. Clair's situation, and yet you of all people ought to be consulted before further action is taken."

Christian listened as Wellington provided a concise, dispassionate military briefing on a situation Christian wanted nothing whatsoever to do with. His tea cooled in his cup, bars of sunlight crept across the thick carpet, and something akin to pity stole across Christian's heart for a man he ought to go to his grave hating.

Eight

STRATEGIC RETREAT WAS A TACTIC IN EVERY COMMANDER'S arsenal, and Sebastian resorted to it shamelessly. If Miss Danforth was in the parlor playing cards with Aunt Freddy, Sebastian was in his study, poring over pamphlets on the cultivation of herbs and flowers. If she took tea in the music room, Sebastian went riding. Avoiding her was not complicated.

Neither was it easy.

"Go to bed, Michael. If the weather holds fair, we'll hack out at first light, and you need your rest."

Michael set aside the volume he'd been reading— Byron?—and rose.

"You and your flowers. Are they really so much more enjoyable than your dreams would be?"

Sebastian's dreams were usually of men in chains, spewing vile curses then begging God to take their lives, moaning for their mothers then begging Sebastian to take their lives. He had been unable to oblige them, and thus the moaning and cursing had gone on endlessly.

"My French lavender is not thriving here. I give

it the best soil, the most careful pruning, the most sheltered start in life, and it does not thrive."

Michael put Byron back up on the shelf where Aunt kept her favorite volumes. "Is your concern financial or sentimental?"

Curious question from a man who struggled mightily to hold himself above matters of sentiment. "It's both. Go to bed. That's a direct order, *mon ami.*"

Michael gave an ironic salute and sauntered off into the darkness of the corridor. Only half the sconces were kept lit, another manifestation of financial worry, and the fire in the grate had been allowed to burn down to coals.

The lavender would not thrive, but it did not die either. Sebastian's fellows at the Society muttered sympathetically, but were either too politically delicate to venture any ideas why this should be or too involved with the appearance of horticultural enthusiasm rather than the substance of it.

He tried for another hour to absorb himself in translating some old Roman doctor's maunderings about the medicinal qualities of lavender, and was making some headway when the door creaked open.

Milly Danforth stood in the gloom, her nightclothes making her look like a pale shade. "Excuse me, my lord. I wasn't aware the library would be occupied."

And yet, even clad in her nightgown and dressing gown, she did not withdraw.

"Miss Danforth, hadn't you best be in bed?"

Alone. Immediately. Dreaming virginal dreams about…her cat, perhaps?

Or Sebastian's kiss from five days ago.

She advanced into the room, gathering a paisley

shawl more closely about her shoulders. "I could not sleep. Why have you let the fire nearly go out?"

With the efficiency of a woman comfortable shifting for herself, she took up the wrought iron poker and moved the coals about, poured more coal onto the andirons, then used the bellows to inspire the flames to life. She finished by tidying up the hearth with the ash broom and dustpan, then replacing the screen and dusting her hands together.

"Perhaps I was trying to save on coal." He would certainly hoard up images of her, auburn braid swinging down her back as she built up his fire.

She gathered the shawl around her again, a pretty blue-and-green peacock silk that contrasted with her plain bedclothes.

"Lady St. Clair knows about the jewels, my lord."

Sebastian took a moment to fathom the mental leaps Miss Danforth had executed. "You think I let the fire go out because I need to economize, so that I might finish replacing Aunt's jewels before she knows what I'm about?"

"She says pinchbeck and paste don't weigh the same as gold and gems, don't feel the same against the skin. She knows when you replace the paste with something real, and she wishes you would not bother."

He ought to say something imperious and French, go back to his old Roman doctor, and shame Miss Danforth into leaving the room. He rose and came around the front of the desk.

"My lavender is not thriving. This keeps me awake at night, but I am like wine, Miss Danforth. I prefer darkness, cool, and calm."

And, apparently, he preferred stubborn little red-headed women who were eager for his kisses and had middle names like Harriette.

She sidled over to the desk and appropriated his seat—an audacious move that left him with another image to memorize. "My aunts' lavender always did well. You've been puzzling over this for some while."

"How do you know?"

"This chair still holds your body heat."

Said in all innocence, while Sebastian's body heat decided to focus behind his falls.

"Why do you come to the library when you can't sleep, Milly Danforth? You've told me reading confounds you late at night."

She glanced up sharply, probably to see if he was insulting her. He wished he were, wished it wasn't curiosity driving his question.

"I like to smell the books. They remind me of my aunts' cottage."

This admission was made as she tidied up the mess Sebastian had created on the desk's surface. She capped the inkwell, set the quill pen in its stand, straightened his papers, and otherwise put to rights the implements of reading and writing that had caused her so much frustration in life.

"You say your aunts did well with their lavender. Did they start their seedlings in frames?"

The fire was giving off more heat, but also light, and that light played with the highlights in Miss Danforth's hair and put a sheen on her paisley silk shawl.

"They started new plants from cuttings, not

seedlings. Aunt Hy said cuttings worked better, and no, the frames were too hot for young plants."

"What do you mean, too hot?"

She opened the ink and dipped the pen. He liked the look of her there, among his things, the pen in her hand.

"The frames are filled with fresh horse manure, and it holds heat for weeks. Aunt said it was too much heat, and too wet."

"What has wet to do with it?"

And was this the real reason she'd come through the cold, dark house? To practice her letters when nobody would be about?

"Lavender is tough—the bugs don't go near it, the blights and rots and such seldom bother it, but too much rain, and it falters."

"*Rain* bothers it?" And here he'd been lavishing water on his plants, thinking to foster luxuriant growth.

She dipped the pen again. "The wetter our summers, the less the lavender grew."

How could he have not known this? How could all those stalwart plant enthusiasts at the Society not have passed this along to him? How could his grandparents, who'd known everything about their herbs, not have imparted this signal fact?

Madam Agronomist looked up from her penmanship. "You are angry. Do not be angry at the plants, St. Clair. Would you like your seat back?"

"You lied to me, Milly Danforth. You did not come down here to sniff books. You came down here to write your name."

And she hadn't let Sebastian's presence stop her.

"One can do both. You are not my conscience, St. Clair. Hadn't you best go up to bed? One hears you clattering out of the mews before the sun is even up."

Did one? Did *one* listen for him clattering out of the mews at such an hour?

He took his time, wandering about the room, though his objective was quite, quite fixed.

"If a man wants to gallop his horse, the early hours are the only ones suited to it. The sun comes up earlier and earlier this time of year, and the park grows crowded."

She went back to her letters, but Sebastian was certain in his bones she was monitoring his progress as he took Byron down then replaced him on the shelf.

"You should speak to her ladyship about the jewels, sir. She is vexed with you for wasting good coin on them."

Sebastian paused to study the fire, which was roaring along tidily.

"They are not her jewels. They are the St. Clair jewels, and she pawned them because I was off larking about in the south of France rather than tending to the duties I was conceived and born to take up."

And she'd pawned each bracelet, tiara, and ring at Sebastian's express instruction.

Miss Danforth considered her letters, her expression similar to when she critiqued a bouquet.

"You were off making war, you mean. Freezing in the winters, starving year 'round, earning the hatred of your countrymen on both sides of the Channel. The English considered you a traitor, while the French resented your competence."

Damn the woman and her casual insights. "More

or less. What are you doing there, Miss Danforth? Waltzing about the page unsupervised, hmm?"

As he closed the distance toward the desk, Sebastian saw that she'd known exactly what he was about, stalking her, and she'd feigned ignorance of his aims adroitly enough to keep him coming closer.

"I'm practicing. Would you like to see?"

Such boldness. He liked her boldness, but the real problem was that she trusted him. Millicent Danforth trusted him bodily, morally, logistically, every way a woman could trust a man, and her trust was a strong aphrodisiac to someone who'd arguably committed treason.

He came around the desk and sat back against it without glancing down at her writing. "Millicent, this will not do."

"You should go to bed, then."

"I want to take you to bed with me. I want to keep you in my bed and make passionate love to you until exhaustion claims us both, then rut on you some more when we've caught a decent nap."

She wrinkled her nose. "You won't, though. Why not?"

Damnation was too mild a fate for such a woman. "You want me to say that a gentleman's honor forbids it. You are longing for me to give you that lie, but I am not honorable, my dear. I am the Traitor Baron, my days are numbered, and those whose loyalty I claim are put in danger."

"Everybody's days are numbered." He heard her aunts speaking, heard the toughness and scorn of old women in her tones, and wanted to scare her out of her complaisance.

"I have been challenged four times in the last six months, Milly. Poison was attempted before that, and recently my horse's bridle was tampered with. Somebody badly wants me dead. So I take you to bed and romp away a few hours with you and get a child on you. Then we must marry, and you become not the discreet dalliance of a disgraced baron, but his widow. Your social doom is sealed by that fate, and I cannot abide such a thought."

Because she deserved better, and because Sebastian could not bear the weight of even one more regret on his heart.

❧

His lordship was trying desperately to shock her, while Milly wanted desperately to impress him with her letters.

"I will not marry you," she said. Not for all the *e*'s, *o*'s, *l*'s, and even *v*'s would she worry him like that. "I am not of an appropriate station, for one thing, and I expect somewhere there's a rule about baronesses being able to read and write. I confess the romping part piques my curiosity."

He swore softly in French but remained close to her, half leaning, half sitting on the desk. This late, his scent was softer, more spice, less sandalwood, and Milly had all she could do to keep her eyes open and not breathe too obviously through her nose.

"The romping part would be the ruin of you." The way he said it suggested romping might be the ruin of him as well, which notion both intrigued and saddened.

"You lecture me when you could be kissing me, and then tell me you have no honor. There's an inconsistency in your actions, my lord—or in your kisses. But no matter. I can find kisses and romping aplenty. I suspect your Mr. Brodie would oblige me easily enough were I simply plagued by curiosity."

She'd shocked *him*, which gave her no satisfaction at all, when she'd been trying to make a point.

"You will not torment Michael the way you are tormenting me, Millicent, and we will not romp."

She tossed the pen aside and moved the inkwell to the corner of the blotter.

"You dratted man, I could not care less about the romping. It's *you* who plagues me. When Vincent kissed me, I wanted to wipe my mouth with my handkerchief. When you kiss me, I want to take my clothes off, and your clothes off too."

He studied his hands, and by firelight, his expression was long-suffering to the point of martyrdom. Milly heard Shakespeare whispering from the shadows, *Will all great Neptune's ocean wash this blood clean from my hands?*

"There will be no taking off of clothes, Miss Danforth. You are merely inquisitive, reckless, befuddled by your curiosity, and quite possibly by grief and"—his expression grew a trifle mean—"loneliness. Many a proper English lady has propositioned me, and do you know what they wanted, Miss Danforth?"

He was near shaking with the force of his ire. "Those gentle flowers of English womanhood wanted me to bind them and beat them. To blindfold them and *play* at being the French colonel. They would offer me the cut direct should I ask them to dance, but they wanted me for their toy in private. I understand the need to use any means available to win a war, but I do not understand this depravity."

Milly perceived that more than outraged, St. Clair was sickened by the propositions he'd received— genuinely shocked and bewildered.

"They did not see you as a person, just as you could not afford to see the English officers as people, but rather, as pawns on a chessboard."

He closed his eyes. "Those Englishmen were my countrymen, and I was a traitor to them. I gained a reputation for knowing how to deal with English officers, for making them yield secrets to me even they didn't know they were keeping."

St. Clair was attempting a confession or a condemnation of himself; Milly wasn't sure which, but she did know she wanted to take him in her arms when he spoke like this.

"Every time you describe your role, you paint yourself as more and more of an animal, and less and less a man." And he let her see more and more of the cost to him for having played that role.

He opened his eyes. "I *am* an animal, a traitorous animal, but I'd rather be honestly viewed as that than as any woman's toy, ever." He touched Milly's chin, so she had to look him in the eye. "*I tortured those officers, Milly.* I studied them, toyed with their trust, and determined how best to wrest from them their dignity, their health, their sanity. Among the English I gained the sobriquet 'The Inquisitor,' and I was very, very good at what I did."

His hand remained under her chin, as if he'd will Milly to repeat his ugly words. His gaze pleaded with her to agree with their import, to accept the truth of his self-characterization.

"And nobody was torturing French officers, were they?" Milly spat. "Englishmen are too noble, too decent, too moral to engage in such activities, even in times of war?" She rose, though she was too short to stand nose to nose with him. "But I forget! Here in England, we torture each other when needs must. I'm told there are all manner of ghoulish devices stored at the Tower for just such purposes. We've tortured Catholics and Jews, witches and imbeciles. Of all the Englishmen engaged in tormenting their fellow creatures, I suspect you were among the few whose justification qualified as typical wartime behavior."

"Milly, please don't shout."

Milly. She loved that he called her Milly, and hated the sorrow in his eyes.

"You are not a diversion to me, my lord. That you think I would consider you thus suggests it's you who cannot keep the role you played separate from the man you are now. I am the paid companion. You are my employer's nephew and a titled lord. You are a decent man, and my regard for you is decent as well."

She'd surprised him with her bold speech, and that felt good. It felt right to set him back on his pins, to punch through his self-absorption.

Which did not explain, not in any way, why she went up on her toes and kissed his cheek—gently, the way she might offer comfort to a friend on a sad occasion.

"You are a man like any other, and they are

silly, bored women whose husbands have neglected them for years. You are not depraved because you considered giving them something of what they wanted so that you might have something of what they offered."

One dark eyebrow quirked, and *monsieur le baron* abruptly joined the conversation. "What does a chaste companion know of such transactions?"

"I know nothing of such transactions, but I know worlds about being lonely and invisible. I'll thank you not to insult me for it."

That was her exit line, but he spoiled it, the wretch. He spoiled it by letting something show in his eyes—not humor, exactly, but tenderness, regret, and possibly respect tinged with self-mocking.

"Mademoiselle is tired and must not be kept from her prayers. *Bonne nuit.*"

He'd caressed the words, making them courtly and old-fashioned, *ma demoiselle*. My lady.

And then he caressed her cheek, one large male hand cradling her jaw against his palm. His touch was gentle, warm, and enticing—also blessedly brief.

"Good night, my lord."

A woman in a dressing gown and nightgown didn't curtsy, not when the hour approached midnight and she'd accosted a fellow in his shirtsleeves by the light of a few candles.

St. Clair's lips quirked—the closest thing to a smile Milly had seen from him. She took the warning and turned to go, just as the blasted, treacherous, infernal rascal blew her a kiss.

More Gallic foolery. His petty flirtation didn't for

one moment hide the fact that he was as lonely as Milly, and even more starved for tenderness.

She picked up one of the few lit candles and left him to his darkness and shadows.

❧

Surveillance was more difficult than Henri wanted to admit, particularly when it involved sitting on a hard bench, hour after hour, pretending to swill ale and eat brown bread smeared with mustard while *not* appearing to stare out a flyspecked window.

The ale grew flat, the brown bread stale, and the mustard—acidic, stinging, not a hint of spice to cut the most abrasive vinegar—was such as no self-respecting French innkeeper would have served to his pigs.

And yet, surveillance gave a man time to think.

St. Clair had walked in the park with a petite sparrow of a woman last week, the same sparrow of a woman who apparently went about with Lady St. Clair. The baroness took the sparrow with her shopping, socializing, and on the Sunday church parade in the park, suggesting either a poor relation had been added to the household, or a lady's companion.

Though St. Clair would not be walking out with a lady's companion—would he?

Henri tore off a bite of execrable brown bread and appeared to study it, when in truth he was watching the progress of a rotund fellow who had shown up twice earlier in the week at about this time.

Too early for a proper morning call, suggesting the fellow was family or wanted to be certain to catch the family at home. Not a tradesman, though—St.

Clair was scrupulous about paying bills when due, and the trades would skulk around back rather than lose custom by presuming on the front door.

As on both previous occasions, Monsieur Well-Fed Englishman rapped on the front door, exchanged a few words with whoever answered, and then a few more words.

Henri left some coins on the table and took his time pulling on his gloves—the English were to be honestly commended for their workmanship when it came to gentlemen's gloves—the better to watch the little drama taking place on St. Clair's front steps.

The argument went on, for it was an argument. The Fat Fellow gesticulated with his walking stick as if it were a drover's staff, and from within the house, the door was drawn closed.

My enemy's enemy is my friend.

This little aphorism was perhaps Roman in origin, so honestly did it summarize one reality of warfare. Henri tapped his hat onto his head squarely, in the English fashion, mentally imbued his walk with an English strut, and quit the Jugged Hare as if late for an appointment.

By maintaining the same attitude, Henri neatly intersected the chubby man's path as that worthy came waddling down St. Clair's steps, muttering under his breath about idiot women and ungrateful cousins.

Henri fell in step beside this beleaguered soul because clearly, like all of God's creatures from time to time, this Englishman was in need of a sympathetic ear.

"My lady, you should know that your companion was closeted with his lordship for a good twenty minutes last night when the rest of the house was abed."

Dear Michael was clearly not happy to be peaching on his employer, while the baroness was ecstatic with his report.

"Which of them do you expect me to scold, sir? They are both of age, and need I remind you, at least one of them has a duty to the title he has yet to fulfill."

Sebastian's bodyguard-stalking-about-as-a-valet picked up the cat stropping itself around his boots. "Shall we conclude they were discussing that duty late at night, behind the closed door of the library?"

"In a manner of speaking, yes."

The cat squeezed its eyes shut and began to purr as Michael scratched its hairy head.

"Baroness, you seek to provide St. Clair companionship, secure the succession, and perhaps even see the young lady well married, but that is not what awaits them."

Lady Freddy had managed the St. Clair holdings for more than ten years without benefit of a baron at her side, or many material resources, and she'd learned in those years whom she could trust and whom she had to watch.

Michael Brodie fell into both categories.

"What aren't you telling me, young man? Sebastian and Milly will soon be head over ears for each other, and neither one is in a position to be picky. In my day, we were more practical about these things. I did not hold the barony together so Wales could fritter away our valuables on his infernal art collection."

George would forgive her for that characterization—he'd always been a tolerant boy when sober, particularly where the ladies were concerned.

Michael wanted to pace. Lady Freddy could sense it in him, the way the switching of a cat's tail presaged a great pounce.

"St. Clair's enemies are not rational," he said. "They do not tell themselves, 'Oh, well, five challenges would be excessive and vindictive, and St. Clair has paid enough for the crime of loyalty to his mother's people. Surely we should let him go in peace to raise up a passel of babies in the grand English tradition.'"

He shifted the cat to cradle it like an infant, and the shameless beast only purred more loudly.

"Michael, what do you know that you aren't saying?"

"Nothing. I hear things, though, rumblings and rumors, and none of them suggest Sebastian's troubles are over."

Well, of course they weren't. "Wellington stood up with me the other night."

Michael left off scratching the cat's chin. "His Grace is said to be an excellent dancer."

In more ways than one, as Lady Freddy could attest. "He gave me a different version of the same warning you're delivering."

Michael paced to the window, which, being at the back of house, overlooked the mews. Soldiers never really lost the need for reconnaissance, good soldiers anyway.

"What did he say?"

"He cautioned me to mind my own business, essentially, because Sebastian's business could become untidy at any moment."

The sunlight streaming in the window showed lines of fatigue at the corners of Michael's handsome mouth and around his eyes. If he didn't soon give up the task of safeguarding his former commanding officer, he was at risk for growing prematurely old.

"What did His Grace mean, my lady? Sebastian's business has been chronically untidy for years."

"That's the challenge in the game we play, isn't it? What did he mean? Arthur and I are old friends, such as one can be friends with such a scamp, and in that context, I believe he was telling me to look after my nephew. Milly Danforth would look after Sebastian better than I ever could."

"Milly Danforth got a dose of cold, hard truth last night. St. Clair explained to her exactly what his role was at the Château, used the words *torture* and *inquisitor* because calling himself a traitor didn't drive the woman from the room."

The cat squirmed, as if Michael might have been holding it too snugly, but rather than set the beast down, Michael shifted it against his shoulder, another posture suited to cuddling infants.

"Michael, those who listen at keyholes are seldom happier for it."

"Those who don't listen at keyholes often live only long enough to regret their virtue. You might want to advertise for a new companion."

Lady Freddy rose from her escritoire and approached the man so intent on bringing old wars into her sitting room. He watched her with the wariness of one who did not entirely understand women.

"He's such a handsome beast, this cat." She ran her

hand over thick, dark fur. "More placid than many of his kind. You should allow him to be a good influence, Michael. He permits himself regular doses of rest and affection, while you eschew both."

"I do not want to see St. Clair's brains spattered across some sheep meadow, but even more, I do not want to see him lose a woman he's come to cherish. You—"

Lady Freddy left off petting the cat and waited, because in the way of men, Michael had finally come around to the point.

"You can take care of yourself," he said, setting the cat on the floor. "Miss Danforth is an innocent. She's a liability to Sebastian because of it, a liability to the household."

"Love is not a liability, Michael, though I have to wonder if this great excess of protectiveness is directed toward Sebastian. He can take care of himself, too, can't he?"

Michael's gaze stayed on the cat as it sauntered out of the sitting room.

"Sebastian cannot protect himself from a woman who regards torture as part of the ordinary course of battle. She scolded him, not for having men beaten and starved and questioned for hours, but for beating himself with his memories."

Sebastian had never starved anybody—except himself, very likely—and yet, this news was fiercely gratifying.

"Stay out of it, Michael. Sebastian will not thank you for interfering, and I shudder to think what Miss Danforth would do should she learn you were eavesdropping and carrying tales."

"It's my job to carry tales, and well you know it."

She did know it, which had probably been another aspect of Arthur's cryptic warning. "So you've done your duty, Michael. I will share this news with the professor, and we'll double the figurative guard. And, Michael?"

He paused with his hand on the door latch.

"Miss Danforth is not your sister. She's not anybody's sister."

He nodded once, an acknowledgment, not an agreement, and left without making a sound.

❧

"I was told I'd find ye here cowerin' among the lilies."

The words were not particularly menacing, but the Scots burr with which they'd been delivered sent a cold, sinking weariness through Sebastian's body.

Sebastian rose, glad he'd at least been alone in the Society's reading room—but for the potted lilies making the place smell like a house in mourning.

"MacHugh."

To say anything more—"You're looking well," "A pleasure to see you," or even, "Good day to you"—would be to invite rage, and Sebastian had had enough rage to last a lifetime.

MacHugh glowered as only a big, mean Scot in a killing temper could glower. "I hear ye've been bragging."

"Then you, or someone else, has heard mistakenly."

Emotion flared in icy green eyes. Surprise maybe, more likely pleasure at meeting with resistance. "My hearing is excellent, Girard."

The name under which Sebastian had traveled while flying the French flag, and a bitter taunt. Sebastian said nothing, but noted that MacHugh was in Highland attire and would likely have a dagger in his right boot.

Though the fellow could kill with his bare hands easily enough.

A movement at the door had MacHugh glancing to Sebastian's left. "Do ye want company for this, Girard?"

The same sort of exaggerated consideration Sebastian might have shown his prisoners. *Sacre bleu*, not again. "I am at your pleasure, *monsieur*."

"So polite." MacHugh fired off a toothy smile at the fellows standing in the door to the reading room—old Postlethwaite, a devotee of the rose, and a nervous young fellow named Chester, who had an avid interest in the sex life of the bean. "Ye lot will keep out of this."

Postlethwaite stood his ground, but the green bean melted away as an enormous, purposeful fist came sailing at Sebastian's jaw. "Name yer seconds, laddie. It's time I was killin' ye."

Sebastian moved his jaw as pain radiated through his neck and shoulders. Nothing broken, a warning shot only, which hinted that MacHugh was not in as much of a temper as his burr and his words might indicate.

And the relief of the blow suggested Sebastian was in more trouble than even MacHugh knew.

"Am I to know the exact dimensions of my transgression, or do I conclude my drawing breath has offended you?"

MacHugh studied the place on Sebastian's jaw that felt like it was turning a nice, rapidly swelling shade of red.

"Ye ran yer bluidy mouth, Girard. I was willin' to

tolerate yer presence among the living as long as the past remained the past, but ye've been telling tales, suggesting I couldna hold m' liquor while in yer dubious keeping, and for that ye mun die."

MacHugh had held a prodigious amount of liquor, attempting to drink Sebastian under the table. The misery resulting to Sebastian had lasted days, though MacHugh had failed to earn his freedom.

"I laced your drinks with laudanum, MacHugh. I cheated. You would never have won free, not even if you drank me witless—which you did."

In his cups—deep, deep in his cups, and aided by the poppy—the Scotsman had mumbled a few facts about a shortage of fodder for the cavalry mounts. Sebastian had been able to send word up the line that the regiment would soon be breaking camp, and had likely averted at least one nasty skirmish between forces all too ready for the winter cease-fire. He'd remembered MacHugh in his prayers ever since, and avoided the near occasion of whiskey.

"Then I'll kill ye for cheatin' *and* braggin'."

MacHugh was not stupid. He was a canny, wily, hardheaded Scot whom Sebastian—may God help him—*liked*.

"I'd *brag* about cheating? About having to cheat?" Having to cheat so one officer at least hadn't been threatened with torture as a means of loosening his tongue. Sebastian had considered the experiment a success—until now.

Green eyes blinked, putting Sebastian in mind of a large, hungry reptile, one capable of breathing fire. "Ye should have kept yer mouth shut, laddie."

Sebastian would not contradict MacHugh directly, lest he be cindered right there in the reading room.

"Why do you suppose I waited more than two years to turn up stupid, MacHugh?"

"Because ye're half-English, and they're a bit slow. Ye're half-French, and they're more than a bit arrogant."

One could not argue MacHugh's logic. "Brodie will be my second. My choice of weapons is bare fists."

A jolly smile bloomed on MacHugh's craggy face— the man had campaigned across the entire Peninsula, endured months of imprisonment, and still had every one of his teeth.

"Clever. Ye want me to have to kill ye slowly, with my bare hands. Ye're an optimistic soul if ye think conscience will prevent me from finishing ye off."

The grin on MacHugh's face suggested Sebastian was a dead soul.

"I am not an optimist. Upon whom should Brodie call?"

With the peculiar courtesy of a furious gentleman assured satisfaction on the field of honor, MacHugh passed over a pair of calling cards, bowed, and withdrew. Postlethwaite bellowed for some ice while Sebastian found a seat among the lilies and, once again, prepared to face death.

Nine

"Bare fists! You'll let that damned Scottish meat wagon beat you to death?"

Milly paused outside the door to the library, Mr. Brodie's words taking her quite, quite aback. She wanted him to repeat them, in part because she'd never met a Scottish meat wagon—she could not possibly have heard that correctly—but also because Brodie had sounded more Scottish than Irish himself.

And then there was that "to death" part, which had to be male hyperbole run amok.

She could not hear Sebastian's reply, for it had to be Sebastian to whom Brodie addressed himself. To the rest of the household Mr. Brodie was unfailingly polite.

When he wasn't snooping through their underlinen.

"Miss Danforth?"

The professor stood on the stairs, looking dapper in his evening attire.

"Sir?"

"I believe Lady Freddy could use your assistance to finish dressing for tonight's card party. She muttered dire imprecations should she be outshone by a Mrs.

Flynn. One fears for her health when such moods overtake her."

The professor's references to her ladyship's décolletage were a marvel of delicacy.

Milly hurried past him up the stairs. "Summer is coming, Professor. We can hope for a mild evening."

"A wiser bet than hoping her ladyship might learn a bit of decorum. My thanks, Miss Danforth."

The professor went sauntering on his way—he was never in a hurry—while voices rose from the library. Milly could not eavesdrop with the professor underfoot, so she hustled up to Lady Freddy's apartment.

"I have told that boy he is to stop this nonsense," Lady Freddy muttered. She sat at her vanity, an aging goddess whose accuracy with a thunderbolt was not to be underestimated. "He's even replaced my pearls with the genuine article, and I haven't worn pearls for decades." She swiveled her guns on Milly. "You could carry off pearls, even with that hair. Pearls in your hair would look quite fetching."

"I have no need of jewels, my lady, and if his lordship wants to replace the St. Clair jewels, then future generations of St. Clairs will likely commend him for it."

The idea that somebody would commend the baron for something struck Milly as appropriate, though she'd rather the praise not be exclusively posthumous.

Lady Freddy dropped her pearls onto a tray of white-and-gilt porcelain. "My dear girl, there will *be* no future generations of St. Clairs at the rate Sebastian goes on. He has a duty to the succession that he should have attended to the instant hostilities ceased, but no, he must break my heart instead while he frets over his *drooping* herbs. What do you think of topaz with my new cream-and-gold ensemble?"

Milly crossed the carpet to stand behind Lady Freddy and consider the image in the folding mirror.

"I think you know more than you should about waging war with silk and jewels, but turquoise or sapphire will go better with your coloring if you're set on wearing the new dress."

"Amber would serve for you," Lady Freddy said. "Though jade would serve better." She fished through the tray and extracted a sapphire bracelet.

"Let me fasten that," Milly said, taking Lady Freddy's left wrist in her hands. "You know, it might be that his lordship cannot see to the succession."

"*Cannot?*"

"War affects some men that way; then too, there are injuries a man can sustain that do not take his life, but take his ability to beget life. There. I think it looks very well on you, ma'am."

Milly sent up a request for forgiveness to the Almighty. Sebastian St. Clair showed every evidence of being in good reproductive health.

Her ladyship admired the bracelet then retrieved its twin from the tray. "Milly Danforth, you shock me. I ought to increase your wages. How could you know of such injuries?"

"My aunts entertained many fellows who served in the Colonial wars. Two in particular were frequent callers. I suspected the gentlemen had an unnatural relationship, but Aunt Hy explained one of them had been injured. The necklace too, my lady?"

"*And* you know of unnatural relationships! My, what a worldly place Chelsea has become. Yes, the necklace too."

They experimented with different lengths of the necklace. Lady Freddy eventually decided it should lie exactly where a young widow might have positioned it—so the gold pendant fell right above her cleavage.

"Have I shocked you, Milly?"

"To my very toes, my lady. I shall endeavor to age every bit as shockingly as you have. The professor will be the envy of all who behold you. Though it might be chilly later on, best tuck a fichu into your pocket, my lady."

Lady Freddy rose from her dressing stool and remained still while Milly unfastened the bracelets and passed her a pair of long white evening gloves. "You'll take the rest of these baubles down to Sebastian to put in the safe?"

"Of course, my lady."

The final touches—refastening the bracelets outside the gloves, adjusting Lady Freddy's wrap just so, choosing a pair of blue silk handkerchiefs edged in gold lace—meant the professor was tapping his toe at the foot of the stairs when Milly eventually shooed her charge off to the Tuesday night card party.

Her ladyship took the professor's arm and sailed out into the night when Lady Avery's coach-and-four pulled up.

"God help Lady Avery and Lord Avery, and anybody who thinks the evening is about cards," Milly muttered as silence settled over the foyer. No raised voices came from the library, even while Milly lingered by the front door, touching up the bouquet of forced white roses and frothy ferns perfuming the air.

She tidied up the capes hanging on the hooks near the porter's nook, leaning in for a whiff of his lordship's greatcoat. She examined her hair—which would never sport pearls—in the mirror and then returned upstairs to set Lady Freddy's boudoir to rights.

Casualties of the battle preparations lay all about, and Lady Freddy's lady's maid was no doubt below stairs, enjoying a much-deserved and much-delayed evening meal. Milly rehung dresses, organized cosmetics, refolded handkerchiefs, and put away a gold lace fichu her ladyship had—purposely?—neglected to tuck into a pocket.

The last task required before Milly could curl up with her embroidery was replacement of the jewels in the safe.

Real jewels. Lady Freddy claimed the pearls were the last of the St. Clair valuables to be restored to genuine status, and they were lovely, lovely jewelry. Each single pearl bore a soft, luminous quality and exactly matched the rest of the rope.

Milly resisted the urge to twine a strand in her hair, and scooped up the lot of rejected gems. She did not knock on the library door, it being past the hour when his lordship usually went out, and Mr. Brodie's entitlement to courtesy being dubious.

"Excuse me, my lord. I wasn't aware you were still at home."

Not only was he at home, St. Clair was only half-dressed. His coat was nowhere in evidence, his cuffs were turned back, and his cravat was gone. He stood and came around his desk, though Milly's sense was that he sought to block her advance into the room rather than to show her the courtesy of rising from his seat.

"Miss Danforth."

"I thought you'd left. My apologies. Lady Freddy asked that her jewels—"

He shifted closer, taking the tray from Milly's hands. "Shall I tell you the combination to the safe, Miss Danforth? You won't have to risk coming upon me of a late night to return them to their proper place."

As if coming upon him was such a hardship?

"I don't want to know the combination." She did, however, want to run her hands through his hair. It stuck up in all directions, as if he'd just risen from a dead sleep, or been sitting at that desk for hours, thrashing through difficult matters.

He set the jewels on the corner of the desk. "Freddy knows the combination, and the professor knows it. I see no harm in you knowing it as well."

As he moved closer to the candles on the desk, Milly could see that St. Clair was tired. He'd been on his horse before the sun rose, coming and going all day, then closeting himself with Mr. Brodie directly after tea.

"I would as soon not be privy to such information, sir."

He nudged aside necklaces, bracelets, rings, and earrings, and picked out a brooch from the pile of beauty on the tray. "Take this."

Milly did not move. "Are you mad? So I can be accused of stealing it?"

Her words did not offend him. Instead, he held

the brooch out to her, the gold setting winking in the candlelight.

"Gold and emeralds, Miss Danforth. Your coloring demands emeralds."

Lady Freddy had said jade should have been her lot. "My coloring might demand emeralds, my lord, but my station in life demands common sense. Put the jewels away, please."

The room did not smell as if he'd been overimbibing, nor was there brandy among the papers on the desk, and yet his gaze held a forlorn quality, something Milly was used to seeing in a muted version.

"I want you to have this, Milly Danforth. The brooch was my mother's, and not part of the St. Clair estate. Giving it to you is simpler than involving a lot of lawyers and documents."

A premonition slithered down Milly's spine, from her nape to her belly. "What document are you working on, St. Clair?"

"Nothing you need puzzle over at this late hour, Miss Danforth." He tossed the gorgeous little brooch aside like so much worthless sentiment. "Come, I will escort you above stairs and order you a pot of chocolate so you might keep your cat company. I cannot believe you prefer the companionship of a feline to that of her ladyship's coven."

He would not let Milly get near that desk. Perhaps he was writing to somebody in France, somebody he ought not to correspond with.

"Put the jewels away first, my lord. They shouldn't be left sitting out to tempt any footman or parlor maid who comes around to tend the fire."

His smile was tired, and all the more charming for it. "As you wish."

He moved aside a painting of the casting of the hounds: a jolly field of squires and their ladies having a nip under the trees while the hounds went sniffing around for the scent of their quarry. He stowed the jewels in their vault, and yet, Milly's anxiety increased.

"Why aren't the dueling pistols on the mantel?"

St. Clair replaced the painting and regarded the hounds nosing about in the undergrowth on the canvas.

"Michael cleans them from time to time. I suppose it's a habit left over from his military days. Would you like some scones with your chocolate?"

What she'd like was some honesty with her baron, but when he took her arm and propelled her toward the door, she did not fight his effort to eject her.

"I didn't realize a valet was charged with maintaining the arsenal."

"There is much you don't realize, Miss Danforth. When you're saying your prayers tonight, your cat purring at your feet, add that to the list."

Perhaps fatigue was making him French, for his consonants and vowels had stolen off across the Channel.

Milly paused with him outside the library, where the scent of roses and greenery wafted on cool breezes from the foyer.

"You're in trouble, aren't you? Either you've spent too much replacing Lady Freddy's jewels or your lavender is failing or you've—"

The bleak humor in his eyes told her she was sniffing in a promising direction. She hadn't guessed the whole of it, but he was in difficulties of some sort.

"I am forever offending somebody, Miss Danforth. This is my fate, and you must not allow it to upset you. I believe on occasion I have even offended you?"

He winged his arm, but Milly could not deal with his lordly flummery, not when two dueling pistols had been sitting on top of their case right beside the jewelry tray.

Had he been reviewing his last will and testament? Was that what the infernal brooch had been about?

"You could marry wealth, my lord. The Germans always have some princesses on offer, the professor would know which ones to ask. A French aristo with no taste for republican government would do. Lady Freddy is desperate for you to have somebody to love."

They paused near the foyer.

"Lady Freddy is desperate for me to have sons. She's worked too long and hard to keep the St. Clair holdings together to see the Crown get its hands on generations of family wealth. And while I am inclined to share her sense of possessiveness—"

Milly could not abide the drawling humor in his tone. She got her hands on *him*. Sank her fingers into his every-which-way hair, plastered herself to him, and kissed his fool, blathering mouth into silence.

"She wants you to have somebody to *love*, you idiot man," she growled against his teeth. "Somebody to *love you*."

He might have argued, except Milly was not turning loose of his mouth. Something shuddered through him, a groan or a sigh, and his arms came around her slowly, then quite, quite snugly.

"Better, my lord."

"My aunt has hired a madwoman."

He was a madman, but he kissed wonderfully, turning Milly's assault into a dance, a twining of tongues, sighs, and bodies that had nothing to do with dueling pistols—at least in Milly's mind.

She would never presume to know his lordship's.

St. Clair's hand cupped Milly's breast from below, a lovely caress, one that inspired her to sink her fingers into the firm musculature of his backside. The urge to climb him stole into Milly's imagination, along with a burning desire to relieve St. Clair of his remaining clothes.

"I'll just get my fich—"

Lady Freddie's voice stopped abruptly as the front door was thrown open, and cold air swirled into the foyer.

"Sebastian, unhand Miss Danforth."

Four little words, but they presaged Milly's ruin. Over her shoulder, she saw the professor intently examining the roses—or studying the scene in the mirror—while Lady Avery and Lady Covington examined Milly and Sebastian.

And Sebastian did not unhand her, for which Milly's knees were grateful.

"Aunt, my ladies, I do beg your pardon. You will forgive me for taking the liberties a fiancé ought not to attempt unless privacy is assured."

Milly's head came off Sebastian's shoulder, only to be shoved gently against his shirt. He was back on his English, and sounding coolly pleased with himself.

"A fiancé?" Lady Avery echoed. "You're snatching your aunt's companion for your baroness, St. Clair?"

Lady Covington produced a lorgnette. "She's a pretty little thing. Not *too* old."

"I am *not*—" Milly began, only to find Sebastian's mouth brushing over hers.

"My dear Millicent is not in the habit of permitting me kisses. I must apologize for having become carried away." And then, murmured right next to her ear, "*Calme, s'il vous plaît, petite tigresse.*"

His petite tigress stifled the urge to bite him. She settled for stomping on his toes, which had no effect whatsoever.

"Blessed saints," Lady Freddy said, clapping her gloved hands. "I own myself relieved to have a simple explanation for a small lapse. Milly, you will go straight up to bed, and, Sebastian, you shall draft the particulars for the professor to send to our friends. Ladies, shall we away? I cannot abide the idea that the Countess Thrall might be winning every hand for want of our steadying influence on the gentlemen."

With pointed looks at Sebastian and Milly, Freddy's companions followed her out. The professor lingered only a moment, his expression bemused.

The instant the door closed, Milly wrestled free of Sebastian's embrace.

"What have you done?! Those, those *women* will bruit it about all over London that we're engaged, and because of a mere kiss!"

"A *mere* kiss?"

Milly paced the confines of the foyer, arms crossed, skirts swishing.

"And Lady Freddy will be so disappointed when there's no ceremony. You should be ashamed!"

"I should be *ashamed*? Of kissing you?"

Milly rounded on his lordship. "I'm well aware that

I should be ashamed for kissing you, my lord. Well aware, but there are employment agencies in York, and a small indiscretion can be overlooked when an unattached, titled gentleman is involved. But now you've gone and—"

Sebastian was smiling at her, and that more than any rousing argument suggested to Milly he might not grasp the situation in all its terrible entirely.

"I cannot marry you, my lord."

"You can kiss me, but you can't use my name?"

"And I cannot marry you. I am a companion, in service, in case you've forgotten." His smile did not falter, so Milly fired her biggest cannon. "*I cannot read.* What baroness cannot even read the menus put before her by the cook? Cannot read bedtime stories to her own children? Can barely follow along in the Book of Common Prayer—"

His smile shifted, becoming tender rather than pleased.

"You can sing to the children instead, tell them stories you make up, or listen to their own fanciful tales. You're resourceful, my dear, and you shall contrive. As a baroness, you will contrive magnificently."

Based on the pride Milly heard in his tone, St. Clair had already dispatched announcements to Lady Freddy's cronies, cried the banns, and said his vows. He was not resigned to this dire turn of events; he was rejoicing in it.

While she…could not read. When St. Clair slipped his arms around her again, Milly leaned into him and tried not to cry.

❧

"MacHugh said you may have as much time as you like to put your affairs in order. He's offended by you, not by the entire St. Clair succession."

Michael could not have sounded more disgusted as he rode along at Sebastian's side.

"So I'm to get a child on my prospective wife, allowing MacHugh the comfort of knowing he won't put Lady Freddy on the Crown's charity when I'm laid to rest? And what if my baroness is so disobliging as to present me with a daughter? Or she doesn't carry the child safely through birth? Am I to put MacHugh off, year to year, until my heir and spare are grown to manhood and MacHugh and I are too old to give a good account of ourselves?"

"Beating each other to death is not giving a good account of anything, and your barony is ancient enough that it likely can be preserved through the female line."

They passed a lilac bush blooming next to a stand of yellow tulips, the lavender and yellow making a cheerful contrast to their dreary conversation. Sebastian bid Fable to pause so his rider might catch a whiff of lilac.

"What does the lilac symbolize to the English?"

"First emotions of love. You don't have to marry the girl at all."

"Yes, Michael, I do. Her reputation was at risk simply because she sought employment in my household, and Aunt's cronies are not about to let my indiscretion remain a secret. Then too, Aunt caught me once before in a similar moment with Miss Danforth."

A similarly lovely moment. Sebastian signaled his horse to toddle on.

"Milly Danforth is a companion, for God's sake. A nobody, a nothing to Polite Society. They'll dine on her bones for a week then go yipping and baying to their next kill. All you did was kiss her, or endure her kisses."

Fable snatched a bite of some leaves hanging over the bridle path.

"Naughty boy," Sebastian chided mildly. "Miss Danforth is a nobody, Michael, but that makes it all the more imperative that my behavior toward her be honorable, which it was not."

He really ought to be ashamed of himself for that, but he was too pleased by the knowledge that Milly Danforth had started the kiss that had resulted in their engagement.

"I'll find somebody to marry the damned woman," Michael spat.

"Dear fellow, on general principles one should not procure a spouse for any female whom one refers to as *the damned woman*. Miss Danforth is not pleased to have me for a husband. I don't think she'd allow any convenient eligible of your acquaintance to so much as kiss her cat."

The turn of phrase was unfortunately prurient, the mistake of a man who'd misplaced his native language for too many years.

"I daresay you won't be kissing her—"

"Hush, Michael. One duel hanging over me is one too many."

Michael turned his horse down the left fork of the path, the less traveled route, the one they always took. "You could apologize."

"No, I cannot. MacHugh struck a stout blow before

at least one witness. He wants no apology from me, he wants satisfaction, though I do wonder—"

He broke off as Fable's head came up. The Duke of Mercia rode around a bend in the path, looking handsome and severe in the early morning light.

Sebastian gave a slow nod and nudged Fable onto the verge. For His Grace, Sebastian would have positioned his horse in the middle of a wet muck pit—and cheerfully dismounted in the same location.

"Mercia."

His Grace checked his horse, a glossy, well-muscled chestnut with perfect manners. "St. Clair." The duke glanced at Michael. "He'll second you?"

"Mr. Brodie has that honor." Again. Michael had seconded St. Clair when he'd met Mercia too, of course. And Pierpont, Neggars, and Cambert, as well.

Mercia switched the bight of his reins from the left to the right side of his horse's neck.

"MacHugh is damned good with his fists, but he's careless—or arrogant. He doesn't close up his defense as snugly as he ought, and he leaves openings. His right is formidable, though he relies on it almost exclusively. Good day."

Mercia touched a gloved finger to his hat brim and cantered off.

The duke's short discourse was astonishing in several regards, not the least impressive of which was that it silenced Michael for a distance of two furlongs. When their path emerged near the sparkling beauty of the Serpentine, Michael found his tongue.

"I must write to my sisters at Blackthorn and ask them whether the wee piggies have sprouted wings."

"Blackthorn is your estate in Ireland?"

Michael was silent for another half furlong, making the day nothing short of miraculous—or damned strange. "My mother's people are Irish, and my sister Bridget married an Irish earl's heir. My sire hails from Aberdeenshire. Hailed."

Hence his Highland attire and his tendency to lapse from a brogue into a burr when in the grip of strong emotions.

In the face of such a revelation, Sebastian trod lightly. "Not much summer that far north."

"What there is has no comparison anywhere in the world." Michael petted his horse, a Roman-nosed bay gelding with a tendency to nip and spook.

"You are homesick, Michael. Many a married man does without a valet."

A gaggle of ladies with their grooms appeared on the path ahead of them, Lady Amelia among them.

"Are you sending me away, *my lord*?"

Holy Mother, preserve me from the pride of the Celt. "I could neither send you away nor summon you to my side unless you wished it, Michael. You cannot protect me from every enraged English officer who wants me dead. Your family must miss you, and they should be your first obligation."

"As your family has been yours?"

Lady Amelia's group passed them single file, grooms bringing up the rear. When it came Amelia's turn to pass him—to snub him—she instead gave him the barest, most infinitesimal nod, her gaze touching Sebastian's for only an instant.

The grooms came along on their unprepossessing

mounts, and Sebastian waited until they'd passed to resume the conversation with his self-appointed conscience.

"You told me not to marry Miss Danforth, Michael, and yet marrying her fulfills both my obligations as a gentleman and my obligations to the succession—to my family. I am mindful of my obligations."

And Amelia had acknowledged him. His engagement to Milly Danforth had become public earlier in the week, and Amelia had acknowledged him.

Michael glanced around, likely making sure nobody else could overhear.

"Do you suppose Lady Amelia feels safe from you now that you're betrothed to somebody else?"

Betrothed was a sweet word, a word full of belonging and hope—also sadness, an emotion Sebastian used to brush aside like so many ashes in a hearth.

"Lady Amelia's group came from that direction," Sebastian said, pointing to a rise off to the north. "She saw no less than the Duke of Mercia acknowledge me with conversation, and hence allowed the smallest crack in her reserve toward me. We should get back to the house, or Lady Freddy will pronounce us late for breakfast. Thank MacHugh for his forbearance, and tell him I will meet him one week after the wedding."

Michael swore in Gaelic and sent his bay forward in a smooth canter, while Sebastian held Fable back to a brisk trot. Lady Amelia had acknowledged him, and yet, he'd rather she'd cut him once more, for instead of indifference, her gaze had held wariness and loathing.

Sebastian was damned sick of people watching him with that same uneasy, anxious gaze, as if he'd drag them off and delight in applying manacles and thumb-screws in hopes of learning how much they owed the tradesmen or what they'd lost at the tables last week.

He kicked Fable up to the canter, and admitted to himself he was marrying Milly Danforth—he *could* marry Milly Danforth—in part because she had never once regarded him with wariness and loathing.

Ten

"WALK WITH ME, MISS DANFORTH." MR. BRODIE winged his arm at Milly, but when she leveled a stare at him in response, he managed to tack on the requisite sop to manners. "Would you mind walking with me for a moment, *please*?"

He was trainable, then. Milly doubted Sebastian would have kept Mr. Brodie about if he were not, though Sebastian—what a delight, to think of him thus—could not be choosy about his familiars.

A daunting thought, when she might well become one of them.

"A few minutes only," Milly said as they turned down between two rows of silvery green lavender. "Lady Freddy will get into mischief if she's left without supervision for very long."

Mr. Brodie looked as if he had wind, or perhaps was trying not to smile. "On a horticultural farm bordering Chelsea?"

"Anywhere. St. Clair and the professor can curb her natural impulses for only so long, and then she must meddle. She'll be telling his lordship what's amiss with his herbs, and the gardener won't dare countermand her directions. She'll tell the lads how to feed that wretched donkey and demand they groom the burrs from the stable cats."

Mr. Brodie bent and snapped off a sprig from a low-growing bush, bringing it to his nose then passing it to Milly. "Does she know what's amiss with his herbs?"

"Only his lordship can puzzle that out, but you did not request this stroll to discuss Lady Freddy's queer starts or his lordship's horticulture."

"I did not. I requested this stroll so I might return some correspondence to you." He produced a packet of letters from an inside pocket and passed them to Milly. "I assume the professor abetted you."

Milly glanced at the letters fleetingly, as if they were contraband, then slipped them into the pocket of her walking dress. To give herself time to sort the emotions rioting through her at the sight of her own handwriting—the professor had helped her only a little with these employment inquiries—she brushed the sprig of lavender under her nose.

"It's a comforting scent," Mr. Brodie said, "having only positive associations."

Wretch. "You are saying St. Clair has been only honorable toward me. What about *my* honor, Mr. Brodie? How am I to behave honorably toward *him*?"

They ambled along, gravel crunching under their feet, the low, shrubby bushes making a pretty green carpet beneath the sun. Despair welled up as the odors of turned earth and stables imbued the very air with bucolic benevolence.

"How is your honor served by tucking tail and

heading for the West Riding, Miss Danforth? Meaning no insult, you will not make St. Clair an ideal baroness. I told him to treat you to a long engagement followed by a quiet, well-compensated jilting. He listened patiently then politely told me to mind my own business."

A capital notion, considering Mr. Brodie had sorted through Milly's belongings and now had taken to sorting through her correspondence. Either Mr. Brodie was a very unscrupulous man, or his devotion to Sebastian was without limit.

Possibly both were true.

Sebastian stood across the field of lavender, head bare, dark hair riffling in the mild breeze as he conferred with his gardener. Milly took a moment to memorize the sight of her fiancé, just another Englishman being conscientious about his land—a handsome Englishman haunted by bad memories, a trying present, and a difficult future.

"I'm not abandoning him," Milly said. "I'm trying to be sensible. I am a semiliterate companion, not a baroness. I cannot read a program at the theater, cannot write out my own invitations."

Not that Sebastian's baroness would have any invitations to send.

"St. Clair has spent at least two hours with you each day this week, working on your letters."

"Are you jealous of me, Mr. Brodie?"

For this notion had occurred to Milly. Such was the influence of a pair of wily old ladies who'd known more of the world than anybody guessed, and such was the puzzle of Michael Brodie.

"I offered to find you another husband to marry you in his stead."

First her letters handed back to her, and now this? Milly took another fortifying whiff of Mr. Brodie's sorry excuse for an olive branch.

"Whatever can you be about, Mr. Brodie? If you agree that I'm not a proper fiancée for his lordship, if you're willing to go to that unimaginable length to thwart this marriage, why sabotage my attempts to investigate employment opportunities elsewhere?"

He was silent for a moment, then gestured to a bench that bordered the lavender. Milly took a seat, though lounging about in the sun without her bonnet would get her a crop of freckles that would take weeks to fade.

"I've changed my mind, that's why. For whatever time he has with you, I think St. Clair could be happy. He doesn't care that you struggle with your letters. I think he likes it, in fact."

The very problem in a nutshell.

"And two years from now, when I am still mistaking *p*'s, *b*'s, and *d*'s, Mr. Brodie? Will his lordship enjoy instructing his poor, stupid baroness then? When I cannot help my children with their letters? When one of my children turns out to share my affliction? *When Sebastian's heir cannot sign his name any better than I can sign my own?* Will he still enjoy pitying his wife then?"

The notion of sending her son off to Eton to be beaten and taunted and made a laughingstock for something he could not help, could *never* help…

A handkerchief appeared in her lap, snowy linen bordered with delicate lace, and monogrammed with the initials *MBO*. Milly had to trace her finger over the big, flourishy *B* to be sure what it was.

"Cease sentimentalizing, Miss Danforth. St. Clair will hire the appropriate tutors and work with the boy himself, the way he's worked with you, assuming he's alive to see his son grow."

Milly blotted her eyes with the handkerchief, the lavender scent on her fingers mingling with vetiver. "You are such a ray of sunshine, Mr. Brodie. One can see why Sebastian treasures your company."

"If you're to marry him—and I hope you do—you should do so with your eyes open. Many would rather he were dead."

"You refer to all those English officers he stretched on the rack? They want him dead?"

"For some of them, it was worse than that."

He spoke quietly, no teasing, no prickliness. The real Michael Brodie had come forth, and Milly liked his quiet reserve far better than his posturing and pride.

She was not as comfortable with the sense of remorse he exuded. Was he sorry for what Sebastian had done, or did Michael Brodie have his own regrets?

"Sebastian doesn't speak of it," she said. "He starts to, then he checks himself, as if my cousin never sent me letters telling me what war is really like. As if my aunts' old friends never reminisced on the same subject."

Late at night, several hours into the Madeira, while Milly embroidered in a quiet corner and hurt for old men who would never be free of their memories.

Mr. Brodie shifted, as if the hard bench pained him. "St. Clair has a talent for knowing when somebody is telling the truth, and he has a talent for knowing how to make them want to tell that truth—to him."

In Milly's experience, this was accurate. Based on very little information, St. Clair had realized she could not read well.

"And these officers, they did not want to tell him anything?"

"Their names, their regimental affiliations—the same information they'd impart if they'd been captured in full uniform. If they told him that much, there was a chance St. Clair could negotiate a quiet and thoroughly improper ransom for them, though he was under no obligation to do so. They knew, though, that the price for that ransom was information."

A sense of dread washed through Milly while, across the field, Sebastian clapped his gardener on the back. "He made traitors of them."

"No, he did not. He had most of them at least nominally beaten by the guards, limited them to scanty rations and inadequate warmth. He fashioned some scheme of pain and deprivation for each man, calculated to most efficiently part that man from whatever scruples guarded his tongue. They each surrendered something to him, and in fairly short order."

"They surrendered their honor, their self-respect, and so they must hate him for it."

"That was his plan and his gift to them—that they suffer at his hands so they might hate him for it enough to survive, rather than hate themselves, but his plan was flawed."

Milly waited for the rest of the explanation, while Sebastian stopped to pet the donkey. The creature would always bear scars, but it held still for a good scratching under its hairy chin—all trust had not been destroyed. There was hope.

For the donkey.

"The flaw in his plan was that he measured his captives by his own standards," Mr. Brodie said. "Had he been taken prisoner and some truth flogged out of him, he would have understood it to be part of the normal course of war. He would not have wasted years later hating his gaolers, or hating himself for his humanity. He might hate the memory, hate all war, but not the people involved."

"These captives of his, they hate him so they need not admit they hate themselves."

"You perceive the problem."

Milly understood that Mr. Brodie's disclosures were made out of a charitable impulse, though from him it was a scarred, battle-weary version of kindness. He was acquainting her with the horror Sebastian endured daily and nightly, because Sebastian was unlikely to burden her with these truths himself.

The donkey butted Sebastian's hand, begging him for one last scratch.

Milly folded up the little handkerchief and stuffed it among her inquires to the agencies in Yorkshire.

"The Duke of Mercia acknowledges St. Clair, Mr. Brodie. Surely that example must carry some weight with the rest of the officers?"

"Mercia was the exception. He gave up nothing, and in a sense, St. Clair guarded him more closely than any of the others—also tortured him the worst, though much of that must lie at the feet of St. Clair's superiors. It's not my story to tell, but you should ask him. Mercia is not to be trusted."

This from a man about whom nobody in the household seemed to know much of anything? "Is anybody to be trusted, Mr. Brodie?"

"St. Clair has the special license."

That was a qualified "yes." Mr. Brodie—was that even his name?—trusted *her*, somewhat.

"His lordship and I are agreed a quiet ceremony will serve best. How do you know I'll not leave him standing at the altar?" Mr. Brodie standing beside him, of course.

This question earned her a smile, a sweet, unlikely, charming smile from a man who snooped, stole correspondence, and was like no valet Milly had ever heard of.

"I can't allow it, Miss Danforth. You've learned to dodge and duck, to bluff when you had to, and to remain out of sight to the extent possible. You would have been a wonderful spy, particularly given that you never forget a word of what you've heard. I've concluded, though, that St. Clair is right."

Across the field, a homely little love-struck donkey watched her new favorite turn and stride in the direction of the bench.

"Right about what, sir?"

"St. Clair could not care less about your penmanship or your letters. What he treasures is your trust, my lady. You are acquainted with the salient features of his past, and yet, they move you to neither pity nor horror. You accept him, and he accepts you." Mr. Brodie rose and extended a hand to her. "Don't you think it's time you accepted yourself?"

Milly rose, shook out her skirts, and tried to pretend Mr. Brodie's question didn't land at her feet like a lit Catherine wheel, sending sparks flying in all directions.

"You stole my employment inquiries because, upon reflection and after trying to talk St. Clair out of this marriage, you think I will make a passable baroness?"

"You will make an excellent baroness, and I only borrowed those inquiries. If you try to send them again, I will not stop you. But ask yourself, Miss Danforth, do you truly want to turn your back on a worthy man who esteems you greatly, and consign yourself to a life of quiet, lonely anonymity? Do you deserve only that?"

He tucked her hand around his arm and patted her knuckles, as if he understood what a troublesome question he posed.

Mr. Brodie was a pestilence of a man, but he'd given Milly insights into her prospective spouse nobody else could pass along, save St. Clair himself. Then too, when he referred to St. Clair, his voice held both respect and affection.

Much as Milly's did. On that thought, she allowed Mr. Brodie to escort her back to the baron's side, the unsent inquiries crackling softly in her pocket.

❧

Across the plot of lavender, Milly led Michael Brodie around the gravel paths. She'd link arms with him and tow him along for a few paces, then pause and bend to sniff at a plant or examine a flower. Michael waited with a patience Sebastian knew was foreign to his nature, then let himself be led off to some other clump of shrubs.

"She's pretty, your lady."

The head gardener was a man by the name of Kincaid, a big, fussy, cheerful soul who'd served on the Peninsula and knew more about hard work than about plants. Kincaid might have been forty, he might have been sixty, and his weathered, sandy blond looks and bright blue eyes would change little if he lived to be eighty. Sebastian had never seen him with clean fingernails or wearing a frown.

"She's beautiful," Sebastian said. "She's also trying to bolt before I can get her to the altar." The professor had passed along that tidbit, resorting to Spanish to convey his message, lest Freddy or one of her spies overhear him.

"Skittish, then. The smart ones know how to lead us a dance, don't they?" Kincaid winked and strode off, a man in charity with the world—and him six months sober, too.

Except Milly did not believe herself to be smart, and Sebastian knew in his bones she hadn't sent inquiries to agencies in the North as any sort of game. He marched himself across the field, intent on securing the would-be fugitive—also on rescuing his friend.

"Brodie, turn loose of my baroness."

Michael's expression was bemused. "She's not your baroness yet, and she says your soil is too damp for your weeds."

Milly straightened and dusted her hands together. "They are herbs, Mr. Brodie, and they keep the fleas from your bed and the infection from your wounds. Show some respect."

Michael's consternation was a lovely addition to a

pretty day. "Listen to my baroness," Sebastian said, taking Milly's hand. "I certainly intend to."

They left Michael among the shrubs, his bemusement blossoming into a smile.

"Michael smiling is an unnerving proposition," Sebastian said as they moved between rows of plants. "Puts one in mind of Lady Freddy going quiet, or the professor lapsing into Russian."

"Marriage to you is an unnerving proposition."

His Milly had such courage. "Marriage to me, or marriage in general?"

"Both."

He closed his fingers more snugly around hers. "You will tell me why."

"You need a baroness whom none will find fault with, St. Clair. I am a nobody, though for the most part, I've been happy in that state."

"Sebastian. You are to be my wife, and that gives me the privilege of hearing you say my name. For years, I was Robert Girard, some fool Frenchman with a reputation for nastiness and no family to speak of. Please call me Sebastian."

"Robert Girard? Those are your middle names, aren't they?"

"They are. Why would you recall something so inconsequential?"

Against his palm, her hand was dusty and warm.

"Your very name could not be inconsequential to me, any more than you've brushed aside my name as a silly exercise in penmanship. Where are we going?"

"Out of the sun." They were engaged. According to the contradictory and labyrinthine rules of proper

English behavior, they could now be alone together for brief periods. Unfortunately, privacy was in short supply on a small horticultural farm. Sebastian led Milly to the drying shed, a building larger than its name would suggest, but upwind from the stables, the fields, and anything else that might pollute the fragrances captured there.

"Come harvest time, this place will be full to bursting with bundled herbs hung up to dry. The scent then is intoxicating."

"It's lovely now." Milly leaned close to an old wooden workbench, sniffing the surface. "That is remarkable."

"It's a cutting table, which you can no doubt tell from the scars, but it absorbs the oils of the plants year after year. Why are you afraid to marry me, Milly?"

She turned and hiked herself up onto the cutting table. She could do that because she was a nobody, a village girl gone into service, not a bloody, simpering debutante. "Not afraid, reluctant. Come here."

Two of his favorite words, when she spoke them. Sebastian moved to stand at her knees. "Have I a smudge on my nose?"

"A bit of lavender in your hair," she said, brushing his temple. "I do like you, you know."

He captured her fingers and kissed them, dust and lavender making the taste of her pleasant and summery. "You're not afraid of me, then?"

She didn't withdraw her hand, and in the light slanting through the old windows, her complexion had a luminous quality.

"Why would I be afraid of you? You're patient with the elderly, clean about your person, kind to abused donkeys, a generous employer, and an inspired teacher of penman—"

He kissed her. Kissed her because she didn't understand the question, though she might possibly understand the answer. "We'll be intimate, Milly. Horrendously, inescapably intimate. Does that bother you?"

He kissed her again, because he didn't want to hear her dithering and dodging. With her aunts as her finishing governesses, it was quite possible that Milly—despite a taste for passionate kisses and a surfeit of courage—did not look forward to the wedding night.

She hauled him closer by his lapels, and damned if he didn't feel her boot hooking around his flanks. "I like being intimate with you, St. Clair."

"Sebastian." He growled this against her mouth, then smiled as her second boot hit him on the backside. "There's more to a wedding night than kisses, you know."

She dropped his lapels, and her boots fell away, leaving Sebastian standing between her spread knees. "I am not uninformed, sir."

"You might well be *mis*informed. Do you look forward to the wedding night?" That wasn't what he'd meant to ask, but she was breathing heavily, her breasts shifting gently in a fashion that directed his blood some distance south of his feeble male brain. "Do you know what happens on a wedding night?"

"One is intimate with one's spouse." She gently dusted the fabric of his lapels, the gesture wifely, but not in a league with her kisses. "One attempts to conceive the baronial heir."

He stepped closer and hauled her forward by virtue

of his hands scooping under her derriere. "One plea-sures one's wife witless."

His motive for providing a demonstration was complicated. He did not want her disappearing to the North, and he did not want her anxious about their conjugal intimacies. Those reasons for sealing his mouth over hers again were real and true.

Also paltry compared to the lust roaring through him.

He wedged himself against her sex, letting her feel the evidence of his arousal, and needing to know she would not shrink away.

"Sebastian—"

She squirmed *closer*. Her hands ran riot over his neck, his ears, through his hair, and down his arms. He hoped she was leaving a trail of dust for all to see, hoped his imprimatur on her would be equally clear as a result of his kisses.

He wrestled with her skirts, shoving them aside enough that he could get his hand on one bare, delec-table knee. "We can't—"

She twisted her fingers in his hair, a compelling, entirely delightful pain. "Talk later; kiss—"

He kissed her like a man dying for warmth and starving for lack of kisses. Kissed her even as he turned her and laid her down on the old wooden table, the window light bathing her in sunshine. He traced her lips with his tongue as she went quiet, flat on her back, one knee propped up, her skirts falling in disarray.

"Hush," he said as he got his coat off, folded it, and tucked it under her head. "I'm not finished kissing you."

Not nearly, though how kissing resulted in a man

climbing onto a table, taking his lady in his arms, and spooning himself around her was not entirely clear. Their dealings shifted, became slower, less desperate, even as Sebastian's fingers reveled in the smooth warmth of Milly's knee…and…thigh.

"No freckles here," he observed, drawing her skirts up higher. "Only perfection." Though even her freckles struck him as perfect, he wasn't about to tell her that.

"I cannot think when you touch me like this, Sebastian. I don't want to think."

Good. A woman incapable of thought was incapable of planning a journey to Yorkshire. Sebastian brushed his hand up the silky inside of her thigh, his fingers drifting through soft, springy curls.

"Lift your knee, love."

He kissed her ear lest she argue, then took her lobe between his teeth and pulled gently. "You understand how one goes—how two go—about conceiving a baronial heir?"

"I do." Even in two syllables, he could hear the caution in her tone. Her understanding was theoretical, at best, while her trust in him, at least in these moments, was real.

Sebastian teased his index finger up the crease of her sex. "You understand that we'll copulate, my cock inside you, my seed spent in your body?"

"Mmm." She moved against his hand, which was answer enough. Sebastian repeated the caress but pressed close enough to find dampness. His cock was rioting behind his falls, pushing snugly against her backside, and clamoring for him to discard boots, breeches, and common sense.

Which would not do. His immediate objective was not to anticipate their vows, but to ensure those vows were taken. He petted her curls, smoothed his fingers against her skin, then went exploring again.

"Close your eyes, Milly. Focus on where I'm touching you."

When she'd complied, Sebastian closed his eyes too, the better to picture the terrain his hand was learning. Soft, pink folds, damp flesh, and a delicate bud...there.

He worked her gently, slicked his fingers over that bud repeatedly, until the dampness grew, and Milly's breathing deepened. She was waiting, but the tenor of her stillness, the way she eased each breath carefully in and out, suggested she didn't know what she waited for.

Fortunately for his nerves, she didn't have to wait long. Milly's body *knew*, even if the rest of her did not. Her hips started a slow rocking in rhythm with his caresses, she nuzzled at his shirtsleeve where her cheek rested against his biceps, and then she was pressing against his fingers, a soft, sighing moan keening past her lips.

"Sebastian... Oh, *Sebastian*."

He withdrew his hand as she went boneless against him, his cheek pressed to her hair. No woman had called him by his real, true name in an intimate moment.

He'd been Robert, Girard, Colonel, St. Clair, and most often no name in particular, but never Sebastian. While Milly drowsed in the sunshine against him, Sebastian unfastened his falls and extricated his cock from his clothes. The scent of herbs, brisk, complex, and pleasant, was stronger, perhaps because the sun hit the old cutting table, perhaps because he'd brought pleasure to the woman he was going to marry.

He tucked his cock between her legs, not coupling, but enfolded by her heat. She scooted back against him, as if she understood what he was about, and brought his hand up to fill his palm with her breast.

"I am remiss," he whispered, planting a kiss on her nape. "I did not pleasure your breasts." She closed her fingers around his, and though her corset posed a damnable impediment, the table was hard beneath them, and dust motes danced thick on the sunshine, Sebastian found both pleasure and relief.

As a soft, sweet release rose up and shuddered through him, tension lurking in all manner of places in his mind and body ebbed, contentment beckoned, and gratitude welled up.

He would live long enough to give Milly a wedding night she'd never forget, and hopefully, never regret— provided, of course, she did not leave him first.

❧

A scent wound among the fragrance of herbs of Provence, an earthy, not exactly sweet scent. Milly lay in the sunshine—this was what it meant to *bask*, she suspected—and conjectured that she smelled the scent of coupling.

"Knee up, my dear." Sebastian stroked a warm hand over her bare bottom, finishing the caress with a brisk pat. Someday, Milly would pat his bottom with exactly the same blend of affection and possessiveness.

"Knee up?"

He showed her, and Milly had to be grateful she

was facing away from the dratted man as he pressed a handkerchief against her privy parts, then positioned her hand over the handkerchief.

"I apologize for the mess, but anything might happen before an engaged couple can get to the altar."

Milly pushed her skirts down, the handkerchief pressed between her legs. "Are you apologizing for more than the mess, Sebastian?"

She posed the question carefully, because in the wake of such—such!—unimaginable pleasure, came emotions neither tidy nor convenient. Milly fought her skirts into submission and rolled to her back, the better to wade into battle with her intended.

He was on his side, propped on his elbow, his hair disheveled, his marvelous green eyes guarded. "Do I need to apologize for more?"

"Yes, I rather think you do." She tidied his hair as best she could, mostly for the pleasure of touching him.

The light in his eyes went from guarded to shuttered. "Apologize, why?"

"I am not particularly literate, but I'm of age, you know. A biology lecture wasn't necessary, though you might have warned me about that other. Not well done of you to ambush your own fiancée that way." Somebody might have warned her, anybody, though she would not have believed them.

He cradled Milly's cheek against his palm. "That other? That pleasure, that closeness, that sharing of intimacies?"

She treasured his touch, which bore a whiff of herbs, musk, and...donkey?

"That bodily surprise. It discommodes one."

He leaned closer. "Does it make one inclined to take marriage vows instead of hare off to Yorkshire?"

The inconvenient, untidy sentiments rose higher. Milly shifted, wrapping her arms around her fiancé and pulling his head down to the breasts he'd neglected.

"I wrote those letters in case you changed your mind, Sebastian. In case you came to your senses, which I fully expected you to do. You won't, will you? Please say you won't. I could not bear to remain near you, knowing you don't care for—"

His tongue swiped up her cleavage, and then his voice rumbled against her heart. "Your letters gave me a start, madam. I can't go racketing about, chasing every fiancée who takes a notion to tour the West Riding. A man has obligations to see to, herbs to raise, an aunt to supervise."

And a donkey to spoil. Milly kissed his temple, having the curious conviction that he'd have come after her at a dead gallop if she'd been on the north-bound stage out of King's Cross.

"You might have tried discussing matters with me, sir. I can be reasoned with, even if you do neglect my breasts."

His shoulders moved. Milly took a moment to grasp that she'd made him laugh, and then she was laughing too. There on the hard table, amid the dust, sunshine, and scents of old herbs and new love, they laughed together.

❧

Dear *Acorn* was a man with problems, and like every man with problems Henri had had the tedious honor to know, an application of spirits provoked a recitation of those problems.

"Frieda says I should have the blasted chit declared incompetent, but that's the perishing problem."

Henri moved the bottle closer to Upton's elbow. "Madame Frieda offers her opinion too freely?" Frieda, whose poor husband had not been permitted conjugal comfort since Wellington had shipped out for Spain.

"Damned right she does." Upton glanced around the taproom, likely to ensure nobody had overheard his domestic treason. Henri had appropriated that uniquely English vantage point, the snug. This cozy corner of the common put Henri in mind of the confessional of his boyfriend, though now, Henri assumed the role of confessor.

"If the young lady is not well in the head, then could your Frieda's plan have merit?"

"It could not." A long, slow burp followed this pronouncement, one of those masculine vulgarities that was nearly melodic and the pride and joy of boys under the age of fifteen when in one another's company. "Milly makes up in memory what she lacks in letters. She can recite the entire New Testament from memory, like a monkey…like a monk."

He enunciated the last word carefully, suggesting Frieda also begrudged her spouse strong spirits in any quantity.

"Even dumb animals can be taught tricks," Henri observed mildly.

"Milly ain't dumb," Upton countered, his head swiveling as a buxom barmaid sashayed by. "The house ran ever so much better when we had the keeping of her. The help did their jobs, the place was clean, the meals decent, the children…"

He took another swallow of brandy that any fool would know had been watered.

"You miss your young cousin, and you are worried for her. Your devotion does you credit."

Upton shifted his considerable bulk on his chair, his hand disappearing under the table in a manner Henri would not dwell on when he sat less than three feet away.

"I miss her, right you are. Vincent has stopped asking about her, though."

Henri was drinking ale, the better to endure Upton's presence with a clear head.

"You say the ungrateful girl has gone into service?" She wasn't a girl. The sparrow was small and plain, but she wasn't a girl.

"Service, of all the queer notions. Vincent was ready to offer for her—he did offer, in a manner of speaking—and she upped and went for a companion. The Traitor Baron's old auntie employs her now, and I'll never get my money."

Henri's grasp of English law was tenuous, but he failed to see how a mother's funds left in trust to her daughter were any property of the daughter's cousin. He tut-tutted the way *his* old auntie would have.

"This must be *very* trying, and after you sheltered the girl for years and saw to her every need."

"For five years, anyway, though Grandfather left a sum for her needs. We spared her no expense, of course, and that meant little dowry was left from

Grandpapa's funds, but who'd want a chit that ain't rigged up right in the brainbox?"

The girl had lived in a poorly ventilated garret on crusts of stale bread, wearing mended clothing. Henri would have bet the same old auntie's last bottle of cognac on it.

"A man with low expectations would take on such a woman, of course, or a saint would. Have a bit more brandy. It's rare to find an Englishman who'll pass the time with a visiting Belgian."

The same auntie would have slapped Henri stoutly for lying about his nationality. Henri would have slapped her back, and had on more than one occasion.

"Fine stuff, this," Upton said, smacking his lips. "Helps a man forget his troubles."

He passed gas, the sound muted by his own sitting bulk, then sighed with contentment, while Henri allowed a pang of sympathy for the sparrow who'd left her cousin's tender care.

"You might consider watching the baron's aunt's comings and goings," Henri suggested, "get a sense of what the old woman does with herself. If she's exposing your cousin to untoward influences, then the young lady might thank you for rescuing her."

"Milly has manners. She's good about the please-and-thank-you business. Not like Frieda."

Poor Frieda, who'd whelped three little acorns for her mighty, flatulent oak.

"You must finish this bottle for me," Henri said, rising as a sulfurous stench came wafting to his nose amid the inn's perfume of fish, beer, onions, and humanity. "I'll tell the proprietor that you are to be served at my expense, and I'm sure if you keep an eye on the aunt, you will soon find compelling reasons to retrieve your cousin. Frieda cannot begrudge you this endeavor, and Vincent will thank you for it as well."

He shrugged into his coat, though the afternoon was warm. "I will look forward to hearing the details of your reconnaissance efforts when we meet next week."

Upton blinked up at him. "Next week?"

"Same time, same day, at this very table. I'll see the sights until then, and you can tell me what I've missed in this great city of yours. Acorn, it has been a pleasure."

Henri bowed smartly, smiled like a whore spotting a half-drunken mark, and put his hat on his head.

"That's *Al*corn, not acorn."

"I do apologize. English is a sophisticated language, and you must excuse my errors. Through conversation with tolerant gentlemen such as yourself, I hope to improve."

*Al*corn looked dazed by that spate of words. Henri left him with the dregs of the bottle, watching the barmaids, and looking like a fat, old hound so far gone with the rheumatism he would not venture far from the hearth even to piss.

Alcorn was a suffering animal in need of a charitable trip to the woods, though first, Henri would earn the tacit thanks of at least two governments, and dispose of the damned Traitor Baron.

Eleven

SEBASTIAN'S BRIDE WAS NOT RADIANT, SHE WAS WORRIED.

"You'll sign your name as legibly as any woman on her wedding day, Millicent. Stop fretting." He'd meant this as a reassurance, but his comment apparently fell short of its mark.

Their nuptials would transpire in the morning, God willing, and then seven days of marital bliss would commence—for Milly at least.

She paused mid-stab at her embroidery. "I'm not concerned about writing my name."

Sebastian's instincts begged to differ. She wasn't worried about the wedding night; yesterday's frolic in the drying shed had reassured him of that.

"You're anxious over something. I can see it here." He scooted to the edge of his reading chair and drew a finger between her brows. "You must learn to share your burdens with me, baroness."

She jerked the needle through the fabric. "I'm not your baroness yet."

Something struck him about the way she hunched

closer to her hoop, the way her cat, cuddled beside her on the sofa, did not purr.

"You are worried your odious cousin will attempt to interfere with the ceremony."

She put the hoop down and scooped the feline onto her lap. Immediately, the beast began rumbling.

"Alcorn can be very determined. Frieda is the more devious of the two, though. She's had to be."

"Sympathy with the enemy is never convenient, Milly, and seldom well-advised, though often unavoidable. I've not put a notice in the newspapers, you know."

Her hand paused mid-stroke over the cat's fur. "You haven't?"

"Most people don't. I have enemies, and they are not above hurting me through you. The more time I have before word of our marriage is generally known, the less likelihood that threat will reach you."

"But Lady Flynn and Lady—"

"Are keeping their powder dry in anticipation of the announcement. When one has played whist as long as Aunt has, one develops a store of ammunition for use in emergencies."

Milly resumed caressing her beast while Sebastian gave her time to put together some of the puzzle pieces: Lady Flynn had been indiscreet at some point in the past. Milly did not need to know that the indiscretion had involved a Russian diplomat who'd shared the occasional bottle with the professor.

"Both of them? Lady Flynn and Lady Covington?"

"Aunt holds a few of Lady Covington's markers, so to speak." Whist being occasionally played for imprudent stakes.

"They seem like such nice women."

She sounded so forlorn, Sebastian shifted to take a place beside her on the sofa, his arm around her shoulders. The moment was sweet, domestic, and laced with sorrow, because a lifetime of such evenings with his wife would be denied him.

He kissed her temple.

"They are nice women. They will deal with each other civilly, and I daresay, the ladies will call upon you to admire your ring and congratulate you on your married state."

Outside, darkness settled over the city like a soft summer quilt, and a heavy wagon jingled past, putting Sebastian in mind of MacHugh's gift of time. A week would not be enough, but then, neither would a lifetime.

"I feel guilty for not notifying my only relations that I'm marrying, Sebastian. They are my family."

"Sometimes, my dear, the kindest thing you can do is leave your family in ignorance." Soon enough she'd be widowed, if not thanks to MacHugh, then thanks to whoever next stepped from the shadows, intent on ending Sebastian's life. Time enough to deal with her family then.

She let her head rest on his shoulder. "You were with the solicitors for quite a while."

"I am to be married tomorrow, which creates a substantial change in my situation. When we come back from St. Clair Manor, you will take your turn with the solicitors too. You will be not only my wife, but also my baroness."

And she would need to sign many documents in

that capacity. Would she think of Sebastian each time she made her signature?

"I would rather be your friend, sir."

Between a pat to the cat's head and a delicate yawn, she had put her finger on the greatest sorrow of their situation, one Sebastian could spare her for the present: She did, indeed, have the potential to be his friend. He would not be marrying her otherwise. In the course of walks through lavender-scented fields, quiet evenings before the fire, and quieter nights of loving, Sebastian might well have found the courage to share with her every shadow on his soul, every regret and hope.

"You're falling asleep, madam. This is no compliment to your fiancé's company."

"It's a compliment to how comfortable I am in his arms. Is there something about this wedding you're not telling me, Sebastian?"

"Yes." This time he followed up his kiss to her temple with a nuzzle to her hair. "You'll be a wealthy woman, eventually. You must plan for your loving family to try to exploit that, and maneuver accordingly."

She was silent, perhaps falling asleep. The weight of her against his side was dear and comforting. "I thought the barony was impoverished."

"The barony struggled badly, but Aunt held matters together. Lately, things have gone much better, in part because I have connections on the Continent for anything I wish to dispose of there. Then too, I had some personal wealth, which my uncle and then his solicitors managed for me. Because I was stuck in France, I was unaware of those funds until after the hostilities were over."

Which was fortunate, or he would have frittered them away too.

"My life was so simple before," she said, bestirring herself to kiss his cheek. "I intend that it remain simple after we're married."

He loved that she cuddled and kissed him so easily, so generously.

"How will you do that? If nothing else, you'll have the infrequent occasion of state, the household duties at St. Clair Manor, and quite possibly a baby to contend with."

"None of which matters much, except for the baby." She set the cat aside. From his expression, Peter did not appreciate being deprived of her lap, and Sebastian could only sympathize. "What matters, the only task to which I must attend without fail, is to love my husband."

She snuggled against Sebastian's chest, which was well done of her. His arms came around her, while grief, joy, a distant sense of Gallic irony, and a sharp twinge of anger collided inside him.

She'd sidled up to the sentiment quietly, avoiding notice but paying attention all the while, and then she'd ambushed him, only a small kiss of warning before she fired her broadside.

Sebastian cuddled her closer. "He's a lucky fellow, this husband of yours. Damned lucky." And he wasn't a coward, either, though he hardly knew in what direction lay the kind, honorable thing to say. "He will make loving his wife his highest priority too."

He kissed her cheek, stroked a hand over her hair, and wondered how much love two people could cram into a week, or a few weeks, before one of those people was left widowed, her love turning to sorrow, then hatred.

∽

The clergyman recruited to perform the wedding apparently understood that excesses of sentiment were not called for, though he was both quick and credibly friendly. Milly spoke her vows sincerely, and when it came time for her to sign the documents, she dipped the quill in the ink pot, blotted the tip, paused…

And panicked.

The professor cleared his throat. Mr. Brodie, looking fierce and handsome in his kilt, took to studying the opposite wall of the library where the hound painting hung in its usual location.

Sebastian, however, appeared amused. "We can pursue an annulment if you're having second thoughts, Baroness."

Mr. Brodie glowered rather gratifyingly at his employer. "There'll be no damned—"

"Mr. Brodie," Milly interrupted. "His lordship is teasing." And he was challenging, and in some male way, also being helpful. The signature would not be binding unless witnessed, so Milly dipped the pen again, wiped the tip on the blotter and…

The letter M was the same shape as a lady's décolletage when her hands were at her side. And i was a simple dance maneuver…

Sebastian began humming a waltz, and Milly's pen picked up momentum. She'd practiced this and practiced it, until her signature became a rote recitation for her hand, and one by one, thirty-three letters flowed onto the page.

"I used to wish my name were Ann," she murmured as she set the pen back in its stand.

Sebastian sprinkled sand over the ink. "And now?"

"I wish our last name did not use the abbreviation."

Our last name. His smile was so proud and naughty, Milly wanted to kiss it—to kiss him, because he understood that she wished for more hours closeted with him in libraries and private sitting rooms. He shuffled papers and presented additional documents to tend to, and on this, her wedding day, that was a sort of kissing too. Michael and the professor appended witness signatures where needed, and Aunt—Milly was to call her Aunt now—herded everybody to the formal dining room for a wedding breakfast.

"You're not eating much, Baroness." Sebastian held up a bite of cake on a fork right before Milly's mouth.

"The sooner this meal is over, the sooner we depart for St. Clair Manor." She took the bite, savoring the sweetness and...lavender in the icing, exactly as she'd requested.

"You will need your strength, Millicent. The day is not over."

He sounded stern, as if he worried about her fainting dead away over a fifteen-minute formality in the library. Milly held a bite of cake up to his mouth.

"I'm not the only one who will need to keep up my strength, Sebastian St. Clair. Did you or did you not promise to make your regard for me a priority in all things?"

"You and your memory." He took the cake from her fork and dispatched the remainder of his serving without lecturing Milly further.

The trip to St. Clair Manor, a rambling pile in the wilds of Surrey, was accomplished by midafternoon. And Milly's *husband*—a lovely word beginning with an *h*, much like Harriette—carried her over the threshold to the cheers of a platoon of servants. Milly endured the introductions to some thirty souls, from the butler to the boot boy, each of whom seemed genuinely happy to see the master married.

As Milly was genuinely happy.

"Shall we retire above stairs, Baroness?"

Sebastian's question was a study in domestic consideration.

"We shall not. It's a beautiful day. We've been shut up in that coach for nearly two hours, and I want to move."

In his morning attire, Sebastian looked quite handsome, also severe—except for the boutonniere of lavender on his lapel.

He winged his arm. "A tour of the gardens then?"

A tour of the gardens—with servants watching from every window, as Milly tottered around in her wedding finery like some…some baroness?

"I will change my clothes, Sebastian, and then you will take me on a picnic. I want to see your favorite place to dream when you were a boy."

Her request—well, it hadn't quite been a request—did not appear to please him. "The most likely spot is a good mile from the house, if you're willing to hop a few stiles."

Sebastian was not usually so dense, but perhaps he was suffering the nerves of a new husband.

"Bring a *blanket*, Sebastian, and some of that food Aunt packed for us, and give me twenty minutes to change my clothes. I suggest you do likewise, because hopping stiles can be hard on wedding finery."

Milly could have managed a blink in the time it took the commander of Castle St. Clair to realign his understanding of her intentions.

"I will meet you on the back terrace in twenty minutes, madam."

Milly made in it fifteen, and the fellow she found pacing before the irises was every bit as handsome as his earlier incarnation, but more relaxed, more *at home*.

"Lead on, Sebastian, and tell me about your parents."

He took her hand, and she hadn't even had to ask. "You're to interrogate me?"

"I'm to be your wife and the mother of your children." How satisfying, to say that in the King's English. Milly wished she could write it as easily, but someday—married to Sebastian—she might.

"When I think of my mother, I think of her in those last months in France. She was not happy, she was not well."

Milly closed her grip on his fingers and tugged him back, slowed him down as he marched them off past a bed of roses not yet blooming. "Tell me of a happier time with her, then. A time when you realized your mama was pretty."

He paused before one lone, precocious rosebud. "She was always pretty."

"Don't snatch it away. Leave it to bloom and show the way for the others. When was your mother happy?"

His stride lost its parade-march quality, and he became a man wandering through a garden on a late-spring afternoon.

"She was overjoyed to go back to France, radiant to at last see her parents, her cousins, her old nurse. I was only a boy, but I recall her standing against the rail on the packet we took to Calais, her gaze fixed on the shoreline of France as if she beheld the approach of heaven. My father stood beside me, beholding her with the same expression she wore watching the shoreline of her homeland."

"They loved each other."

Milly was careful to survey the garden as she drew this conclusion. Talk of love made Sebastian go quiet. One had to deal with the topic casually, with every appearance of unconcern. She attributed this to a dearth of such expressions of regard in his life, rather than to a lack of receptivity on his part.

"They loved each other passionately. A boy can't know that, but looking back, I can only imagine what my father suffered, to part from her when she fell ill. Her last thoughts, her last words were of her love for him. I never got to tell him that."

Milly waited while Sebastian unlatched a gate in the garden wall, the pause giving her a moment to check an anger directed at two people who'd been more absorbed with each other than with their only child.

"I will make you a promise, Sebastian," she said as she took him firmly by the hand. "If I lie dying at some point, while our young son endures that trial in a strange land without the comfort of your presence, I will use my last breaths to assure him that he's a wonderful boy. I will tell him how proud I am of him, and how much I have loved being his mama."

She would write those sentiments down, too, somehow. A boy needed them, and a mother ought to know that.

Sebastian's arm fell across her shoulders. "My baroness is fierce."

"Your wife is fierce." So was his friend, though Milly would not force that sentiment on him. "Did you always grow hops in this field?"

For a man who'd been away from England for more than a decade, he was well-informed regarding his acres. This field was suited to pasture, being good soil, but too rocky to plow easily. That one had always been the tenant's common potato field, being thin-soiled even after repeated marling.

He vaulted the stiles one-handed, a display of casual athleticism common to any boy raised in the country, then turned and offered Milly his hand with gallantry country boys never learned.

With each field, each stile and stream, Milly became more and more convinced that all the trials and losses visited upon her earlier in life had been wiped away by the great gift of the person of her husband.

Though the loss of him… She snipped that thought off, because today was her wedding day, and anything or anybody seeking to take Sebastian from her would have to overcome her defense of him first.

Sebastian led her down a grassy lane running between parallel avenues of oaks, until they reached an old overshot grist mill, with lavender, lilacs, and honeysuckle growing in a riot around its whitewashed walls.

Along the stream, blankets and a basket sat in the shade of the oaks.

"This is where you came to dream."

"I called it planning my life. I intended to be the best Baron St. Clair ever seen. I would write famous speeches, I would advise the king himself, and impress the entire world with my swordsmanship."

He spoke with affection for that boy. Reluctant affection, but affection.

"I would have been happy to write my lessons," Milly said, leading him toward the blankets. "Now I am happy to share some victuals with my husband."

She was happy to share the day with him, to share his land with him, to share his memories with him. As Milly let the peace of the surrounding glade seep into her soul, she would be happy to share herself with him as well.

❧

The occasional duel was apparently not enough to keep a man's instincts sharpened when it came to ambushes. Such were the deadening results of a few years on the fringe of London Society.

"We're to picnic here?" Sebastian asked. "Wouldn't you rather take your meal where the sun can reach us?"

Because the footmen had laid out the blankets—a thickness of three old quilts—in the dappled shade near the stream. The meal—assuming his wife allowed him to eat between her questions—would thus take place right beneath one of the best climbing oaks a boy had ever discovered.

Milly snapped off a sprig of honeysuckle, sniffed it, then passed it to Sebastian. "For this meal, my first private meal with my husband, seclusion suits me better. Does the mill still function?"

Sebastian breathed in the scent that symbolized the bonds of love. Honeysuckle was like his wife: a quietly lovely exterior hid a more beguiling and intangible beauty than one suspected.

"The mill ought to work. Local lore is that it dates back to Good King Hal's day. We had a succession of dry years, though, and my father and a few of the other landowners thought it prudent to build a mill powered by livestock rather than water. The mill closer to the village is larger, but this one could serve when that one's at capacity."

Milly went after a cluster of lilacs next, the buds not entirely open.

"Will you make love with me here, Husband? Somewhere you were happy, somewhere a happy memory would be within our reach as the years go by?"

Deliver me from village girls when spring is at its height. He took the lilacs from her and led her to the blankets.

"Baroness, you are very bold on your wedding day."

"I am very happy on my wedding day. Did you know lilacs stand for first emotions of love?"

Yes, he had known that. He paused to strip a few inches of lavender leaves from a bush and held them out to her. "Lavender is for distrust."

"Lavender"—she upended his hand, so the leaves fluttered to earth—"is for making soaps, sachets, and money. What do you suppose is packed in that hamper?"

He did not care what was in the hamper. He

cared very much that Milly should not trust this happiness she mentioned so casually. Sooner or later—perhaps within the week—she would have to deal with being the Traitor Baron's wife, or—more likely—his widow.

Milly knelt on the blankets, reminding him of another picnic they'd shared. "You are brooding, Sebastian. Do you regret marrying me?" She passed him a bottle of wine along with her question.

A snippet of schoolboy Latin assailed him: *in vino veritas.* "I will never regret marrying you, though you…"

She sat back, a knife in one hand, a small loaf of bread in the other.

"Yes, yes, I know. I will regret marrying you. You are a bad, wicked man, treason personified, the shame of three peerages and probably many a colonial society as well. Open the wine, and we'll toast the depths of your disgrace."

The bottle in his hand was one of a few shipped back from France years ago, before Napoleon had barged his way onto Britain's list of crosses to bear.

"Milly, I'm sorry." So inadequate; so sincere.

She fished another crock out of the hamper and lifted the lid.

"Strawberries. Just for today, Sebastian, might we please not dwell under the cloud of your sorrows and misgivings? Might we pretend you're any other handsome fellow about to make love with his wife for the first time? You do intend to consummate the vows, don't you?"

The strawberries went back into the hamper, the lid of the crock clattering against the container. She passed him the knife, though what he was supposed to do with it was a mystery.

Sebastian had upset his wife. She hid it well, probably between a wedge of cheddar and some sliced ham yet to make an appearance on the blanket, but Sebastian was ruining her wedding day.

Their wedding day.

Between one lovely, scented spring breeze and the next, Sebastian's emotions shifted from a need to protect his wife against the sentimentality of the day, to a need to cherish her for her tender emotions. Regardless of the outcome of the next duel, and the next—of all of the duels—Sebastian would never have another wedding day. Of that, he was certain.

He set the wine aside unopened, tossed the knife into the hamper, and crawled across the blanket.

"Kiss me, Milly St. Clair."

He should have asked for her kisses. Of all the questions he knew how to find answers to, that question— "Will you kiss me?"—he could not ask. The best he could do was to nuzzle her jaw, the way her cat might have importuned her for attention—both playfulness and determination in his flirting.

"We're to eat first," she said, angling her chin away. "My husband has turned up moody, and I would not impose on him."

"You should make me beg," he said, running his tongue over the rim of her ear. "Your husband is an idiot who hasn't sense enough to be grateful for the blessings that fall into his very lap. I am given to unhappy moods, and I do apologize. I would not burden our wedding day with them further. I shall make love with you, Wife. I will probably do little else for the next week, at least. You may consider that another one of my famous priorities."

The allusion had the desired effect of tipping up the corners of her mouth. "Some of your priorities are laudable, Sebastian. Will you open the wine?"

She was being coy, for which he adored her. The breeze stirred a lock of her hair across her mouth just as he leaned in to kiss her, so he ended up kissing silky strands as well as her lips.

"Hang the wine."

He muttered the words against her mouth. She drew back enough to extricate her hair from between their lips. "You might need the fortification."

Yes, he might. Later.

"Kiss me, Baroness. Today is your wedding day, and you're fretting over the menu."

He made a menu of her, kissing her to her back, where she clearly had wanted to be, then feasting on her shoulders, her collarbone, her jaw, the few inches of skin revealed above her neckline. Everywhere, she was warm and fragrant and *his*.

And yet, a man—a husband—ought not to presume. He crouched over her on all fours, as winded as if they'd been wrestling, not kissing.

"Shall we consummate our vows here, Milly? Is this the memory you want of your wedding day?" Because whatever memory she sought, he'd try his utmost to give it to her.

She cupped his jaw then stroked a hand down over his chest. "Yes. Here. Now. Right now."

Sebastian felt those words, felt the shape of them

as Milly's mouth moved, and something inside him broke free. His life was a shambles, but this moment, these sentiments of tenderness and desire between him and his wife, they were real, pure, and good.

His hand had gone to the falls of his breeches when the first cold, wet drop slapped the back of his neck. Several more raindrops pelted him before reality penetrated his incredulity: the elements were not in agreement with Milly's wishes—or his own.

"Grab the blankets, Wife. If we're quick, we can move our feast before we're soaked to the skin."

He snatched up the hamper, and they dashed for the mill as the shower intensified. While they weren't soaked to the skin, the moment, at least for Sebastian, had lost its bloom with damnable predictability.

◆

Milly laid out two thick blankets on the threshing floor. Ancient oak was not the softest bed upon which to consummate a marriage, but neither was it any more solid than her determination.

"A passing shower," she said, taking a place on the blankets. "Get down here, Sebastian, and make yourself useful."

Her husband apparently recognized a tone of command and left off scouting the mill's interior. "Useful?"

"I did not bring a shawl, this place is drafty, and you give off warmth." He gave off sadness, too, and an exasperating sense of resignation. "You never did open the wine."

Hang the wine, he'd said. Milly had no doubt it was

a fine vintage, which would be handy if she could ever retrieve her husband from the memories, doubts, and guilts that had also apparently found their way into the mill's gloomy interior.

"You are cold?" he asked, prowling away from the enormous grinding stone at the center of the building.

"I will soon take a chill. Sebastian, how is it you were called upon to torture English officers?"

From his arrested expression, Milly surmised that she could not have captured his attention any more effectively had she torn off her clothes.

"An interrogation is my penance for not making love to you in the pouring rain?"

She patted the blanket, and he came down beside her as she lied through her teeth. "We were merely kissing. Has no one asked you this question?"

She gathered from the set of his jaw that no one had been presuming enough—or stupid enough—to ask him, and yet, of all people to entrust with tormenting British officers, a former English schoolboy was not a logical choice.

"I was good at it." He fitted himself around Milly's back, so his knees were hiked on either side of her. Of course, she could not see his face as she curled against his chest.

She did not need to. The bleakness in his words filled the entire grist mill.

"Yes, but why *you*? Was it a test of your French patriotism?"

His lips brushed her hair. Milly encircled his waist with one arm, closed her eyes, and felt Sebastian arranging the third blanket over them.

"At first, maybe it was a test, but not entirely. I'd gone into Toulouse to meet with my superior, a nasty little man by the name of Henri Anduvoir. He'd had an English prisoner beaten nearly beyond recognition, and still, the fellow had told them nothing except his name and rank."

A hint of an accent had crept into Sebastian's words—the vowels broadened, initial consonants softened: 'ee'd told hem nawthing...

Milly kissed her husband's throat, where these words had to be choking him.

"But you did recognize him?" Thunder rumbled at a benign distance while the rain drummed on the roof and Milly waited for Sebastian to answer.

"I did not immediately recognize the captive. Anduvoir had the man's name, and I realized I'd spent a couple of years at school with an older brother. They shared a family resemblance, same blond hair, same build..."

Something in his voice implied not much of the man's face had remained untouched as a result of the beating he'd sustained. Milly clutched her husband more tightly. "Tell me."

Sebastian's chest heaved up with a slow sigh, and Milly thought he'd keep his memories locked inside him, like the poison they were.

"The fellow I'd known, Daniel Pixler, Viscount Aubrey, was the oldest of four boys, one hell of a batsman, and a decent chap. This was the youngest boy, Damien. I knew they had a sister, one sister. She was the youngest, and a bit slow. Daniel had written to her each week, printing the words for her."

"A good brother, then." A very good brother who

did not require a woman to read well in order to hold her dear.

"I gambled that Damien was cut from the same cloth as Daniel, and told Anduvoir to stop criticizing England's mad king, and fat, nancy prince, whom any boot boy was free to criticize and regularly did. I told him to stop beating a man who could no longer feel the pain, a man for whom each blow only fortified his resolve to remain silent."

Beatings could do that. Milly knew this from experience, and Sebastian had reminded her of it when they'd walked in the park.

"What did you do, Sebastian?"

The next kiss landed on Milly's brow. "In a sense, I was the one who broke." Then more softly, "I was always the one who broke."

Sebastian was broken, Milly did not argue that, but she doubted he'd been the one to spill England's secrets before her enemies.

"I could not endure what I saw before me, could not tolerate seeing a man—a good, decent soldier, regardless of his nationality—made to suffer because he'd forgotten his jacket in some tavern. They would spare his life—Anduvoir was not about to give up such an intriguing and valuable toy—but they would…"

The things human beings could do to one another once decency had been cast aside in the name of some national delusion were the stuff of old men's nightmares.

"You did not allow him to become Anduvoir's pet depravity."

Another big sigh, but to Milly, the quality of it was different, more weary, maybe a touch grateful that she'd not made him illuminate the darkest corners of his memory for her.

"I told him to insult Pixler's sister, as violently and vulgarly as he could. Told him how to threaten the girl by name, described the family seat where she lived, so Anduvoir could suggest her safety hung in the balance. I insisted that an offer of private ransom be put before the man as well, a sincere offer. For hope to be an effective torment, it must be grounded in reality. Anduvoir was as greedy as he was cruel, and my plan was…successful."

Success had never been achieved while bearing such a razor-sharp blade of irony. Sebastian's plan had worked out well for this Anduvoir demon, for the *République*'s coffers, and even for Mr. Pixler, who likely strolled the grounds of the family seat with his sister to this day.

Milly pushed Sebastian to his back and straddled him. "You preserved Damien Pixler from becoming Anduvoir's pet depravity, but condemned yourself to that torment instead."

She uttered the words because she could not bear to make him say them. Beneath her, a soldier felled by memory stared up at the beamed ceiling of the dusty old mill.

"Not immediately. The next time Anduvoir caught an officer out of uniform, he miscalculated, and the prisoner died without offering up any information. The fatality was a boy, barely sixteen. My guess is he had nothing to give, but a general got wind of it and had all the English officers sent to me if they were caught without the protection of their uniform."

Milly silently cursed astute generals, war, France, Anduvoir, and boys who joined up before they learned to shave.

"Love, don't cry." Sebastian kissed her cheek, where a stupid tear was tracking down toward her chin. "Please, don't cry. It was long ago and far away, another time, another country."

His voice was rough, the accent banished. Milly lashed her arms around his neck, knowing that for Sebastian, these awful memories, the experience of them, was no farther away than the great, ancient grinding stone at the center of the mill.

The thunder came again, closer, as Milly sat up and fumbled with the fastenings of her dress. She'd purposely chosen something simple, a garment that let her unfasten a few buttons and get at the front laces of her country stays.

Sebastian remained silent, but his eyes, so cold and distant, gradually warmed. "You'll take a chill."

"We'll keep each other warm." When she'd wrestled her dress off and was wearing only her chemise, Milly started on her husband's cravat. "We have blankets, and nobody will come looking for us until the storm passes. Let me do your cuffs."

He allowed her to remove his waistcoat and shirt, their clothing becoming an untidy pile near the edge of the blankets, until Sebastian grabbed her dress and his shirt and wadded them into a pillow. He let her plow her fingers through the dusting of dark hair on his chest, let her feel his hands shaping the contour of her breasts.

"Your touch is warm, Husband."

And he was becoming aroused. Milly knew this because she sat upon the part of him most honestly able to communicate such a development.

"I am glad you married me, Millicent St. Clair. Glad of it, and I always will be."

Ah, finally. Milly hadn't been sure, hadn't known if she was a blessing or another burden to him, hadn't dared hope his sentiments matched her own.

"I'm glad too. You will please now exert yourself to make me even more glad."

She added that last because already she had learned that her husband responded to a tone of command, even if the words were half-whispered and full of wonder.

Twelve

"MERCIA, YOU MUST CELEBRATE WITH ME!"

Christian folded down his newspaper to regard former Captain Lord Prentice "Pretentious" Anderson grinning at him with a sense of bonhomie usually reserved for a much later hour.

And for much closer acquaintances. "Anderson."

Anderson stuck a pale hand in Christian's face. "I'm to be a papa, again. Her ladyship told me at breakfast, said kippers would not be on the menu for some while. Sure a sign as ever there was. She can't abide kippers when she's on the nest."

Christian rose from his reading chair, his irritation with the captain and with the day fading marginally. "That is splendid news. This will be your third?"

Anderson gave a ponderous wink. "Third time's the charm, not that I don't adore m' girls, but a fellow has a duty, dontcha know."

Christian, being a duke without extant male progeny, did know, though he wouldn't trade his daughter for all the trees in Surrey. Anderson was beaming at the books encircling the club's reading room as if the entire burden of gestation and childbirth was one he'd personally undertaken in service to the succession.

"You're having champagne?"

"Told the steward to bring up the best," Anderson said. "The fellows are in the dining room, but somebody recalled you were hibernating in here."

Hibernating. Christian was serving out a sentence handed down by his duchess, to get out and enjoy the day. Her Grace was likely stealing a nap, rest being of paramount interest to a woman in anticipation of a blessed event.

"One drink, then. A man deserves to celebrate such good fortune." And as Anderson's former commanding officer, however briefly, Christian was obligated to celebrate it with him.

"Say what you will about the damned Frenchies," Anderson observed as they quit the sanctuary of the reading room, "they brew fine drink. Suppose that's why we let some of them live, what?"

Christian remained silent, because precious few men, precious few young men, had survived France's bid for glory. The ones who'd survived had been lucky, and damned brave.

The crowd in the dining room had clearly been alerted to Anderson's happy news. Glasses were full, the noise level rising with one bawdy toast after another.

"Mercia! It's an occasion indeed when you deign to join us." Lord Hector Pierpont's voice held the grating good cheer of a man masking self-consciousness with lubricious manners. "Steward, another bottle for His Grace!"

Christian accepted a drink—he'd said he would.

"Give us a toast, Your Grace. Like old times, eh?" somebody called.

Wellington believed in reassembling his staff periodically at Apsley House for social dinners. He trotted out the full Portuguese service and the best wines, an occasion for men who'd shared a war to take a step in the direction of sharing peace.

Christian had dodged every invitation thus far, and intended to keep dodging them indefinitely.

He held up his glass and waited for order to assert itself. "To our ladies. May they weather their challenges as safely as we have weathered ours."

His duchess would have been proud of his restraint. He did not disrespect good wine by downing it all at once, another feat of which his duchess would have approved.

After a beat of silence, a general chorus of, "The ladies! Hear, hear!" greeted Christian's sentiments. He stood on the periphery of the group, sipping his drink while more toasts were raised.

The steward was a shrewd little fellow from Alsace, and had known better than to disturb the best vintages for this impromptu cricket party. The wine was good, though, and for the first time since Christian had dragged himself from the Château, the company of his former fellow officers was not entirely objectionable either.

He'd learned to accept any measure of progress, however small. Learned from his duchess.

"So, has MacHugh asked you to second him?" Anderson had sidled away from the group to join Christian lounging against a doorjamb.

The name MacHugh brought to mind a big, tough, hardheaded Scot, though hardheaded Scot was a redundant term in Christian's experience.

"Has MacHugh insulted somebody's daughter? I never took him for a fool."

Unlike Anderson, whom nobody would mistake for clever.

"Not hardly," Anderson said, tossing back a gulp of champagne. "He's taken offense at Girard's maunderings—though I suppose we're to refer to him as St. Clair these days."

Christian set his half-full glass aside as a sharp twinge afflicted his left wrist. "I beg your pardon?"

Anderson glanced about over the rim of his glass. "I had a hand in things, if you must know. That Henri fellow said I was the best suited to it."

The champagne curdled abruptly in Christian's gut, though half the French nation answered to the name Henri.

"Anderson, join me for a moment at the window." He took his former subordinate none too gently by the arm and steered him away from the group. "Has MacHugh challenged St. Clair?"

His lordship straightened with the exaggerated dignity of those inebriated while the sun yet shone.

"He most certainly has. A few words over a tot or two of whiskey, and MacHugh was ready to permanently solve the problem of St. Clair for two grateful governments, not that I told him that. He'd likely make a hash of it just to be contrary if I had. Pierpont blundered badly, but he never was very accurate with a pistol."

More glancing about followed these disclosures as a shout went up from the group across the room.

Christian didn't particularly enjoy being a duke; it was simply his lot, like being blond, tall, or Church of England rather than a Dissenter. One didn't quibble with it, but one did learn to exploit its benefits. He took Anderson's empty glass from his lordship's hand and let a silence spread beneath the raucous drollery of the other men.

And then, when Anderson realized awkwardness was upon them, Christian posed his question in the tones of a titled superior officer whose patience was ebbing. "What's afoot, Captain?"

"Old Hookey hasn't told you?"

"Wellington is off in Hampshire, dealing with household matters."

The gears of Anderson's mind ground forward slowly, but they moved in the direction Christian had known they would.

"St. Clair is an embarrassment," Anderson said, enunciating carefully, as if he'd repeated this to himself many times. "An em-barr-ass-ment to two governments. Henri and I, we're the fellows to set things to rights. Clever chap, Henri—subtle, for a Frog."

"Describe Henri."

Anderson gave a description that fit exactly the worst of the specters haunting Christian's nightmares. He suspected the same specter haunted St. Clair's as well.

"So you lied to MacHugh, goaded him into challenging St. Clair, and are trusting to the Scot to see to the killing of an English peer?"

"A traitor baron who won't be missed. Prinny's never shy about taking on an estate or two left begging for an heir, not that I'd want credit for my part. I told the Frenchie this was my last contribush—my last part in it. St. Clair hasn't bothered anybody since Waterloo, after all."

Since Toulouse had fallen, though "bothered" was a spectacular euphemism for what St. Clair had got up to in the years prior to the False Peace.

"You're smart to keep this to yourself, Anderson. You can't breathe a word to anybody. Not Pierpont, not your lady, nobody. When is the duel to take place?"

Across the room, a song started up, a dirty little tune about plowing the fields of France, probably no worse than the French infantry had sung about the fields of England, but it increased Christian's need to quit the premises.

"I dunno when they fight, but it's to be a bare-knuckle encounter, of all things. MacHugh will finish him, I've no doubt. I expect MacHugh is giving Girard—St. Clair—time to get the wifey in an interesting condition first."

Wifey. That Anderson's brain could allow a peer of the realm and avowed traitor to have a *wifey* was a telling comment on the cramped dimensions of his intellect.

"When did St. Clair take a wife?"

Some of Anderson's inebriation seemed to fall away. "This morning, probably right about the time my lady was denying me a plate of kippers. I like kippers. I'll miss them."

"Order yourself a plate of kippers to go with your

champagne. And you must not say another word to anybody regarding this situation with St. Clair."

Anderson brightened. "Kippers and champagne? Suppose I shall."

He turned to go, but Christian stopped him with a hand on his sleeve. Once, Anderson's life had been Christian's responsibility, and a dearth of intelligence was no more a man's fault than a ducal title or a French mother.

"In future, I'd avoid this Henri fellow, Anderson. It strikes me as curious that England would turn to a Frenchman to dispatch one of our own. We've plenty enough talented officers on hand to see to such a thing, if needs must."

Anderson blinked, and in the space of that blink, Christian perceived that Anderson himself had come to the same conclusion, and then, having no alternative short of admitting gross stupidity, had rejected it.

"Avoid him, I shall. I'll be too busy deciding what to name my heir and missing my kippers."

He sauntered off, a fool in charity with the world and intent on committing the gastronomic equivalent of treason by washing his kippers down with champagne.

❧

Milly did not know how to retrieve Sebastian from Toulouse, London, or whatever sad, safe place he'd gone. She cuddled down to his chest. "I am cold. The temperature has dropped considerably."

Sebastian grasped the blanket and wrapped it more closely around her. "You're intent on consummating our vows now, aren't you, Baroness?" He sounded amused, which was an improvement over his earlier mood.

"Sooner would suit me better than later, Sebastian, and the idea that each of your twenty-nine servants will know exactly what we're about when we retire this evening…it unsettles me. I never thought to be a baroness, you know."

"My apologies for the imposition. I thought you said there were thirty servants."

"The boot boy, Charles, must be presumed innocent of marital intimacies."

Sebastian's chin came to rest against Milly's temple. "You recall his name. You would have made a good commanding officer."

He'd no doubt meant it as a compliment, though Milly could not hear anything military as flattering.

"Sebastian, you must lead this charge. Perhaps, in future, when I am more accustomed to my—"

His kiss was soft, reassuring. He would lead the charge, but a full-out gallop was not where they'd start. "Let me get my breeches off. If we're to consecrate the mill with marital intimacies, a fellow wants to be out of uniform."

He probably felt her cringe at that analogy. Milly now knew that only officers captured out of uniform were tortured. She pitched off of him onto the blankets, grateful somebody had thought to provide them three.

Sebastian stood to remove his boots, stockings, and breeches. From the way he went about it, a snowstorm could have been howling and he would have been equally impervious to the elements.

"You are wonderfully put together, sir."
Wonderful—had such a prosaic word been applied to
the Apollo Belvedere? Sebastian was perfect proportions on a generous scale, his musculature in evidence
as he tossed his breeches onto the clothes pile.

And for a man who'd spent years soldiering, he had
no visible scars.

"Shall I strut my wares, Baroness?"

She allowed him to leer, because he was trying to
set her at ease. Trying to give her a few moments to
gather her courage.

"Your wares are adequately in evidence, though
they do me no good wandering about the threshing
floor." Milly delivered her lecture with the blanket
held firmly to her throat, and Sebastian's leer became
a smile—a tender smile.

He settled beside her and let her have her blanket—
his nudity, the cold, the cavernous space apparently of
no moment to him.

"I wonder if in the history of this venerable mill,
anybody has ever put this threshing floor to the use
we contemplate."

Thunder cracked, a loud, startling clap, followed
immediately by a flash of lightning.

"It's private here," Milly said, extricating her right
arm from the blanket to brush Sebastian's hair back from
his eyes. "And I desire my husband's intimate attentions."

Mostly. A small, spinstery part of her sought
reassurances, not that those intimacies would be
pleasurable—they would be, eventually—but that
desiring them was not unladylike.

Un-baroness-like.

"An honest woman is worth more than rubies."

He'd mangled his Proverbs. Milly did not quibble, though, because honest and virtuous were close enough, also because Sebastian had lifted her blanket and insinuated himself beside her.

"I think it is you, Milly St. Clair, who must warm me." He arranged himself over her, directly over her, braced on his knees and forearms. "Though I warn you, madam, I will not be rushed."

Words did not come biddably to heel. Milly's body was blanketed by a large, warm, naked husband, his thighs between hers, his hard belly against her softer flesh, his chest inches from her beating heart.

A woman who could not read well was accustomed to being caught up short and forced to rely on wits instead of words; nonetheless, Milly felt a thread of unease.

"Tell me what to expect, Sebastian. Tell me what you expect of me. My aunts were forthright, but one needs details, not sly looks and—"

"One needs to trust one's husband. Kiss me."

Sebastian waited above her, as settled in his posture as the grinding stone that had been turning, turning, for centuries in the center of the mill. Trusting Sebastian should have been easy, and yet, Milly hesitated—because he did not trust her.

He trusted no one, and that offended Milly on his behalf.

She lifted her hips and spread her legs, watching as Sebastian absorbed her overture.

He kissed her cheek. "Love, you will part me from my reason, and that is not well-advised for our first encounter." He kissed her other cheek, and Milly understood these for the opening salvos they were. She relaxed and let go of another increment of anxiety, because Sebastian was making plain that *not rushing* was for her benefit.

With her fingertips, Milly traced the muscles on either side of his spine. "You could rush just a little, Sebastian, couldn't you?"

"No, I could not. I want you mindless with need for what I can give you, and such an undertaking will not be accomplished with haste." Oh, how very English he sounded, how lordly and patient. "You smell good, like lavender sachets. You must have washed…"

Milly had washed. Had used five precious minutes to freshen up, and her last coherent thought was gratitude that she had.

"You taste like lavender," Sebastian went on. "Here." His tongue lapped at the spot beneath her ear where Milly had dabbed a bit of *eau du bain*. "And you taste worried. Don't worry, Milly St. Clair. These are among the few moments in a marriage nobody is required to manage or worry over."

He'd let her have some of his weight, a much-needed comfort as Milly gathered herself to him. His cock—old women could delight in shocking language—was hard, smooth, and warm against Milly's belly, and the way Sebastian pressed it against her suggested this part of him did not need delicacy from her.

Milly's hands trailed lower on Sebastian's back, until she felt the muscular contour of his derriere beneath her palms.

"I like that," Sebastian growled against her ear. "I like that you're bold and curious, that you want this."

This. Milly had no experience with *this*. *This* made her breasts feel heavy and her spine as flexible as an old rope. "I want *you*, Sebastian. I want children with green eyes and dark hair, I want—"

He covered her mouth with his, like an incoming tide, and even as Milly welcomed his kiss, she had the sense he'd needed to stop her words. His tongue touched her lips, bringing with it a hint of mint.

Part of his five minutes above stairs had been spent on his tooth powder, which made Milly smile as that same tongue—a *hot* tongue—traced her teeth. "Open, Milly St. Clair. Kiss me the way a village girl kisses her swain."

She clutched at his backside, involuntarily at first, so naughty were his words, and then experimentally. "Even your fundament is muscular."

When she did it again, Sebastian shifted up so Milly was tucked more firmly beneath him. He could kiss her lazily from this angle, braced on his elbows as if he were a freight wagon whose brake had been set. The slow tour he made of the inside of her lips suggested he could take all afternoon acquainting himself with her mouth.

Milly used both hands on his backside this time, anchoring herself before she touched her tongue to Sebastian's. He returned the caress, the way duelists would test each other's reactions with a beat and rebeat of their swords.

"Again," he whispered. "Take your time."

The wind gusts picked up, and the tempo and volume of the rain against the mill's roof rose, while amid the blankets, Milly went from warm to hot. That

Sebastian could be so in control of himself was both reassuring and exasperating.

She squirmed, pressing her breasts against his chest, and he groaned with an answering pressure.

Like a village swain kisses his damsel. She pulled his hair rather than struggle for the words, holding him still so she could possess his mouth. When Sebastian broke the kiss and cradled her head against his shoulder, they were both breathing hard.

Milly waited, the rain pounding down outside a perfect metaphor for the tumult inside her. They were not finished. Heaven help her, they were not even started, and already, she was struggling against the urge to weep.

❧

Sebastian rested his chin on his wife's crown and mentally grabbed for some…some restraint. Thank God his path had not previously crossed that of any village girls, if Milly's kisses were an indication of how they went about their pleasures.

He'd have marks on his arse from the way she clutched at him. Marks he'd delight in knowing she had put there.

"Stop wiggling." He delighted as well in her name: Milly St. Clair. She'd think him daft if he appended it to his every remark.

"Wiggling is part of it," Milly replied, tracing her tongue up his throat. God abide, she was a fast learner. "Perhaps you'd care to demonstrate?"

The way she patted his backside…affection, command, protectiveness, and desire, all in one small, warm caress.

"Not until you stop thrashing about."

The slow undulations of her hips ceased, like an ocean going quiet as the wind died. And yet, like an ocean, Sebastian could feel currents moving in her even when the surface of her appeared calm.

He shifted his weight to one elbow, took his cock in one hand, and nudged among her damp folds. "Do not think of moving."

An intended command came out sounding like the plea that it was. Milly kissed his throat and brushed her hand over his arse.

Reassuringly?

He pushed forward cautiously, assured himself he'd located the proper trajectory, and hitched himself over her.

"Sebastian, I want—" She grabbed two handfuls of his backside and gave him a solid squeeze.

"Hold on as tight as you please. It helps me…" Helped him resist the urge to charge headlong.

"I want to move. I *need* to move. It isn't fair that you're moving…"

He quieted her with a shallow rhythm, a slow, gentle invasion and retreat that would last as long as he needed it to. "Move, then. Never let it be said I was unfair to my bride."

What followed was a conversation of bodies new to each other, and in some sense, new to the business of lovemaking. For Sebastian, anything but a mindless rogering between strangers had been beyond his reach for years, and for Milly…

He was her first, her only. No man had even kissed her before he'd appropriated that privilege for himself, and that…suggested he had judgment superior to any of the Englishmen strutting about old Albion.

She delighted him, with her hair pulling and arse grabbing, but now that the moment of consummation was upon them, she delighted him with her trust. Her maneuvers were delicate, questions rather than commands. A flex of her hips here, then a pause. *Have I got that right?*

He answered as civilly as enthusiasm would allow, with incrementally deeper thrusts. *Perfect. You're perfect. Again, please.*

Rhythm took over, not his, not hers, *their* rhythm. Milly's sighs fanned past Sebastian's neck; she hooked her ankles at the small of his back.

He could hear her body awakening, could sense passion overcoming all her caution and self-restraint, and the wonder he felt to witness her transformation aided his control.

"You'll not rush me, love." A vow, one that ought to be included in the wedding ceremony.

"You'll not… Oh, *Sebastian*."

Sebastian understood torment in all its forms. As Milly unraveled beneath him, bucking into his thrusts, mashing her face into the crook of his shoulder, moaning softly against his neck, he had his first experience with the bliss that lay on the far side of torment.

For her, he could endure the sharp, burning ache of unfulfilled desire. For her, he could go quiet, stroking his hand over her hair, cherishing her in silence while his body clamored in vain for its own satisfaction.

Her moment was his, her pleasure his goal and his glory.

"Sebastian St. Clair." She kissed his jaw. "You… You… I shall cry now. Please tell me it's permitted. Nobody warns one, nobody even hints…"

He gathered her close, cradled the back of her head in his palm, and became her personal handkerchief. For an instant, he entertained the possibility—the fear—that he might have hurt her, but the way Milly moved—like a houri far gone in her bliss—banished the notion.

"Again, Wife."

Her grip on him became desperate. "Not again. I could not bear—"

She bore it. She bore it with such unbridled enthusiasm that it was likely a good thing old mills were built on double foundations. She bore it as the thunder rumbled, the rain beat down, and every corner of Sebastian—heart, soul, mind, and strength—gave itself up to furthering and then sharing in her pleasure.

When he was certain Milly's body had wrung from him the greatest satisfaction he could give her, he let himself fly free, let himself pour into her not only his seed, but everything he was or would ever be.

And for a moment, for a procession of moments wrapped in old wool and a new wife on a hard oak floor, Sebastian felt *light*—he felt both weightless and illuminated from within, as if he were radiance itself.

He did not know how long he drifted in that light, how long he lay collapsed on his wife, filleted of all worry, all intentions, all past and future. Milly's hand drifted through his hair like a benediction; her breathing gave his own exhalations their rhythm.

"I'm crushing you."

She murmured something about wheat being ground into flour, of all things, but made no move to push him off. Sebastian managed to hike one knee—a knee somebody had abused, come to that—under him, enough to give Milly some space.

"Stay." Her word was clear enough, as was the way she wrapped a hand around the back of his neck. "Please."

She rubbed a damp cheek against his jaw, reminding him that he'd made her cry. He wiped her cheeks with a handy shirttail, then tucked her under him and prepared to beg. "You're my wife now. I'm your husband. I forbid you to cry."

Beneath him, she chuckled, which was inordinately reassuring. Women—tenderhearted women—sometimes cried in bed. Men, by contrast, cried after battles, if they were lucky enough to survive.

Milly had known a few battles. He kissed her nose.

"That's better." He rolled with her, which untangled his softening cock from her body but also put her straddling him. "I neglected your breasts again."

She tried to bat his hands away from her neglected parts. "Sebastian, hush, and don't be difficult."

He did not feel difficult. For the first time in years, he felt *easy*. He wrapped the blanket up over her, lest her mortification at his frank appreciation for those breasts set the mill afire.

"Do you feel like a wife now, Milly St. Clair? Like a baroness? Will I do as a husband?"

The scent of sex mingled in the air with the scent of the passing storm, old grain, and spring flowers. The fragrance of the moment was unique, as unprecedented as the ease with which Sebastian drew breath and the temptation he felt to laugh.

"I feel like *your* wife," she said, a little peevishly. "Also like having a short nap."

The lady clearly wanted to hide, to find some quiet and safety in sleep, and some peace from him and his mischief. That Sebastian knew this told him Milly was, in truth and already, his wife.

"Sleep, then," he said, tugging her down to his chest. "You've earned your rest, and I've earned the right to hold you while you slumber. We'll attack that hamper when you've napped."

She ducked her head against his shoulder, but not before he saw her smile at his gallantry. In moments, she was breathing regularly, her weight warm and comforting over him.

Beneath him, some knot or gnarl in the oak floor made a nuisance of itself in the vicinity of his left buttock. Sebastian moved a few inches without disturbing his wife, but had the odd thought as he dozed off that oak leaves symbolized bravery.

Married to him, Milly would need her courage.

And married to her… Sebastian's sense of lightness dimmed as sleep drew nearer. Married to Milly, he would need the ability to treasure each moment, to hold shadows and duels and memories at bay, lest he ruin for himself and his wife the gift of whatever time they had together.

❦

"I know when somebody feigns sleep or unconsciousness, and you, Madam Baroness, are no longer asleep."

Sebastian spoke so close to Milly's ear as to tickle her with his words.

"Does your observation have a point?"

Because a point was rising between them, a husbandly, loverly point Milly found as intriguing as the ease with which she lay sprawled naked on her baron.

"You have to be hungry," he said, kissing her ear. "I certainly am." Another kiss, brisk, like a pat to a horse's neck before directing it to trot away from the stable yard.

"You are hungry." Milly lifted herself away from the warmth of his chest, let the blanket fall from her shoulders, and stretched, *lazily.*

Sebastian goggled at her Neglected Parts for an instant, then tried to hide his fascination.

"I *am* hungry," he said. "Breakfast was ages and some exertion ago. We'd best locate our attire lest a searching party find us as God made us."

He sounded disappointingly determined. Milly gathered the blanket about her but didn't move off of him. "Can one make love only once per day? Is this another pertinent fact nobody tells a woman until she's taken a husband?"

"*Taken* a husband?"

Sebastian's tone curdled the edges of Milly's sense of well-being and wonder. "Don't sound so amused. You *took* a bride, as best I recall."

He brushed a stray lock of hair back over her shoulder. "And she took me, you are quite correct. Now I would be pleased if she'd allow me to provide her some sustenance."

His touch had been gentle, but something in his words

rankled. Milly moved off of him—being a bride was not the most dignified undertaking—and realized Sebastian had subtly implied that lovemaking was not sustenance.

She fussed the blankets and appropriated Sebastian's shirt. "You didn't answer my question. Do we make love only once at a go? Must we eat between rounds, sleep, dress, receive callers, that sort of thing?"

He found his breeches and pulled them up, but left half his buttons undone. "I could make love to you until neither one of us could recall how to walk or why we'd want to. Do you care for strawberries?"

While Milly sorted through her feelings, Sebastian plundered the hamper. He was all that was considerate, offering her the choicest strawberries, encouraging her to swill a fine, fizzy vintage directly from the bottle, and buttering her bread for her. As picnics went, this one would do.

And yet, he tugged the shirt closed over Milly's breasts and fastened two of the buttons. He sat two feet away, neither facing her nor touching her. For a man who professed to be famished, he only picked at his food and downed rather more than his share of the wine.

"The rain has stopped," Milly said, declining more wine. "The paths back to the manor will be soaked and the trees dripping."

Sebastian paused, the bottle two inches from his lips. "I can carry you, if you're concerned for your hems."

Milly was concerned for her marriage. Already, and for reasons she could not articulate, she was concerned for her marriage.

"The countryside is beautiful following a

late-afternoon shower. The sun comes in at the right
angle to illuminate everything, and we might even
see a rainbow." A rainbow would be a good omen,
and Milly felt the need for one of those on her wedding day.

Sebastian corked the bottle without taking the
final sip. "We might. I would wish that for you,
Milly St. Clair."

His expression was sweet and solemn, and suf-
ficiently hard for Milly to look upon, that she crawled
across the blanket and tucked herself against him.
"Sebastian, *what's wrong?*"

She hadn't wanted to ask him, hadn't wanted
to pester him. A wife was supposed to know her
husband and respect his privacy. They hadn't even
been married a day, and already she was begging him
for confidences.

"If I tell you nothing is amiss, you will be hurt,"
he said, gathering her against his chest. "I do not
want you to be hurt, and yet, I don't know how to
answer you."

At least he wasn't pretending, or worse, condescend-
ing to her. "Talk to me. I won't allow you to have your
shirt unless you try to talk to me, Sebastian."

The rain no longer drummed on the roof, but the
stream, swollen from the cloudburst, could be heard
rushing past beyond the mill's walls.

"I could take you again, Milly, right now, and then
again after that. A man's passion usually requires some
time to recover—not long for a young man, though I
hardly consider myself young—but you…"

Sebastian was feeling his way, threshing through the

words, separating truth from platitude in a way that cheered Milly.

She kissed his chest, felt the beat of his heart with her lips. "But I?"

"I am a stranger to pleasure, Milly." His hands on her back could not have been more cherishing. "I know torment. I know how to use pain and deprivation to show a man his most frightening truths, I know how to wrap suffering around an experienced soldier so it consumes him the way ivy obscures then obliterates even a church made of stone. I know how to present death as a longed-for blessing. And then along comes Millicent Danforth, and this…"

He was trying so hard, and yet Milly could barely comprehend his words for the horror she felt on his behalf. "Tell me."

"I am wary of the pleasure you bring me. I don't understand why you are not wary too, of me, of this marriage, of this pleasure." Then, more softly, "You should be."

Milly relaxed against him, because in his words she found a thread of hope.

"Wariness and a care for your own survival is why you yet live, Sebastian. I am all at sea, too. One might even say I am frightened, and yet, I would not trade the past hour with you for any safe, comfortable, predictable path I might have otherwise chosen."

Because she was wrapped in his arms, Milly felt the tension go out of him, though his tone still held some detachment.

"We will muddle on, then, though I wish you'd let me have my shirt back, despite how fetching you look in it. My grandmother made it for me, the last of her handi-work I have, and I wear it only on special occasions."

Milly's baron was wary, but also courageous. The occasion was special, indeed. She passed him his shirt and cast about for something to say that would reward his trust.

"I would have a promise from you, Sebastian."

For a few moments, he hid in the process of putting his shirt on, but then he held out his wrist for her to fasten the cuffs.

"Vows weren't enough? Making love with you here, despite the abuse to my knees isn't enough? You must have promises too?"

"The vows were lovely, else I would not have recited them to you." She slid the sleeve button through the hole and reached for his other hand, though she missed sorely the modesty his garment had provided her.

"What promise do you seek from me, Milly?" His tone said he'd put his wariness aside, but not out of reach.

"The next time we make love, you must not neglect my breasts. I will have your word on this."

He gave her his word, his mouth, his hands, and enough pleasure that, for Milly, the walk back to the manor held rainbows, despite the shadows lengthening across the fields.

Thirteen

LADY FREDDY STOPPED PRETENDING TO READ THE
latest copy of *La Belle Assemblée*, which was an insipid
publication, appropriate only for fidgety young girls.

"Do you suppose they'll make a go of it?" she
muttered.

The professor tapped a pencil against the blotter,
though she doubted he'd been making any progress
with his latest code—he hadn't written a single digit
or letter for twenty minutes.

"Theirs is a complicated undertaking."

He was always honest with her. Their partnership
thrived on such honesty, and yet, Freddy resented him
mightily for it just then. "Sebastian is besotted."

The professor had sometimes worn a beard as a
younger man, when he'd wanted to appear Continental
or hide his youth. Freddy could tell from the way he
stroked his chin he might wear a beard as an older
fellow too, and be all the handsomer for it.

"A romantic nature can make matters more difficult," he said. "Miss Danforth—Millicent—hides a
tender heart as well."

More honesty. "I wish to hell I didn't have such a tender damned heart."

He rose from his escritoire and took a seat beside her, all uninvited. This was fortunate, because tenderhearted people were often too stubborn and self-reliant for their own good.

"The St. Clairs have never wanted for courage," the professor observed. "That will serve Sebastian well in the coming days. And nights."

He had such a lovely smile. The warmth started in his eyes, and sometimes, particularly when they were in public, it remained only there, a beauty Freddy alone was allowed to see. When they were private, though, that smile advanced like a sunrise, cascading down his physiognomy until the corners of his mouth tipped up and a subtle impishness suffused his features.

"Will you ever ask me to marry you again?"

Oh, where in perdition had that question come from? Getting old wreaked all manner of havoc with one's dignity, and yet it created a sense of urgency too.

The smile became muted, as a sunrise becomes mere sunshine and unremarkable to most as a result. "Perhaps I shall, though I have a tender heart too, you know."

Tender heart, tender hands. A lady of dignified years ought not to dwell on such things lest she make a fool of herself. Freddy picked up her magazine, which at least had pictures she could study. "I wish I knew what Arthur was up to."

"Thus sayeth his duchess, frequently. The word is he's off at Stratfield Saye, getting the place organized and making peace with her over household matters."

This was part of the reason Freddy and her professor

should not marry. An aging bachelor of Continental extraction who made his living as a gentleman of letters could linger over a pint in any tavern, stroll down any street, do business in any shop. The second husband of a widowed baroness was precluded from many behaviors useful for gathering information.

"Wellington has left peace on the home front very late in his agenda," Freddy said, though his duchess was not the most scintillating exponent of Irish aristocracy. She had waited twelve years for her man while he kicked up his heels in India, nonetheless, and had produced his heir and spare as required, despite his conquests off the battlefield.

A woman, even a duchess, or, say, a baroness, did the best she could.

The professor took her hand, which he would not have done had Sebastian and Milly been underfoot rather than safely tucked away in Surrey. "I can send Wellington a message by means other than post."

"And tell him what? An old flirt from his days in India wants an accounting?"

"Tell him you're worried. Tell him you're tired of all the games and stratagems, the war is over, and you'd like some answers."

The hour was not late, and yet Freddy felt fatigue washing through her, resonating with the professor's words.

"I *am* tired. Sick and tired. I can only imagine what Sebastian must be feeling. Milly will have her hands full."

Freddy suffered a soft kiss to her knuckles.

"You do not want to know what Wellington's

answers might be. This is your tender heart at work.
Wellington is a gentleman. He's had several years to
deal with Sebastian, if that were his intent. Ney was
permitted a civilian life, and Sebastian was by no
means a field marshal. You have no reason to assume
the worst."

All very true, and no comfort whatsoever.

"There's to be yet another duel," Freddy said, getting to her feet. She crossed the room rather than see
the pity in the professor's eyes. "MacHugh, that great,
strapping Scotsman with the nasty mouth."

The professor rose as well, but let Freddy be the
one to blow out the candles, one by one.

"Michael says MacHugh is not noted for his
swordsmanship or his ability with a pistol, my dear,
and his mouth is nasty, but as Scotsmen go, he's reasonable enough."

"Bank the fire, if you please." MacHugh was not
reasonable. He was cold-blooded, which was the worst
sort of temperament for a man with a mortal grievance.

"The servants will tend to the fire, and I will escort
you above stairs. If you cannot cease fretting, then
send Michael down to Surrey on reconnaissance. He's
scaring the maids with his dark looks and muttered
Gaelic. He too worries that Sebastian will come to
harm in his wife's arms."

Freddy took herself into the chilly corridor and let
her escort trail behind rather than wait for him to hold
the door for her.

"Sending Michael down to St. Clair Manor would
be an excellent notion, if I were exclusively concerned
for Sebastian. You men…"

Except that wasn't fair. The entire time Sebastian had been at war in France, the professor had been in England with Freddy, waiting and hoping while pretending to do neither.

The professor took her hand in his—he'd always had warm hands—and wrapped her fingers around his elbow. "I most humbly beg my lady's pardon if my surmises are in error."

Wretch, though his teasing was more welcome than his patronizing.

They gained the first landing as Freddy admitted to herself she was truly weary, and not merely tired of worrying for her nephew. "In the morning, I will dictate a note to Milly, and you and Michael will deliver it for me."

"Isn't sending both of us a bit obvious?"

"Sending either one of you would be obvious," Freddy said as they neared her sitting-room door. "Sending you both suggests I want you and Michael out of my hair for a day, which is nothing but the simple truth."

"Ah. Of course."

In those few syllables, Freddy heard a hint of male uncertainty and felt an unbecoming gratification that she could still outthink her professor on the occasional detail. "For tonight, however, I would love to hear some poetry before I retire, assuming you're not too fatigued?"

He opened her sitting-room door, the warmth of the room greeting Freddy before she'd taken two steps.

"My dear, I am never too tired to read poetry to you."

He was reading to her from Dante's *Divine Comedy*, the language beautiful for all Freddy didn't bother to translate half of it, when it occurred to her that the professor was waiting for Sebastian's situation to resolve itself before he proposed again.

Sitting beside the man who'd endured wars with her, Freddy closed her eyes and worried.

❦

Milly had never appreciated how a marriage—any marriage—was the sum of myriad decisions of myriad sizes, one after the other, day after day, night after night.

And each decision could either strengthen the marital bond or weaken it.

"You don't expect me to sleep alone, do you?"

Sebastian clearly had anticipated exactly that. He jerked the belt of his dressing gown closed and kept his hands around the ends of the belt, as if he'd draw out the moment while he formed a reply.

Milly rose off the sofa flanking the fireplace in his bedroom. "Sebastian St. Clair, I am your wife, not some servant to be summoned when your conjugal urges come upon you."

She spoke as if she were annoyed, when what Milly felt was fear. Sebastian looked so wary, so burdened by her presence in his bedroom after dark.

"You could summon me," he suggested, and the daft man was serious.

"I would summon you every night, and then I would beg you to stay with me, Sebastian. We are *married*."

He gave the belt a final, solid jerk. "I take it Alcorn and his lady passed each night snuggled in each other's arms, and so you think even among those whose domiciles permit separate chambers—"

Milly advanced on him, unwilling to hear any more meanness from a mouth she'd kissed only hours earlier. "Alcorn and Frieda have separate rooms. I do not aspire to emulate their situation in any regard; moreover, they have no requirement for an heir."

"Do you think frequent copulation requires that we share a bed? I can assure you, marital relations can be undertaken in a variety of locations and at various times of day, as our recent trip to the mill proves, Baroness."

In his voice, Milly heard a hint of the imperious French colonel, and something…something nearing exasperation. She matched it with an exasperation of her own.

"I want to sleep with my husband, Sebastian. If you find my company objectionable, you should not have married me."

He said something under his breath, in French.

Which was the outside of too much. Milly took the last two steps so she could jab a finger at his chest. "Speak English. If we're to have our first argument, we'll at least have it in the same language."

He trapped her fingers in his, his grip warm. "I am sorry. I had not realized I spoke French." He kissed her knuckles with his eyes closed, the way a Papist would kiss a rosary or sacred relic. "I do not want to argue with you, Milly."

"You do not want to sleep with me. Why?"

He stroked his fingers over her knuckles. "I married a stubborn woman."

"Determined," Milly said. Also worried, for him.

"Give me a reason to abandon you each night, and if it's a sound reason, I'll accommodate it. My parents never spent a night apart once they married, and I would hear them as I fell asleep, talking over the day's events or reading to each other. Their voices would grow quieter and quieter as my fire burned down."

She'd forgotten this. Forgotten thousands of nights, each one the same, each one a piece of the pleasant, unremarkable puzzle that was her life before she'd been orphaned.

"You have so many good memories." Sebastian tugged her by the wrist back to the sofa and took a seat beside her. "Did they become bad memories when your parents died? Did those memories torment you by illuminating the magnitude of your loss?"

She curled up against him, and he obligingly wrapped an arm around her.

"I never thought of it like that. Your English boy-hood soured on you that way, didn't it?" Because he'd traded a happy childhood, not for the grudging charity of relations, but for a war in which he had no allies.

He was quiet for a long time, while the fire settled on the andirons and Milly kept questions behind her teeth.

"I have nightmares, Milly. I thrash and mutter in my sleep. I wake up in a cold sweat, screaming obscenities in two languages. I cannot promise you would be safe, were I to waken in your embrace."

And worse than all of it—which was awful enough—Milly sensed he was ashamed of himself for allowing his dreams to be haunted.

She shifted, so she was straddling his lap. "I cannot abide this, Sebastian."

"I am sorry. I should have told you before we married, I know, but one doesn't—"

Milly cradled his jaw with both hands, so he could not elude her kiss. "I cannot abide that you must suffer this way. Is it the same dream each night?"

Her kiss or her question seemed to foil his flight of self-castigation. "Often it's the same, or it's variations on the same theme."

"You will tell me, please."

"So we can share my nightmares?"

Milly brushed his hair back from his temple, where he'd turn gray and distinguished long before she would consider abandoning him to his nightmares. "So I can understand."

He lifted her off of him, carefully, and set her on one end of the settee. Before Milly could lodge her protest, Sebastian lay down on his side, his head pillowed on her thigh. He crossed his arms over his chest, as if settling in for a nap.

"This is cozy," Milly said, stroking his shoulder.

"You will recall I tried to spare you this recitation, Baroness."

She fiddled with the silky dark hair at his nape. "You will recall I am your wife."

His smile was faint, fleeting, and sad.

"At the same time it became clear to me that the English advance across Spain would not stop, and that France's cause was doomed, a duke came into my keeping. An English duke, and a man of more mental fortitude than you will find in six lifetimes did you spend them scouring the entire earth."

He fell silent for a time, staring at the fire while Milly traced the shape of his ear.

"My duke was the reason I could keep Anduvoir cowed, the reason the guards never rebelled, the reason the other prisoners had time to heal in body and spirit. Before I could set him free, it became the duke who tortured me, and not the other way around… The pain that man could endure would have felled all the rest of Wellington's staff put together, and for a time, it felled me."

"Mercia?"

"Mercia. Christian Donatus Severn. On his silence rested the safety and well-being of every Englishman, Frenchman, dog, and cat at the Château. I could not turn my back without my own guards, my own commanding officer, attempting to break him, and they all failed. Thank God, they failed, for any success on their part would have seen the end of my role as the authority over captured English officers."

"Mercia acknowledges you." Though it made little sense, given what Sebastian was disclosing.

"He had enemies more diabolical than a mere provincial French army colonel with a foul temper and a sharp knife, and after a time, I think Mercia understood that my intent was not to destroy him."

"Others sought to destroy him?"

"They were not successful."

The fire threw out a decent amount of heat, and yet Milly was chilled. As shadows danced and flickered across Sebastian's features, she tried to grasp the delicacy of his position: the English had hated and feared him, the French had resented him and exploited him, and likely had not trusted him either. In every direction, someone had been invested in Sebastian's failure and his disgrace.

Despite all, he'd appointed himself both tormentor and guardian of his English countrymen and somehow kept both his skin and his sanity intact.

"You knew the French cause was lost, but you did not abandon your post, because you had to protect this duke."

"I had to protect my people, and that included Mercia and the other prisoners. What Anduvoir would have done to them defies your worst imaginings—rations grew short, tempers shorter. The prisoners were half-starved, and the soldiers treated not much better. What I did to Mercia in those months does not bear contemplation, though I often think of little else. I decorated him with scars, Milly, the way others would draw a pattern on a canvas, to the point that the knife became his comfort. And then I took that away from him, too."

He fell silent, which was fortunate, because Milly had been ready to cover his mouth with her hand. A knife could not be a comfort, and yet, Sebastian somehow understood it as such, and the silent duke had as well. Mercia had not been Sebastian's only prisoner, but Milly gathered His Grace had become the focus of Sebastian's memories.

She linked her fingers with her husband's. "I recall the day I first understood my place in Alcorn's household. The tweenie was ill."

Sebastian shifted, nuzzling Milly's thigh. He did not turn loose of her hand.

"The weather was beastly, miserably cold, and sopping wet," she went on. "We'd gone shopping, and when the maid could carry no more packages for Frieda, I was expected to carry them."

And somehow, she was to carry them without anything getting wet, except, of course, Milly, her hems, her last good bonnet, her boots, everything.

"I did not at first understand why it was necessary for Frieda to make all those purchases on that particular day. Not until I dropped something—a parcel of pins, something small—and was stoutly cuffed for my clumsiness. She never struck me when Alcorn was about, but she clouted me soundly that day."

Sebastian rubbed his fingers over her knuckles, else Milly would have given up the recitation. Compared to the hell Sebastian had endured, Frieda and Alcorn were trivial aggravations.

"I can't believe your cousin stopped there."

"She did not. When we returned home, she passed me her boots and said that in the tweenie's absence, I would have to clean them. She spoke an apology, while rendering my status that of unpaid boot boy." The stench of horse droppings on a wet, miserable day tried to penetrate the warmth of the sitting room. "We'd come in from the mews, and Frieda had not been careful where she stepped."

Or she had been careful, cruelly careful.

Sebastian untangled their fingers, sat up, and produced a handkerchief. "Marriage to me is making you lachrymose. I forbid these tears, Wife." He slipped an arm around her shoulders.

"I do not understand you," Milly said, blotting her eyes and taking comfort from the scent of his linen. "How can you not *hate*, Sebastian? How can you not hate Mercia? Hate the French, Wellington, your parents, everybody, and everything? I hated my cousins.

I hated them bitterly. Frieda did not have to treat me thus, and Alcorn could have put a stop to it."

This was her wedding day, and these were not memories she wanted touching any part of her wedding day.

"Hate serves a purpose," Sebastian said—or recited. "Hate can lend us strength, but the loan always come due eventually, and the interest is usurious. I do hate Anduvoir, though. I hate him like I'd hate a rabid dog whose illness only makes him harder to kill. He delighted in destroying the recruits, in finding excuses to flog the unwary. The entire garrison dreaded his inspections, myself and the whores included. I believe he would have cheerfully staked me out for the English to find, but I was able to negotiate ransoms for some of the British officers—contrary to all regulations—and even Henri understood the necessity for coin."

"Coin…for him? What of the *République*? What of the bad rations, what of winter in the Pyrenees?"

Sebastian's silence was explanation enough. He might have forgiven his superior for being severe, ill-tempered, and violent, but not for stealing the windfall of an illegal ransom from his own men.

And that garrison had included women and children. Milly curled closer to her husband's side, craving the warmth of his body. "Don't stop hating Anduvoir, Sebastian."

A kiss brushed her brow. They remained thus for some time, until the fire burned down and the hour grew late.

"I don't still hate Frieda."

"Prisoners who escape can afford to be generous

regarding their incompetent captors. Mercia must be extending me the same clemency, because he alone remained silent under my tortures. Are you ready to come to bed?"

Milly bit back a comment about Mercia being generous toward a competent captor, but Mercia himself likely did not comprehend the debt he owed the ill-tempered French colonel with the sharp, clean, careful knife.

"I'm ready to come to bed."

He scooped her up against his chest, carried her to their bed, and made love to her, sweetly, slowly, and thoroughly, before Milly fell into an exhausted slumber, her arms around her husband.

When they rose in the morning, Sebastian reported that he'd slept soundly through the night—as had Milly.

❧

"You couldn't give me a single day to enjoy wedded bliss with my bride?" St. Clair gestured with the teapot, for he and his baroness had apparently been having a late breakfast on the back terrace when their guests had arrived.

A very late breakfast.

"No thank you." Michael extracted a silver flask from his waistcoat and arched an inquiring eye at his employer. One took only so many liberties when imposing on newlyweds if the husband could easily kill an intruder, and the wife…could slay him with a look.

Some days, Michael hated each and every detail of his tiresome, convoluted existence.

"Feel free." His lordship, while declining the proffered

flask, appeared inebriated on the sight of his wife strolling among the roses with Professor Baumgartner.

"Lady Freddy is having an at-home today." Michael might have used the same lugubrious tone to explain that Napoleon was missing from Elba, along with a quantity of soldiers, ships, and ammunition. The last thing needed at this point was a gaggle of hens clucking and pecking about the London premises.

Though Michael well knew that normality was the surest form of camouflage.

"And you could not simply remain in your garret, writing letters home or polishing your single pair of decent boots?"

The question did not merit an answer. Across the garden, Baumgartner flashed one of his rare smiles, appearing to share in St. Clair's besottedness with the baroness amid the sunshine and flowers.

"Have you ever wondered what it would be like to have peace?" Michael asked. "True peace, not this war by stealth and indirection you've endured since coming home."

Which Michael had endured as well.

St. Clair stopped ogling his wife long enough to examine his guest. "You look tired, Michael."

Marriage had done nothing to dull St. Clair's perceptiveness, though it had apparently robbed him of his wits.

"You have a duel to the death scheduled for Tuesday next, my lord. I watch your pretty baroness inspecting your gardens, and I want to get blind drunk—or put period to your existence myself."

His lordship sat back, looking relaxed, handsome,

and not exactly well rested, but—confound the bastard—pleasantly exhausted.

"MacHugh won't kill me," St. Clair said gently. "He wants to teach me a lesson is all, and I am happy to be his pupil. I owe him that much reparation."

The flask came out again, and this time Michael drained it. "Does she know?"

The baron took a sip of his tea then peered at it as if somebody had forgotten to add sugar, say, somebody too busy staring at his new wife. "Have a scone, Michael. You and Milly both prefer them with raisins."

"Fuck the scones. You haven't told her. The woman has married a dead man, and you did not think to warn her."

St. Clair apparently decided to play a round of Gracious English Lord, buttering a scone, putting it on a little blue, gold, and white Sèvres plate, and passing it across the table to Michael.

"Rather than make threats upon the chastity of the breakfast pastry—or on my life—why don't you ask me what Freddy sent you here to find out? She dispatched you both, not because she's having an at-home—the professor gathers all manner of news at Aunt Freddy's at-homes—but because she wanted to ensure you could separate me from my wife for the duration of one conversation, at least."

"Or perhaps, separate your wife from you."

Conflicting loyalties were something St. Clair had appeared to handle easily, while Michael... He took a bite of a wonderful, flaky scone and tried not to choke on homesickness.

When he could speak again, Michael addressed the twelve raisins yet visible on and in his scone. "I may have seen Anduvoir."

St. Clair poured a cup of tea, added cream and sugar, and passed it across. "One either sees a fellow or one doesn't, my friend."

Michael tore off another bite of scone and paused to count the raisins remaining. "Have you ever, in any language, referred to me as your friend before?" And why in bloody hell must he do so now?

"Marriage agrees with me." Marriage also put a smile on St. Clair's face, the like of which Michael had not seen previously. The smile was not ironic, mocking, bemused, resigned, or any of the other sophisticated expressions St. Clair put on and off like so many masks. This smile was…sweet.

"Marriage to that woman would agree with any man who possessed a modicum of sense," Michael said. "Though if MacHugh doesn't kill you, and Miss Dan—your wife—learns of the duel, she likely will."

"Women do not understand gentlemanly honor."

Yes, they did. They understood it for the asinine display it generally was. If Michael could apologize to his family for one thing, it would be for the gentlemanly honor that had kept him from home for nearly ten years.

"If I did see Anduvoir, he's lost weight, shaved his beard, and tried to lighten what remains of his hair."

"Easy enough to do, and he was rather better fed than the rest of us." Which, given the state of things when Toulouse finally fell, was reason enough to hate the man.

"He's grown bold, if it was he. Both he and the baroness's cousin have taken to lurking at the Jugged Hare by the hour. The patrons have confirmed that Upton's tab is being paid by a Frenchman."

Across the gardens, the baroness had paused by a bed of lavender. She plucked a sprig and passed it to the professor, who tucked it into his lapel.

"Do you suppose, Michael, you might have passed news of this sighting to me *before* I put Milly at risk by taking her to wife? Or do you forget what Anduvoir is capable of where anybody small or helpless is concerned?"

Michael had heard that same offhand, bored tone in the interrogation room after one of Anduvoir's visits. St. Clair's indifferent drawl hid an arctic fury.

"You're protective of her? Married one day, and you're protective of the lady already? I am encouraged, St. Clair. Perhaps under her good influences, you will one day soon become protective of yourself."

Though years at the Château, fretting over the fate of the chickens and traitors in his care hadn't done much to hone St. Clair's instincts for self-preservation.

"And you are protective of me," St. Clair said, "but you waited days at least, perhaps longer, to warn me of Anduvoir's presence on my very doorstep. One wonders why."

One would have an answer—St. Clair was a bloody genius at inspiring answers—and yet Michael hesitated.

"I wanted you to have one day with her, one day to sample what life could be if matters ever came right. Your wedding day at least should not have been darkened with Anduvoir's shadow." Baumgartner laughed at something the baroness said, the sound hearty and startling. "I'd forgotten Baum could laugh. The Germans usually have a wonderful laugh, and they aren't afraid to direct it at themselves."

"Like the Scots." St. Clair set about buttering another scone, Michael having apparently demolished his first one. "You know, I have lost the habit of thinking in French. I still turn to it for profanity, particularly if a lady is present, but my imagination now speaks English."

When Michael said nothing, St. Clair held out the buttered scone, this time not bothering with a plate.

"Michael, you are lying to me about your reasons for withholding this information regarding Anduvoir. You wanted me to have a proper wedding day, but your sentiment has put an innocent woman at risk, and for that, you of all men need a better reason than simple tenderheartedness."

"No more for me," Michael said. "Too many raisins. I very much wanted you to have a proper wedding day, or wedding night. I thought *she* was owed that much, at least." May God help the woman.

St. Clair took a bite of the scone. "We both enjoyed our wedding day, for which I do thank you. Should you be serving me your notice, Michael? Heading North to see all those sisters and clansmen and gillies who worried so for your continued good health? At the least, some summer leave is in order, don't you think?"

Rather than start smashing porcelain, Michael took his flask out again and recalled too late the thing was empty. "Are you sending me away for safekeeping, or because you no longer trust me?"

"Why did you keep Anduvoir's presence to yourself? I can understand you were not sure it was he and you did not want to believe it could be he, and yet my baroness can be used against me in a manner my aunt's companion could not."

"You have never once erred in your ability to identify and deal with an enemy, St. Clair, but you have far less experience with allies. I'll not go North until the duel with MacHugh is resolved, if even then."

The baroness, looking fetching in pale green edged with violet, was leading Baumgartner back toward the terrace. Michael pretended to watch that cheery tableau while the baron scrutinized him.

"If you in any way bring harm to my wife, Michael, I will kill you without a thought. This is a solemn promise. You may pass that along to whoever may find it of interest, for I'd hope they are protective of you as well."

Michael made no reply, for to protest would be to lie to a man who'd saved his life more than once, and to acknowledge the comment would admit that Michael's loyalty did not lie exclusively with his employer.

Fourteen

"YOU DID NOT APPEAR IN CHARITY WITH MR. BRODIE."

Sebastian considered prevaricating. Milly was not an experienced rider, and managing her horse meant she could not quite as easily manage her husband.

"I am not in charity with my aunt," he replied. "She sent not one spy, but two, the very day after you and I spoke our vows. Did she think we'd not manage our own wedding night?"

Milly fiddled with her mare's mane. He'd put her up on Folly, a lovely little chestnut Arabian whose smooth gaits made up for a lamentable tendency to flirt with even mature geldings.

"Your aunt is in the habit of worrying about you, Sebastian. She'll not stop merely because a wife has stumbled into your path."

"No, she must add you to her list of people she worries about. May I assume the professor interrogated you?"

He bent forward to duck under a low-hanging branch. Because the mare and the woman were both smaller than their male counterparts, Milly did not have to duck.

"The professor was charming. He got his answers without asking any difficult questions. Did you know he once proposed to your aunt?"

Answers to which questions? "I did not. How did you pry that out of him?"

The mare made a feint at nipping Fable's shoulder. "Bad girl," Milly chided. "I asked him. I asked if, now that I have taken over the job of lady-most-concerned-with-your-welfare, would Lady Freddy allow somebody to acquire the same post with regard to her?"

Fable, poor lad, was not oblivious to the mare's overtures, but danced off a few paces, looking more confused than annoyed.

Sebastian petted his gelding. "And his reply?"

"He regarded himself as already assigned to that post, happily so, but awaited the lady's realization of it. They love you, Sebastian, and I think you hardly realize it."

The horses settled, while Sebastian's thoughts did not.

"I know they love me. Aunt's steadfastness was sometimes all that sustained me when I was in France. She found ways to get letters through, news of home, the occasional small frippery or memento. My debt to her is substantial."

For the first time, riding along with his wife at his side, Sebastian also admitted—to himself—that his debt to Lady Freddy was infernally tiresome.

Have you ever wondered what it would be like to have peace?

"She owes you too," Milly said, drawing back on the reins when Folly would have made another try for Fable's attention. "Your aunt is one of those ladies for whom an embroidery hoop is a type of shackle. She must be managing things, involved in larger affairs, and challenged by matters beyond petty gossip and fashion. If she were a vicar's wife, she'd be running the parish. If she were a man, she would have bought her colors."

"This puts her in my debt?"

"Your exile in France allowed her to manage the barony, gave her a challenge at a time in life when becoming a widow might have made her desperate and stupid. Lady Freddy likely understands this and feels indebted to you accordingly. Another nephew would have seen his affairs in the hands of anybody else rather than let an aging female make the important decisions."

His affairs had been in the hands of trustees when he'd come of age in France, but Freddy had guided those trustees, as best Sebastian could ascertain.

"I have never once, not in my mind, not in any language, applied the word *exile* to the time I spent in my mother's homeland."

"I hardly see why not. If you'd been a duke's son, you can bet somebody would have negotiated for your return. Frenchmen were stranded here, too, and the French are surpassingly practical."

Fable came to a halt, though Sebastian did not ask it of him.

"You're saying my aunt *stranded* me in France?" Once the thought intruded on his peace, the idea sat in his mind with the cold, leaden immobility of an ugly possibility.

"Of course not. I'm saying your aunt thrived on the challenges created by your absence, and likely prayed for your safety every night. A woman's reach will always have limits, compared to a man's. Is he supposed to be eating those?"

Fable had snatched a mouthful of leaves from some shrub. Sebastian could not think of the English name for it, though it was not noxious.

"No, he is not. The mare's company has overset him. Come along, you." He nudged the beast with his calf. "What questions did you answer for the professor?"

A casual observer might have concluded Milly was more cargo than equestrienne. She was inexperienced on horseback, true, but she had the knack of leaving the horse in peace as long as it behaved. One day, she would be an excellent rider, if she so chose, the kind of rider a horse trusted and took care of as it might a member of its own herd.

"I assured the professor I was happy with my choice of husband, assured him I anticipated many happy years as your baroness. I assured him your treatment of me had been all that I might have wished for as a new bride."

He'd asked her for a single rose, and she'd flung an entire bouquet at him. "You might have simply told him you were content."

"I am by no means content. Contentment is for children, the elderly, and those who've earned it. When we have a nursery full of happy, healthy children, and they are each excelling at their letters, then I can be content. When I can curl up in the library of a chilly afternoon with a novel by Mrs. Radcliffe, then I will be content. When you no longer suspect everybody and everything of nefarious motives, then I will be content."

And each of her roses came with thorns.

"Often, people have nefarious motives. I have them too." And now he'd have to consider that Freddy had left him in France for purposes he could not fathom, a thorny undertaking indeed.

"You never did tell me why you were unhappy with Mr. Brodie," Milly observed.

The mare resumed her doomed efforts at flirtation, though Fable was apparently more interested now in spying another bush of forbidden fodder. "What makes you think I was unhappy with him?"

"You were drinking tea, and your aunt told me you cannot abide the stuff. Then too, Mr. Brodie looked like a guilty schoolboy made to copy Bible verses and go without his pudding."

Or like a sergeant assigned drill duty when he'd been promised leave.

"I like tea. I particularly like a hearty black, with a touch of gunpowder in the blend. Occasionally, I'll flavor my tea with bergamot, which I learned from an Italian who passed through the Château on the way to some Papist cathedral in the North of Spain."

They'd come to the oak avenue that led to the mill where, in Sebastian's mind, their marriage had begun.

"You like tea, but you deny yourself the pleasure of it," Milly concluded. "This makes no sense. Tea is not a vice nor, for an English peer, an extravagance."

"Forgoing tea is a habit," Sebastian said slowly, "a habit of such long-standing, it barely requires effort to maintain. Tea is English. Coffee is French, and my life depended on my becoming French. I was careful to disdain tea."

Milly drew her mare up and peered down the row of oaks. The vista was beautiful, in a bucolic, English way that made Sebastian's chest ache.

"Your life depended on your being perceived as French. My hope would be that instead of becoming English or French, your efforts are now bent in the direction of becoming Sebastian, Baron St. Clair, and my husband."

"Shall we visit the mill?" He wanted to, wanted to make sure it was still there, still available for a private interlude, if his wife were so inclined.

"No. I have wonderful memories of that mill, but I'd like to see another place you frequented as a boy, and I want to make wonderful memories there, too."

"Madam, this estate covers thousands of acres, and the smile I see on your face can only be described as naughty. I am but one man, and no longer blessed with the stamina of youth. I suggest you moderate your ambitions."

Her smile was also enchanting. Enchantingly naughty. Too naughty for Sebastian to think of how few places they might make memories before Tuesday next.

The mare used her tail to whisk a fly off her quarters, which inspired Fable into a sizable dodge sideways.

"And I suggest you stop ridiculing my ambitions and choose us another destination," Milly said. "What lies off in that direction?" She'd pointed with her whip toward a sheep-dotted rise to the east of the park.

"Our very own ruins lie that way. Some say it was a watchtower for spotting Romans, Vikings, and other nuisances, others say it was some sort of Druid mound converted to a cow byre. Part of it looks like a circle the gods knocked askew."

"You played there as a child?"

"Endlessly." Though he'd forgotten that. Forgotten that he'd imagine centurions far from home—brave, brawny, dark-bearded fellows longing for their airy piazzas and sunny Mediterranean shores.

"Then that's our next destination, but, Sebastian?"

"My dear?" He'd almost called her "my love." He waited for her reply while they turned their horses toward the rise, away from the mill.

"I still do not entirely trust Michael Brodie, though I like him."

Sebastian reminded himself that his baroness had appropriated a place in his bed as if he owed her his very nightmares. Fainthearted, Milly St. Clair was not, and he loved her for it.

"I've known Michael for years, and for many of those years, I would have said he was my only friend." But was he an ally? Had he ever been?

"He's a good fellow, but sometimes good fellows cannot entirely choose the paths they take."

"Delicately put." Sometimes good fellows could not even choose what countries they dwelled in or fought for. "Why don't you trust him, Milly?"

"I'm not sure. He warned me that any woman who mattered to you could become a liability to you, like an Achilles' heel."

Michael, Michael, Michael…though in truth, Sebastian approved of his initiative. "He was being honest, Milly. You know I've fought duels. Not all my enemies are as honorable as the English officers I've met over pistols."

Her mare, perhaps thinking they were turning for

home, picked up the pace of her walk. "I'll have no more of that pistols-at-dawn nonsense, Sebastian. You've a succession to see to, and a wife who can barely read a menu. Freddy isn't getting any younger, and in any case, the war is over."

He assayed a husbandly smile. "No pistols. I do understand." Which left swords, bare fists, knives, whips...

"Do not humor me, Sebastian." Her tone was a trifle sharp. "I woke up today and found I am a baroness. This was not in my plans, and I'd be cross to find it so, except I also woke up next to you."

She'd woken up mostly under him. He'd woken up mostly inside her. All three times.

"No pistols, Milly. You have my word, and don't be concerned about Michael. He and I get along well, in part because his mother was Irish and his father Scottish. Like me, Michael is a mongrel."

"Which accounts for why he has a brogue sometimes and a burr at others."

She fell silent, though Michael would be appalled to realize she'd heard his slips—and heard them, she had. Milly did not read easily, but she listened prodigiously well.

"Do you notice anything else about Michael that makes you uneasy?"

She fiddled with her reins, she petted her horse, she looked all about, as if trying to recall how they'd arrived to their present location.

"Yes." In one syllable, she conveyed her reluctance to find fault with her husband's fellow mongrel. "If he'd desert the English cause when he was a duly commissioned officer, and the war was mostly going in England's favor, what's to stop him from deserting your cause eventually too?"

If he hasn't already. "Michael will be leaving soon to visit family in the North, if that's any comfort to you. Shall we let the horses stretch their legs a bit?"

And if Michael did not care to visit family, then Sebastian was left in a quandary: Was he better off knowing exactly where Michael was, and when he came and went, or would he benefit from having Michael out from under his roof, up to who knew what, and on behalf of who knew which government—or clan?

Milly's mare cantered off, and Sebastian followed, admiring his wife's seat and the fearless way she allowed her mare to go thundering over the countryside.

⤫

The professor had explained to Milly in one of their penmanship sessions that English was a large language, a language that did not discard the old in favor of the new, but instead added to its arsenal of vocabulary. The Romans had come and gone, and much of their language had been added to that arsenal, similarly with the Anglo-Saxons and Jutes, the Vikings and the Normans. As a consequence, most any thought requiring expression in English words could take a variety of forms.

A husband could also be a spouse or a marital partner. A dog could, depending on one's regard, be a canine, a hound, a companion animal, or a mongrel.

And of all the words available, in English, in any language, the only description Milly could find appropriate to her domestic situation was "fallen in love."

She had fallen in love with her husband. He had not intended this result—theirs was a pragmatic union born of his honor and her lack of alternatives—but he was the cause of it.

After making love at the ruins, they'd fallen asleep the previous night entwined in each other's arms, talking, kissing, petting, and talking some more.

Sebastian had been physically sick after the first time he'd taken a knife to Mercia, and the second.

He'd been unable to attend his grandmother's funeral, because his commanding officer, the dread Anduvoir, had been threatening to make an inspection of the Château.

He'd considered emigrating to America rather than assuming his baronial responsibilities, but concern for Freddy had stopped him.

With each confession, Milly became more Sebastian's wife and more in awe of the man she'd married. Also more determined to see that he somehow laid claim to the happiness he was due.

"That field there"—Milly gestured with her whip—"that's where you should try some lavender. It's well drained, gets plenty of light, and lies on the southern exposure of the hillside."

Fable sauntered along, apparently oblivious to whips, mares, and other aggravations.

"That area has always been pasture," Sebastian said. "I suspect the ground is rocky."

"All of England is rocky," Milly retorted, "except for the parts that are boggy, which this is not. Get the sheep off it after harvest, marl it thoroughly, then plow up a portion this spring and see how your plants do."

He did not dismiss her suggestions out of hand, as most other men would have. He petted his white horse—who sported a streak of green slobber on its shoulder, courtesy of Folly's dubious affections—and glanced back toward the manor house.

"If we put lavender in here, the prevailing breeze would blow the scent back that direction, and we could see the entire crop from the family wing."

Milly remained silent, because Sebastian's commanding-officer mind grasped such details with a speed and thoroughness Milly could only marvel at.

"We'd need a drying shed," he said as their horses wandered down the lane bordering the pasture. "A wooden structure, because stone attracts cold and damp."

His command post in France had been a pile of stones.

"A small wooden structure," Milly said. "You can add on as the size of the crop increases."

"We have time to build something before next summer."

The lane widened, it being one of the primary routes into the village. Milly listened to her husband think out loud, loving the sound of his voice along with the characteristic rigor of his plans.

He made love with the same focus, the same intensity of purpose.

"You sound very English, you know." She'd meant it as a casual observation, maybe even a compliment, but Sebastian drew rein in the middle of the lane.

"When haven't I sounded English?"

His intensity was focused on her now, so Milly searched her memory for details. "Do you recall when you came upon me in the music room, and the roses were in the wrong vase?"

From his expression, he knew exactly which encounter she referred to.

"You made an English flower arrangement," she went on. "Symmetric, and every stem just so, but you sounded...Continental."

"I sounded French." He did not permit himself an emotional reaction to her observation, which Milly took for a reaction in itself. "When else?"

She wanted to tell him it didn't matter, but to him, it did. It always would.

"When we walked in the park and you asked me about Alcorn." He'd been not only French then, he'd been the commanding officer, in charge of the garrison.

Sebastian sat taller in the saddle, as if he wanted to see farther. "And what about when we went to Chelsea?"

"English," Milly said. "You kiss and flirt in English, sir."

His smile...oh, she lived to see such a smile on his face. Happy, rascally, smug, and very male. "How could you know such a thing?"

"I am an English baroness, lest you forget, married to a peer of the realm and soon to be mother of the next Baron St. Clair. I know an English kiss when my husband gifts me with one."

Or dozens. Milly touched her heel to the mare's side rather than belabor such a point in the very lane.

"Soon to be mother of the next Baron St. Clair? We've been married less than a week, madam. Do you know something else you ought to be telling your English husband?"

"I know we indulge in marital relations with a frequency that will yield inevitable results, given that we both enjoy great good health. Will you plant the lavender?"

They debated whether they could propagate enough plants from cuttings in what remained of the growing season, and whether those cuttings could be safely wintered over in the experimental farm's small propagation house. All the while, Milly tried not to watch her husband's mouth, his hands on the reins, or the muscles of his thighs as he rode along.

"We're not the only ones enjoying a pretty day," Milly said as another couple approached on horseback. The gentleman rode a big sleek chestnut, and the lady was on a pretty gray. Two half-grown mastiffs gamboled along beside the horses.

Beside Milly, Sebastian's demeanor shifted, though she could not have said how. Fable sensed the change as well, and left off making halfhearted swipes at the foliage along the lane.

"Milly, I cannot vouch for—"

"St. Clair." The Duke of Mercia touched his hat brim. "Baroness. Good day."

He'd brought his horse to the halt, and so had the lady. A beat of silence went by—this was the man who crafted silences sturdier than a granite garrison—before Milly realized the pause in conversation was harmless, even polite.

"Sebastian, I believe His Grace is waiting on introductions."

Another infinitesimal increment of quiet, while Milly's words penetrated the tension her husband gave off.

"I beg your pardon, Your Grace. Your Graces." He tended to the civilities, and Milly was pleased to note he did so sounding quite English.

"We're visiting a property Mercia inherited from a cousin," the duchess explained. She was a small blond lady who watched her duke the way Milly probably watched Sebastian. "We're having the dower house demolished, and I wanted to see that."

Within minutes, the men were riding ahead, and the dogs had disappeared into the hedges, leaving Milly to make small talk with…a duchess.

"You wanted to watch a building being torn down, Your Grace?"

Perhaps duchesses were given to eccentricity. One heard about inbreeding in the aristocracy.

"I want Mercia to blow it up. I was married to the property's previous owner before His Grace made me his duchess, and those were not happy years."

Did everybody arrive to adulthood incarcerated by memories of misery?

"Then you should schedule the demolition for nighttime, Your Grace. The explosion will be like fireworks, and the ground will be more damp, so there's less chance of any fire spreading."

"Splendid notion!" Their horses ambled along the pretty country lane for some yards before the duchess spoke again. "I wanted to hate your husband, you know. Wanted to arrange a slow, painful, disfiguring death for him. Several deaths."

This duchess was not eccentric, but she was apparently quite fierce. "You have revised your opinion of St. Clair?"

"I'm considering it. Mercia seems to respect him, which I cannot fathom, but one doesn't rush some discussions. I know whatever the tally between the two of them, Mercia regards the balance as even. There was a duel…there was supposed to be a duel, but they came to an understanding instead."

Her Grace fell silent, a habit she'd perhaps learned from her handsome spouse, or from those difficult years.

"I know Sebastian has dueled, but he's promised me he's done with that. He has no heir, you see, and I have much to learn if I'm to be a proper baroness to him."

Ahead of them, Sebastian was pointing at the well-drained, south-facing field, and the duke appeared to be offering suggestions.

"I think you are already a proper baroness to him," Her Grace observed. "You genuinely care for him, don't you?" The duchess was puzzled to find it so. Her expression didn't suggest it so much as her tone of voice.

"I am smitten, Your Grace. Sebastian has endured much, had no allies through any of it, and still grapples with the results of decisions he had no hand in. He needs no defending, but he deserves loving."

Her Grace adjusted her whip. "He tortured my husband, among others. If you could see—"

Mercia had come to find the knife a comfort. Milly still did not fathom what Sebastian had meant, and she might never.

"I *can* see. I can see that Sebastian's choices haunt him, and I can see that every man he held captive is now strutting around on English soil, nursing a grudge with more care than you likely shower on His Grace's heir."

Somewhere, it was likely written in elegant, flowing, thoroughly indecipherable prose that one didn't interrupt a duchess. Her Grace apparently hadn't yet read that tract, because she offered Milly a smile, a conspiratorial, purely friendly smile, and she stopped fussing her whip.

"You are quite ferocious, Baroness, and you sound like my husband. I cannot like the man you're married to—I cannot understand him—but I like you, and I'm glad he's married. For everybody's sake, at some point the past must be allowed to become the past."

"Thank you, Your Grace. I begin to wonder if anybody knows Sebastian, or if all England is content to hate the person they think he is."

"You don't hate him, and he's given up dueling for you, so he must hold you in considerable regard."

Excellent points. "He also married me when he did not have to. Is your mare of Arabian extraction, Your Grace? She has a beautiful eye."

They shared perhaps a quarter mile more of small talk before the duchess reminded her duke that they'd promised their daughter a visit at teatime. Their Graces made their farewells and turned down a shaded lane, the duke bellowing for the dogs, who came panting and barking to his side.

Sebastian sat on Fable, still as a garden statue. "Mercia named one of those enormous beasts Dimwit."

Milly could not divine the significance of this observation. "Apparently so. I didn't catch the other one's name."

Sebastian turned only his head, so his horse still faced down the lane traversed by Their Graces. "Was the duchess decent to you?"

"She was quite friendly." Also quite frank, and she hadn't invited Milly to call upon her. Then too, acknowledging an upstart baroness on a back road when one's husband asked for an introduction was no guarantee of safe conduct at the local assembly.

Sebastian resumed watching the duke and duchess until a bend in the road took them from his sight.

"Mercia offered me the loan of his propagation house. Said his mother was quite the rose gardener, and the building sits mostly empty. Her Grace—the current duchess—also enjoys gardening."

Still, he watched the empty lane.

"Sebastian?"

"My love?"

Gracious. "The next step in the dance is you send them over some rose cuttings from our gardens. The white ones with the extraordinary fragrance. Your gardener will know which ones."

"My mother brought those with her from France."

"All the better."

Now he gave his horse leave to move forward, turning Fable back the way they'd come.

"You called them *our* gardens. His Grace asked if you might call on his wife. Said she wasn't permitted any friendships in her first marriage, and hasn't developed the knack for finding them yet in her second."

The consternation in Sebastian's eyes made sense now.

"Am I to befriend a lonely duchess all on my own? I, who haven't even the knack of baronessing yet myself?"

"You are. I'm sure the lady has no use for me, though Mercia would probably tolerate me in small doses over a tot of brandy." They traversed the lane in silence for some time, while Milly contemplated plain Milly Danforth from Chelsea, former poor relation, lady's companion, and schoolroom failure, taking tea with a duchess.

A fierce duchess and a ferocious baroness. They'd get on famously.

"Something is different about Mercia's regard for me," Sebastian said as they crossed one of the numerous St. Clair sheep meadows.

"Perhaps marriage agrees with him. Her Grace is protective of him."

"Marriage agrees with me," Sebastian muttered. He glanced around, as if hoping one of the sheep might have said the words.

"One has wondered, St. Clair." He wasn't professing undying love, but as Her Grace had said, some conversations ought not to be rushed.

"Marriage to you agrees with me," he said, clearly this time. "I hadn't thought myself much of a bargain, as husbands go, but I seem to be rising to the challenge—aren't I?"

He tugged at his hat brim then glanced back in the direction they'd come. Back toward the duke who'd suggested their wives might call on each other.

"As husbands go, I would not describe you as any sort of bargain." Milly's words had the desired effect of recapturing Sebastian's attention. "As husbands go, you are an absolute treasure." And then, because his expression had gone bashful and dear, she found the courage to add, "I *adore* being your baroness."

The ruin came into sight, the one that offered all manner of privacy amid sun-warmed stone.

"Mercia no longer looks at me as if all he can see is the knife in my hand," Sebastian said. He glanced down at his black-gloved hands, which held reins, nothing more.

"Someday, I hope you can see yourself just as clearly, Husband, for I already do."

⤜⤏

"St. Clair is not as easy to hate as I'd like." Gillian, Duchess of Mercia, offered this observation as she and her spouse rounded a bend that would take them from St. Clair's sight.

"Your conclusions astound me, my dear. You said not one word to St. Clair beyond 'good day, my lord,'" Mercia observed. "Is it possible these dogs are still growing?"

"For another six months, at least." Though His Grace would have to do much better than that if he wanted to distract his wife. "Once the pleasantries were concluded, you neatly prevented me from asking St. Clair how he slept at night after the horrors he perpetrated on your person, or how he justified drawing breath, after all the miseries he inflicted on officers defending the interests of his native soil."

Christian Severn had learned much about silence, but one thing Gilly knew for a certainty: he would never use silence as a weapon against her or their children. And yet, he would choose his words, sometimes choose them slowly.

"I suggested to him that you and the baroness might strike up an acquaintance."

"Her, I liked, but why would you make such an overture, Christian? They are besotted. Where she goes, St. Clair is sure to follow."

His Grace stretched up in his irons, as if saddle weary, though they'd traveled less than thirty minutes from the stables.

"He won't be following his baroness if he's dead. St. Clair has been challenged again, and the fellow who called him out is lethal on a bad day, not some strutting boy prone to ranting when in his cups. They're using the same location where I met St. Clair, not even bothering to keep the arrangements discreet."

Not every husband would confide such a thing in a wife, much less in a duchess.

"You feel responsible for this." Christian's sense of responsibility was bred in the bone, unshakable, and—in Gilly's opinion—not entirely rational. "Explain this to me, lest I develop a headache trying to fathom the Stygian abyss that passes for male reasoning."

Ahead of them, the dogs caught the scent of something fascinating, for they both went dashing off into the undergrowth amid a great lot of flapping ears, sniffing, and woofing.

"I was the first to challenge him," His Grace reminded her. "Called him out at his very club, with witnesses all around."

Gilly's mare wanted to chase after the dogs, so Gilly had to check her rather firmly. "And then you stood down, the both of you."

Christian whistled for the dogs, a piercing shriek

that startled the horses and did not agree with Gilly either. Nor did it produce any dogs.

"The gentlemen of Polite Society do not know that St. Clair and I reached an accommodation, but until I challenged him, he was permitted to live quietly, resuming civilian life like the rest of us." After a moment of watching the undergrowth to no avail, His Grace added softly, "Wellington has forbidden me to interfere."

In terms of precedence, Mercia outranked Wellington, who for all his military successes was merely a *first* duke.

"Wellington is no longer your superior officer, Christian. If you wish to interfere, you'd be within your rights to ascertain why Wellington has taken a hand in matters. What can those dogs have found?"

"Running riot, no doubt. This time of year, the young of many species lurk in the hedgerows."

The mastiffs were both enormous and too immature to have any self-restraint around fawns, baby rabbits, fox kits—all of them helpless and unsuspecting, much like St. Clair's brand-new baroness.

"Lady St. Clair believes her husband is safe from honorable gentlemen who want to blow his brains out. I do not like that she's being deceived, Christian. She pronounced herself smitten with the brute."

His Grace let forth another ear-piercing whistle and bellowed for the dogs by name in what his daughter called his Papa-Is-Vexed voice.

"He's smitten with her too, though I doubt he realizes it. Said 'his Milly' likes to garden. I can ask Wellington for more details, though Old Hookey doesn't take well to pestering."

A rustling in the bushes suggested the mastiffs were heeding the duke's summons.

"Consider this, Christian: the Baroness St. Clair will not take kindly to being widowed a week after saying her vows, and the aggravation that was Bonaparte will pale compared to the wrath of that woman if harm befalls her baron, particularly if those who could have aided him did nothing."

"You don't even like him."

"True." The dogs emerged from the hedgerow some yards up the lane. "But I love you, and you feel responsible, so you must bother dear Arthur, regardless of his temper. You haven't refused his most recent invitation, you know."

His Grace heaved a martyred sigh. "Another hail-fellows-well-met at Apsley House?"

Gilly gave him the date, upon which, she knew for a certainty, he had no other obligations.

"You see before you a doomed duke, then. Some matters do not admit of handling by post. What is that smell?"

As the dogs bounded closer, tongues lolling, plumed tails swaying in the breeze, Gilly caught the same sweet, noxious odor. "Whatever it is, it's quite dead, and your dogs have thoroughly rolled in it, Your Grace."

"*My* dogs?"

"You brought them into our home."

They argued agreeably all the way back to the stables, though when they went into the house, Gilly penned an acceptance of Wellington's invitation—His Grace's penmanship being deplorable—and Mercia signed it. He grumbled, he complained, and he generally tried his duchess's patience first—and then rewarded her patience generously—but he did sign it.

Fifteen

"I DO NOT UNDERSTAND THIS." HENRI AFFIXED A PER-plexed look to his features and studied the scarred table, into one corner of which some philosopher of the grape had carved the words, "Fuk the Frogs."

"She's married him," Upton reiterated. "Married a damned baron, and her the closest thing to a dimwit."

Upton sounded more bewildered than affronted, as if barons were immune from mating with dimwits, when in Henri's experience, intellectual abilities were the last thing a titled lord considered in a prospective spouse.

"I thought women required the permission of their next of kin before taking a spouse in this most civilized country. More ale?" The women of France, of course, no longer tolerated such interference, which was fortunate, given that few adult Frenchmen were extant to do the interfering.

"Please. Milly's of age. She's damned on the shelf, in fact, or she was, so she can marry where she pleases. Mrs. Upton is in quite a taking, quite a taking indeed."

Hence Mr. Upton's refuge in this cozy tavern.

Henri lifted a hand to signal the barmaid. "Your

lady, she is not pleased to have a baroness in the family?" Because what was wanted here was not wallowing in self-pity, but action.

"Any other baroness would do famously," Upton said, swiping his finger around the rim of his tankard then licking the wet digit. "Milly has gone and married the Traitor Baron, though, and that's rather a different thing altogether."

"Ah."

Upton was marginally sober—the man could hold prodigious quantities of ale—and he was sly, but not particularly astute. The single syllable—a bit knowing, a bit commiserating—provoked him to turning an annoyed gaze on Henri.

"What? I'm not in the mood for any of your Frenchie subtleties, sir. Mrs. Upton in a taking is a formidable challenge to a man's peace."

"The ladies have no strategy." Henri fell silent while the barmaid replenished Upton's drink, but he waved her away rather than befoul his own palate with any more English ale.

"The ladies have a damned lot of strategy, most of it intended to keep a fellow from his marital bliss, if you know what I mean. My wife is the only lady to have three children and remain almost a virgin."

Suggesting Mrs. Upton was a formidable woman even when *not* in a taking. "You must show yourself the wiser person, and congratulate Millicent on her nuptials."

Henri offered this suggestion with careful diffidence, because Upton was a pawn who could be led but not pushed.

"Congratulate her? You mean send around some fussy note? The damned girl can barely read."

"She's a baroness now. She'll have a secretary or a companion, somebody who handles her correspondence."

Henri was counting on it.

"Mrs. Upton ought to be the one to send such a letter, and she'll swim the Channel in her stays before she offers Milly any congratulations. The girl's portion was half the means…"

Upton took a judicious gulp of his ale, but he'd confirmed one of Henri's favorite theories of human behavior: it all came down to money. Henri's own motivations were rooted at least partly in pecuniary concerns, though France's best interests would not be damaged when Henri's goal had been achieved—not much.

"Do you know why the baron turned traitor?" Henri asked.

"Haven't the foggiest."

And Upton wasn't inclined to wonder how Henri knew, which was a lovely oversight on Upton's part.

"England abandoned him. I have puzzled on this, you see, because you English take the succession of your titles quite seriously. St. Clair is the last of his line, and if he'd been killed or convicted of high treason, then his estate would have reverted to the Crown. At one time, it was a wealthy barony, while the Crown is not so wealthy, hmm?"

The debts incurred by the Regent and some of his siblings would have occasioned a revolution in any other country—particularly when the common English man or woman typically faced jail for even minor debt.

Upton took another gulp of ale, belched, and then seized upon the heart of the matter.

"Milly is the Traitor Baroness now. That's not good, not even for her."

Such compassion for a woman who'd probably been little more than slave labor in Upton's nursery. She would likely thank Henri for his efforts before matters were concluded.

"You must warn her, then."

This time, Upton took the bait. "Warn her about what? She can't help but know St. Clair's past. Even if she can't read the papers, she'll hear the gossip in the man's own house. The aunt's received, and you can bet Milly's heard plenty already, trailing that old woman about in Polite Society."

Henri used the ring finger of his left hand to trace the lettering carved into the table. "Your dear cousin knows of his past, but you must warn her of his future."

"I'm not a damned fortune-teller—" Upton's gaze fell on the lettering. "What do you mean? And speak plainly, for I must return to Mrs. Upton's side before supper."

Another burp followed, this one musical. Flatulence was sure to ensue directly, so Henri spoke quite plainly.

"Even among my countrymen, it's known that St. Clair has been challenged to several duels, and has come away unscathed each time. He faces another challenge, though, and the man he meets this time is noted for his ability to fight in close quarters. By this hour on Tuesday, your cousin could well be widowed."

"The nobs and their damned duels…"

"Even a traitor baron makes provision for his baroness, should she be widowed."

Henri spared a moment's pity for this Millicent creature. Henri had not seen her at close range, but Upton described her as plain by English standards, none too bright, illiterate in a land that took to heart at least the reading of its Bible, and no longer young. She was ideally situated to overlook St. Clair's numerous shortcomings, and provided she was fertile, St. Clair was probably happy to overlook hers as well.

"You're saying Milly will come into some blunt, if St. Clair's killed."

Henri traced the letters again, the smooth feel of the ancient wood oddly comforting. "She well could, but nobody will warn her of her husband's approaching folly. If the other fellow dies, St. Clair could face charges of murder, and his lady will want to distance herself from any further scandal, I'm sure." More to the point, Mrs. Upton wouldn't care for it.

"Tuesday, you say?"

"I have it on reliable authority. And your Milly has nobody else in the entire world who will explain to her the depth of her error regarding this marriage."

Upton tilted sideways on his chair, and predictably, a low, rumbling noise escaped. His gaze, however, was fixed on the table, so Henri could watch as thoughts linked up in the murky recesses of Upton's mind and became conclusions.

"I'll drop her a note, and Milly will see who her friends are. Mrs. Upton never understood the girl, but Milly isn't entirely stupid, not about common sense things."

"Milly will appreciate your honesty, and if her baron is killed, she will know to whom she can turn in her grief."

Henri did not expect St. Clair to be killed in a round of fisticuffs—far from it. St. Clair was big, fit, quick, and hard to kill, for Henri had tried on several occasions to accomplish just that goal. Before a court martial, at the hands of an impoverished whore, and by direct means.

St. Clair needed killing before certain decisions of Henri's came to light. The sullen Scot might see it done, but Henri was not about to depend on such means, not when the field of honor had proven so hospitable to St. Clair in the past.

"Milly's not here," Upton said, gesturing vaguely in the direction of the St. Clair town house. "Off in Surrey with her baron, probably ordering maids and footmen about when she's not flouncing around in the St. Clair jewels and dreaming of new gowns."

"So send word to her in Surrey."

For this was the vital contribution Upton could make to the game. He could summon the baroness from the family seat and bring her back within range of Henri's grasp. The arrival of a lone Frenchman in the wilds of Surrey would be remarked by all and sundry, and doubtless come to St. Clair's attention. If Henri was to acquire the baroness for his own purposes, she must be brought back to Town, and before Wellington's next gathering of his officers.

Another occasion of flatulence ensued. "Suppose I could."

"If she were my cousin, I would feel honor bound

to put the truth at her misguided feet. You'd think St. Clair would have had enough of killing his countrymen when he served the Corsican." A slight, necessary exaggeration of St. Clair's record of service.

Upton grimaced, downed the rest of his ale, and rose. "I've never shirked m' duty where Milly's concerned. Wretched girl has been nothing but trouble."

Henri rose as well, and clapped Upton on a beefy shoulder. "She is luckier than she will ever know, to have family as devoted as you."

Because such affection was likely outside of Upton's experience, Henri twinkled a smile at his friend for good measure. Upton looked momentarily confused, slapped his hat onto his head, and waddled out, muttering about "Tuesday next" and "disobliging women."

❧

The foot of the adult male was an interesting appendage and surprisingly susceptible to tickling, but Milly knew she was in a sad case indeed when she missed Sebastian's feet in her lap. In less than a week, Milly and her husband had developed the habit of repairing to the library after dinner. Sebastian would read to her, his head or his feet in her lap.

When she'd had her fill of stroking his ears or examining his toes—his second toe was the longest of the batch on both feet—he'd pass Milly the book, and she'd take a turn at thrashing her way through some Wordsworth or Byron.

Sebastian was endlessly patient with her, always correcting and never scolding. He said she was improving, and Milly had to agree. Once, he'd asked her if she recognized the shape of the words without being able to recite the letters, and the question had proven insightful.

So now, when Sebastian had left for London and Milly had the evening to herself, she repaired to the library and prepared to trudge through a stack of correspondence.

"You are not Peter," she informed the red-and-black cat curled in the opposite chair. "You aren't even purring."

The cat formed a perfect oval against the cushions, and the chair had been angled to catch the fire's heat. Milly doubted the beast was even awake, while Peter—or Sebastian—would never have abandoned her for anything so prosaic as an evening's nap.

"Sebastian is meeting with the solicitors tomorrow, and said he ought to be home by sundown. I should have gone with him."

Except he'd decided to travel to Town on horseback to make better time and take advantage of the full moon, and Milly's equestrian confidence wasn't up to a moonlit ride the entire distance to London.

Or maybe her confidence as a baroness had failed her. Sebastian had taken her upstairs directly after dinner and made slow, silent love to her, then kissed her forehead and slipped into his riding attire while Milly had watched and tried not to feel abandoned.

"Trust is complicated," she informed the cat. "And difficult. Reading is difficult too, though it was once impossible. Would you like to hear some of my correspondence?"

The very tip of the cat's tail moved once.

"A hearty endorsement." Milly picked up the first epistle, a single folded sheet that bore, of all things, Alcorn's sprawling, untidy hand.

"Felicitations, no doubt, and a scold or two." Milly pried off the seal, wondering why, if congratulations were to be extended, Frieda had not troubled herself to make the overture. Frieda had a daughter, after all, a cheerful girl who might someday have need of a titled aunt.

Milly fell silent as she read. When she finished the note, she went back over it again, word for word, to make sure she had the correct sense of Alcorn's letter, and then—much to the cat's apparent displeasure—she started bellowing at the top of her lungs.

❦

"Bloody goddamned rain." And bloody goddamned coffee, because the kitchen staff at the town house had prepared only coffee for Sebastian, their habits being driven by his own. A hot cup of tea would have been ever so much more soothing to his belly.

Michael drew his horse up. "You've dueled in the rain before."

"With pistols," Sebastian replied, bringing Fable to a halt. "How likely is sloppy footing to make a difference when a man knows his powder is dry, and all he must do is turn, aim, and fire into the boughs?"

"So change your choice of weapon."

"We did not bring the pistols or swords. Bare knuckles it will be. If I survive this, remind me to order the kitchen to throw out every bean of coffee in the larder."

Michael swung off his beast and ran up his stirrups. "You aren't generally nervous before a dawn meeting."

"I am not nervous, I am frustrated." Sebastian climbed off his horse, which made him more *frustrated*. Riding into London by the full moon, tossing and turning the night away, and rising before dawn to a damp and chilly morning did not agree with his joints—another legacy of his years at the Château.

"What has you frustrated?"

"This business with MacHugh. It won't solve anything. A half-dozen others, at least, can come after me should MacHugh fail to kill me."

Michael paused in the act of loosening his gelding's girth. "I thought MacHugh didn't want to kill you."

"He doesn't. Not really. If he kills me, I won't have to suffer the results of all the damage he plans to inflict on me. Make sure the rules stipulate no blows below the waist."

"With an attitude like that, I hope your affairs are in order."

They fell silent as MacHugh and his seconds rode into the clearing, the same place, ironically, where the Duke of Mercia had chosen to spare Sebastian's life.

"I will greet my counterparts." Michael tied his horse's reins to a convenient sapling, and would have crossed the clearing to confer with the kilted associates flanking MacHugh, but Sebastian stopped him with a hand on his arm.

"Tell Milly I'm sorry."

Michael's features lost their typical veneer of irritability, becoming downright bleak. "For?"

"I am sorry I did not tell her…" The words felt

foolish and impotent. At that moment, Sebastian's whole life felt foolish.

"You did not warn her she might go to bed a widow tonight?" Michael took Fable's reins and tied them to the same sapling.

"I did not tell her I love her." Had not told her she deserved much better than a traitor baron, and had not told her so many other things that now seemed far more important than allowing MacHugh to indulge a Scotsman's injured pride.

"If you love her," Michael said, "then knock MacHugh's arse in the mud, and go on a tour of the Continent with your lady wife. At least give her a few babies before she's widowed, so she isn't left on the charity of the Crown."

Milly would be well provided for from Sebastian's private wealth, though that gave him little comfort.

"Acknowledge MacHugh's seconds. The ground will only become muddier the longer we wait to deal with this unpleasantness."

Something an intelligent man might keep in mind when he deceived his new wife.

MacHugh was draining the contents of a silver flask, his seconds keeping their backs to Sebastian. As Sebastian shed cravat and coat, Mercia's words came back to him: MacHugh was good with his fists, but overconfident. Didn't mind his defenses, and overused his right.

Or words to that effect. Milly would have been able to quote His Grace word for word. Sebastian's shirt came off next, and then his boots and stockings. The ground was cold and slippery beneath his feet, and the occasional rock or root would no doubt make the footing even more interesting at precisely the wrong moment.

As Michael conferred with the kilted bear holding MacHugh's horse, Sebastian focused on the gnawing ache that had plagued him since he'd ridden away from St. Clair Manor the previous evening.

Ridden away from Milly.

What he felt did have some frustration in it—would Wellington's minions never stop bothering him?—but also despair, and a quality of homesickness. He'd endured this feeling for years at the Château, until he had nigh choked on it with each thick, bitter cup of coffee he'd downed.

The feeling was worse now though, when, as Michael had said, Sebastian could dream about a real peace, one that included a wife and children.

"MacHugh's ready," Michael said, shifting Sebastian's boots so low-hanging branches gave them some protection from the rain.

"Did you offer an apology?"

"Tried that. No luck."

Sebastian passed his signet ring over. "Any words of advice?"

"Stay the hell alive. You're the last excuse I can use to put off going North."

Sebastian willed his body to relax, despite the damp and the chill. "I will make every effort to oblige you. Do I assume one of those skirted mastodons is a surgeon?"

"The shorter one. MacHugh thinks he owes it to your widow to clean up your corpse before he sends you home to her."

"Most considerate of him. Let's get this over with."
They walked forward into the clearing as MacHugh
tossed his flask to his second. "You'll tell Milly?"

"Bloody hell. Yes."

A damp, drippy silence went by while Sebastian
studied the terrain. The left side of the clearing rose
slightly, suggesting the ground might be less boggy.
Rocks jutted toward the right, rocks a man would
not want to fall against but ought to maneuver his
opponent into.

"Your lordship, good morning," MacHugh said,
swaggering into the clearing. "Brodie says we're not to
kick each other in the balls, which suggests—contrary
to all rumor and inference—you have a pair."

MacHugh's version of civilities.

"You're not to bite me, either, MacHugh, lest the
taste of my treasonous flesh fatally poison even so stout
a constitution as yours. Shall we chat away the morning, or be about our business?"

Any conflict had a psychological aspect that a com-
batant ignored at his peril, so Sebastian had allowed
a hint of a French accent to slip into his words, the
better to goad MacHugh.

"My thanks for the reminder," MacHugh said.
"Gentlemen?"

The seconds paced off a circle of sorts while
Sebastian mentally reached for the detachment he'd
worn like a shroud for five years. MacHugh did not
want to kill him—though somebody did—and when
this morning's inconvenience was dealt with, Sebastian
intended to find out who.

‰

"If milady would slow down," Milly's groom panted, "it's barely light."

"This is as light as the day will likely get," Milly said, tossing her ruined bonnet off into the bushes. "Why does this wood have to be so perishing large?"

She took stock of her surroundings, comparing it to the Duchess of Mercia's description. The clearing could not be far, but had Her Grace said it lay to the left of the rise or to the right?

"I should at least have tried to write down the directions," Milly muttered. Or asked Her Grace to write them down, to print them, even, because Milly's humiliation at making such a request could not possibly compare with her fear for her husband's life.

Or her despair at his betrayal.

A horse whinnied from among the trees to the left of the rise.

"This way," Milly said, hurrying off. Her boots slipped and nearly went out from under her in the mud, while the groom, exercising a damnable quotient of prudence, trailed her at an increasing distance.

Thank goodness Fable was snow white, because without the beacon of his coat among the wet greenery, Milly might have missed the clearing. As it was, she half slipped, half clambered down a bank, stopping short at the sight before her.

Michael Brodie stood off to the side, looking positively martyred, and two other fellows in kilts bore similarly pained expressions. In the center of the clearing, Sebastian and another fellow were stripped to the waist and pounding away at each other.

No, not at each other. The fellow in the kilt was

pounding on Sebastian, who ducked, feinted, and dodged as many blows as the Scot landed.

"Fight, damn ye, St. Clair!"

"I drugged your drinks. I didn't give you a fair chance," Sebastian panted back, just as another blow landed on his jaw. He'd jerked back, but the sound of a fist on flesh was enough to make Milly's gorge rise.

"I mean to kill ye, and I'll not—bluidy blue blazes!"

Milly saw when the Scot caught sight of her, because he trotted backward, away from Sebastian, and let his fists drop.

"Get away from my husband, you, you *meat wagon*." Milly tromped up to the Scot and planted her hands on her hips. "What would your wife say about this stupidity? Does she know you're out prancing around in the rain in nothing but a kilt, intent on killing a man who was not to blame for your capture?"

"Milly—"

She rounded on her husband, who'd spoken her name in quiet, patient tones.

"Quiet, please, your lordship. This fellow owes me an answer." She turned back to the Scot rather than behold the sight of Sebastian's red and puffy jaw.

"Be she daft?" The Scot spoke over Milly's head, the consternation in his voice real.

"I am not *daft*, I am *married* to the most impossible man in the realm. A man who did not capture you, did he?"

Sebastian's opponent eyed Milly as if she might be something worse than daft—as if she might be *right*.

"Nay, he did not, but I was turned over to him the next day."

"And this is his fault? If you'd come across a French officer out of uniform, would you have wished him good day and gone whistling on your way?"

He widened his stance. "That's not the point. The point is St. Clair brought it all up again, before another officer, and I willna, I *canna* allow—"

"Another officer," Milly spat. "Some other officer caught with his breeches around his ankles while he made the acquaintance of a French maid. Some other fellow St. Clair did not capture, did not relieve of his uniform, and did not ask to have thrust into his keeping."

"Milly, please."

If she looked at Sebastian, she'd cry. She'd cry and throw herself against his wet, naked chest, where, if she weren't mistaken, other bruises were soon to manifest.

"Go home, sir," Milly said to the meat wagon. "Unless I miss my guess, the same arrogance that had you running around behind enemy lines without your uniform is responsible for causing this folly today."

She ruined the effect of this pithy observation by swiping a lock of wet hair from her eyes.

"St. Clair, I dinna mean to make her cry. We said no blows below the belt, but this—"

The wretch was pleading with Sebastian. While Milly stood blinking furiously in the rain, Sebastian's hand landed on her shoulder.

"Perhaps, MacHugh, you will see the futility of further attempts to settle our differences through pugilism. I am sorry that you've been upset, and I did not breathe a word to anybody of what passed between us in the officer's mess at the Château. I was not proud of my tactics, but your disclosures spared both sides a final useless skirmish—or worse—before the winter camps were set up."

MacHugh rubbed his jaw, an angle of bone that looked like it could hold up to a solid kick from a plow horse without sustaining damage. "That's all?"

"Nothing more. I will not insult your temper by swearing it, but you have my word."

Tears ran hot down Milly's cheeks, like the anger trickling through her as the men exchanged reminiscences of war. MacHugh's temper would be nothing compared to hers, though it was some consolation that Sebastian would be alive to suffer her wrath.

A second hand landed on Milly's opposite shoulder. She wrenched away.

"The woman is protective of ye," MacHugh observed. "I expect she'll deliver ye a thrashin' far more punishin' than what I might have done."

"She will," Sebastian said, and perhaps the man still possessed a shred of common sense, because he'd answered in earnest.

"I wanted ye…" MacHugh regarded Milly as he spoke. "I wanted ye to know the keen despair of having lost, St. Clair. Lost your honor, your wits, your little part of the war. And for nothing. It haunts a man."

Milly knew that despair. She swiped at her hair again and tried not to think of how good it might feel to lay about with her fists—at the Scot, at Sebastian, at Michael trying not to look worried as the rain dripped from his hat brim.

Sebastian spoke softly. "It does. Haunts his every waking and sleeping moment."

MacHugh bellowed to his second, "Ewan, my flask."

A silver flask came sailing through the air. MacHugh caught it in an appallingly large hand. He took a drink and held it out, not to Sebastian, but to Milly.

"My apologies, mum. A slight misunderstanding, ye see. No harm done. A tot will ward off the chill."

Milly wanted to hurl the flask at him, wanted to bellow and rage and scare the horses, except a sip from the little flask would eliminate one threat to Sebastian's welfare.

"We all make mistakes," Milly said, tipping the flask up. "Some of them more serious than others."

"Aye." The Scot's expression might have borne a hint of humor. Milly did not care that he was amused, did not care that he was perhaps impressed, or even that he might have pitied Sebastian his choice of wife.

"St. Clair, I bid ye good day, and"—he gave Milly an appraising look—"I bid ye good luck."

He bowed slightly to Milly and stomped off, leaving her with the flask and the temptation to pitch it at his retreating backside.

"Don't," Sebastian said, easing the flask from her grasp. He'd moved up behind Milly and spoken softly. She could feel the heat of him, could catch a whiff of his sandalwood scent over the smell of damp earth and wet greenery.

He turned her by the shoulders and wrapped his arms around her. "Say something."

She rested her forehead against his bare, bruised chest, emotions and words tangling up in her throat.

How could you?

Why did you?
How am I ever to trust you?
"Take me home."

❧

Sebastian walked out of the clearing half-naked, sopping wet, and barefoot, none of which mattered. He climbed into Milly's coach and took the bench across from her, though she was just as wet as he.

"Who told you?"

She kept her head turned to gaze out the window, but because she wasn't wearing a bonnet, her profile answered him handily enough. It didn't matter which helpful, misguided soul had told her about the duel; it hadn't been Sebastian to give her the news.

"Alcorn. He sought to reveal to me the depths of my folly in marrying a man who apparently duels for recreation. I am to turn to him for guidance. He holds out hope the marriage can be annulled."

If she'd been seething, bitter, infuriated, or hysterical, Sebastian would have been less alarmed, but Milly was calm, terribly, unreachably calm. Sebastian recognized her achievement because he'd endured years of such calm in the mountains of southern France.

"You're angry." And she was no longer crying.

"I am disappointed. I will weather this blow, having managed similar tribulations in the past."

The idea that Sebastian might have anything in common with the relatives or the fiancé who had treated her so shabbily helped him locate his own temper. "You are capable of mendacity, too, Milly St. Clair."

His use of her married name elicited the barest, least voluntary flinch, which made his temper flare up like a glowing ember finding a fresh breeze.

"Had your aunt asked me, I would have told her plainly I read very poorly. She did not ask and did not include literacy among the qualifications required of her companion. Does it hurt?"

Her question confused him because her chilly reserve hurt him far worse than MacHugh's fists had.

"Your jaw, your chest, all those bruises coming up where MacHugh pummeled you. They have to hurt."

Now that she'd drawn his attention to them, Sebastian mentally inventoried his injuries. "None of it's serious. MacHugh was still investigating my responses rather than truly attacking."

"How fortunate. Why didn't you go after him, too?"

She wanted to analyze an altercation that now meant nothing.

"When they challenge me, I make no resistance. It's what they want, to have me as helpless as they were."

She swiveled her gaze to regard him, and he wished she hadn't. "You are an idiot." Her eyes held a spark of emotion. Not indignation, but maybe—God spare him—pity.

"I am an idiot who has survived five challenges in less than a year." Though somebody was determined that there be five more, which also, at the moment, did not matter.

"When you choose not to fight back, you are not helpless, Sebastian. You are controlling matters every bit as much as you did at that awful fortress in France, maybe more. What they want is a chance to meet you on fair terms, and to assure themselves that unbound, on the field of honor, in a fair fight, they could acquit themselves honorably, win or lose. You're right that they don't want merely to kill you, they want to kill you honorably, and you deny them that."

She would confound him with her philosophy, and the coach had already left the park.

"Milly, none of that matters now. What matters is that I owe you an apology, and that I love you."

Cold, wet, and coming off the excitement of battle, his body wanted to shiver. He prevented this by an act of will and forbade himself the comfort of a woolen lap robe around his shoulders.

"What are you apologizing for?"

Women. Any answer he gave would be inadequate.

"I apologize for not telling you that I was to meet MacHugh, though I'll not ask your permission before defending my honor."

Her calm went from cool to glacial, suggesting Sebastian had given an answer that wasn't merely wrong, but rather, disastrous. He shifted to sit beside her and wrapped his arms around her. She permitted it, but when Sebastian kissed her cheek, her skin was as chilled as his own.

"How would it have changed anything if you'd known I had this meeting with MacHugh?"

"One confides one's burdens in one's friends."

Because he held her, Sebastian could feel more tears in her clamoring for expression, and could feel her resolve building by the moment.

He struck at her verbally, even as he held her more closely. "You would not have tried to stop me?

Would not have locked your bedroom door to me until I agreed to surrender my honor to you? Would not have sulked, brooded, and given me one more thing to worry about?"

She relaxed, implying his words were an egregious blunder, which he'd known even as they were leaving his fool mouth. He lied when he implied that Milly's concern for him was an inconvenience. He treasured her protectiveness like the last flint and tinder in his possession when a long, cold winter had already gripped the land.

A shudder passed through her, maybe cold, maybe despair.

"I have no bedroom door to lock against you, Sebastian. Had I known your life was imperiled, I would have made love with you *more*."

Sixteen

"I'VE ORDERED YOU A BATH," SEBASTIAN SAID. "I'LL not have you taking a chill in addition to risking your neck on the field of honor."

Milly could not watch as Sebastian peeled out of his wet breeches. He was all over gooseflesh, badly bruised, and worried about *her* taking a chill.

"Doesn't it strike you as the least bit hypocritical that you should fear for my well-being, Husband, but deny me the privilege of fearing for yours?"

Stark-naked, Sebastian hunkered before the fire, added coal, used the bellows with a vengeance, and then rose to face her. His hair was a mess, bruises decorated his belly and chest, and his jaw was slightly swollen on one side.

He was also half-aroused, which shouldn't have been possible. "Let me get you out of that dress."

Milly turned her back, because in her haste to leave St. Clair Manor, she'd let one of the maids help her with her clothes, and the dress Milly had yanked out of the wardrobe buttoned in the back.

"You should use the bath first, Sebastian."

"Hold still." Perhaps his fingers were clumsy with

cold, perhaps he was in no particular hurry. When he'd assisted her out of her clothing on previous occasions, it had never taken him this long.

Milly moved away as soon as she felt her dress gaping in the back. "Thank you."

"You'll wear your stays into the bathtub?"

"Possibly. I am that upset, you see." She hadn't meant to say that. She'd meant to be civil.

"Then yell at me, curse, break things, and let the entire house hear of it, but don't shut me out. You have every right to be upset."

"Unlace my stays, please." She hated asking, hated standing still while Sebastian struggled with knots made impossible by the wet.

"To hell with this." He produced a knife from somewhere and sliced at her laces. Even as they fell open, Milly's breathing still felt constrained.

She bunched her damp clothes in her fists and kept her back to him. "You shut me out, Sebastian. You shut me out in several regards."

"I tried to keep you safe, to keep you apart from all the…to keep you safe." He spoke from immediately behind her but did not touch her.

Milly moved away, rummaged in the wardrobe for her only dressing gown—she'd used one of Sebastian's at St. Clair Manor—and took it behind the privacy screen. She remained hidden away, removing her sodden attire, untangling the rat's nest her braids had become, and trying to find solid ground in a marriage gone pitch dark and boggy.

When she emerged, Sebastian was also wearing a dressing gown, and a full tub steamed before the fire.

"You first," Milly said, unwilling and unable to disrobe before him.

He looked prepared to pick a fight so they'd have something to wrestle with besides his lying to her, and letting some fool Scot beat him to flinders.

"My feet are filthy. After you."

His conscience ought to be what troubled him, not his dirty feet.

"Sit on the hearth," Milly said, picking up a flannel from the stack piled near the tub. To her surprise, he obeyed her. She poured hot water into a washbasin, dipped the cloth and wrung it out, then knelt before her husband.

His feet were cold, of course. Milly started on the right, wrapping the hot, wet flannel around toes she'd been missing just the evening before. "You've a sizable scratch, here," she said, drawing her finger along the side of his arch.

"I can't feel it. You don't have to do this."

She unwrapped his foot and wiped at the muddy spaces between his toes. "Why did you tell me you would engage in no more duels, when you knew of at least one?"

Sebastian closed his eyes, as if she were whipping his soles, not bathing his feet. "I said there would be no more pistols at dawn, and I spoke the truth. As the party challenged, I can select the weapons, and I will eschew pistols henceforth."

Milly rinsed and wrung out the cloth in the basin, muddying the water.

"You lied by omission then. I can assure you my sense of betrayal does not abate because you were lawyerly in your untruths. Why lie at all?"

This time, she wrapped the hot cloth around his arch.

"Most gentlemen would not burden their lady wives with such information."

His heels were callused, something Milly had noted during evenings in the library. "You are not most gentlemen, Sebastian. The real reason, if you please. Did you think I would leave you?"

Would he have missed her, or been relieved at her absence? He was a reluctant husband, for all that his efforts to assure the succession had been enthusiastic.

As had hers.

"I wanted to spare you, wanted to preserve you from tossing and turning all night, offering desperate, useless prayers by the hour, choking down your morning tea while you waited for news. Ask Lady Freddy how agreeable such a course is, for she's had to suffer it too many times in the past year."

Under the guise of wrapping his clean foot in a dry cloth, Milly hugged her husband's foot against her middle.

"You would have me believe your lying was a form of consideration, Sebastian, but earlier, you reminded me that I've lied too." She used the basin again, needing to finish before the water cooled. "Give me the left one."

"You were desperate," Sebastian said. "You needed employment if you were to avoid your cousin's schemes. I understand that."

Milly started on the second foot, which, thankfully, was free of abrasions.

"Do you also understand that lying about mortal combat and lying about an ability to read well are not the same thing at all? You gave me a false promise that you would not duel, then deceived me again as to the nature of your business in Town. Had Alcorn not written that note, had I not been able to wrest a location from Their Graces, had the moon not been full…"

She scrubbed at his foot even when she'd removed all the mud.

"I've apologized, Milly, but I do not control who challenges me. How can I make you see that these men will not cease trying to redeem their honor by the only means available to them? This one I had beaten, that one deprived of water, MacHugh I drugged, another who was so fastidious was made to lie chained in his own—"

Milly stopped this recitation by virtue of wrapping her arms around her husband's waist.

"You did not capture them. You did not wrest their uniforms from them. The war is over, and has been for some while. Those officers are all walking about as free men, and yet you are trapped in that miserable garrison. Do you know that a properly timed blow to the chest can stop the heart from beating?"

He held her, while Milly waited for him to say something, to say anything honest and true. She waited for him to tell her that he'd never wanted to marry her; he was weary of living; he had more duels scheduled for the very next week.

She felt his lips graze her forehead. "The water's getting cold, Wife."

Yes, it was. Milly rose and wrung the soiled cloth out with particular force.

"Did you even have an appointment planned with the solicitors?"

He bent to unwrap his right foot. "Of course, I did."

He'd scheduled such an appointment, because the best lies were packaged in mundane truths, and he folded up the damp, clean flannel so very carefully lest Milly see that truth in his eyes.

"I'll be meeting with the solicitors myself," Milly said, moving toward the door. "And your presence will not be needed."

He rose, looking pale, angry, hurt, and…damn him, *dear*.

"Take the professor with you, or Michael. Don't attempt to puzzle through legal documents alone, and don't sign anything you aren't absolutely comfortable with or sure of."

"I'll take Aunt Freddy. You'd best tend to your bath. The water won't be warm much longer."

❧

Milly had known exhaustion of the spirit often, when she could not face another day in the schoolroom, when Frieda's temper was particularly short, when word of Martin's stupid death had come and nobody had told her until after supper.

Exhaustion of the spirit could ease with time, good company, a few kind words, and rest. As she succumbed to slumber in the bed she'd yet to share with her husband, she said a prayer that exhaustion of the heart could heal as well.

The next impression to grace her awareness was of Sebastian climbing in beside her—an answer to her prayers? He wrapped himself around her, the scent and feel of him already a bodily comfort after only a week of marriage.

"Are you awake?"

How she hated the hesitance in his voice, and how she nearly hated him, for risking death without even telling her. She tucked herself against him.

"Do not attempt to reason with me, Sebastian."

"I do love you."

What manner of love had no trust in it? What manner of love insisted on remaining alone with every fear and burden?

"We are in need of wisdom, Sebastian, not flowery sentiments."

They also needed patience, compassion, and a host of other strengths, but Milly wanted desperately to give him the flowery words back, to explain to him that her anger was a well-dressed, articulate version of innumerable screaming terrors.

Terror that she might have lost him to a Scottish lout with too much pride and even more muscle.

That she might not trust her husband, not now, not ever.

That tomorrow he might face death again, and all because circumstances had conspired to put him in a situation where every possible choice had cost him dearly.

Milly kissed his brow, as he'd kissed hers before departing for London. "I am very, very angry with you, Sebastian. Enraged and disappointed."

He kissed her mouth, humbly, if a man could kiss humbly.

"You terrify me," she whispered, kissing him back.

"I have married into a war where everybody is held prisoner and the fighting never ceases."

Sebastian shifted over her, exactly where the most unhappy, desolate part of her wanted him, exactly where he was *not* entitled to be.

"Please, Milly."

He might have held her to him by force, by reason, by legal arguments and promises of wealth, and yet, they were barely touching. Sebastian poised above her, willing to be banished from the bed and from the marriage.

She knew then the dubious honor of having broken a strong man, and knew as well that Sebastian's plea— for understanding, for forgiveness, for time—left her broken as well.

She could not allow him to imprison himself in his endless war without even a single ally.

"You belong to me, Sebastian." Yes, she was hurt and angry, also confused and in need of solitude, but on this point, she would have his concession.

"I belong to you. Wholly to you," he said, some of the tension draining from him. "I always will."

Milly pushed at him, and he collapsed onto his back as if winded. She climbed over him, needing to follow up his concession with stern kisses that turned tender, and then passionate.

"Sebastian, this doesn't—"

He kissed her to silence and shifted them again, so he was above her, poised to join their bodies.

"We'll talk," he said. "Later. I understand that. We'll talk all you please."

He fell silent on a single, desperate, transcendently gratifying thrust, and Milly gave up on philosophy, strategy, and even thought. She put her rage and fear into her loving, her desperate need to protect him, and her consternation about how to protect herself.

He was ruthless, drawing out her satisfaction into a blend of pleasure and torment that inspired Milly to torment him right back. Never was marital discord so intimately prosecuted, until Milly understood that Sebastian needed her surrender, as she'd needed his.

They were allies, not captives, so she gave herself up to his loving, enduring pleasure upon pleasure, until Sebastian shuddered in her arms, and silence at last reigned over the battlefield.

∽

"The women have been gone for hours." Michael, predictably, was the one to voice the complaint Sebastian also felt.

Baumgartner twirled a quill pen at the desk in the town house library. "Lawyers are not usually motivated to be efficient. St. Clair, you should pay a call on Mr. MacHugh."

Sebastian stopped staring into the library's fire long enough to note that the professor was serious. "Why?"

"Because," Michael said from his perch in the window seat, "MacHugh is not a hothead, not some fired up, titled puppy drunk on his expectations. Somebody goaded him into challenging you. Somebody lied to him convincingly enough that he'd risk his life over pistols or swords—and put your life in jeopardy as well."

Lied to MacHugh, as Sebastian had lied to his wife, for reasons he himself was no longer entirely sure of.

"Somebody badly wants me dead," Sebastian said. "And my wife is out running around the City with no one but Giles and Aunt Freddy to keep her safe."

"St. Clair," the professor said, tossing the feather to the blotter, "pay attention to your man. He makes sense. Talk to the officers who challenged you, and a pattern might emerge."

And that pattern could lead straight to Michael, or straight to the Iron Duke himself, in which case emigration to Patagonia might extend Sebastian's years on earth.

"Mercia could be behind it." Sebastian rose from the couch rather than keep the library's tray of decanters in sight. "My instincts have been spectacularly wrong on occasion."

"Your instincts are superb," Michael muttered. "They always have been."

Suggesting what? Sebastian could not read Michael's expression, because the man was staring out the window. Again.

"Fine, then. When Milly gets back, tell her not to wait dinner for me. I'm off to call upon MacHugh."

Professor and valet exchanged a glance Sebastian could easily decode.

"Perhaps I should go," Baumgartner said. "Or at least go with you. As an observer. I'm feeling decidedly Germanic, and perhaps even princely, now that I consider the matter."

Michael let loose a particularly profane curse in Gaelic, an oath Sebastian hadn't heard for more than a year.

"It's him," Michael said, springing off the window seat. "It's Anduvoir. I know it." Sebastian and the professor joined Michael at the window. "That fellow leaving the tavern on the corner, the one with his hat at the wrong angle."

"He's too far away to be sure," Sebastian said, but the hair on his arms and nape was prickling disagreeably. "It could be him." Anduvoir prided himself on the creative use of heel lifts, costumes, and cosmetics, but something in the arrogance of the walk, the angle of the hat, the attitude of the walking stick was definitely Continental.

"It's him," Michael said, moving swiftly toward the door. "I know that little shite's bullying swagger."

"Michael!" Sebastian's voice stopped him at the door. Michael turned, impatience in every line. "Don't let him see you. If he's here, there's a game afoot, and his games usually end up deadly for those who least deserve it."

"He'll not catch sight of me."

Michael was gone, a wisp of lethal Celtic smoke dissipated on the spring air, but Sebastian spoke aloud anyway. "Be careful. For God's sake, my friend, be careful."

The professor remained to the side of the window, where light and shadow would not reveal his presence unless a person knew exactly where to look. "Brodie can take care of himself, but you do realize our womenfolk are abroad without us, and now Anduvoir is loose in the same city?"

Dread curled into a hard ball in Sebastian belly.

"I made Anduvoir rich and earned him more than one promotion. He has no reason to bear me ill will."

The words were like a child's prayer, equal parts fantasy and hope.

"Anduvoir bears every living creature ill will," the professor said. "He's a putrid excrescence on the face of humanity. My guess is the French won't mind should we find a dung heap to fling his remains upon."

"I would mind. I served France for five years without once taking a human life. My wife would not be pleased were I to turn up murderer now."

Baumgartner gave a shrug that looked far more Gallic than German. "So don't tell her. Lady Freddy and I long ago came to the realization that discretion is not only prudent on some occasions, it is also kind."

For all the pragmatism in Baum's words, he seemed uncomfortable with them. And well he should.

Amid the panic swirling in Sebastian's gut, and the dire possibilities crowding his mind, he found a point of stability.

"I would tell my wife if I'd gone after Anduvoir. Milly would want to know. She would rather endure my truths than my self-serving attacks of kindness. I realize that now."

She would deserve to know, because her loyalty was that reliable, and because Sebastian could not afford cowardice where she was concerned. He only hoped he had a chance to explain that to her.

"Michael's on his tail," Baumgartner said softly.

Out on the street, as Anduvoir strolled around the corner, a big, shambling character in a disreputable coat sauntered after him. The disreputable character paused to buy a nosegay from a flower girl, a useful ploy for reconnoitering the street and for giving a man something to hold before his face should the need arise. The fellow tipped a battered hat at the flower girl and disappeared from view.

❧

"Where the hell is my wife?"

Sebastian's tone assured Freddy he was no longer her indulgent, faintly amused nephew. He was a tormented man.

"I have no idea." Freddy wrenched off her gloves. "She deposited me in the mews then had John Coachman drive her elsewhere. If I never meet with another solicitor again, it will be too soon."

Rather than face more questions to which she hadn't any answers, Freddy made a try for the stairs.

"You will join me in the music room," Sebastian said, voice cracking like a whip. "And do not think for one instant that a megrim or any other petty drama will spare you my company. Anduvoir is in London."

Freddy paused, hand on the newel post because she needed the support to remain upright. "Henri Anduvoir is in London?"

"Michael spotted him and went in discreet pursuit. The professor is taking a few pints at the tavern on the corner in hopes of learning more. You are coming with me."

He spun on his heel with military precision, no proffer of a polite escort, no waiting for Freddy to gather her wits. More than she'd feared the English troops, more than she'd feared winter in the French Pyrenees, more than she'd feared Wellington himself, Freddy had feared Henri Anduvoir would be the death of her nephew.

So she swept into the library, head held high. "Do you know it's Anduvoir? Frenchmen in London are common enough these days."

Sebastian glowered at a painting of puppies playing tug-of-war with a hunting whip.

"Michael was certain, and if the impulse to cast up my accounts is any indication, I am certain as well." He ran his finger across the bottom of the frame, as if checking for dust. "Somebody should notify the foreign office, or Wellington."

Sebastian did not like to even say the duke's name.

"You would notify His Grace?"

"Henri is a scourge whose menace transcends national boundaries, and thanks to me, he's a wealthy scourge, much respected in a certain strata of French society. What transpired at the solicitors?"

"I hardly know." Freddy took the seat at Sebastian's desk, for several reasons. A wall at one's back was generally a safe proposition, the desk commanded a good view of the entire room, and it afforded some protection against whoever might come charging in the door—or across the room.

"I have no patience, Baroness. None. My wife might well be running away from me, right into Anduvoir's waiting arms. Do you know what he'd do to one of Milly's strength of will? She has no allies, no safe harbor, no one whom she feels she—"

"Whom she feels she can trust," Freddy finished for him. "And you know the exact contours of such misery."

Knew them only too well. Freddy very much wanted to get drunk and give His Grace the Duke of Wellington the rousing set down he richly deserved.

"Where is my wife?"

"I expect John Coachman can tell us when he returns. Milly closeted herself with that dusty little fellow who worked for her aunts, while I kicked my heels in an anteroom and was roundly ignored by a bunch of children masquerading as law clerks."

Sebastian focused on a point above Freddy's left shoulder. "You did not read her any documents?"

"Not a one. She was with the solicitor for ages, and need I remind you she was exhausted before we departed for the City. I'm fairly certain she had documents in her reticule when we left."

Sebastian was exhausted too. The grooves around his mouth, the shadows under his eyes, the tension in his posture were proof of his need for rest.

"You will make a series of social calls," Sebastian said. "Start today, now, with MacHugh." He listed several other names, each one a former prisoner of his who'd challenged him unsuccessfully.

"I am happy to ask these fellows for the details regarding who goaded them to their foolish bravery, but aren't you concerned they'll say you're hiding behind my skirts?"

"I am hiding behind your skirts," Sebastian snapped. "I'd bloody wear skirts down the middle of St. James's Street if it would bring Milly home to me safely, but I can't leave this house until she's been located. If she comes home to find me gone—"

"You're afraid she'll pack her things and slip away permanently."

Long ago, Freddy had been Sebastian's confidante, the harmless older relation to whom a boy could confess his dreams and troubles. That boy was as dead as many of Wellington's brave soldiers, and Freddy did not know whether to blame the duke or the French—or herself.

"I am afraid of that very possibility, Aunt: that Milly will leave me, and then she'll try to make her way, without coin, without much ability to read, without a character, without friends…while my enemies, whom I taught a great deal about torture and interrogation, lie in wait for her. How does a woman keep herself safe when she can barely read street signs?"

"The solicitor treated her quite well, all bows and good manners. He did not treat her as if she were a penniless bother. Milly knows how to command respect."

Though what a miserable measure of the situation, that Freddy was reduced to offering a solicitor's manners as a comfort.

The door banged open, and Michael strode in, looking like some Midlands drover after the sheep had been delivered and before the drinking had concluded.

"It was Anduvoir. I followed him to his rooms in Bloomsbury, and he's traveling under a fictitious last name. He's gained weight and lost hair."

Milly's cat came strolling in behind Michael, who closed the door when the animal had made its stately progress into the room.

Sebastian swore creatively in French and English both.

"Milly hasn't come back. Aunt, please send a footman to retrieve the professor. We must make plans, and you must make calls."

She was being dispatched like a recruit taking messages to the officers' mess, a punishment for having failed so badly on the outing to the solicitors. Freddy scooped up Milly's cat, which had gained weight and *not* lost hair since joining the household.

"I will be gone within the half hour, Sebastian, and I will find you some answers, you may depend upon it." She owed him at least that—some answers, not all the answers.

Freddy deposited the cat in Sebastian's arms, and couldn't resist a single blow in her own defense.

"The way you feel now, sick with dread and worry, afraid anything you do to remedy the situation might make it worse? I felt that way for years, about you, and you came home in one piece. Remember that."

For an instant he looked puzzled.

"The coach is back," Michael said from his post at the window. "I don't see the baroness getting out of it."

Freddy left to execute her assignments. She'd had a chance to say her piece, which was as much as any condemned prisoner was allowed.

❧

Sebastian watched his only relative leave, and cuddled Milly's cat as if the damned beast could bring him some comfort.

"Does Aunt think I didn't worry for her? Didn't fret nightly the French would make off with her for some stupid lark? Didn't treasure her every letter? For God's sake, I love the woman—"

He sounded more French the more exhausted and indignant he became—the more desperate he felt.

Michael scratched the cat's chin, and a predictable rumble began.

"Shall I tell Lady Freddy of your love when Anduvoir has sent you to your dubious reward?"

"Sod yourself." The most English foul language Sebastian knew, words he could lay claim to honestly. "I told Milly I loved her, but I botched it."

The pity in Michael's gaze was hard to look upon, but even when Michael dropped his hand, the cat kept purring.

"How can a man botch telling the woman who loves him that he loves her too?"

"To Milly, I used the words as a weapon. I let the wrong instincts guide me."

"Truth can be a powerful weapon."

"A husband's truth, possibly, not an inquisitor's. An inquisitor deals in threats, manipulation, fear, and false hope."

"You never dealt in false hope."

They were arguing history, and miserable history at that, while Anduvoir was skulking about Mayfair and Milly was without protection.

"Enough, Michael. I'm off to find John Coachman. Ask the professor to wait for me."

A lift of Michael's eyebrow suggested he knew damned good and well Sebastian was excluding him from the interview with the coachman. Michael's loyalties had become suspect, and bringing Anduvoir to Sebastian's attention would be a convincing way to allay those suspicions.

Sebastian passed him the cat and headed for the mews.

Only to be radically disappointed.

"She got out at a hackney stand in Piccadilly," John Coachman said. "Cabs lined up in the street, patrons lined up on the walk. You can get a cab to pretty much anywhere from Piccadilly, my lord, including to King's Cross."

From whence the postal coaches took the Great North Road to points varied and distant.

Sebastian wanted to wring the old man's neck. "She gave you no indication of her direction? She popped out of the carriage and simply sent you on your way?" Milly might well have behaved exactly thus.

"She said I wasn't to worry, but to go directly home."

The coachman wasn't to worry. The *coachman* wasn't to *worry*. The dread congealing in Sebastian's chest acquired a new intensity, and a veneer of admiration. Whatever course she'd set, Milly was confident in it.

"What direction did the hackney stand face?"

"Northbound," the coachman said.

"T'weren't northbound."

Giles, Sebastian's largest footman, shifted from foot to foot two yards away.

"Now see here," the coachy said, drawing himself up. "You're not to interrupt your betters nor even to take notice of 'em without permission, young man. His lordship weren't asking you—"

"Why do you say it wasn't northbound?" Sebastian asked.

"We had to turn the coach around, and while we did, her ladyship crossed the street and hailed a westbound cab. I heard her holler to the fellow to take her to Chelsea, and she had a little satchel with her. I waved to her, and she waved back."

A woman utterly broken in spirit did not wave at

her servants across a busy thoroughfare. A fraction of Sebastian's unease relaxed.

"You're sure she said Chelsea?"

"Aye, milord. Driver answered her clear as day, 'Chelsea, it is!' Probably wanted to show the other fellows he'd landed a good fare."

Milly had been safe and happy in Chelsea; she'd had allies there. Of course, she'd seek comfort in familiar surroundings when her marriage was no comfort at all.

"Thank you, Giles. Walk with me, if you please."

As Sebastian traversed a short distance down the alley, he sorted through options. His first impulse was to retrieve his wife the way he'd pursue an escaped prisoner. She was his wife, and she belonged with him—belonged *to* him, and he to her. Except that sentiment bore a noticeable stench, not of loyalty or protectiveness, but of command and possessiveness.

His second impulse was to throw a saddle on Fable and tear out to Chelsea, which notion bore more than a whiff of desperation.

"Did her ladyship seem upset, Giles?"

"Tired, not upset." Giles was quite sure of his conclusion. "I have six sisters, milord. Her ladyship weren't in a taking. Them lawyers would try anybody's patience."

"Describe the satchel."

Sebastian listened with half an ear, because he knew well the little traveling bag Milly had appropriated from his wardrobe. He'd carried it to France as a boy, and brought it home from France as a man. The satchel was battered, sturdy, and stored with lavender sachets when not in use.

A third option emerged in Sebastian's mind, this one having a certain difficult rightness to it—a punishment to fit the crime, or a well-crafted penance. He was to do exactly as he'd expected his wife to do if she'd learned he'd gone off to a dawn meeting, and her all unsuspecting.

He was to sit at home and *do nothing* except worry and trust to her luck and her judgment. Chelsea was, after all, where Milly had kissed her husband for the first time, too.

Seventeen

WITHOUT PEOPLE TO LOVE IT, THE COTTAGE WAS NO longer home. Milly had not even a cat to share that realization with. Despite a lack of appetite, she was making an evening meal of bread and cheese, when she heard a knock on the kitchen door.

"Sebastian."

Though if he'd come for her, Milly was at least resolved they'd arrive to some understandings before she returned to his household. She tidied the crumbs off the table, touched a hand to her hair, and opened the door.

"Your ladyship." Giles bowed low, an incongruous gesture given that he was in a workingman's rough clothing rather than footman's livery.

"Giles, good evening. Is anything amiss?"

He came up smiling. "That's what I was to ask. His lordship sent me to make sure you didn't need anything."

Milly needed her husband's trust, she needed sleep, and she needed courage. She glanced behind Giles, half hoping to see the St. Clair town coach in the alley.

"I wasn't sent to fetch you unless you want to be fetched, mum. The dog cart is waiting up at the corner."

"You're not to bring me home?" Not that she'd allow any but her husband to escort her.

"Not unless you'd like to go home, but I am to bring you this." He hefted a familiar-looking wicker basket.

"You may set it on the counter." Milly stared at the basket long enough to know Peter was not among its contents, which was some reassurance. "How did you leave his lordship, Giles?"

Giles set the basket on the counter. Crockery within the wicker tinkled at the shift. "He be in a taking, you ask me, and ain't nobody never seen his lordship in a taking."

Oh, dear. "His hair is sticking up in all directions, he can't hold still, and he sounds very English?"

Giles apparently found the basket worthy of study too. "He be cursin', ma'am, in English and Frenchie both."

Protectiveness and guilt tugged at Milly's resolve.

"The tavern halfway down the block on the high street serves a wonderful summer ale, Giles. Perhaps you'd enjoy a pint and then check back with me?"

He bowed again. "Always did enjoy a good summer ale."

When he was gone and Milly had put away her bread and cheese, she considered the hamper. Darkness was falling, though the moon would be up in less than two hours. She could return to Mayfair safely enough with Giles's escort…if she had to.

She opened the hamper and lifted a book from among the contents. The title was not easy to decipher, but Milly recognized a capital *M*, and kept puzzling it out, just as she'd puzzled out every word of the bill of sale she'd signed earlier in the day.

When she realized she was holding a copy of *The Mysteries of Udolpho* by Ann Radcliffe, an ache started up in her throat. A letter in Sebastian's flowing hand fell from between the pages of the book.

As she stumbled, trudged, and groped her way through her husband's letter, Milly began to cry.

Dearest Milly,

I have betrayed your trust, and for this I can only apologize. The habit to protect those I care about is of long standing, and at times has been all that has sustained me, my only lodestar. I am blessed with a wife who can protect herself better than most, who is resourceful, resilient, and capable of making her own sound decisions. I see this, now.

I pray you will decide to resume your place beside me, and promise you most solemnly that I have presumed on your forgiving nature, at least as regards my past, for the last time.

No more duels, Milly. I vow this. No more contests of honor, not by sword, pistol, fists, whips, knives…none of it. No more lies to spare me difficult explanations, no more assuming my secrecy shows regard for any save myself. The debt to my past must be regarded as paid with interest if I am, as you say, allowing it to rob me of a future, much less a future with you.

I await your response, but urge you not to rush. Your answer matters to me so very much, I will be as patient as you need me to be.

I've learned that my enemies are abroad right here in London, old foes who would harm any I care about in their effort to harm me. Be careful, my love. Bad enough I jeopardize your regard with my present folly. Don't allow the enemies of my past to jeopardize your person as well.

I remain your most loving husband,
Sebastian

❦

Milly wore an old frock, one stored in the trunks Alcorn and Frieda had apparently not found in the attic. With Giles beside her in his everyday dress, they were just another young couple, tooling about in a dog cart, likely going into Town to visit relations or do some afternoon shopping.

She had waited the entire morning and even into afternoon, as Sebastian had suggested—not ordered—and her only course remained to return to her husband.

Though she was still angry with him. One heart-wrenching note did not a marriage repair. She understood better now why separate bedrooms might have some appeal, though the thought rankled.

"Traffic be a right bear," Giles said. "Makes a man miss the village."

"Would you rather work at St. Clair Manor, Giles?"

As he handled the reins with the competence of a country-bred man, Giles's ears turned red. "The city ain't so bad."

Milly recalled his affection for one of the maids, and had the happy thought that being Sebastian's baroness required skills other than reading menus or arguing with one's spouse. Two servants could transfer households as easily as one, provided the young lady was willing.

As the cart rattled from Knightsbridge to the shady perimeter of Hyde Park, Milly admitted she was not traveling into London because she was ready to forgive and forget. She was ready to listen, and to be listened to.

Which might not be enough.

"Mayfair has some of the widest streets in London, and yet the traffic here is some of the worst. Makes no sense a'tall," Giles groused.

"We'll be home soon," Milly said, and part of her could not wait to see her husband again, while another part of her dreaded a difficult confrontation.

Giles slowed the cart to accommodate a dray turning across an intersection before them. "What do you suppose Lady Freddy be doing out strolling without the professor?"

Milly pulled her thoughts off the speech she would deliver to her husband and followed Giles's gesture with the whip. Lady Freddy was indeed on the arm of a strange man, or rather…

The fellow was portly, well dressed, and fairly dragging Freddy along by the elbow. Because the couple was across the way and up the street, Milly did not shout out a greeting to Sebastian's aunt.

When she might have waved, she checked the impulse. Cold slithered down her spine, the same cold she'd experienced reading Alcorn's helpful little note. Sebastian's enemies were loose in London itself, and would use any means to harm him.

"I think he has a weapon pressed to her side, Giles. Lady Freddy's in danger. His lordship warned me—"

"Then we'd best get help," Giles said, asking the horse to pick up its pace.

"No, Giles. That fellow will make off with Freddy, and we'll never find her. Turn the cart when next you can and then hop out. You alert his lordship."

Giles's expression went from affable footman happily in service, to sturdy young fellow not about to countenance foolery. "His lordship won't like it, milady. He'll sack me, and properly so."

"His lordship will not like his aunt being carried off to France, or the war office, or wherever that man is taking her. I am the Baroness St. Clair, and I am ordering you to do as I say."

Giles did not slow the cart.

"Please, Giles. I'll be careful. Dressed as I am, I'm just another village girl about my business, and nobody will remark this cart." Up the street, the man escorting Lady Freddy turned her down a side street. "I'll follow them. All I'll do is follow them. Tell his lordship that."

Giles passed her the reins. "I'll expect a decent character from you when he sacks me."

"A glowing character, and he won't sack you."

Giles was out of the cart before the horse had halted. He loped off in the direction of the St. Clair town house, while Milly clucked to the horse and tried to look as if she drove unescorted through the streets of Mayfair as a matter of course.

The fiction was barely supportable, but as she followed Aunt Freddy and her dubious companion northward, the traffic became less fashionable and neighborhoods became less grand.

Also utterly unfamiliar.

❧

"Describe the man with my aunt." Sebastian saw the effect his captain-of-the-guard inflection had on his footman, and tried for a more moderate tone. "Giles, your position is not in jeopardy, but my aunt, and very likely my baroness, are. Was the fellow well dressed?"

Giles had found him in the music room, and Sebastian wanted answers before Michael or the professor joined them.

"He were well dressed, top hat, and fine coat, but they were walking away from us, so I couldn't see if he had a watch chain and such. He did have a cane."

A sword cane, likely, or a piece with a weighted handle. Old bones broke so easily.

"Anything else? What drew your eye to him in the first place?"

Giles's brow knitted. The fellow wasn't stupid. He was, in fact, shrewd enough to know a less than creditable answer to his betters would result in both disbelief and ridicule, and yet, Sebastian dared not prompt any particular answer.

"You must have sensed something…?"

"He walked funny, like a woman trying to draw a fellow's notice."

More than dress, more than accent, more than any other detail, Giles's observation confirmed that Aunt Freddy had fallen into Anduvoir's clutches.

"What was my baroness wearing?"

Giles described a worn brown dress, years out of fashion, one that might blend in well anywhere in London *except* Mayfair. As Sebastian noted the details of Giles's description—Milly was an attractive woman, maybe especially to a young footman—another part of Sebastian reached for the ability to think without feeling, to make decisions based on facts rather than emotion.

Viewed in this light, Milly's decision to pursue Anduvoir was exactly the same sound judgment Michael had shown the previous day, and yet Sebastian wanted to throttle her for it. She did not know who or what she followed. He could only pray he had the chance to throttle her.

"Has the baroness returned?" The professor's question was casual as he stood in the music-room door, but his posture was alert, an old hound catching the scent of trouble.

"She has not. Giles, you're excused. Say nothing to anybody of this, and that includes—"

Michael appeared at the professor's shoulder. "I saw Giles return on foot, and it is by no means his day off." An accusation rather than observation.

Giles hurried from the room, and a silence took root in his wake. Michael had deserted his Highland unit to join Sebastian's guard at the Château. No sane man had joined the French cause as the English offensive across Spain had picked up momentum.

Neither did a sane man remain in the employ of a traitor universally loathed by all of Polite Society.

Abruptly, Sebastian had no more time to gather information, to consider, to equivocate.

"Michael, you are either a traitor to the traitor, or you are my friend."

"I am your friend." The answer was swift, certain, and exactly what a traitor would say. Michael's expression, though, wasn't pugnacious, but rather, damnably understanding. "We can debate my loyalties for what remains of the day, or we can solve whatever problem has you mad enough to kill with your bare hands."

Sebastian examined his hands, which had formed into fists. Many mornings, he and Michael rode the most remote paths of Hyde Park's several hundred acres. Michael had had myriad opportunities to murder the Traitor Baron, if his intent were that simple.

His deeper motives would keep for another day.

"Anduvoir has Aunt Freddy, and Milly is in pursuit of them. I need a map of Bloomsbury."

"Give me five minutes," the professor said, spinning on his heel. "The library is full of atlases."

Michael bent to pick up Milly's cat, who appeared to have no qualms about the man's uses or his loyalties. "I am not your enemy, St. Clair. I might have been at one point, but—"

Sebastian waited for the damned cat to start purring, but it leaped from Michael's arms, hit the floor with a solid thud, and stropped itself against Sebastian's boots.

"You needed at least one friend," Michael went on. "A man can endure much, if he has one true friend. I'm not French, I'm not English, and that seemed to qualify me for the position."

Which left the question, who was Michael's friend, for Sebastian could not regard himself in that light because…

One confided one's burdens in one's friends.

"Aunt said Captain Lord Anderson is responsible for inspiring both MacHugh and Pierpont into challenging me. I suspect the others would also admit he had a hand in resurrecting their patriotic indignation."

"Anderson is a buffoon," Michael replied as Sebastian scooped up Milly's pet. "He's a good choice as a pawn, though. He looks the part of affronted military dignity, but for God's sake, he spent less than a fortnight at the Château. That cat likes you."

Michael sounded more puzzled than peeved, but then, the cat was not particularly French or English, either. The beast was purring and bopping its head against Sebastian's chin.

"Peter is a defender of the hearts of women. His regard is worth having, but let's see where the professor has got off to with that map."

Fifteen minutes later, Sebastian had finally located the damned map in an old survey atlas. Michael found the street where Anduvoir's rooms were, though the atlas gave it a different name.

"It's a rooming house, is my guess," Michael said. "One main entrance front and back, as if it used to be a dwelling for a family of some means. Three stories above the street, a tavern to the immediate left, a book shop to the right."

Sebastian set the atlas aside, having learned all he could from it.

"We have about an hour of light if he's taken Aunt to his rooms." Time for him to arrive there, and time for Milly to get the hell home. No matter how often Sebastian silently cursed the clock, and no matter in which language, Milly was not yet safely home. "I want to rescue my aunt, but I need to find my wife."

And God help him, God damn him and God help him, if he had to choose which one to protect.

"They were on foot," the professor observed. "If he were intent on leaving the City, Anduvoir would have jumped into the nearest hack."

Beyond the library, a door slammed elsewhere in the house.

Milly. Please, let that be Milly.

She came pelting into the library, no bonnet, no gloves. "Sebastian! Thank God you're home. There's a man, he's French, he has Aunt Freddy, and you must listen to me."

The cat vaulted onto the desk an instant before Milly slammed into Sebastian's chest. Michael closed the door, and the professor sank into a chair.

"It's all right," Sebastian said. Now that he held his wife safe in his arms, everything that mattered was all right. "We know who he is, we know how he thinks. We know, and we'll get Aunt out of there before the moon rises."

Milly pulled back enough that Sebastian could see the desperation in her eyes. "No, Sebastian. Whatever you do, you must not go to your aunt's aid. That's exactly what he wants, and you must not accommodate him. It's you he wants, and you he's determined to see killed."

❧

"Of course, it is." Sebastian sounded almost amused, and Milly wanted to pummel him—just as soon as she'd held on to him as tightly as her strength allowed and breathed in his sandalwood scent and kissed him to within an inch of his life.

"Shall I ring for tea?" Michael asked.

"No!" Sebastian and Milly answered in unison, Milly in a near shout, Sebastian in implacable tones of command.

"We haven't time," Milly said. "This man, this Frenchman, wants you to come looking for Aunt Freddy. He wanted to take me, but Freddy went out to cut some roses. His plan is…"

His plan was damned clever. Clever enough to work.

Sebastian nuzzled at Milly's temple, a soft, soothing gesture. "Let's sit, shall we?"

"I want to pace, Sebastian. I want to break things. He's awful, that fellow. I think even Aunt was more scared than angry around him."

Milly felt rather than saw the glance this comment provoked among the men.

"Did Anduvoir see you, Milly?" Despite Sebastian's calm tone, Milly knew the question was fraught.

"No, he did not. I overheard him as he strutted and preened about his room. It's a pleasant afternoon, and his room is at the back of some little house thirteen streets from here. He left a window open."

To sit beside Sebastian, to hear his voice and feel him solid and strong beside her, was exactly what Milly had been craving since seeing Aunt Freddy abducted. His presence gave her the strength to call upon her memorization skills, the skills honed in a dozen cold schoolrooms and hundreds of long evenings by the fire with her aunts.

"His plan is as follows—he wanted to impress Aunt

Freddy with it, or intimidate her. He has notes waiting for you all over London, sending you on a game of fox and geese to rescue Aunt. He has paid people to deny you ever came to retrieve these notes, the first of which he will have delivered right here."

"He's been watching us," Michael said. "Bloody hell, I should have seen—"

"Michael." Sebastian hadn't raised his voice or even put much emphasis on the single word, but Michael fell silent.

"The point of this haring about is for you to be unaccounted for this evening, while Anduvoir himself assassinates the Duke of Wellington, an act for which he will see you blamed. He'll use more notes, and some sort of poison, so that Wellington collapses before a good two dozen of his former officers at some regimental dinner. Sebastian, Anduvoir has many samples of your handwriting, and he sounded…*gleeful* to contemplate you being hanged for murder."

"And such a murder," the professor murmured. "The last thing the French would do is stir up a hornet's nest this grand."

"Which leaves us with why Anduvoir is getting up to such tricks, and how we can stop him and retrieve Freddy from his clutches."

Milly felt Sebastian's lips as he spoke against her temple, and yet, beside her, his body had undergone a change. He was not relaxed; he was not calm. He'd gone into a state of battle readiness beyond calm.

He rose and drew Milly to her feet, wrapping his arm around her. "There being nobody else well suited to the task, I shall present myself at Wellington's little fete."

"They'll kill you," Michael said. "If you burst in uninvited on the lot of them, their dress swords at hand, the liquor flowing freely, they'll fall upon you like a pack of dogs, and Wellington himself may not be able to stop them."

Sebastian's chin rested on the top of Milly's head, while she clung to him.

"I am exhausted, Michael," he said. "Weary to death of defending myself against all comers for actions that were the best I could manage at the time. My whereabouts will be impossible to deny if I attend this party, and my presence at Wellington's table the only defense I can make. Then, too, I might be able to save His Grace's life."

Michael and the professor argued with him and swore and argued some more, but Sebastian's plan made a kind of dreadful sense.

When it had been decided that Michael, the professor, and Giles would retrieve Aunt Freddy as soon as darkness had fallen, Milly found herself alone with her husband—her doomed husband.

"You've been very quiet," Sebastian said, leading her over to the desk. He sat back against it, positioning Milly so she stood between his legs. "Talk to me, Milly."

"I want to go with you."

He kissed her, and in that kiss—sweet, tender, full of regret—he informed her that her daft notion would never form part of his plans.

"The less you're associated with me now, the better. My suggestion for when this is all over is for you to retire to St. Clair Manor and enjoy being the Baroness St. Clair. You will be wealthy, you know, and you have a life estate in the dower house, regardless of what the Crown does with the succession."

"I want no wealth, Sebastian. I've some money of my own, as it turns out. I want to grow old with you, to name our babies, to——"

Another kiss. "Milly, I know. I wish…I did not want you to hate me. I did not want my troubles to become yours. I did not want to leave you alone."

The regret in his voice was piercing and genuine. Milly wanted to shake him to silence lest he break her heart.

"I love you." Milly did not regret the words, only the circumstances under which she'd said them. "I love you because you are not hiding this awful business from me. You are not shutting me out as if I hadn't a brain in my head. I love you because you could be catching a packet for somewhere far away right now, throwing your clothes into a trunk, grabbing the jewels, and fleeing, but that would only mean this nasty Frenchman has won, after you've fought so hard and so well against that very outcome."

He pulled back and studied her for a long moment, his expression curious, not one Milly had seen him wear previously. "You understand."

"I hate that you're put in this position, but yes, I understand. Have you your knives?"

"I will not leave this house without them."

"I'll help you change. You must be quite the baron when you show up at this party, Sebastian, quite the English baron."

He held her for one more instant, a moment in

which Milly fought back all the arguments she had for joining him on that packet, sending him to his club rather than on this doomed outing, or trying to lock him in their rooms until this madness had passed.

Except that way would lead to more madness, more duels, more nasty Frenchmen, more war waged against Sebastian's honor and his right to a peaceful old age.

"Come," Milly said, stepping back and taking him by the hand. "None of your expensive cologne tonight either. You will reek of bay rum and English respectability, and make these men listen to you."

While she would have his bottle of scent to torment herself with through all the years of her widowhood if they killed him instead of listening to him.

∿

"Sir, you haven't an invitation."

Wellington's staff was formidable, but no match for Sebastian's resolve. "I have misplaced it, along with my patience. Where is His Grace?"

Something about Sebastian's tone must have convinced the butler that here, despite a lack of uniform, was an officer expecting to be obeyed. "His Grace is in the kitchen, seeing to the final prep—"

"Get to the kitchen and tell him to not sample a single dish, most especially the mushrooms, not even one."

The butler, a stocky fellow who could easily have passed for a gunnery sergeant in livery, blinked.

"Go, man! Your master's life may depend upon it." Rather than linger in the foyer, Sebastian dashed past the goggling footmen and headed for the stairs. A commotion above stairs could get His Grace's legendary nose out of the soup pot faster than any bowing and scraping servant's summons.

"But, *sir*! You haven't an invita—"

"Fetch me the duke!" Sebastian bellowed over his shoulder.

He did not know the layout of Apsley House, but the dining room was readily apparent from the noise and merriment issuing from it. Sebastian forced himself to slow to a walk, a dignified, unconcerned, baronial walk.

And he tried not to think of Milly, sending him on his way with a kiss "for luck."

She had not forbidden him to attempt this, and he wasn't sure he could have thwarted her wishes if she had.

Sebastian said a short prayer for his wife's happiness and sauntered into the Duke of Wellington's formal dining room.

"What the deuce!"

"Damn me, if it ain't St. Clair."

"You mean Girard."

Conversation stopped as Sebastian paused near the door. "Good evening, gentlemen. Don't let me interrupt you."

The sound of a sword being drawn scraped through the ensuing silence, while Sebastian noted food had already been placed on the table, including several plates of sautéed mushrooms.

"St. Clair." The Duke of Mercia gestured from his place near the head of the table. He looked elegant and relaxed even while he glared murder at Sebastian. "Best hare off, sir. Not your type of gathering."

Mercia had rank, and so the rest of the mob might

follow his lead. He also had the presence of mind to remain seated, rather than provoke a full-out charge on Sebastian.

"It's *exactly* his type of gathering," somebody said as another sword was drawn. "It's a welcome St. Clair should have been given months ago in some dark alley full of garbage and offal just like him."

Mercia's gaze darted to the door, suggesting footmen might be creeping up from the corridor.

"Captain Anderson," Sebastian called over the rising murmur of ill will. "Let's talk about garbage and offal. You've recently been keeping company with my former superior officer. You might know him only as Henri, or perhaps as Henri Montresslor or Henri Archambault. To me and some of your fellows, he was Henri Anduvoir."

Anderson turned so the sideboard was at his back. "I know of no Henri Anduvoir." He tossed back a drink, while the room again fell silent.

"Short, balding, well fed. He plucked at your pride and told you a pack of believable lies without ever offering any proof of his rank or authority. Probably told you he represented the entire French nation, without any orders, letters, or corroboration—and I wouldn't eat that mushroom, Dirks. Might give you a nasty, permanent bellyache."

Dirks put the mushroom down and wiped his fingers.

"You're the one who's lying," Anderson retorted.

Mercia set his drink aside and rose. "Anderson, perhaps you'd like to reconsider your words."

"I'm under orders," Anderson said, drawing himself up. "St. Clair is an embarrassment to two sovereign nations."

The assemblage apparently agreed with this conclusion as more swords came into evidence. Mercia mouthed the word, "Go," though Sebastian wasn't about to turn his back on this mob.

"I've met this Anduvoir. Rather wish I hadn't." The speaker was a lean fellow of about six feet. He wore a captain's uniform.

"Mr. Pixler." Sebastian bowed, though the man was his social inferior. "Good evening."

"You say Anduvoir is here in London?" Pixler asked.

"Then we'll kill him too," somebody volunteered.

"Not until you hear me out," Sebastian retorted. "The lot of you are being manipulated by a Frenchman whose only loyalty is to his own schemes. Anderson goads you into challenging me, thinking he's following some obscure orders, and you risk your lives to settle a score that His Grace put to rest decisively at Waterloo."

"Time somebody put you to rest," Anderson sneered. The uniformed rabble around him seconded that sentiment, and Mercia's gaze became resigned.

Sebastian was about to reach for his knife when the sound of a bottle breaking against the edge of the table galvanized the two dozen brave fellows around him.

"Not a fair fight, gentlemen," Mercia observed, though the comment hardly helped matters.

"As if he was fair to us," Anderson said, brandishing a sword that looked more functional than decorative. "For two weeks I suffered his attentions, and I'm lucky I can sleep at night."

The quiet in the room shifted, and Sebastian sensed movement behind him.

"One hears you've been doing something other than sleeping at night, Anderson," said the Duke of Wellington. "And that your lady wife is to be congratulated accordingly. Gentlemen, stand down."

For perhaps the first time in a long and distinguished military career, the Duke of Wellington was not immediately obeyed. Nobody sheathed his sword; nobody stepped back.

"He's left us with more nightmares than any man has a right to, Your Grace." Pierpont offered that retort, and the men closest to Sebastian edged nearer.

Wellington did not look amused. "Are you countermanding a direct order, Captain?"

An ugly silence spread. These men were no longer under Wellington's command, and yet, they were guests in his home and had served under him, some of them for most of their adult lives.

And still, not one soldier heeded the duke's mandate.

Eighteen

A LOUD CRASH SOUNDED TOWARD THE BACK OF THE room, where a second door led to adjoining parlors. All heads turned to see a porcelain vase in shards on the floor.

"If you won't listen to His Grace's common sense, you will listen to mine."

"Her again. I thought ye said she wasna daft," came from another corner.

Milly swept forward through the officers, her cloak a magnificent green velvet, her red hair an artful cascade, jewels flashing at her throat, ears, and wrists.

"Baroness." Wellington himself bowed over her hand, and the mood in the room abruptly shifted from ugly to…awkward. A lady had invited herself to a summary execution, and that, in the opinion of every officer there, *would not do*.

Milly curtsied prettily but none too low to the duke, then turned to survey the room.

"When a child is caught being naughty, he invariably blames his governess or his mama or his puppy, but seldom his own poor judgment. You fellows similarly blame St. Clair for your capture, but I tire of pointing out that he captured none of you. He deprived none of you of your uniforms. He challenges none of you to these *stupid* duels, and if this keeps up, I will inform your ladies of your foolishness."

Swords lowered. The men in the room looked anywhere but at Sebastian's wife.

"My dear baroness," Wellington said. "If you'd permit an old soldier to have the floor?"

Milly nodded—regally—and Sebastian wanted badly to kiss his wife, also to pitch her out the nearest window if it would keep her safe.

Wellington sauntered forward, to the head of the table. "You fellows heard the baroness, and now you will do me the courtesy of listening to me as well."

His Grace picked up a plate of sautéed mushrooms, apparently intent on snitching an appetizer.

"Don't, Your Grace!" Sebastian fairly bellowed the words. Milly regarded him with consternation, suggesting even summary executions required a certain etiquette. "Don't touch those mushrooms. Anduvoir fancies himself something of a gourmand, and he's been known to use poison."

Wellington regarded the morsel in his hand. "And you know this, how?"

"He tried to poison me shortly before Toulouse fell."

"Oh, St. Clair." Milly crossed the room to take his hand—his left hand, which would leave his right free to reach for his knife, should he need to defend her. "Your own commanding officer. Why would he do that?"

Wellington pitched the mushroom back onto the

tray and wiped his fingers on a linen serviette. "I can shed light on that, if my officers will be so good as to sheathe their swords?"

Metal scraped; Mercia took his seat. Over by the sideboard, glassware tinkled, as if someone had resumed pouring drinks.

"Pixler was the one to alert us to your location," Wellington said. "Your aunt knew you were in the south of France somewhere, but you'd been careful not to reveal your position in what correspondence she'd had from you."

"For obvious reasons," Sebastian said. Milly's fingers tightened around his hand.

"Just so," His Grace replied. "You could not have the baroness importuned for such intelligence. Bad enough we gentlemen must choose between duty to our loved ones and duty to the Crown. No need to put the ladies in such a position—and yet, I did. Would somebody find a chair for my guest and his baroness?"

The duke's courtesy—referring to Sebastian as a guest, having chairs fetched—set off an alarm in the back of Sebastian's mind.

"We'll stand," Milly said. "And we really can't be staying."

Sebastian did kiss her, right on her helpful mouth. "Your Grace was saying?"

"We learned from Pixler where you were, and we also learned the boy would have died without your intervention. The beating he took was severe, true, but he said that was more Anduvoir's doing than yours. Then came the ransom request."

Sebastian realized too late the direction the duke's recitation might take.

"Many officers were unofficially ransomed, Your Grace. The French needed coin badly, despite the official position."

"True enough, but not every officer whose family lacked the funds to ransom him found the lady of the house sitting down to whist across from your dear aunt. Seems Lady Frederica had a prodigious run of bad luck when she opposed Pixler's mother, and somehow, I gather this is not news to you."

Milly's arms around Sebastian's waist went from protective to necessary, lest his very knees buckle. "How did you learn of that?"

Nobody was ever supposed to know, save Freddy and the professor, and nobody would have believed—

"I didn't figure it out until the third or fourth occasion of such a coincidence, and then I noticed other patterns as well. Nobody died at your hands, St. Clair, and some weren't even beaten, and yet you had a reputation for reducing a man to tears and plucking all his secrets from him."

"At least one secret from every man," Sebastian said, but he'd nearly whispered the words, while his worlds—his French world and his English world—collided. "I demanded one secret to show my superiors, lest somebody else, somebody worse, be given my command."

He was at risk for babbling out all of his own secrets, so when Milly kissed him on the mouth, he shut up.

"Yes, you extracted from each officer foolish enough to be found behind enemy lines out of uniform

one bit of information—more from a few of the loqua-
cious ones—and you found a way to return them to
us more or less whole. This one you ransomed with
funds from your own pocket, that one you slipped into
a clandestine prisoner exchange, the other escaped after
a productive interrogation session—such a pity—and
was not recaptured."

His Grace appeared to study a wine goblet half-full
of a pretty ruby claret, and the only sound in the room
was Milly sniffling into Sebastian's handkerchief.

"Every officer you tortured came home,"
Wellington said softly. "Even Mercia, whose circumstances were complicated, indeed. I concluded you
were a far greater asset to England in your French
garrison than you could have been anywhere else."

"Nobody else—" Sebastian did not know whether
to be grateful for, or furious at, Wellington's recitation.

"Nobody else figured this out? Your aunt clearly
had more than an inkling, and she begged me to
extricate you from a situation that was obviously difficult and dangerous for you. You were and are a peer
of the realm, the Baron St. Clair, a man serving in a
war zone, who lacked legitimate male progeny, and if
anybody should have been offered safe passage home,
it was you."

"Yes," Milly said, eyes glittering. "Exactly, and yet
you left him there on that miserable pile of rocks, left
him without an ally, without any support, and then let
these imbeciles challenge him to duel after duel. How
could you, Your Grace?"

She voiced Sebastian's own questions, because
incredulity was quickly giving way to rage. The anger

trickled into him, a warmth and sense of rightness to it he'd craved for years.

"Lady Frederica and I reached a compromise," Wellington said. "I sent you a guardian angel, so to speak, and he had orders to offer you safe passage if your life were imperiled. Brodie's first message back to us was that your life was imperiled daily by your own superior officer, by the advancing English, and by the conflicted loyalties that demanded you abuse your peers to ensure they remained in your care. He requested permission to extricate you from the Château, and I put the matter to your aunt."

The room was quieter than a graveyard in the middle of a winter night.

"You made an old woman choose between her only living male relative and the safety of British officers held captive at my garrison," Sebastian said, slowly and clearly, as if the words pronounced sentence on Wellington rather than verified his strategy. "Freddy chose for England, and I remained at that garrison, torturing men I ought to have served with, bankrupting my birthright and my reason, while the same old woman was left to contend with neglected estates, dwindling resources, and no family at her side."

Had Milly not been weeping softly against his chest, Sebastian would likely have strangled Wellington right then and there. Not an entire regiment of officers would have stopped him. He would have strangled him for Aunt Freddy, for Milly, for himself, and for the men who'd challenged him, for they had been put at risk every bit as much as he.

While Sebastian frankly clung to his wife, he spared a thought for what Freddy had gone through, for the impossible choice she'd faced, much like the impossible choices Sebastian had faced.

Mercia rose. "You were betrayed," he said quietly. Over Milly's head, Sebastian saw him looking around the room, seeking any who would argue that conclusion. "You are no traitor to England, though England surely betrayed you. I am profoundly sorry for it."

Mercia saluted with his wineglass. One by one, the other officers rose and offered a silent toast, until Wellington himself lifted a goblet.

"Sir, I salute you for your aid in the capture of one Henri Anduvoir, a criminal wanted by his own authorities for embezzling monies due the *République* as spoils of war—substantial sums, as it turns out."

His Grace paused for a considering sip of claret. "The French asked for our aid, which took no small toll on their pride. Anduvoir was here to see you killed—you had put those sums into his hands to be delivered to his superiors—but Anduvoir also sought to plant evidence that you had stolen that money, too. I hope you consider matters between you and the Crown acceptably addressed after this day's work, for the Crown considers itself in your debt."

Sebastian managed to ask the only pertinent question. "You have Anduvoir in custody, then?"

"We do. Brodie reported the address by messenger earlier today and demanded my aid in seeing your aunt to safety. Seems a certain Frenchman tried to interfere with the King's men when about the King's business. Dreadfully stupid of him. Mortally stupid, I should think."

"Don't think it," Milly snapped. "Make sure of it, if you please."

"I rather agree with the lady," Mercia drawled.

A chorus of "hear, hear" followed, though to Sebastian, the words and the goodwill they embodied rang hollow. The only solid thing in his awareness at that moment was the woman who still held on to him for dear life.

"St. Clair, will you and your lady stay to enjoy the meal with us?" Wellington asked.

His Grace was extending an olive branch, and though the officers might be willing to let the past remain in the past, Wellington's overture presaged not merely tolerance, but acceptance.

Approval, even, from the most respected subject of the British Crown. Though this might for years have been the answer to prayers Sebastian dared not admit to even himself, now it mattered not in the least.

"I think not," Milly said. "St. Clair, I am quite fatigued. If you would please take me home?"

Sebastian did not glance at Wellington or Mercia, or anybody else who might have ventured an opinion, for the lot of them could go to blazes.

"Of course, my dear. Events have been wearying in the extreme."

She took his arm, but they did not escape without Mercia—the man certainly knew how to make his opinions known—instigating a round of applause, in which Wellington himself joined.

❦

Milly forced herself to loosen her grip on Sebastian's hand. "Tell me you are not about to run down this street, tearing your hair and screaming French obscenities."

"I am not."

He walked along beside her, while Milly stifled the impulses she'd just named. For a good two dozen yards, she managed to hold her silence.

"Sebastian, how *are* you?"

He kissed her knuckles. "Quite well."

Milly lasted a dozen yards this time. "Talk to me, Husband, or so help me, I will lose my reason."

Right there in the street, with fashionable carriages rumbling past on the way to an evening's entertainment, Sebastian stopped and wrapped her in his arms.

"I am walking out of the Château again, but this time, I am taking my heart, my soul, and my future with me. The prospect will take some getting used to."

Milly caught a whiff of lavender from the small bouquet she'd affixed to his lapel not two hours earlier. "Will you take your baroness with you?"

His arms slipped away, and he resumed walking, not even taking her hand.

"What nonsense is this, Wife? We're married. I was thinking of moving to Patagonia with you."

Milly held her ground as he strolled off. "Sebastian, I *left* you. I purchased my own establishment in Chelsea as insurance, in case our difficulties could not be resolved. I'm worse than Wellington, who was at least trying to win a war."

His lordship came stomping back to her side.

"You did not leave me. You shut me out, in the

same manner I had first demonstrated to you. We are done with such folly. Did you read my letter?"

She'd memorized his letter. "Yes. The letter was very prettily written."

By the light of the streetlamp, Milly saw that her answer had baffled him.

"You came home on the strength of a pretty letter? I bare my soul to you, offer my most profound and heartfelt sentiments...?"

She did not want him marching off into the darkness, so she took his hand. "The letter was very nice, but the book decided me."

Sebastian allowed her to tow him in the direction of their home. "You came back to me for *Mrs. Radcliffe*?"

"I came back to you because my heart and soul were in your keeping, and if your sole fault was protectiveness toward me—a protectiveness which was apparently well-founded—then I stand guilty of the same transgression toward you. I could not leave you to deal with those enemies you referred to by yourself, and I could not forgive myself if I'd added to your worries when your enemies were skulking about London itself."

He looped her arm through his, as a proper escort would, or as a man intent on preventing a woman from fleeing might. "Mrs. Radcliffe told you that?"

"Yes."

Milly's husband had more patience than she, because he let her wander along at his side in silence until they were nearly home.

"We have all of Mrs. Radcliffe's novels in the

library, you know." He offered this as they tarried on the steps of the town house, Sebastian two steps higher. Milly could see his face in the shadows of the porch light, could see he was asking a question.

"I cannot read well," Milly said. "I never will. This does not matter to you, much as your military past does not matter to me, though anything that troubles you troubles me as well. I have longed for the ability to curl up with a novel on a rainy afternoon, swilling tea before a crackling fire while enjoying a rousing tale of love and adventure."

"I want that for you too. I wanted it for you in Chelsea if I couldn't provide it to you in Mayfair. I hoped you'd understand that."

Milly touched the lavender on his lapel. "It's a silly dream, to indulge in such a pastime. More than I ever wanted that rainy afternoon, I want a tale of love and adventure with you. You will read to me, Sebastian. You will deal with children who perhaps don't read so well. You will guard my heart and allow me to guard yours. I will go to Patagonia with you, of course I will, if that dream can be ours."

He came down the steps and enveloped her in his arms. "I will love you. I do love you."

Milly twined her arms around him. "And I love you."

She didn't know how long she stood on the steps, reveling in her husband's embrace, but the door opened, and Michael stood in the entrance, the light from the foyer turning his blond hair into a nimbus.

"I don't know about all this talk of moving to Patagonia," he said, "but Lady Freddy's in the music room, threatening to decamp for the Continent, and

the professor isn't having much luck talking her out
of it."

⚜

Sebastian was not about to face Freddy without
reinforcements. He tucked Milly against his side and
headed for the music room.

"You, I will deal with later," he tossed over his
shoulder at Michael.

Michael, the imbecile, flourished a salute and fell in
behind them.

"Sebastian, you must not be too hard on Aunt.
She's old, and she is more tenderhearted than she
seems, and you—"

"Hush," Sebastian said as he held the music-room
door for his baroness. "We will deal with this."

Lady Freddy sat in the middle of the sofa, while the
professor stood sentry duty near the piano. "She thinks
you will throw her out," Baum said, a German accent
much in evidence.

"For what? Conduct unbecoming?"

Freddy's head snapped up. "I'll go. You need not
indulge in dramatics, though I will take a few days to
make my farewells."

She launched off the sofa, while Baumgartner
looked increasingly distraught.

"Where will you go?" Sebastian asked. "France?"

"I hate France, and while we're about it, I very nearly
hate England," she said, pacing to the window, turning,
and pacing back. "Wellington left the decision in my
hands, you see, and what was I to do? If you came home,
you'd want to buy your colors anyway, and then—"

"There I'd be," Sebastian finished for her, "wondering if I'd shot Cousin Luc today, or made a widow of Cousin Lisbette. Perhaps if the invasion of France were successful, I'd be treated to the sight of my men torching *Grand-père's* estate, or pillaging his vineyards. What a fine treat that would have been."

Freddy stopped fluttering around the room. She pretended to study a bouquet of bloodred roses, while her eyes filled with years and years of grief.

"Or you would have stayed here, humoring an old woman's fears, hating your duty to the succession, worrying for your mother's people. Here, you had only me. In France, you had aunts and uncles, cousins, grandparents. Do you know how many letters I started, asking you to come home?"

"Too many," Sebastian said.

"*Liebchen,*" Baumgartner murmured, "this serves nothing."

"We'll tour the pumpernickel courts," Freddy said. "They're a friendly lot, and my German is passable."

"I'll not have you deserting at this late date," Sebastian said, "though if you truly want to muster out, say, for a wedding journey, I'll consider it."

Milly looked worried, and Sebastian's heart felt none too sturdy, because his words seemed to have no effect.

"I suppose I could tolerate Italy, if we must winter there," Freddy informed the roses. "Italian servants are insolent, though. I will probably deal with them very well."

Sebastian strode over to the window and seized his aunt gently by the shoulders. "You will go nowhere you don't wish to go."

She blinked up at him, looking small, old, dear, and uncertain.

"I will go wherever I please, in any case, young man, but when your only paternal relation leaves you to deal with torture and treason on some frozen pile of French rocks, when she might instead have had you brought home with a full pardon, then you are entitled to your sulks and pouts."

Rather than torment himself with her uncertainty, Sebastian wrapped her in a careful hug, the way a boy might hold a pretty bird caught fluttering against his window.

"I will sulk and pout past reason if you abandon me now."

Up close, Freddy smelled of roses, and in his arms, she was tiny.

"You foolish boy, don't you understand? *I left you in France.* My brother's only son, and I left you there, and then you began that dangerous business with the money, and I knew—I knew—you would never come home, while all those other boys, those wretched, pompous *English* boys—"

Milly passed Freddy a wrinkled handkerchief, while Sebastian closed his eyes and swallowed past the ache in his throat.

"I am an English boy, sometimes wretchedly pompous—ask my wife if you don't believe me—and I am home safe and sound. Cease with your dramatics, Baroness, and stop trying to manipulate me with your tears."

His insults were of more use to his aunt than his handkerchief. She pulled out of his arms and sashayed over to the sofa. "Explain yourself, Sebastian. This exchange grows tedious."

The professor settled on one side of her, Milly on the other, while Michael pretended to straighten a stack of music.

"I did not understand that Michael was serving an English master," Sebastian said when Aunt had assembled her court. "Did not even suspect it until recently. From time to time, he'd ask if I thought about returning to England, and intimated that he could see such a thing done. He was most insistent, I assure you. I would list difficulty after difficulty, and for each obstacle, he had a solution. There were pardons, quiet, informal prisoner exchanges, diplomatic accommodations, impunities, all manner of magic wands Michael was certain would be waved on my behalf. I never once took him seriously."

Michael left off fussing the music.

"I tried, my lady," he said with creditable long-suffering. "I did try, repeatedly. St. Clair would not leave the Château, though I knew if I presented St. Clair under Wellington's very nose, we'd have had no trouble. Believes in the peerage, does Old Hookey. He believed in St. Clair's honor, too, more's the pity. I came very close to taking your nephew captive, not for his benefit, but to spare my own poor nerves."

While Michael exhibited a propensity for convincing fictions, an exchange of handkerchiefs was under way, like so many flags of truce. The professor slipped his linen into Milly's hands, while Aunt traced the initials on Sebastian's handkerchief. Sebastian saw that Milly was pleased though, relieved and smiling through her tears.

He had the odd thought that breeding women could be lachrymose.

"So you see, Aunt, Wellington put the decision to you. Michael repeatedly put the decision to me, and my judgment was in accord with your own. If you leave my household, I hope it will be because the professor seeks to make an honest woman of you, or because you've a sudden longing for sauerbraten and pine forests."

Freddy looked at the roses, at the music Michael had stacked, at the little square of cloth in her lap, and—fleetingly—at the professor.

"I hate sauerbraten, and if we've beaten this subject to death, I will allow the professor to escort me up to my sitting room."

She marched off the field on the professor's arm, which meant Sebastian could settle in beside his wife.

"Shouldn't you be off petting a cat?" Sebastian asked Michael. "Or perhaps making plans to leave for Scotland?"

"When Anduvoir's on a packet for Calais, bound hand and foot or in a coffin, then I'll leave for Scotland."

Sebastian kissed his wife's cheek, in part because he had to, and in part because such overtures stood a chance of embarrassing Michael into a retreat. "I thought you had a wife or a fiancée secreted in the Highlands."

"A bit of both actually." Still the man sat upon the piano bench.

Milly lifted her head from Sebastian's shoulder. "Both, Michael?"

"We do things differently in Scotland."

"And you haven't seen this woman in how many years?" Sebastian asked.

Michael stood, his expression not that of a man anticipating a romantic reunion. "If I *had* offered, even once, to get you off that godforsaken rock pile, would you have come?"

Lavender-scented fingers settled over Sebastian's mouth. "Don't answer that," Milly said. "He didn't offer, and you were both very kind to poor Freddy."

"I have a cat to pet." Michael bowed to them and departed, closing the door quietly behind him. Though he'd tried to hide it, he'd been smiling as he left the room.

Milly subsided against Sebastian, and if he'd had the ability to purr, he would have.

"A wife and a fiancée sounds complicated. I wonder if I should be flattered that Michael chose my company over theirs."

"You'll miss him. We'll visit him, once he's sorted out his ladies. You had an ally you did not understand as such, and Michael has been more alone even than you."

Yes, poor Michael, guardian angel at large.

"I owe him an enormous debt, which I can never repay, and so on and so forth. At the moment, I've had rather enough of duty, honor, debts, and deceptions. May I please read Mrs. Radcliffe to my wife?"

He thought maybe she'd fallen asleep, so long did it take that wife to respond to his question.

"Mrs. Radcliffe can keep, for now," she said, kissing the corner of his mouth. "I had rather we put the evening to a different use, sir."

Alas for Mrs. Radcliffe, in the years following, when the Baron St. Clair offered to read to his wife, she frequently declined his literary generosity in favor of those different pursuits. While Mrs. Radcliffe was neglected, the St. Clair nursery became full to bursting, the quiet of the household entirely cut up by the laughter of the children and the many blessings of a lasting and well deserved—if noisy!—peace.

The Laird

The third installment in the Captive Hearts series

by Grace Burrowes

New York Times Bestselling Author

He left his bride to go to war...

After years of soldiering, Michael Brodie returns to his Highland estate to find that the bride he left behind has become a stranger. Brenna is self-sufficient, competent, confident—and furious. Despite Michael's prolonged absence, Brenna has remained loyal, though Michael's clan make it clear they expect him to set Brenna aside.

Now his most important battle will be for her heart.

Michael left Brenna when she needed him most, and then stayed away even after the war ended. Nonetheless, the young man who abandoned her has come home a wiser, more patient, and honorable husband. But if she trusts Michael with the truths she's been guarding, he'll have to choose between his wife and everything else he holds dear.

Praise for Grace Burrowes:

"Grace Burrowes has quickly become one of my favorite historical romance authors. The stories she tells will capture your heart and mind."—*Night Owl Reviews*

"Burrowes has a knack for giving fresh twists to genre tropes and developing them in unexpected and delightful directions."—*Publishers Weekly*

For more Grace Burrowes, visit:

www.sourcebooks.com

About the Author

New York Times and USA Today bestselling author Grace Burrowes hit the bestseller lists with her debut, The Heir, followed by The Soldier, Lady Maggie's Secret Scandal, and Lady Eve's Indiscretion. The Heir was a Publishers Weekly Best Book of 2010, The Soldier was a Publishers Weekly Best Spring Romance of 2011, Lady Sophie's Christmas Wish won Best Historical Romance of the Year in 2011 from RT Reviewers' Choice Awards, Lady Louisa's Christmas Knight was a Library Journal Best Book of 2012, and The Bridegroom Wore Plaid, the first in her trilogy of Scotland-set Victorian romances, was a Publishers Weekly Best Book of 2012. All of her Regency and Victorian romances have received extensive praise, including several starred reviews from Publishers Weekly and Booklist. Darius, the first in her groundbreaking Regency series The Lonely Lords, was named one of iBooks Store's Best Romances of 2013.

Grace is a practicing family law attorney and lives in rural Maryland. She loves to hear from her readers and can be reached through her website at graceburrowes .com.

the
TRAITOR

GRACE
BURROWES

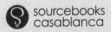
sourcebooks
casablanca

Published by Sourcebooks Casablanca, an imprint of Sourcebooks, Inc.
P.O. Box 4410, Naperville, Illinois 60567-4410
(630) 961-3900
Fax: (630) 961-2168
www.sourcebooks.com

Printed and bound in Canada
MBP 10 9 8 7 6 5 4 3 2 1